ONE RAINY NIGHT

RICHARD LAYMON

LEISURE BOOKS NEW YORK CITY

A LEISURE BOOK®

February 2000

Published by

Dorchester Publishing Co., Inc.
276 Fifth Avenue
New York, NY 10001

ISBN 0-8439-4690-3

RAVE REVIEWS FOR RICHARD LAYMON!

"Laymon always takes it to the max. No one writes like him and you're going to have a good time with anything he writes."

—Dean Koontz

"If you've missed Laymon, you've missed a treat."

—Stephen King

"Laymon is Stephen King without a conscience."

—Dan J. Marlowe

"Laymon's writing's super-tight and characters well detailed and believable, which makes the savage termination of so many of them all the more shocking! The unbridled joy of a delightfully fertile and *wicked* imagination at work."

—*Terrorzone*

"Laymon is an American writer of the highest caliber."

—*Time Out* (London)

"Laymon is unique. A phenomenon. A genius of the grisly and the grotesque."

—Joe Citro, *The Blood Review*

"One of the best, and most reliable, writers working today."

—*Cemetery Dance*

"I've read every book of Laymon's I could get my hands on. I'm absolutely a longtime fan."

—Jack Ketchum

"Richard Laymon has become for me one of a small handful of must-read horror novelists."

—Robert Devereaux

"A brilliant writer."

—*Sunday Express* (London)

Other *Leisure* books by Richard Laymon:
BITE

To Wren and Ida Marshall,
two of the best people I know.
May the luck of the Irish
be with you always.

The Killing Ground

This is pretty goddamn crazy, Hanson thought. But he didn't climb down.

The chainlink fence surrounding the football stadium of Lincoln High School shook as he made his way upward. Its mesh let out tinny chinging sounds that seemed terribly loud in the stillness of the November evening. But Hanson doubted that anyone would hear the noise.

The nearest houses were out of sight beyond the stands at the far side of the stadium. Behind him, an empty field stretched toward the distant classroom buildings. The stadium itself seemed deserted.

The sounds of the shaking fence would be heard by no one. Hanson knew that. Yet they unnerved him just as surely as the crunch of dry leaves underfoot might unsettle a man making his lone way through a graveyard in the dead of night. His heart pounded. Sweat seemed to run out of every pore. His arms and legs trembled.

Climbing the fence was easy. Being here was not.

At the top, he hurled himself over the rail. He dropped the nine feet to the grass, landing with his knees

3

bent to absorb the impact. He felt the jolt mostly around his waist, where gravity tugged at his gun belt. Jostled leather groaned and creaked. Cuffs and ammunition rattled inside their cases. Standing up straight, Hanson gave the belt a couple of pulls to bring it back up where it belonged.

He rubbed his sweaty hands on the front of his shirt.

Well, he thought, you're here.

Now, if he only knew *why*.

He walked slowly over the grass, eyes on the north goal post straight in front of him.

He was kidding himself if he thought he might find anything new. The boys had gone over the area thoroughly last night, and again in daylight. They'd photographed, picked up, tagged and taken away everything: the poor bastard himself, his clothes, matches and cigarette butts, the gasoline can, candy wrappers and other shit that probably had nothing at all to do with the crime, even some of the sod surrounding the main standard where the kid had been tied. There'd been talk of taking the goalpost, as well, but the chief decided against it. They had stripped off the charred remains of the padding for evidence.

Hell, there was nothing left to find.

But Hanson, patrolling the neighborhood, had found himself circling the high school, slowing his car each time he had a view of the distant goalpost and staring out his window at the damned thing. Finally, he'd parked in front of the stadium.

And left the car without even radioing in.

Crazy.

As he crunched across the cinder track, Hanson wished he'd made the call. He could've given Lucy a phony location, claimed he was taking an early break for chow.

Would've been worse, lying to her.

He planned to marry the woman. You don't lie to someone you love.

Better this way, he thought. Besides, she'll probably cover for me if anything comes up.

The grass felt soft and springy under his shoes. He walked through the end zone, the goalpost jarring slightly in his vision. He stopped just outside the circle where the grass had been removed. He stared.

Again, he wondered why he was drawn to this place.

He'd seen murder victims before. Though not many. And only one, Jennifer Sayers, who'd met an end this brutal. She hadn't been burnt like this boy. Tortured and raped. Her mutilated body had given Hanson plenty of nightmares, but he'd never made a secret trip to the section of woods where it happened.

Somehow, this was different.

Yeah, he thought. Somehow. Maxwell Chidi was a black kid. That's the difference, right there.

When does a black guy become a nigger? When he leaves the room.

Hanson used to laugh at stuff like that. Shit, he used to *say* stuff like that.

That's why I'm here, he realized.

Guilt.

They did it to the kid because he was black. White people. They got themselves a nigger.

Hell, you're just guessing. It might've had nothing to do with that. We aren't in Alabama, here. Could've been a perfectly ordinary motive. Jealousy, greed. Maybe the kid was a pusher, could've been skimming and . . .

Right. He was black, therefore he was a pusher.

That's the kind of thinking . . .

The stadium lights came on.

Hanson flinched, sucked in a quick breath. *Oh, Jesus!* He whirled around. He scanned the stands on both sides of the field. Nobody there. But he knew he'd been caught.

Stay cool, he told himself.

Probably just a maintenance man. Might not even know I'm here. Yet.

Hell, I'm a cop. I've got business here.

He still saw no one.

Somebody turned the lights on.

Maxwell . . .

Oh, right. Sure.

But his skin prickled as he imagined the dead boy staggering through a passageway of the stadium, coming toward the field. A black shape shuffling through the dark. Rigid all over, arms sticking out, stubs of fingers hooked like claws. No face at all. Just a black, earless knot above the shoulders. With teeth.

He thought he could hear the slow shuffle of Maxwell's charred feet on the concrete, hear his crisp skin cracking as he moved, see it flaking off and drifting down from him like dead leaves.

Gonna getcha, white man.

Quit it! Hanson told himself.

Though he knew he was letting his imagination run wild, he snapped his head from side to side, eyes darting to the grandstand openings. Three on each side. Dark holes. Tunnels leading to the rear, to refreshment stands and restrooms, to exit gates in the fence.

Stop this. You're just spooking yourself. Maxwell's dead in the morgue, not . . .

Across the field, a figure emerged from the nearest passageway.

A white man in dark green coveralls. A grounds keeper? Hanson sighed. He felt as if all his strength had drained away. The effort of standing up straight made him tremble.

The guy raised an arm in greeting, then climbed over the rail and leaped down to the grass area on the far side of the track. He took all the impact with his left leg while he kept his right leg high. Then he was standing on both feet, and walking toward Hanson with a limp. 'Evening, officer,' he called.

Hanson nodded a greeting.

The top of the man's head gleamed in the stadium lights. The hair around his ears was gray. His lean face was weathered. He looked wiry and tough. Keys jangled at his side as he hobbled closer.

'Toby Barnes,' he said, and stuck out his hand.

Hanson shook it. 'Bob Hanson.'

'Just got here, Bob. I saw your car out front. Mind if I ask how you got in?'

'I had to come over the fence.'

Toby looked relieved. 'Glad to hear it. I was afraid some idiot might've left a gate unlocked. Sorry I wasn't around to let you in.'

'No problem.'

'Anyway, I thought you might appreciate some light on the subject. I was on my way over to the school. I'm the head of maintenance, you know, gotta keep my eye on the cleaning crew. Bunch of no-good loafers, most of them.' Toby turned his eyes away from Hanson and frowned at the goalpost. 'Terrible,' he said. 'Any ideas who did it?'

'We're working on it. I just thought I'd stop by and try to get the feel of the situation.'

'I suppose you were out here last night.'

'Yeah.'

'Must've been pretty grim. I've seen my share of crispy critters, you know. Bakersfield Fire Department till a roof dropped out from under me.' He slapped his right leg. What it smacked through the trousers didn't sound like skin. 'Never a pretty sight. That's one aspect of the job I sure don't miss.'

Hanson, who'd taken a liking to the man right away, now felt a grudging admiration. 'They couldn't pay me enough to be a fireman,' he said.

Toby nodded. His eyes stayed on the goalpost. 'Think it was kids?'

'I don't know. Seems likely.'

'We haven't got any Klan here that I know of.'

'No.'

'It's the sort of thing you might expect from the Klan. Really gives this burg a black eye.'

'Did you know the boy?' Hanson asked.

'I've seen him around school.' Toby faced him, frowning slightly. 'We've only got a handful of coloreds, you know. This Chidi, he wasn't at all like the others. A tall fellow, kind of handsome, and he talked funny. I guess he came from one of those islands. Jamaica, Haiti, someplace like that. It was none of this "hey, bro, mutherfuh," stuff. He talked like he had breeding, you know?'

'How did he get along with the other students?'

'Well, from what I saw, he didn't have much to do with the other black kids. The rest of them were always hanging around together. I guess that's only natural. But I don't think I ever saw Chidi with them. When I saw him, he was always with white kids. White girls, mostly. It seems like the girls really took to him.'

Hanson felt his heart quicken. 'Anyone special?'

'Yeah, there was. I don't know the girl's name, but I could find it out for you. The past couple of weeks, they've been hanging all over each other. I wouldn't be at all surprised if she wasn't putting out for him.'

'Well, now,' Hanson muttered.

'Yeah, I can see how a thing like that might rub some folks the wrong way.'

'This is . . .'

They both jumped and threw their heads back as the sky seemed to explode. For an instant, Hanson thought a mid-air collision had occurred over the stadium. But what he saw was a searing bright flash of lightning, branched like a giant tree, ripping down through a canyon of dark, piled cloud.

The roar faded. It left his ears ringing.

'Jesus-smoking-Christ,' Toby blurted.

The rain came down.

It dropped like a shroud over the stadium lights, blocking out all but the faintest yellow glow.

A moment after the lights dimmed, the shower hit Hanson. Big, hot drops that pelted his face and shoulders. They made his skin tingle. They seemed to sink in. They warmed him. He suddenly felt a strange, wild rush of excitement.

Toby said, 'Holy shit.'

Hanson and Toby stared at each other through the faint jaundiced light, the dark shower and the mist that now drifted around them – condensation, probably caused by the hot rain sluicing through the cooler November air.

Toby looked as if someone had dumped a bucket of ink over his head. Only his eyes and teeth were white. More teeth showed as his lips curled.

Hanson popped the snap of his holster guard and snatched out his revolver as Toby lunged at him, snarling. The man's fingers clutched Hanson's neck. Thumbs dug into his throat. He rammed the muzzle of his .38 into Toby's belly and jerked the trigger three times fast. The blasts pounded his ears.

Toby staggered backward, folding at the waist.

The fourth round smacked through the crown of his bald, black head. He sat down hard, skidded on his rump, and came to a stop sitting up, drooping over his outstretched legs.

Hanson gave himself a small running start, and punted Toby's face. He hoped he might send the head soaring like a football. In spite of his power and follow-through, however, all he managed was to slam the man's back against the ground.

As Hanson's right leg reached the height of its kick, his left foot slipped on the wet grass. He flapped his arms, gasped, and flopped on his back beside Toby. Jarred by the fall, he lay motionless for a while. The rain felt very good. This was like sprawling out in his bathtub with the shower on, but this was better. He holstered his weapon, then spread out his arms and legs. Moaning, he squirmed with pleasure.

As his head turned, he saw Toby's body close beside him.

Wow, he thought. Sure wasted that son-of-a-bitch.

He laughed. Feeling the rain in his mouth, he opened up wide and stretched out his tongue. The rain felt thicker than water. It tasted, he thought, a little bit like blood.

Just a little bit. A mild coppery flavor. Very subtle.

It made him long to fill his mouth with the real thing.

Hanson rolled over, pushed himself up, and crawled. He stretched out, belly down. Elbows against the soft, wet grass, he grabbed Toby by the ears. He lifted the man's head. He clamped his mouth to the bullet wound and sucked.

A Hard Rain's Gonna Fall

1

Earlier that evening, while patrolman Bob Hanson was still cruising the streets near Lincoln High and just more than an hour before his bullets ripped out the life of Toby Barnes, Francine Walters sat down on her living room sofa. She pulled the TV tray closer as the six o'clock Eyewitness News came on. While the lead-in music played, she polished off the scotch at the bottom of her glass.

'Good evening, everyone,' said anchorwoman Chris Donner. 'At the top of our news, investigators continue to probe last night's grisly murder of seventeen-year-old Maxwell Chidi, a student at Lincoln High in the nearby valley community of Bixby. The body of the black youth was discovered in the newly completed Memorial Stadium by . . .

'Mark my words,' Francine said, 'that boy was up to no good. He probably had it coming.'

'Shit,' Lisa muttered.

Francine snapped her head toward the girl. 'What? What did you say?'

Lisa glared at her from the rocking chair. 'I said

that's shit. You don't know what you're talking about.'

'I know good and well what I'm talking about, young lady, and don't you dare speak to me that way. What's gotten into you? You haven't been fit to live with ever since you climbed out of bed this morning.'

The anger seemed to melt out of Lisa's stare. She opened her mouth as if to say something, then closed it again. Her lips mashed themselves together. Their corners trembled. Her chin, dimpled and discolored with the effort of thrusting up her lower lip, began to shake. Her eyes filled with tears.

'Lisa?'

'Just leave me alone.' She scooted back her rocking chair. But not far enough. As she got up, her thighs bumped the edge of her dinner tray. Not hard, but the collision jostled the tray and capsized her glass, which tumbled over the edge, flinging out its contents of ice cubes and water. The glass hit the carpet with a soft thump.

'*Now* see what you've done!' Francine snapped.

Letting out an anguished sob, the girl ran from the room.

What the *hell's* the matter with her? Francine wondered. Damn it!

Carefully, she moved her own tray aside. As she stood, she heard a door slam shut. It sounded too near to be Lisa's bedroom door. Probably the bathroom, just off the foyer.

She stepped past Lisa's tray and picked up the glass. Squatting, she gathered ice cubes off the beige carpet. Thank God it was only water, she thought. She dropped the cubes into the glass. If Lisa'd been drinking milk or Pepsi . . . and you can thank your lucky stars her lasagna didn't end up on the floor.

Francine set the glass on the tray, then went looking for Lisa. She felt hot and squirmy inside. God, how she hated this kind of thing.

But this episode didn't seem like one of her daughter's typical tantrums. Something more serious. Maybe something to do with the death of that black kid.

I shouldn't have smarted off about it, she thought.

Just as she'd suspected, the bathroom door was shut.

'Honey?'

'Leave me alone.' From the girl's high, shaky voice, Francine knew she was still crying.

'Are you OK?'

'No.'

'I'm sorry I lost my temper, honey. Come on out, now, all right? You have to be at the Foxworth's in less than an hour.'

'I can't.'

'They're counting on you. Come on out and finish your dinner.'

Seconds later, the lock pinged and the door swung open. Lisa's face was red, her eyes bloodshot, her face gleaming with streams of tears. Sobbing, she rubbed her runny nose with a Kleenex.

Seeing the girl this way, Francine felt her own

throat tighten. Her eyes burned as they filled with tears. 'What is it?' she asked.

'*Oh, Mom*!' She lurched forward, threw her arms around Francine and hugged her fiercely. She gasped for air. Spasms jerked her body. 'I loved him,' she blurted. 'I loved him so bad and they killed him.'

2

Denise Gunderson, done with her cheeseburger, folded the paper plate in half and dropped it into the waste container. She took a chocolate chip cookie from the freezer side of the refrigerator. Munching on it, cupping a hand under her chin in case of crumbs, she wandered into the front room.

'And what have we here?' she asked, her voice muffled by the mouthful of cookie.

She knew what she had here: a plastic bag containing the three video tapes she'd rented that afternoon. But whenever she was alone in the house, she liked to talk to herself. It broke the silence.

She sat on the floor and crossed her legs. She poked the remains of the cookie into her mouth, then brushed her fingers against the leg of her sweatpants. The noise of her teeth crunching the frozen cookie sounded a lot louder than the soft whispery rustle made by the bag as she spread it open. She took out the tapes and examined their titles. She had *Watchers*, *Near Dark*, and *The Texas Chainsaw Massacre*.

Shaking her head, she laughed softly and muttered, 'Fine, wholesome family entertainment.'

But Tom would love them. He'd probably seen them already, but that wouldn't faze him at all.

'Now, if you've just got the guts to call him.'

The clock on the VCR showed 6:11 p.m.

If you're going to call him, Denise thought, you'd better do it now. Before he goes out somewhere.

Trying to ignore the unpleasant pounding of her heart, she got to her feet. She walked back into the kitchen and stared at the wall phone.

She felt awfully shaky. Drops of sweat slid down her sides.

'Oh, man,' she muttered.

If Mom and Dad find out I had him over . . .

They had one hard and fast rule: *no boys in the house when we're not home*. So far, Denise had never broken the rule. She'd been tempted, but the fear of being caught (even innocently watching television with the guy) had always prevailed.

Tonight, however, there was no chance of her parents walking in. They were spending the night with friends in Tiburon, which was a two-hour drive from Bixby. They'd phoned at 5:30 just to make sure nothing was amiss. And Dad, who loathed driving at night, was not about to head for home before daylight. Their actual plan was to leave Tiburon in mid-afternoon.

Still, something could go wrong. A neighbor might

spot Tom coming or going. His car might break down in the driveway, immovable, stuck there till Mom and Dad showed up. An earthquake might hit, trapping Tom in the house with her. 'Or caving in our beans,' she said, and chuckled. 'Screw it, call him up.'

She rubbed her clammy hands on her sweatpants. She took a deep breath. Then she reached for the phone and its sudden clamor rammed her breath out.

It's Tom, she thought. He must be psychic.

She lifted the receiver. 'Hello?'

'Is this Denise?'

Not him. A woman's voice, vaguely familiar. 'Yes, it is.'

'This is Lynn Foxworth. You sat for us a few months ago?'

'Sure.' Oh, no, she thought. But she forced herself to sound cheery as she said, 'Kara's mother.'

'I really hate to bother you with this, it's such short notice. I just feel horrible, even asking. And please, if you already have plans for tonight, that's fine, maybe you can suggest someone else. But we're in an awful bind. We have seven o'clock dinner reservations, and I just this minute got off the phone with Francine Walters. Lisa's mom? Lisa – it was all arranged for her to sit for us, but, I don't know, Francine was awfully upset. It seems she just found out that Lisa was with that murdered boy last night. There was a dance after the game? Anyway, Lisa apparently has some idea about who did it, and Francine's rushing her right over to the police department. Apparently she's afraid that, you know, somebody might try something with Lisa. To keep her from talking? Scary stuff. I guess it's just as well she *isn't* coming here. Not if *killers* might be after her, or something. Can you believe it? Anyway, now we're stuck without a sitter and I'm really at my wits' end but I thought, if you don't already have plans. Kara really likes you, and I know you only did it as a special favor last time because of your folks, but . . . can you help us out?'

Denise wished she'd let the phone keep ringing.

'I sort of had a date,' she said.

'Well, he could come over here. God, what am I saying? I'd certainly never suggest such a thing to someone like Lisa, but . . . I know how trustworthy you are. It might not be much fun for your friend, but it'd certainly be OK with us. We've got all kinds of good snacks, soft drinks.'

This, Denise thought, is one desperate woman.

'We shouldn't be very late. Maybe ten or eleven?'

'Well, I don't know about having my boyfriend there, but I'll come over. What time do you want me?'

'We should leave the house no later than ten till seven, so any time before that.'

Denise glanced at the kitchen clock. Six-fourteen.

'If you haven't eaten yet . . .'

'No, I just finished.'

'I was going to say you could eat here, but . . . Oh, Denise, you're a lifesaver. I can't tell you. This is great.'

'Glad to help. I'll see you in a while.'

'Would you like John to pick you up?'

'No, that's not necessary. But thanks.'

'Oh, don't thank me. You're a lifesaver, you really are.'

'I'd better get ready to go.'

'Right, right. Great. We'll see you in a few minutes.'

'Fine. Bye-bye.'

Denise hung up.

She thought about the rented movies. She thought about Tom. She felt cheated and sad.

'It's not the end of the world,' she muttered.

Maybe a blessing in disguise, she thought as she headed for her room to change clothes. Keeps me from breaking the 'house rule.' Keeps me and Tom from being together for hours, alone in the house, and maybe things would've gotten out of hand.

Maybe I *wanted* things to get out of hand.

God's way of saving me from temptation.

Or giving me the shaft.

3

Patterson, manning the front desk, leaned forward and smirked when Trevor Hudson entered the station. 'When are you gonna get a life, Hudson?'

'I just couldn't stay away,' Trev said. 'I know how you pine for me.'

'Your ass and my face, pal.'

'If you say so.' Trev made his way past the end of the counter, smiled a greeting to Lucy, and was almost to his desk when Patterson turned around, frowning.

'I meant that the other way around.'

'Oh? OK.' He pulled out his swivel chair and sat down.

'I mean it, though. This is Saturday night, man. *Date* night, you know? You oughta be out somewhere getting lowdown and hairy.'

'I'd rather be here with you,' he said, and winked at the burly sergeant.

Lucy, at the dispatcher station off in the corner, looked over her shoulder grinning. 'You'd better watch what you say, Trev, or you'll have Patty sitting on your lap.'

'Sit on mine, honey,' Patterson told her. 'Better still, on my face.'

'Don't you wish,' she said, then turned away as a call came in.

Trev slid open his top drawer. He took out a coupon for a dollar off a family size pizza at O'Casey's, dug his wallet out of a seat pocket of his jeans, and folded the coupon. As he tucked it into his wallet, he shook his head at the absurdity of dropping by here for a dollar-off coupon.

Nothing absurd about it, he told himself. He had to drive right past the station, anyway, on his way to O'Casey's. And a buck is a buck.

But his stomach fluttered a bit as he stuffed the wallet back into his pocket and he knew that his real reason for picking up the coupon had less to do with thrift than with procrastination.

A delaying tactic.

Maureen might not even be there. This *is* Saturday, and she'd been on the job each time Trev had gone there during the past week. It only stood to reason that she wouldn't work every night.

On the other hand, the dinner hour on a Saturday evening is probably O'Casey's busiest time. And it's a family business. She'd come to town for Mary's funeral, three weeks ago, and turned up waiting on customers when the pizzaria reopened. According to her brother, she was staying with Liam and planned to remain indefinitely, taking care of her father and helping out with the business.

So it didn't make sense for Maureen to take off Saturday night.

She would be there, all right.

And Trev planned to do more, this time, than exchange a few friendly words with her and gape at her while she made visits to other tables. He planned to ask her out. And he wasn't sure he had the nerve.

She likes me, he thought. I know she does.

It was more than her cheerful, wise-cracking banter. She talked to all the customers that way. But she didn't look at the others the way she looked at Trev. When her eyes met his, their gaze seemed to sink into him as if searching deep inside, looking for something, wondering about him, and they seemed to hold a soft challenge.

She wants me to ask her out. And she's wondering

why I haven't, yet. Wondering what's wrong.

I've got to do it, Trev thought. Tonight. Now.

But he remained at his desk, staring past the deserted desks toward the door of the interrogation room.

Come on, he told himself. Get up and go. Do it.

'You all of a sudden into meditation?' Patterson asked.

Trev looked around at him. 'Just thinking,' he said. 'Try it, sometime.'

'Try eating dirt,' Patterson said. And was about to say more, but someone apparently entered the station just then, so he turned to the front.

Trev looked at the wall clock. Six twenty-five.

He'd been going into O'Casey's at eight, midway through his shift. If he showed up this early, Maureen might not be on duty yet. Maybe he should wait a couple of hours.

Don't be such a damn chicken!

He rolled back his chair. As he started to rise, he heard footsteps behind him. He stood and turned around. Patterson was striding toward him, a serious look on his face. In a hushed voice, he said, 'Since you're here anyway, maybe you'd like to handle this.'

Trev saw two females, an adult and a teenaged girl, at the other side of the reception window. 'I was just on my way out.'

'It's about the Chidi case. You're more up on it than me.'

'Well, I was there last night.'

25

'The girl knew Chidi. Sounds like they were going together.'

'OK, I'll talk to them.'

What the hell, he thought. I was looking for an excuse. And this might be a break. Shouldn't take long, and Maureen might not be there yet, anyway.

'You won't regret it,' Patterson said, then rolled his eyes upward and pursed his lips. 'Couple of knock-outs. Maybe you'll get lucky.' Resuming a solemn expression, he turned away. He headed toward the women and said, 'Officer Hudson will see you. If you'd like to step in.' He nodded toward the opening at the far end of the counter.

Trev met them there. He sized them up quickly, decided he didn't much like what he saw, and gave them a smile that he hoped was reassuring. 'Thanks for coming by. I'm Trevor Hudson.'

The older woman, probably the girl's mother, narrowed her eyes as if she expected Trev to give her shit and rather hoped he might try. 'Francine Walters,' she said. Her raspy voice was as hard as her looks. She appeared to be about forty, but Trev had seen this type before, and they always appeared older than their years. Her hair was bleached blond. She needed to do the roots. Too much eye makeup. Lipstick too bright. A lean, drawn face with wrinkle lines in the wrong places. It was a face that hadn't smiled much, that spent too much time scowling or giving off sarcastic smirks. 'This is Lisa,' she said.

'Hi, Lisa.'

The girl didn't look up. Her head was lowered, her

shoulders slumped. Her hair was the same silvery blond as her mother's, but her roots didn't show.

'Come on back here,' Trev said, 'and we'll talk.'

He led the way toward the interrogation room. 'We don't want to end up on the news,' Francine said to his back. 'We don't want it all over town.'

He opened the door and held it for them.

'Is that understood?' Francine asked.

'We'll try to keep it between the three of us,' Trev said.

The girl gave him a wary glance as she stepped by. She'd been crying, and her face looked freshly scrubbed. Trev imagined that she might be a beautiful young woman if she ever smiled. She was shorter than her mother, but had the same build – hips and breasts that seemed too prominent for her otherwise slim figure. She probably kept the high school girls in a constant state of envy and the boys in heat.

She wore a pullover sweater that might have fit her a couple of years ago. She'd probably bought it too small, just as she'd probably bought the blue jeans pre-faded and pre-slashed. The legs of her jeans, fashionably ripped and frayed, made it look as if she'd been attacked by a knife-wielding midget.

A cloying odor of perfume swept past Trev as she stepped through the doorway.

A more exotic perfume followed Francine. Not as sweet, dark and wanton, mixed with odors of whiskey and stale smoke.

Trev stepped into the room. 'Please, sit down. Could I get you some coffee? We've got a soda machine, Lisa. Would you like a Pepsi or . . . ?'

'Can we just get on with it?' Francine asked.

Nodding, he closed the door. Through the glass, he saw Patterson leer at him, pump his fist, and mouth something that looked like 'Va va va voom.'

Thinks he's doing me a favor, sending me in with these two. Knockouts. Right.

I could be sitting at O'Casey's, right now. I could be talking to Maureen.

He turned to the women. They were seated facing the table, their backs to him. He stepped behind them. He picked up a legal pad from a stack at the end of the table, then swung a chair out past the corner and sat down. He wanted to keep it informal. He didn't want the table in the way. He told himself that it had nothing to do with wanting a better view of Patterson's knockouts. He crossed one leg, rested the legal pad against his upthrust knee, and said to Lisa, 'I understand that you knew Maxwell Chidi.'

'Yeah,' she said. She glanced at him, then looked the other way to check on her mother who was nearly hidden from Trev's view on her far side. She then did just what he expected. She scooted her chair away from the table, far back until it bumped the window sill and she no longer separated Trev from her mother.

Then both women turned their chairs toward him.

'They were going together,' Francine said. 'I didn't know a thing about it. The last I heard, she was still going with Buddy Gilbert.'

Trev plucked a ballpoint from his shirt pocket and

wrote down the name. 'How long were you seeing Maxwell?' he asked the girl.

'A couple of weeks,' she said without looking at him. Her eyes were fixed on the knee of her jeans, where she was fingering her skin through a ragged slit. There were more gashes higher up.

'She just kept me totally in the dark,' Francine said, taking a pack of cigarettes from her purse. 'If I'd known, I would've put a quick stop to it. You'd better believe it.' She shook out a cigarette. Tapping its filter against the table, she said, 'It's not that I'm a bigot or anything.'

'Sure you aren't,' Lisa muttered.

'That's right, I'm not.' Glaring at the back of her daughter's head, she jabbed the cigarette into a corner of her mouth and fired it with a Bic. 'But I think I've been around awhile longer than you, young lady, and I think I know a few things you don't.' The cigarette jerked up and down as she talked. Lisa kept fiddling with the tear at her knee. 'One thing I know is a girl like you starts going around with a black guy, it means trouble. And I was right, wasn't I? Wasn't I?'

'I guess,' Lisa murmured.

'You guess. The boy's dead, isn't he?'

Lisa nodded.

'Think he'd be dead if he didn't start going with you?'

'Lisa,' Trev said, 'do you know who murdered him?'

'Not exactly.'

'Tell the man what you told me.'

She glanced up at Trev, then frowned at the rip in her jeans. 'I think it might've been Buddy and his friends.'

'Buddy Gilbert,' Trev said.

'Yeah. See, he didn't like it when I broke up with him. Then there was the dance after the game last night. In the gym? Buddy came in with his friends. They were all drunk, you know? Buddy tried to cut in and dance with me and I told him, you know, to get lost. And he started . . . He got real nasty. He called Maxwell . . . like every name in the book. You know?' She raised her eyes to Trev as if curious to see his reactions. 'Nigger, coon, jigaboo, spade, spearchucker, jungle bunny. That kind of thing? And he got really crude about how black people are supposed to have bigger dicks?'

'*Jesus*, Lisa!' her mother snapped.

'Well, he did. Like that was why I dumped him for Maxwell.'

'You don't have to announce it to the goddamn *world*!'

'It's all right,' Trev told the girl. 'What happened then?'

'Well, Maxwell just stood there and didn't say anything, and Mr Sherman – he's the vice principal? – he came over and kicked Buddy and his friends out.'

'Do you know the names of Buddy's friends?'

'Sure. Doug Haines and Lou Nicholson.'

4

Lou didn't want to be here. He wished he were in his own home, in bed with the pillow covering his face. But when Buddy calls and says come over, you come over.

Hell, maybe it was better not to be home. Here, at least, he wasn't alone. There were sure to be some wild times, what with the five of them together and Doug's folks over at the club. And the booze. One way or another, maybe he'd be able to forget about last night. At least for a while.

And then, as if his hopes were being answered, he *did* forget about last night. Because Sheila, his girl, chose that moment to sit down across Buddy's lap. She bounced on it playfully and fingered his left ear. 'How are we supposed to have a party when you haven't got a gal?'

'Who says I haven't got a gal?' Buddy rubbed his hand over the back of her sweatshirt.

They're just kidding around, Lou told himself. But he suddenly felt hot and squirmy inside.

Sheila smiled over her shoulder at him and said, 'I think my fella's getting jealous.'

Lou shrugged. 'Who, me?' Stupid! He wanted to grab her by the neck and throw her off Buddy's lap.

Facing Buddy again, she slipped her fingers through his hair. 'I guess Lou doesn't mind.'

'Who's talking about you?' Buddy grabbed a handful at the back of her sweatshirt. When he let go, Lou heard the bra strap whap against her skin. She flinched and yelped.

'Hey!'

Doug and Cyndi laughed from the other side of the sofa, and Lou felt a surge of relief.

Sheila scurried off his lap, being careful not to spill her rum Coke. 'Aren't *you* nice,' she said. 'I was just trying to cheer you up.'

He grinned at her as she backed away. 'That cheered me up.' He looked at Lou and raised his eyebrows. 'Did that cheer *you* up, Louie?'

Lou couldn't hold back a smile. 'Yeah, sure did.'

'What a bunch of assholes,' she said. Shaking her head and laughing, she twirled her middle finger through the air. Then she sat on the floor in front of Lou's chair. He leaned over and rubbed her back. 'Anyway, we've gotta find a gal for Buddy and get her over here.'

'I've got a gal,' he said.

'Who, Lisa?'

'That's right.'

Doug, sitting on the far side of Cyndi with one hand behind her back and the other holding a vodka tonic, hunched forward to look at Buddy. 'Guess she's all yours now, huh?'

'Yep. Now that Maxi-pad's gone to that big jungle in the sky.'

Cyndi laughed and said, 'That's terrible.'

'Sick,' agreed Sheila.

Lou wondered how the girls would react if they knew who'd *sent* Maxwell to that big jungle in the sky.

'Yeah,' Doug said. 'We should be ashamed of ourselves, joking about such a tragedy.'

'But anyway,' Cyndi said, 'I happen to know that Lisa's babysitting tonight. So she couldn't come over even if she wanted to.'

She wouldn't want to, Lou thought. Christ, Lisa *had* to know it was Buddy and us, or at least figure it might've been.

'You oughta just forget about her anyway,' Sheila advised. 'I mean, I know how you felt about her and all, but shit, she dumped you . . .'

'For a nigger,' Doug added.

'Yeah, well I'm not done with her yet.'

Uh-oh, Lou thought. Nobody spoke. The silence seemed heavy.

Buddy set his empty glass on the table. 'I don't know about the rest of you, but I'm starving.'

'Now you're talking,' Doug said.

'What've you got?' Sheila asked.

'You think I'm gonna *cook* for you slugs?'

'A couple of us could run over to McDonald's,' Lou said, 'and pick up some stuff. Me and Sheila could go.'

'I feel too comfy to move.' She leaned back against the padded front of Lou's chair, lifted an arm and rested it across his thighs. Bending her elbow, she curled her hand over his knee. He felt the side of her breast pressing against his leg.

'Yeah, shit,' Cyndi said. 'Why don't we call out for something?'

'Chink?' Doug suggested.

33

'Yuck,' Cyndi said.

'What about pizza?' Buddy asked.

'All *right*!' from Cyndi.

'Yeah!' Sheila.

'Fine with me,' Lou said, not quite so eager to rush off for McDonald's now that Sheila was leaning on him. He moved his leg slightly to rub it against her breast. She did nothing to stop him. In fact, she squeezed his knee.

Lou was suddenly glad to be here.

He started caressing the side of her neck.

His mind was on Sheila while the others discussed how many pizzas to order, what size, what to have on them. He was only vaguely aware of Buddy leaving the room to phone in the order.

Sheila's neck felt like warm velvet. He wished there wasn't so much clothing between her breast and his leg – the corduroy of his pants, her sweatshirt, the rather stiff fabric of her bra. Still, through all that, he could feel her breast's springy firmness.

And she wasn't giving him any grief at all.

This might get really interesting, he thought.

Then Buddy returned to his place on the sofa. 'All set,' he said. 'The pizzas'll be here in about half an hour.'

Doug checked his wristwatch. 'That'll be ten after seven,' he said. 'Don't know if my stomach can last that long.'

'Let's get some more drinks,' Buddy said.

5

Denise eased her car up against an empty stretch of curb in front of the Foxworth house. She shut off the headlights. After dropping the keys into her purse, she raised her left wrist and turned it until the face of her watch caught the faint light coming in through the windshield.

Twenty till seven.

She'd made pretty good time, she thought, considering that she'd had to change clothes and brush her hair before leaving home.

If Lynn and John don't dawdle around, they shouldn't have any trouble at all getting to the restaurant for their seven o'clock reservations.

She climbed out of the car, locked its door, and hurried toward the house thinking she really should've worn a jacket.

It's not *that* cold, she told herself. She unclenched her teeth and tried to stop shivering, but the night air seemed to be sliding right under the hanging tails of her chamois shirt, rising like chilly water against her skin. If she wasn't going to wear a jacket or tuck in the shirt (who on earth tucks in a chamois shirt?), she could've at least worn a T-shirt under it. Too late for that now, she thought.

On the front stoop, she jabbed the doorbell, then pressed the heavy shirt against her belly to keep out some of the chill. She stood rigid, waiting.

What's taking them so long? They're supposed to be in a big rush.

She pressed her legs together. She rubbed them against each other, her corduroys making soft whissy sounds.

At last, Lynn opened the door. 'Come in, come in. Oh, you're such a lifesaver. I can't tell you.'

Denise stepped into the foyer. She managed not to sigh as the inside air wrapped its warmth around her.

'We're almost ready to step out the door,' Lynn told her. 'Let me show you a few things real quick-like-a-bunny.' To Kara, she said, 'Look who's here,' as she hurried by.

'Hi there, Kara,' Denise said.

The nine-year-old, cross-legged on the floor playing a video game, looked over her shoulder, smiled, and mouthed a silent 'Hi.' She had an amused expression that seemed to say, 'Can't interrupt Mom when she's on a roll.'

'We'll be at the Edgewood, did I tell you that?' Lynn continued as Denise followed her toward the kitchen. 'We shouldn't be very late. If you want to let Kara stay up, that's fine. Whatever. Or get rid of her. And if you want to invite your friend over, fine. The refrigerator's all stocked and we've got plenty of snacks in the cupboard. Kara can show you everything.' They reached the kitchen. She stopped just inside the entry and put a hand on the wall phone. 'Here's the phone,' she said. 'If anything comes up, you can reach us at the restaurant. The number's right here.' She tapped a long, tapering fingernail against a note pad beside the phone. 'And here are numbers for the police and fire department, just in case. God knows, you shouldn't need those.' She faced Denise, smiling. 'So, any questions? I feel like I'm forgetting something.'

You're forgetting to calm down, Denise thought. But she shook her head. 'I can't think of anything.'

'Good, good. I can't tell you how glad I am you're here. This is kind of a very big deal tonight, and . . . do you think I look all right?'

'You look terrific,' Denise assured her.

Lowering her voice, she said, 'Just between you and me and the fencepost, John thinks this dress is too . . .' She grimaced and rolled her eyes upward. 'What shall we say . . . flamboyant?' She twirled around once.

The glossy, royal blue gown had only one shoulder and sleeve. The top angled down sharply from the shoulder and didn't cover much of her right breast before it passed beneath her armpit. It slanted down the same way across her back. The hem of the skirt appeared to be cut at the same angle, descending from just above her left knee to just below her right. She wore high heels that matched the dress. No nylons, but her legs had a good tan.

The way the fabric hugged her body, Denise was pretty sure the woman didn't have a stitch on underneath it.

'I hope it's warm in the restaurant,' she said.

Lynn grimaced. 'My God. Am I indecent?'

'You look fabulous. Really.'

She lowered her head to study herself. 'It *is* awfully . . . I have a nice cable-knit shawl. I have a *stole*, for that matter. A mink stole. It's gorgeous, but John has a thing about me wearing it.'

'He's against fur?'

'He's against "conspicuous consumption." He thinks if I wear a mink somebody'll knock me on the head and run off with it. A lot of good it does, having nice things . . .' She clutched Denise by the upper arm and looked her in the eyes. 'I'll get my shawl. I should've thought of it, myself. It's just the thing. You're precious.'

'Well, thanks. You might want to wear a coat, too. It's kind of chilly out.'

'Oh, I will. I'll do that.' She laughed. 'I'm not a total flake, you know.'

She let go and hurried out of the kitchen.

Denise watched her swish away.

She couldn't blame John for having doubts about that dress.

But God, the gal looked awesome in it. Tom would climb the walls slobbering if he ever saw me in something like that. He'd never get the chance. Mom and Dad would take turns killing me.

She went into the living room and sat on the floor beside Kara. The girl pressed a button on the control device that she held on her lap. On the television screen, little Mario halted his run and Bowser the dragon froze in mid-air, a burst of fire about to leave its mouth.

'That's OK, go on,' Denise said.

'Oh, I've got it on pause.'

'It's good to see you again,' she said, and gently squeezed Kara's shoulder. 'Been a while, hasn't it?'

'Since May first. You haven't sat for me since then.'

Trust Kara to know the exact date. 'Well, I came to your birthday party, didn't I?'

'Do you want to see the video tape? It's really neat. We can watch it right now. I'll go ahead and commit.'

'Commit what?'

'Suicide. Kill off Mario. I've only got two left, anyway. I think I'm jinxed. It's terribly difficult to concentrate with Mom running around acting crazy. She *always* acts crazy when she's going out.' Kara leaned closer and spoke softly. 'Dad doesn't even want to go. Of course, he never wants to go *anywhere*, but he really doesn't want to go to this thing tonight. I'd tell you the whole story, but I don't know it. Sometimes, they try to keep things from me. It's very annoying. I'm sure glad you're here instead of Lisa. She's OK, I guess. But she's a little weird around the edges, if you know what I mean, and she's constantly on the phone with her boyfriends. Constantly. It's very difficult to carry on conversation with her. Myself, I think maybe she hasn't got a lot of furniture in her attic.'

Denise laughed and shook her head. 'Boy, you haven't changed.'

Kara, beaming, raised her eyebrows. The fine blond hair of the brows barely showed, but the muscles above her eyes sent curved ridges and valleys climbing her forehead. 'That's good, isn't it?' she asked.

'It's terrific.'

'Well, we're off,' Lynn announced.

Denise looked around. Lynn wore a knee-length camel coat, carried a blue clutch bag in one hand and a fringed, white shawl in the other.

'How are you doing, Denise?' John asked, following his wife into the room.

'Just fine, thanks.'

'It's nice to see you again. I thought you'd retired from sitting.'

'She's just doing this tonight as a special favor,' Lynn told him.

He shook his head, smiling. He was a big, heavy-set man who always seemed friendly. Denise was glad to see him again. He wore a blue blazer and gray slacks. His necktie wasn't quite straight. It swung down as he bent over and frowned at each of Denise's arms. 'Which one did Lynn twist?'

'This one.' She raised her right arm, the hand limp and dangling.

'Better have that looked at.'

'Well, we've got to be off.' Lynn stepped past Denise, crouched and kissed Kara. 'You behave yourself,' she said.

'I will.'

John kissed her. 'Yeah,' he said. 'No torturing Denise with toothpicks.'

Kara smirked and rolled her eyes upward. 'Oh Dad, you're so weird.'

'Have fun, you two,' he said, and followed Lynn toward the door. 'We shouldn't be very late.'

Kara watched them. When they reached the foyer, she waved.

'You might want to put the chain on after we're gone,' John called. He opened the door and followed Lynn outside.

As the door began to swing shut, Kara shouted, 'THEY'RE GONE! LET'S PARTY!'

Denise heard a burst of laughter from John. Then the door bumped shut.

'I'll go ahead and commit so we can look at the tape. Or do you want to play some *Mario*?'

'Maybe later. I'll go and put on the chain.'

As she started to get up, Kara said, 'I'll do it,' leaped to her feet and ran for the door.

6

'I'm glad to see your mood's improved,' Lynn said as John backed his car out of the driveway.

'Looking forward to a good dinner.' He steered onto the street and started forward. 'We could've had that at home, of course, and without the hassle. I imagine Kara and Denise will have themselves a great time.'

'So will we.'

'We'll see.'

'This is a wonderful opportunity. I just don't know why you're so reluctant. I know one thing – if they offered to do a big write-up on *me* in a national magazine, I'd jump at the chance. Can you imagine? They may even want to put you on the cover.'

'Thrills.'

There would be no picture of him on the cover of *People Today* magazine, or inside it. John planned to make that clear, soon enough, but he figured he might as well postpone the announcement. Let the snoops make their pitch. Let Lynn enjoy herself for a while longer. Have the dinner, and then drop the bomb. She was bound to flip out.

What do you mean, you won't do it!

'Do you know what I think might happen?' Lynn asked. 'I think, when the story gets out, *every*body will want your paintings. You'll probably even have offers to do exhibits. Wouldn't that be fabulous? Can't you just imagine walking into a gallery in Beverly Hills or San Francisco – maybe even in New York?'

'My stuff sells fine right now,' John said.

'Oh, come on.'

'And if people are going to buy my work, I'd much prefer they buy it because they like it, not because it was painted by the guy who stopped some jerk from plugging Velma.'

'Veronica.'

'Whatever. If I'd known this was gonna happen, I maybe would've looked the other way.'

'Don't say that even joking, John. You did a wonderful, heroic thing, and you deserve recognition for it. My God, the woman has *platinum* records. She's a *legend*. And you saved her life.' Lynn was silent for a moment. Then she said, 'I still can't believe you didn't tell me about it.'

'I knew you'd make a fuss.'

'You spend one day by yourself in San Francisco and save the life of a *legend* and you don't even tell your own wife. I have to find out from strangers.'

'They weren't supposed to find out, either.'

John had thought, for more than a week after returning home, that he'd gotten away clean. Then, the call came. Apparently, some damn paparazzo had followed him to the car after he broke that crazy bastard's arm and fled through the crowd. He'd never gotten a photo of John's face, but a snapshot of the car revealed its license plate number, and either the freelancer or someone at the magazine got his identity through the DMV. The call had come from an editor, who wanted to send out a staff writer and photographer to do a feature article on him. An exclusive. *Passerby Confronts Gunman, Saves Life of Rock Superstar.* John's 'Thanks, but I'm not interested' only seemed to make the editor more persistent. But John had held his ground, stuck to his refusal.

He was taking a shower half an hour later when the editor called again. This time, Lynn had answered the phone.

Thus, a dinner tonight at the Edgewood with a

writer and photographer who'd come a long way for nothing.

'And I just can't *believe* you told the man you wouldn't let them do the story,' Lynn said. Then she sighed. 'Of course I believe it. Thank God he called back, or . . .'

'Why do you think that lunatic tried to shoot Veronica?' John asked, speaking softly, knowing how Lynn would freeze up if he raised his voice. 'Because she's famous. Do you think he would've gone after her with a gun if she'd been a nobody? There's a lot to be said for anonymity. John Lennon would probably still be alive today if he'd been a TV repairman.'

'Now you're being just plain ridiculous. Nobody's going to shoot you, for crying out loud, just because *People Today* does a story about you.'

'You never know. Some nut might read it and get pissed off because I interfered.' He wasn't especially worried about that, but he'd had time during the past week to think of a few matters that *really* worried him. 'There's something else. They'll want to run photos of us all. So maybe your picture turns on some pervert, and he decides to pay you a visit.'

'Oh, for God's sake.'

'Do you think such things don't happen?'

'I certainly wouldn't know, but . . .'

'I'll tell you one thing, there's no way I'm going to let them put a picture of Kara in that magazine.' Or you either, he thought. Or me. Not a chance. If they try to so much as print our names, I'll hit them with a suit for invasion of privacy.

'You're paranoid,' Lynn said. 'You're absolutely paranoid, do you know that?'

'I just don't think we should call attention to ourselves,' he pointed out, still managing to keep his voice low and calm. 'Which is why I got out of there after nailing that bastard in the first place.'

'Which is also why I'm not wearing my mink tonight and why I can't have a Porsche and why you don't even *try* to sell your good stuff and why we'll be spending the rest of our lives living off your father's inheritance.'

Though her words hurt him, he muttered, 'That's right.' Why argue? She *was* right, and he knew it.

'Some cruds swipe a jacket off you when you're fifteen years old, and we have to spend the rest of our lives paying for it.'

'They almost killed me.'

Lynn fell silent.

'Because they wanted my leather jacket.'

'I *knooooow*.' She'd lost her spunk. Her voice came out quiet and pleading. 'But John, you don't stop buying leather jackets because of something like that.'

'You do if you're smart.'

'You don't dig yourself a hole and hide in it.'

'Come on now, honey, we aren't exactly living in a hole and hiding. There's a big difference between that and simply trying to keep a low profile.'

'We'd be living like hermits if I didn't constantly keep after you.'

'No, we wouldn't.'

'You'd probably prefer to be invisible, if you had any choice in the matter.'

He forced out a chuckle. 'Now, there's a neat idea.'

'It'd be perfect for you. The invisible man. The ultimate in anonymity.'

'Why didn't *I* think of that?'

He *had* thought of that. Often. He was sure he'd never told Lynn, though. It was his pet fantasy, being invisible, and he'd always kept it to himself. Not exactly something you share, your desire to vanish from sight.

But if he ever stumbled onto a Genie, that would be his first wish. And the only wish he would need.

He wouldn't want to be invisible all the time, of course. To be able to change at will, that'd be the thing.

He'd never again have to worry about the creeps of the world chosing him for a target. You can't hassle, rob or murder someone you can't see. That part, he knew, was cowardly. The other part of being invisible, which appealed to him just as much, had nothing to do with cowardice but seemed even more shameful.

As a teenager, his favorite daydream had involved sneaking invisible into the girls' shower room after gym class. He hadn't given up that daydream. But now his fantasies more often involved young women, not teenagers. Watching them undress and bathe.

Invisible, he could do other things, too: eavesdrop, steal anything he might want, wreck havoc on his enemies, even commit murder. Not that he would. He had no desire at all to do any of those things, and rarely gave them a thought. His fantasies included very little beyond spying on women in the shower.

But that was enough to prevent him from ever breathing a word of his secret desire to Lynn or to anyone else.

She would consider him a latent Peeping Tom, a sicko for wanting to do that. For desiring invisibility to avoid the attention of creeps, she would figure him for a paranoid coward.

She's already got that part figured, John thought as he pulled away from a stop light and realized he was only a block from the Edgewood.

He accelerated through the intersection, then swung his car to an empty space at the curb.

'Now, come on,' Lynn said. 'They've got valet parking.'

'It won't kill us to walk for two minutes.'

'God, I get so tired of this.'

'It'll save a couple of bucks.'

'That isn't it, and we both know it. For crying out loud, who'd *want* to steal this heap?'

'I just don't want some stranger driving it around.'

'Yeah, right.' She thrust open her door and climbed out.

John met her on the sidewalk. She took his hand, looked at him and sighed. 'It's not that I mind walking, you know.'

'I know.'

'It's just the way you're always trying to avoid things.'

He managed a smile. 'You should be used to it, by now.'

'Well, I'm not. It irks me more and more all the time.'

'I'm sorry.'

'And the one time in years you stand up and do something terrific, you don't even want anyone to find out about it.'

'I'm here, aren't I?'

'Under duress.'

Maybe I should let them do the article, he thought as he walked with Lynn through the chilly evening. He checked his wristwatch. Seven o'clock on the nose and the restaurant was just ahead.

It would make up for a lot in Lynn's eyes, if I go along with the damn thing. And they'll probably do some kind of story whether or not I cooperate. No threat of a lawsuit was likely to stop a powerful magazine like that.

But the consequences.

There probably won't *be* any consequences.

Beneath the restaurant's portico stood a young man wearing a red jacket and a ponytail. Waiting for customers to come along and turn over their cars. The glance he gave John made it clear he didn't appreciate people who parked on the street.

John blushed.

Can't even go out for dinner without someone giving you grief.

He pulled open one of the heavy double doors, and held it wide for Lynn. The foyer of the Edgewood was nearly as dark as the night outside.

Lynn stopped and unbuttoned her coat. John took it from her, and she stuffed her shawl down one of the sleeves.

'Aren't you going to wear that?'

'I don't think so. It's nice and warm in here.'

Everyone in the restaurant would probably end up staring at her. Men with dreams of invisibility were likely to fantasize about watching *her* shower.

'I think you ought to wear it. That dress is awfully revealing.'

'Oh, don't be such a stick in the . . .'

A slam of thunder shut off her voice.

Downpour

Toby Barnes, gunned down at the north goalpost of Memorial Stadium by patrolman Bob Hanson, was the first to die that night when the black rain fell. He was far from the last.

The rain caught Ethel Banks while she backed away from the tailgate of her station wagon with two sacks of groceries clutched to her chest. She nearly dropped them when the thunder crashed. She did drop them when the warm rain fell on her.

'Oh dear,' she muttered.

She bent over the split bags, thinking she ought to pick them up, and was surprised to notice how dark the night suddenly seemed. Maybe the bulb in the pole lamp by the driveway had burnt out. But the two sacks and the exposed groceries grew even darker as she gazed at them.

They seemed to be turning black.

Steam swirled up around them.

'Isn't this peculiar,' she said.

Even more peculiar was the way she suddenly felt. Normally, Ethel would've been rushing for the house to get away from such a downpour. But she found herself enjoying it so much that she couldn't bring herself to move. She stayed as she was, bent over, letting the rain mat down her hair, run down her face and neck, soak through the back of her sweater, the seat of her skirt and panties.

It made her feel . . . strange.

Hot and strange and full of a restless urge that she couldn't quite focus on. She ached to do *some*thing. But what?

'Ethel?' The rain was loud, smacking the concrete, drumming on the car, pattering on the paper sacks and the plastic wrappers of toilet paper and Wonderbread that had spilled onto the driveway. But the voice was louder. 'Is that you? What's going on?'

She looked up. Through the mist and shrouds of black rain, she saw a vague figure in the doorway. 'It's me, Charlie,' she called.

'Well, don't just stand out there. You'd better get inside before you're soaked.'

'I'm coming,' she called, and stood up straight. 'I'm coming,' she repeated, striding toward the open door. 'I sure am, Charlie,' she muttered as she started to run, head tilted back, smiling into the rain. She didn't see the front stoop. The single step tripped her, sent her sprawling. She slid on her belly across the slick, painted concrete.

'My Lord!' Charlie gasped. 'Are you all . . . Why, you're as black as the ace of spades! What the devil's going on?'

Ethel scurried up, lunging forward.

Charlie yelled, 'Hey!' an instant before her head struck his groin. *That* let the wind out of him! Ethel hugged his legs, driving him backward as he doubled over her. His rump hit the marble floor of the foyer.

She shoved her face between his legs, filled her mouth with the crotch of his slacks and his pal, Mr Pete, and chomped.

Charlie jumped and shimmied as if he'd stuck his finger in a socket.

Ethel clambered up his twitching body. She sat on his chest and grabbed his ears. Using them for handles, she bounced his head off the floor. The first couple of times, it sounded like someone dropping a coconut. Then the sound softened to wet, sloppy smacks as if the back of his head might have turned into a sirloin steak. One that hadn't been broiled yet. All floppy and juicy.

Willis Yardly signed his credit card slip, tore off the top copy, and fingered the rest of it into the trough under the window. He stuffed his credit card into his wallet, then took out a dollar bill. He used that to buy a Twix candy bar for his son, Jimmy. The boy liked to come along to the filling station and make his own selection, but he had the sniffles so Mandy kept him home this time.

While Willis waited for change, he folded his copy of the slip. He stuffed that, along with the Twix, into his jacket pocket. His hand came out with a pack of cigarettes, a book of matches.

The drive home would give him time for one smoke.

Better not light up in here, he thought.

He took his change, dropped it into a pocket of his trousers, and pushed through the door. Outside, he shook the pack to jostle some cigarettes through the opening. As he raised it to his mouth and pinched out a cigarette with his lips, he noticed the woman at pump number one.

She wore a clear plastic glove so she wouldn't soil her hand with the messy job. Obviously, she didn't enjoy pumping her own gas.

Willis wondered if he should offer to do it for her.

She'd probably think I'm trying to pick her up.

She looked good, bending over like that. Her faded jeans were pulled taut against her rump. Her blue T-shirt was so tight that he could see the bumps of her spine and the outline of her bra. The bottom of it had come untucked in back, baring a strip of skin to the chilly night.

She must be freezing, Willis thought.

Maybe I *should* offer to help.

He took the unlighted cigarette from his mouth, slipped it into his pocket (it'll probably pick up pocket lint), and stepped off the walkway beside the office. He took one stride before thunder shook the night.

The woman jumped.

The rain came down, masking the bright lights of the Mobil station, splashing its heat onto Willis as he hurried toward the woman with a strange excitement.

She was dry beneath the island's roof. No longer pumping gas. Standing up straight with nozzle by her side, a look of shock on her face as Willis came out of the rain.

'Jesus!' she gasped.

'Let me help you with that,' Willis said, reaching for the nozzle.

'You're all *black*! What the hell kind of rain . . . ?'

He yanked the nozzle from her grip. His other hand grabbed the front of her T-shirt. He shoved her, slamming her back against the trunk, holding her down with his fist thrust hard against her chest.

She opened her mouth to curse him or scream.

He shoved the spout inside it. He squeezed the trigger. Gasoline flooded her mouth, splashed out. She thrashed on the trunk, choking, eyes squeezed shut, hands clawing at the nozzle.

Willis pulled the spout from her mouth and hosed her face, her T-shirt. He rammed the spout into her belly. She bucked under his straight arm and gasoline exploded from her mouth.

Stepping back, he let her slide off the trunk. Her knees hit the concrete. She fell forward and caught herself with her hands.

Willis soaked her down some more.

Then he dropped the nozzle, fished his match book out of the pocket where it rested beside the Twix bar, and lit a match.

His hands and arms flamed, but he managed to toss the match.

It blew out on its way toward the woman.

So he crouched and touched her hair.

Chet Baxter was waiting in line beside his girlfriend, Christie Lord, to buy a ticket for the seven o'clock showing of *Out Are The Lights* when the thunder boomed. They both flinched. Laughing, Chet squeezed her against his side. She smiled up at him. The lights dimmed. As the hot, exciting rain pounded down on his head and shoulders, Chet watched her face go blotchy then disappear except for the whites of her eyes and teeth.

He grabbed her wet, hanging hair. Before he could yank her head back to expose her throat, her fingernails ripped open his cheek. Crying out, he clutched her wrist.

Someone smashed against them. Hanging onto Christie, Chet tumbled to the sidewalk. She came down on top of him, snarling, thrusting her head down at his face, teeth snapping.

Suddenly, she looked up.

Chet clutched her throat with both hands.

'No,' she gasped. 'Wait. Let's get *them*.'

He ached to choke the life out of the bitch, but her words made him hesitate. He relaxed his grip for a moment, and she lurched free. She scurried backward, crawling off him. 'Them,' she said again.

On her knees, the sodden black spector thrust an arm straight out and pointed. 'LET'S GET *THEM*!' she yelled.

Chet sat up, ignoring the alarmed voices and outcries of those behind him – those at whom Christie was pointing. Instead, he watched the eight or ten struggling figures beyond her back. Some were down on the sidewalk, pounding and ripping at one another. Others were still on their feet. Chet saw one man slamming the face of a teenaged boy against the top of a fire hydrant. He saw a woman clamped to a storefront wall by a man's forearm across her throat while the guy rammed a pocket knife into her belly.

'LET'S GET THE DRY ONES!' Christie shouted.

It seemed like a fine idea to Chet. It seemed fitting, somehow.

Apparently, the idea appealed to the others as well. They ceased their struggles, let go of one another. Some fell to the sidewalk. Some didn't get up. Those were left behind as the faint shapes of the others approached.

With Christie and Chet in the lead, they rushed under the marquee. The dry ones were already in flight, a few racing away, running out from under the shelter and into the rain themselves, but most seeking the safety of the theater, yelling as they pushed through the glass door, knocking aside the flustered teenaged boy whose job was to take their tickets.

One man remained in front of the ticket booth, shouting at the girl inside the glass enclosure to hurry. As he reached into the opening for his ticket, Christie smashed his head against the glass. The glass didn't break. Not that time. But Christie, Chet and a pregnant woman used the man for a battering ram, driving his head against the ticket booth until the glass disintegrated.

They hurled the man aside. The pregnant woman fell upon him.

Inside the booth, the ticket girl was turning in circles, her eyes bulging, her mouth hanging open. She looked as if she wanted to make a dash for the theater entrance, but a rain-blackened man was trying to rip open the locked door at the rear of her enclosure. And others were already rushing through the lobby.

Her back was turned when Christie leaned in, grabbed the shoulders of her blazer and wrenched her off her feet. Chet reached in to help. Together, they dragged the shrieking, kicking girl onto the counter. Her flapping arms struck the edges of the glass, slashing her sleeves and breaking off jagged shards. When she was halfway out, Chet put a headlock on her. Christie jerked the girl's blazer, popping its single fastened button away, then tore open the blouse.

Her skin was pebbled with goosebumps. Her breasts shook as she squirmed. Her nipples were visible through the black lace of her bra, pink and jutting.

Christie split the girl's belly with a blade of glass.

Entrances

1

Maureen O'Casey, with three family-sized pizzas stacked on the passenger seat of her Jeep Cherokee, stopped beneath a street light to check her map of Bixby.

She looked for Mercer Lane. She'd set out from the pizza parlor certain that she knew where to find it. But the street had turned out to be Merced, and she realized she didn't have the foggiest notion where Mercer might be.

Her brother, Rory, would probably be able to drive there blindfolded. He'd been delivering pizzas for six years, ever since the family moved here from Modesto. Except for occasional visits, however, Maureen had spent those years in San Francisco doing graduate work and later writing books for children. Her visits had provided her with knowledge of Bixby's general layout and quite a few of its streets, but not Mercer.

Maureen found her ignorance annoying. She liked to feel in control of whatever situations presented themselves, and she was definitely not in control of this. She should've anticipated that she would be asked, sooner or later, to make deliveries. But she hadn't. Rory's illness had taken her totally by surprise, and totally unprepared to fill in for him.

'Ah-*ha*! There you are, you little bugger.'

Mercer appeared to be only three blocks from her present location.

She folded the map, tossed it onto the dashboard, and made a U-turn.

With any luck, she would make the delivery and be back at the restaurant by seven-twenty. That would give her forty minutes to spare, but of course her father would likely ship her right off on another errand. And then another.

'Buck up,' she told herself. 'It's not the end of the world. Consider it an intermission.'

Though she wouldn't be seeing much of Trevor tonight, he would surely pop in tomorrow.

That wasn't much consolation. She'd been looking forward to tonight, had even discarded her usual jeans and blouse for a dress, all the better to attract his eye.

Well, she would find time to drop by his table no matter what. Slip off the coat, first. Have a few words with him.

Maureen made a left turn, then smiled. Suppose she invited him to come along? He's off duty tonight, isn't he?

I don't want to scare him off.

Cop or not, he's obviously a timid man. The poor blighter might go into cardiac arrest if I try to drag him off with me . . . But not if I plead for his help. After all, I'm the new girl in town and don't know my way around – who better to help me navigate the foreign streets than a policeman?

How could he possibly refuse?

She laughed softly. 'Am I brilliant, or what?'

Stopping at the next intersection, she leaned toward the windshield and peered at the corner sign.

Mercer!

She turned right and drove along, delighted with her scheme. It wouldn't be an actual date, but they'd finally have a chance to be alone with each other. Guiding her around town, Trev was bound to get over his jitters. Before long . . .

She spotted 3548 painted on the curb, and pulled over.

Just to make sure of the address, she plucked the order slip off the top box. This street was darker than the other. She turned on the overhead light.

The address was 3548 Mercer, just as she'd remembered it. The order had been placed by someone named Buddy.

This is it, all right.

Maureen shut off the lights and engine. She dropped the keys into her coat pocket, swung open her door, then lifted the three white cartons off the passenger seat. Slipping a hand under the bottom box, she felt the heat. In spite of her small detour, the pizzas hadn't cooled off.

She climbed out of the Cherokee and knocked its door shut with her rump.

As she stepped over the curb, she noticed three motorcycles parked on the driveway. She wrinkled her nose. These didn't look like the cute little bikes a family might use on weekends. These were burly machines – hogs, choppers – steel mounts for tattooed men with skulls emblazoned on the backs of their denim jackets.

Or boys who like to fancy themselves tough, Maureen thought as she strode toward the lighted front porch of the house.

She was pretty sure she wouldn't find a band of savage bikers here. Even in Bixby, where real estate was cheap by California standards, a home like this must be worth at least a hundred and fifty thousand.

More than likely, the pizzas were for the son and his friends.

If bikers *had* taken over the place, they wouldn't be ordering out for . . .

Overhead, the night seemed to explode.

Maureen cringed.

'Oh, wouldn't you just know it,' she muttered, and started to run for the porch.

The rain came down before she got there. When she felt its heat on her head, she stopped.

Hey, she thought, this is nice.

Bending over, she set the pizza boxes on the walkway at her feet. She took off her coat, stretched out her arms, and tilted back her head to feel the rain on her face. In seconds, her dress was soaked and clinging to her body.

A warm tremor spread through Maureen. She felt an urge to strip naked and roll on the grass. But a different urge was stronger.

Just ahead, to the left of the front steps, she saw the faint shapes of rocks along the border of a garden. She hurried over and tugged one loose from the soil. She felt so good, squatting in her soaked clothes, that she was reluctant to stand up again.

But she pictured herself swinging the rock, smashing a face to bloody pulp. The image of that stirred Maureen to action.

She carried the rock back to the walkway, set it on the sodden black cardboard of the top box, and lifted all three pizzas.

Grinning, she climbed the steps. At the door, she shifted the load, bracing it up with her left hand, the edges of the boxes against her chest to keep them steady. Her right hand removed the rock and used a corner of it to ring the bell. 'Pizza!' she called.

She lowered the rock. She pressed it against her right buttock, out of sight. In her eagerness, she bobbed up and down on the balls of her feet.

The door opened.

'Pizza!' she shouted into the face of the teenager. The kid, a big muscular guy with brushed up hair and a garden of raw pimples on his chin, looked glad to see her. For half a second.

'What the *fuck*!'

She swung the rock, aiming for his chin.

His arm shot up. Maureen's wrist struck it. Pain flashed up her arm. The rock flew from her numb fingers, missing him and clumping the door frame and bouncing off as the boxes of pizza hit the stoop.

She tried to duck, hoping to retrieve the rock, but

67

the kid clutched the front of her dress. He jerked her forward. She stumbled over the threshold. Felt herself being turned and thrown off her feet. The kid's scared face was above her for a moment. Then her back slammed the floor. As her breath exploded out, the impact snapped her head down.

It made a terrible thud. In the instant before she lost consciousness, Maureen saw her brain as a grenade going off, blowing fire out her eyes and nose and ears.

2

'My *God*, what was that!' Francine blurted, hand scurrying over the table top to retrieve the cigarette that had leaped from between her fingers.

Trev himself had flinched at the sudden muffled roar. Lisa must've jumped an inch off her seat, and her breasts had bounced dramatically under the tight sweater.

'I hope it was just thunder,' Trev said.

Lisa studied the ceiling as if she expected it to come down.

'*God*,' Francine said again. She clamped the cigarette between her lips. It jiggled. She took only one pull, then crushed it in the ashtray.

'It isn't suppose to rain,' Lisa muttered, still frowning at the acoustic tiles above her.

'I'm sure there's nothing to be concerned about.' As Trev said that, he turned his head. Out in the other room, Patterson looked concerned. The man was scowling, saying something as he walked toward Lucy at the switchboard. Lucy was shaking her head and shrugging.

'Anyway,' Francine said, 'about protection for us.'

Trev faced her again.

'My daughter's a witness . . .'

'Well, she's certainly provided valuable information.' He looked at Lisa. 'Is there anything else you want to tell me about last night?'

Shrugging, the girl shook her head. She resumed her study of the frayed knee of her jeans.

Trev turned his eyes to Francine. 'Would you like to step out the door for a minute?'

'No, I would not. Lisa has nothing to say that can't be said in front of me.'

'I've already told you everything,' Lisa said, her voice pouty. 'I'm not keeping any big hot secrets, if that's what you're getting at.'

Trev glanced through the glass in time to see Patterson stride around the end of the front counter. Probably going out to make sure it *had* been nothing but thunder.

He looked again at the girl. 'Well, you've been very helpful, Lisa, and I really appreciate it.'

'I know they killed him,' she said.

'But you never saw Buddy or his friends after they were escorted from the dance?'

'That's what I told you.'

'And the last you saw of Maxwell was when you kissed him goodnight in the school parking lot. Then you left his car to go back to your own car, but didn't see . . .'

'I didn't really look around. They might've been there, and I just didn't see them. You know? They could've had their motorcycles hidden behind something. Some buses were parked over at the side.'

'You've got to give us police protection,' Francine demanded. 'We can't just walk out of here and go on our merry way. Those boys will come after Lisa. I know it.'

'I doubt if they'll have the opportunity,' Trev told her. 'We'll pick them up tonight and bring them in.'

'Oh great,' Lisa muttered. 'Then they'll *know* I blabbed.'

Trev gave her a smile, then tapped the top page of the legal tablet resting on his leg. 'I've got a whole list of people who saw those guys acting up at the dance. Buddy and his friends won't know you're the one who talked to us. I certainly won't tell them.'

'They're not stupid,' she said.

'They *are* stupid, or they wouldn't have murdered that young man. If they did it, they're going down. You can bet on it.'

Francine smirked. 'Who are you, Sergeant Preston of the Yukon?'

'No, ma'am.'

'I've got it. Joe Friday.'

'Two of my favorite cops.'

'I'll just bet.'

Standing, he slid the pad of paper onto the table. 'We'll have a talk with Buddy, Doug and Lou tonight, and see how things develop from there.'

'And you'll let us know what happens.' It wasn't a request.

'Of course.'

As Francine and Lisa got to their feet, Trev stepped past them. He opened the glass door. 'I really appreciate your taking the time to come in about this. And Lisa, if you think of anything else that might . . .'

The noise that pounded Trev's ears, this time, was not thunder.

He jerked his eyes toward the blast and saw Lucy's chair lurch backward, hurling her away from the switchboard as the base of her skull erupted, splashing a red mess at the floor.

'Down down down!' he shouted, sinking to a squat in the doorway and reaching for the off-duty revolver at his side while the black thing on the other side of the counter (is that *Patterson*?) fired a round into Lucy's chest that sent her chair flipping over. She tumbled out of it, legs flying up, and hit the floor in a backward somersault.

Then Patterson's gun was aimed at Trev. He heard himself yell 'SHIT!' as explosions smacked his eardrums and a slug whizzed by his face and some of his bullets missed but two struck Patterson high in the chest and another punched through his throat and Patterson flopped out of sight behind the counter.

Gasping for air, Trev switched the empty gun to his left hand. He grabbed the metal doorframe with his right hand and pulled at it to drag himself upward. When he was standing, he looked over his shoulder. Francine was on her hands and knees, staring up at him with wild eyes. Lisa hadn't dropped. She was frozen upright behind her mother, fists pressed to her cheeks.

'Are you both OK?' he asked. He could barely hear himself through the ringing in his ears. And he didn't need to ask the question. He could see that they hadn't been hit. 'Stay right here,' he said.

He staggered through the doorway and headed for his desk. It seemed like a great distance away. He kept glancing at the counter, though he doubted that Patterson was capable of popping up and firing (fuck, you shot his throat out).

As he walked along, he emptied his cylinder. Brass casings clattered against the floor.

From the top drawer of his desk, he removed a box of cartridges. His shaky hands dropped two of them while he tried to reload. At last, he managed to fill the cylinder and snap it shut.

Glancing back, he saw Francine in the interrogation room doorway with her arm around Lisa. They both looked dazed and sick.

He walked over to Lucy. She was sprawled facedown in a spreading swamp of blood.

The switchboard was a panel of blinking lights, a call on every line.

What's going on?

Trev leaned across the counter.

Patterson was stretched out on his back, revolver

on the floor near his right hand. His eyes and teeth were still white. His throat and chest were bright red. His shield gleamed silver. Some blue showed below the knees of his uniform trousers. Otherwise, the man was black.

Wet and black. Like an oilman in the movies who has struck a gusher and stood in its downpour.

'Did you get him?' Francine called.

'I got him.'

'Who was it? Why did he shoot that woman and . . .'

'He was the desk sergeant,' Trev said. 'I don't know why he . . .'

'The man we *talked* to?'

'Yeah,' he said, and climbed over the counter. He dropped to the floor at Patterson's feet. 'Stay put. I'll be right back.'

For a moment, he considered taking Patterson's revolver or at least kicking it some distance from the body. But he didn't want to disturb the crime scene. Patterson was in no shape to use the revolver, anyway, and the gun was almost certainly out of ammunition. So he left it there and hurried toward the station doors.

'Don't go out there!' Lisa shouted.

Patterson went out, he thought. Patterson came in wet and black and shooting. Doesn't make any sense at all.

The double doors were blue painted metal, each with a square window of bullet-proof glass at head level. From the other side came a faint hissing sound like rain striking pavement. He cupped his hands to one of the panes, and peered out.

Something was wrong with the lights. The walks, driveway and parking strip in front of the station should've been bright under the sodium arcs. Instead, they were barely visible. He could make out the faint smudges of two cars – his own and probably Francine's.

Trev released the door's catch and stepped back. With his right foot, he flung the door open. The sounds of the falling rain came in, along with a mild breeze. He sniffed, wondering if he might detect fumes, but the air smelled fresh and clean.

As the door started to swing back, Trev stopped it with his shoe.

The area of walk directly beyond the door, sheltered by an overhang, appeared to be dry. But he decided not to risk stepping outside.

Patterson went out, and look what happened. Had the black stuff *made* him act that way? Hardly seemed likely, but something had sure screwed up the man's head. He'd gone out normal, and come in homicidal and covered with black fluid.

It must, somehow, have to do with the rain.

The light spilling out through the doorway didn't reach far enough to show Trev the color of the rain.

But if the falling water wasn't black, what was that all over Patterson? And why couldn't he see the parking lot lights?

Trev toed down the metal stop to keep the door from swinging shut, then stepped outside. He took a few strides. Halting a yard from the edge of the over-hang, he stared at the curtain of falling water. It looked dark, all right. But hell, the night itself was dark.

Though he couldn't be certain that the rain was black, it was obviously warm, for he saw a faint, pale mist rising off the walkway ahead of him and the grass that bordered it.

He pulled a folded white handkerchief from his pocket. He shook it open, then wadded it into a ball and tossed it underhand. The cloth unfurled. The instant it passed into the shower, it ceased to be white. Trev watched a sodden black rag drop to the walkway.

'Holy shit,' he muttered.

He rushed back inside the station.

3

Kara didn't jump, but her face pulled a contortion that made Denise laugh: eyes wide, forehead rumpled, nose wrinkled, lips twisted sideways. It was the kind of expression, Denise thought, that this particular girl might put on her face if she just happened to notice a boogeyman leering at her from the darkness of a closet – a weird mixture of fright, disbelief and amusement

'You'd better hope it doesn't freeze that way.'

Kara didn't say a word, but Denise had no trouble at all deciphering the exaggerated motions of her lips and tongue. *What. Was. That?*

'Either thunder or the end of the world, take your pick.'

Kara screwed up her face again, then let it settle back into place and said, 'Which one would you pick?'

'Thunder, I imagine.'

'Me, too. Though I'm not especially fond of thunder, either.' She pressed the mute button on the VCR's remote and sat very still for a moment.

Denise heard the soft, windy sound of rain falling on the roof.

'It must be raining cats and dogs,' Kara said. 'I hope they don't hurt themselves. If it *really* rained cats and dogs, you know, the cats would all land on their feet. But I'm not sure the dogs would fare so well. They would probably break their necks, don't you suppose?' A smile spread across her face. Leaning toward Denise, she said, 'And just imagine the mess they'd make on the lawn. Toes-up dogs everywhere you look, not even to mention all the *elimination.*'

'Not a pretty picture,' Denise admitted.

'A gross-out of major proportions, that's what I think.'

'Probably won't happen, though.'

'Do you know what? Maybe I should round up

some candles. We just might lose the juice, you know. That happened two years ago, the day after Thanksgiving.'

'Your mom and dad would have to eat in the dark.'

'Ooo, yuck, they might come home early and ruin our fun.'

'Maybe while we've still got juice we should make the popcorn.'

Kara frowned upward for a moment as if deep in thought. Then she snapped her fingers. 'Hey, I've got it! Let's make some popcorn!'

'Weird kid.'

Kara pressed a button on the remote to shut off the tape of her birthday party, and a regular show appeared on the television. She bounded off the sofa. Denise followed her through the dining room to the kitchen.

There, Kara rushed around gathering the popper, the plastic bowl, a measuring cup, popcorn and oil and butter and salt. She arranged them all on the counter, plugged in the cord, dribbled oil into the pot, and dropped in three kernels.

'That should be enough for you,' Denise said. 'But what about me?'

'We need to wait for these to pop so we know the oil's ready and . . . Oh, right. As if you didn't know. Honestly, you're as bad as my dad. Come with me.'

'Where to?' Denise asked, following her from the kitchen.

'I've gotta ride the porcelain trolley.'

'Huh?'

'I've gotta *pee*.'

'And that requires my presence?'

'I'm not going in there alone. It's storming out. What if I'm by myself and we lose the juice?'

'While *you're* losing the juice.'

Kara laughed. 'If you were on *The Gong Show*, I'd gong you for that.'

'You're a cruel little thing.'

'Yep.'

She's not all that little, Denise thought. Her slender build probably made her look taller than she really was, but the top of the girl's head seemed to be almost level with Denise's shoulders.

It was odd, having to accompany her to the toilet.

She's only nine, Denise reminded herself. In spite of her height and rather grown-up behavior, she's still just a kid. A kid who doesn't like storms. A kid who's afraid of the dark.

At the end of the hall, Kara said, 'You don't have to come in if you don't want.'

'I appreciate that.'

Kara turned on the light, entered the bathroom, and stepped out of sight behind the open door. 'Don't go away.'

'I won't.'

She heard a rustle of clothes, then splashing sounds.

'Mom said it'd be all right if you wanted to invite your boyfriend over. Would you like to do that? I think it might be neat. What's his name?'

'Tom.'

'Is he nice?'

'He wouldn't be my boyfriend if he was a jerk.'

'Well, I should hope not. Why don't you see if he wants to come over? He could have popcorn with us, you know?'

'Well, I don't know. The storm and everything.'

'It might be nice to have a guy around, especially if the lights go off.'

'You just want to steal him from me.'

'No, I don't.' She sounded disgusted by the thought. 'Boys are a pain in the neck. All they ever talk about are P-38s and M-16s and F-17s. Guns and planes and tanks and stuff. As if I even know what they're talking about. As if I care.' Denise heard her spin the toilet paper roll. 'But I really think you ought to phone Tom and see if he wants to come over and have some popcorn. How far away does he live?'

'A few blocks.'

'Does he have a car?'

'His parents do.'

The toilet flushed. 'Well, he can drive over, then. He won't get very wet.'

'I don't know, Kara. He might just want to talk about P-38s and things.'

'If he does, we'll send him packing.' She stepped around the door, zipped her jeans and reached for the light switch.

'Aren't you going to wash your hands?'

She grinned. 'Didn't get anything on them.'

'How about washing them, anyway? You're going to be sticking your hand in the popcorn bowl.'

Kara sighed, then went to the sink. She didn't use hot water, but she did use soap. As she dried her hands, she said, 'Besides, it's not fair that you didn't get to go out with him tonight.'

'That's OK.'

'You can phone him from the kitchen. I'll take care of the popcorn.'

It would be nice, Denise thought as she walked down the hallway with Kara. Though she didn't regret her decision to babysit, she'd found her mind straying while she watched the videotape of the birthday party, found herself imagining how it would've been if she'd stayed home and Tom had come over.

With Kara here, she could spend the time with him and not have to worry about matters getting out of hand.

'Maybe I'll do it,' she said as they entered the kitchen.

'All right!'

'No harm in calling, anyway.' She lifted the handset of the wall phone. While she punched in Tom's number, Kara hurried to the popper and checked inside. As the phone rang, Kara scooped a cupful of kernels out of the jar. She dumped them into the pot.

A woman's voice said, 'Hello?'

'Hi, Mrs Carney. This is Denise.'

'Oh, how are you? Tom's right here. Hang on just a sec.'

Kara covered the popper, then turned around to watch. *Is he there?* she mouthed without speaking.

Denise nodded.

'Hey, Denny,' Tom said.

'Hey, how's it going?'

'Pretty good.'

'I'm over here sitting for Kara Foxworth. That dynamite kid I told you about?'

Kara drew her head back, giving herself a double chin and beaming.

'I was just thinking about you,' Tom said.

'Something good, I hope.'

'Wondering what you were up to. I figured you were all alone at home, you know, with the storm going on and everything. Man, did you catch that thunder?'

'Who could miss it?'

'I thought the house was going to come down.'

'Have you got an umbrella?'

'Why? What's up?'

'Well, Kara here is awfully eager to share her popcorn with you.'

Kara made a face and jammed her fists against her hips.

'You want me to come over?' Tom asked.

'Yeah. I mean, I know it's miserable out, but if you could make it over here without getting yourself drenched . . . Kara's parents are out to dinner, so they won't be very late. And they said it's all right for you to come over. We could watch some TV, have some popcorn and stuff.'

'Sounds great. Hang on a minute, I'll see if it's OK.'

Denise heard his phone clatter against something. 'He's checking with his parents,' she told Kara.

'You didn't have to say it was *my* idea.'

'It was your idea.'

'Well, stilllll.' In the pot behind her, popcorn began to burst with soft explosive sounds and a general clinking of kernels hurled against the walls and lid.

When Tom returned to the phone, he said, 'It's OK with them.'

'Really?'

'Yeah. They're not overjoyed about me going out on a night like this, but I told them we wouldn't be driving around in it. I'm supposed to go straight to your house, and come straight home afterward.'

'Nobody's there.'

'Hey, if they knew you were babysitting, there's no way they'd let me come. As far as they know, you're at home with your folks and we're just going to stay there and watch the tube.'

'Liar liar, pants on fire.'

That seemed to amuse Kara no end.

'Necessity is the mother of deception,' Tom said. 'So, what time do you want me?'

'As soon as you can make it. The popcorn's gonna be ready in about five more minutes.'

'I'll be as quick as I can.'

'Get here while it's hot.'

'I'll try. See you.'

'See you,' she said, and hung up. To Kara, she said, 'He's on his way.'

4

'What's going on?' Francine sounded more angry than frightened, as if she hadn't come to the police station in hopes of being shot at, and blamed Trev.

'I don't know,' he said. He stepped around the end of the counter. 'The rain's black out there.'

'That's ridiculous.'

'Look for yourself if you want.'

Francine shook her head. She and Lisa had come out of the interrogation room and were standing among the desks, holding hands. Lisa's gaze was fixed on Lucy's body. She looked as if she might get sick.

'You two keep an eye on the door. If someone comes in, speak up fast.' Trev moved in between Lucy's overturned chair and the switchboard.

'What are you doing?'

'I'm gonna see what some of these calls are about.' The headset lay on the floor where it had fallen when it flew off Lucy. Trev pulled it up by the cord and put it on. The earphones had a built-in microphone that curved around in front of his mouth.

He pressed a button on the switchboard. One of the lights stopped blinking and he heard a line open.

'Hello? Hello?' A woman's voice, high-pitched.

'Bixby Police Department.'

'You've gotta send a car! Quick! God, where've you been? There's a madman trying to break in. I shot at him. He tried to come in a window, but I shot at him. I

83

don't think I hit him, but he's still out there. I'm all alone and he's trying to get me!'

'Could you describe him?'

'He's black, that's all I know.'

'A Negro?'

'No. I don't think so. He's just got black stuff on him, I don't know. What does it matter? I need help!'

'Give me your address, please.'

'4329 Larson.'

'Got it. Hang on, I'll contact a patrol car.'

'Hurry! Hurry!'

Trev picked up the radio mike and fingered the speak button. 'All units, report.' He released the button. Waited.

'Oh my God!' the woman squealed. 'Oh my Jesus! He's . . .'

Trev cringed as gunblasts hit his ears.

Then the woman was sobbing. 'There's . . . there's no hurry any more. You can . . . take your sweet time now. He's dead. I shot him dead. Oh, Jesus. Where *were* you?'

'We've got troubles here, too. Are you sure the intruder's dead?'

'Oh, yes. Oh, yes. Oh, yes.'

'OK. Now, we'll have a car there as soon as possible. In the meantime, just take it easy and try to stay calm.'

'Ho ho. Calm, yes. Jesus.'

'And don't go outside or let anyone into your place. There's something strange going on.'

'You're telling me? Oh, I think I've already noticed. Strange?'

'And don't touch the intruder. That black liquid on him . . . it may be dangerous. It may be contagious.'

'What, you think I'd *touch* him? No, I don't think so. No, I don't think so. What do you mean, contagious? He was sick?'

'I just don't know. I think the rain might be making people crazy. Look, I've got to go now.' He disconnected.

He realized he'd told the woman that he would send a patrol car and she shouldn't let anyone in. Good move, he thought.

But no response had come from the radio.

He activated the mike again. 'Anybody out there? Hanson? Yarbrough? Gonzales? Paxton?'

The crackle and hiss of white noise came from the receiver. Nothing more.

'Where are you guys? This is Hudson. Talk to me, damn it!'

Nobody answered.

He took another call, this one from a man.

'You better hustle some troops over here, pal. Man, I never seen nothing to beat it. Place is going wild.'

'Where are you calling from?'

'My shop on Third. Jiffy Locksmith? I go to leave and, man, there's a fucking riot going on in the street. Must be a dozen of 'em, yelling and running around getting soaked, bashing in windows. Shit! They're killing folks, man. Honest to God. I seen 'em run in the fucking doughnut shop across the street, and they just started tearing into the folks in there. Killed every last one of 'em, far as I could see. So, you gonna send in the army, or what?'

'I'm afraid we don't have anyone to send right now.'

'Figures. Well, don't say I didn't give you the poop.'

'Just stay in your shop and try to keep out of sight. We'll try to send help, but . . .'

The man hung up.

Trev felt numb. O'Casey's was on Third Street, just two blocks south of the Tastee Donut shop.

If I hadn't procrastinated, damn it, I'd be there right now.

Oh God, Maureen, what've I done to you!

He pulled out his wallet. His hand trembled as he removed the pizza coupon.

The dollar-off coupon gave the phone number.

All the lines were busy again, so he disconnected one and punched in O'Casey's number. He listened to the ringing.

'Come on, come on,' he muttered.

It rang fifteen times before he gave up.

He flung the headset down. Francine, on the other side of the counter, whirled around.

'I've gotta go out,' he said.

'In the rain? You can't do that.'

'Watch me.'

5

'My name's Peggy, and I'll be serving you this evening.' Peggy, John noticed, wore a frilly peasant skirt and a bodice that left her shoulders bare. Her breasts bulged over the top of the laced, corset-like garment, and it occurred to John that a deep breath might pop them right out of it. The hostess near the front door had sported a similar costume. He supposed Lynn's dress wasn't so bad, after all, with everyone running around in those outfits. But he still wished she hadn't given up her shawl to the cloak room girl. 'Would you care for something from the bar?'

'Do you think we ought to wait for the others?' he asked Lynn.

'Oh, let's just go ahead.' Smiling up at Peggy, she asked for a margarita.

'Would you prefer that with or without salt?'

'With, please.'

'And I'll have a Mai Tai,' John told her. When the waitress was gone, he said, 'Maybe we'll be lucky, and they won't show up at all.'

'Now, don't be that way.'

'Are you sure we've got the right night?'

'I wrote it on my calendar. Seven o'clock, November eleventh, the Edgewood.'

'Maybe it was supposed to be at seven *a.m.*'

'I hardly think so. I'm sure they'll be along shortly.'

'Shortly, and wet,' he said. He hoped they didn't have umbrellas. It would serve them right. If they'd been here on time, they would've missed the downpour. He didn't even know the people, but they irked him. Not only were they butting into his life, but now they were late for the dinner they'd supposedly arranged and they hadn't even bothered to make reservations.

The Edgewood was a popular restaurant, so the lack of reservations might've forced them into a long wait. No thanks to their absent hosts, they'd been spared that. Luck was with them, and there had been several empty tables.

John looked around, wondering if the pair from *People Today* had arrived on time, after all, and simply neglected to mention they were expecting him and Lynn.

We might all be here at separate tables, he thought. That'd be swift. All of us go ahead and eat our dinners thinking we got stood up.

He saw three parties of four. Wouldn't be any of those. Couples sat at four other tables. Among them, he recognized Steve and Carol Winter. That left three pairs of strangers – men sitting across from women.

'Was this Dodd character supposed to be with a man or a woman?' he asked.

'He mentioned a photographer, but I'm sure he didn't say whether it was male or female. Why?'

'I'm just wondering if they're already here.'

'I suppose that's possible, isn't it?' An eagerness seemed to come over Lynn. Her head swiveled as she scanned the diners to either side, then she twisted around in her seat. Facing John again, she said, 'I don't know. What do you think?'

'Well, I'm not about to go around asking.'

'It's pretty unlikely, I suppose. These people were all here before us. I'm sure, if one of them were Mr Dodd, he would've told someone he was expecting us.'

'You'd think so. But then, you'd also think they might've made reservations.'

Peggy arrived with the drinks. John watched the bulges at the top of her bodice while she bent over the table, and Lynn started in on her. 'You know, we're supposed to be meeting some people here. A Mr Dodd and someone else? None of us know each other from Adam, and I'm concerned there may have been some kind of a mixup. They may already be here, for all we know.'

'I'll be happy to check with the hostess for you,' Peggy said.

'Would you, please? That would be wonderful. And in case they haven't arrived yet, they'll be looking for us when they do show up. John and Lynn Foxworth? You might want to give the hostess our names, and warn her to be on the lookout for . . .'

'HEY!'

The woman's distant, alarmed voice hushed the restaurant. The quiet undertones of conversations and laughter and tinking of utensils ceased. In the silence, John heard clanks and clatters from the kitchen area and the piped-in music of an orchestra playing 'Send in the Clowns.' Waitresses halted. Diners turned in their seats. From somewhere near the front came a crash as if a heavy piece of furniture had been knocked over.

Then a sharp cry of pain that ended the shocked silence.

'My God!' Peggy blurted.

'John?'

He shook his head and gazed toward the front. The foyer and doors – and whatever might be happening – were out of sight beyond a corner of the dining area. Waitresses and a few guests started rushing that way.

'I'd better . . .' he muttered, shoving back his chair.

'No, stay here. Don't involve yourself in . . . John!'

'I'll be right back.'

He hurried along with the others, passed the corner and saw a waitress tugging at the arm of a wildman who sat astride the overturned hostess station and bounced on it, pounding the heavy wooden lectern against the chest of the young woman pinned beneath it. Her scarlet face was twisted with pain. Her breasts *had* popped out of her bodice, and they shook as she strained to shove away the punishing weight.

The man, sodden and black (it's the parking attendant who gave me the dirty look, John realized), flung the clinging waitress off his arm. As she stumbled backward, a guy in a sport coat shot his foot out, ramming the lunatic's shoulder and knocking him off the lectern. That man and two others threw themselves onto him.

John tumbled the lectern off the hostess. He knelt beside her. Wheezing for breath, she drew up her knees and hugged her ribcage. Her teeth were bared and she whipped her head from side to side. John took off his blazer. He covered her from waist to shoulders.

'Are you all right?'

'Move out of the way,' a man said. 'I'm a doctor.'

He crawled aside. A gray-haired man crouched and swept John's blazer to the floor. 'You'll be fine,' he said in a gentle voice. 'What's your name, dear?'

'Cassy,' she gasped out.

'Cassy, I'm Dr Goodman. I'm sure you'll be just fine.' With a pocket knife, he severed the laces down her front.

She raised her head off the floor to see what he was doing.

'Nothing to be alarmed about, Cassy. I'm just going to take a look. I won't hurt you.' He spread the bodice. The girl flinched and gasped as he fingered her lower ribs where her skin was red. 'Uh-huh, uh-huh.'

John watched her breasts jiggle as she twitched. They were small and firm. The creamy skin just above her nipples was seamed with indentations left by the tight garment. Her nipples were erect. John felt heat spreading through his groin.

He was suddenly glad he'd been forced to come here, tonight.

Then he felt guilty about it and looked away.

The attacker was squirming on the floor a couple of yards away, one man sitting on his chest, others holding down his arms and legs. John realized that quite a few people were yelling, shouting questions and commands.

'Have you got him?'

'Call the police! Somebody call the police!'

'What'd he do?'

'*Look* at him!'

'How's the girl?'

'Why's he all black like that?'

'What's going on?'

'Is everybody all right?'

'Somebody fuckin' call the cops!'

'Probably just some bruised ribs,' the doctor said, his voice soft and calm through the mayhem. 'Maybe a couple of hairline fractures. Nothing to be especially concerned about, I should think, but we'd best get you to the ER for some x-rays.'

John looked again as the doctor covered her with his blazer.

'Just lie still for the time being.'

The waitress who had tried to pull the attacker off Cassy came over and squatted down. 'Are you OK, hon?'

'I'll live.'

'Christ, what got into Bill? What got *on* him?'

'I don't know. But thanks for coming to the rescue, Joyce.'

'No problem, hon.'

'Did he hurt you?'

'Naa. I'm fine. You take care of yourself,' she said, then straightened up and turned to the crowd surrounding the man.

Dr Goodman turned his head toward John. 'And you are?'

'John Foxworth. I was just eating here.'

'Why don't you watch out for her, John, while I

go and phone for an ambulance?'

'I don't want an ambulance,' Cassy said. 'I'll be OK in a minute. He just . . . knocked my wind out. I'm feeling . . . a lot better.'

'Be that as it may,' Goodman said, 'I think it would be wise to have you checked over.'

'I'll stay with her,' John said.

Goodman patted his shoulder, then pushed against it as he uncrouched.

The moment he was gone, Cassy shook her head. 'I don't want any ambulance.' Holding the blazer to her chest, she started to rise.

'I'm not sure you ought to do that.'

Ignoring him, she sat up. The top of her costume slid off her back and dropped to the floor. She scowled at the man who'd attacked her.

Her scowl looked troubled and confused, not angry.

John had spoken to her briefly when he entered the restaurant, but he'd been too preoccupied to notice much about her appearance. Now, he found himself staring at her. He guessed she wasn't much older than twenty. She had a small, faint scar on her right cheekbone. Like a nick that a sculptor might've given his statue because he found it too perfect and felt the need to give it a small flaw for a touch of humanity and vulnerability. Her hair was glossy black. It was very short, cut in a style that reminded John of Peter Pan.

He imagined himself painting a portrait of her. A nude, of course. Right. When hell freezes over. A, she would never go for it. B, Lynn would pitch a fit. C, the temptation to do more than paint her picture . . .

If only he were invisible . . .

John forced himself to look away from her.

People were gathered around her assailant. Through a narrow gap, however, John saw that he was facedown. Some men were using their belts to bind his arms behind his back and lash his feet together.

'God, why did he do that to me?'

John shook his head.

'He just ran in and attacked me for no good reason. We've always been friends. It's like he went crazy or something. God! I don't get it. And what's that all over him?'

'I don't know.'

She looked at John. 'Can I keep your jacket for a while?'

'Sure. Go ahead.'

'I don't know why that man had to *cut* my costume. I'll have to get new laces and . . .' She sighed. 'I suppose everyone here got an eyeful.' Apparently, however, she didn't care much. Or figured there was no more reason for modesty. She took the blazer away from her chest. John managed not to moan as a rush of heat surged through him. He knew he should look away, but he couldn't. Cassy swept the jacket behind her, pushed her arms through the sleeves, then overlapped the front and held it shut. She smiled at him. 'Hey, this is nice and warm.'

'Well, keep it as long as you like.'

One side of her lip curled up, showing her teeth. 'I wonder what I'm supposed to do now.'

'Well, the ambulance . . .'

'Screw that. But I can't very well greet customers like this.'

'I don't think anyone would expect you to. Not after what happened.'

'I'm sort of the "acting manager" tonight.'

'This isn't exactly business as usual. Why don't you come over to our table and have a drink? Just relax until the cops show up and take that guy away. Somebody else can watch the door for you.'

'I don't know,' she said, still frowning. 'Yeah, OK.'

She started to get up. John stood quickly, took a gentle grip of her arm, and helped her to rise. When she straightened herself, she grimaced and bent over slightly and clamped her arms against the lower part of her ribcage.

'Are you all right?'

'Maybe I *should* have those x-rays.'

Both the front doors flew open at once. The cluster of people blocked John's view, but not for long. With shouts and squeals, some dropped to the floor cowering and others scattered, fleeing toward the dining room or the cocktail bar at the other side of the restaurant. Some stayed to fight.

One man tumbled backward when a camera slammed the side of his head. The woman wielding it rushed after him, dropped her knees onto his chest as he struck the floor, and pounded his face.

John shoved Cassy toward the dining room. 'Get away from here!' he snapped.

Nobody was coming to the aid of the fallen man. The woman kept battering his face, holding her camera by its zoom lens and swinging it down like a club.

Her hair was matted down and black. Her dripping face was black. So were the shoulders of her trench coat.

As John hurried toward her, a man in a corduroy jacket staggered backward and collided with him. The impact knocked the man sideways, turning him. Blood shooting from his torn throat splashed John's shirt.

The guy who'd done it to him was still up, the waitress Joyce riding his back and twisting his head while he struck out with his fist at two men who were keeping their distance. His fist bristled with metal. Keys. Three of them squeezed between his fingers, sticking out like little daggers.

John stumbled over the feet of someone kneeling on the floor, lurched forward and almost stepped on the ruined face of the man he'd come to help. As the woman raised her camera for another blow, he kicked. The toe of his shoe smashed her throat. The camera flew from her hand. She was lifted off her knees and thrown onto her back. Choking, she clutched her throat. She bucked and twitched.

The man was down, now, Joyce still on his back. Someone stomped his key hand against the floor and he cried out. Joyce scurried off him, and the two men kicked his head until he stopped moving.

'WE'VE GOTTA LOCK THE DOORS!' John shouted. 'LET'S LOCK THE DAMN DOORS!'

He remembered that Cassy was the acting manager. She'll know where the keys are.

He whirled around. 'CASSY!'

6

Trev didn't waste time searching the station for rain gear. It was unlikely that he would find anything useful. The weather had been dry for the past two weeks, and he knew that clear skies had been predicted for the next several days. Besides, even if he could find an umbrella or raincoat, he wouldn't have trusted them to do the job.

Whatever was wrong with the rain to make it black and apparently turn people into killers, he suspected that a single drop touching exposed skin or even seeping through clothes might be enough to contaminate him.

So he headed straight for the janitor's closet. There, he found a box of plastic garbage bags. He brought it out, and spotted Patterson's Stetson on a corner of the sergeant's desk. He tried it on. The cowboy hat fit loosely, but it would do. He took the hat and bags to his desk.

'What *are* you doing?' Francine asked.

'Gotta make a rain suit.'

'You can't be serious about going outside.'

He rushed past Francine and Lisa. In the top drawer of Lucy's desk, he found a pair of scissors and two rolls of strapping tape. He took them back to his own desk, then pulled out a garbage bag. He shook the bag open. Hopping, he thrust his right foot to the bottom. Then he rolled his chair back, sat down on it, and stretched out his covered leg.

'You've got to be kidding,' Francine muttered.

'People are running amok out there.' With his scissors, he started to cut off the bag so it reached only as high as his groin. 'I've got a friend who might be in trouble.'

'What about us?'

'That's up to you. You can either stay here or come along.'

'Oh, fabulous.'

He wrapped the plastic around his ankle and leg. 'I can lock the doors. I'll get you some firearms.'

'Mom, we can't stay here.'

'There're *bodies*.'

'I'm well aware of that.' Trev cut off a length of tape, and cinched the bunched up bag around his ankle. He bound a yard-long strip of tape several times around his thigh, pulling it tight. Tight enough, he hoped, to prevent it from slipping down. When he finished, his right leg was encased in layers of green plastic.

'That isn't going to stay up,' Lisa said.

'I don't know,' he muttered. He pulled out a second bag and shook it open.

'If you're gonna do that, you oughta wear your pants *over* the bags.'

He looked up at Lisa.

For the first time, he saw her smile.

'That's a good idea. Thanks.' While he ripped the tape loose, Lisa squatted by his foot and tugged at the bag. She tore it down his leg and flung it aside.

Trev swung a foot up across his knee and grabbed his sneaker.

'No, leave your shoes on. You won't get them on over all the plastic. Put the bags *over* your shoes, *under* your jeans.'

'You done this before?' he asked.

'Not hardly.'

As he unfastened his belt and pants, Francine said, 'We'll have to go with you.' Something was different about her voice. She no longer sounded snotty.

The change in her, Trev thought, probably had to do with the way Lisa had suddenly decided to pitch in and help.

'Fine,' he told her. 'I can pull my car right up to the door so you won't get wet.'

When his jeans were off, both women crouched in front of his outstretched legs. He felt a little uncomfortable, sitting there in his Jockey shorts. Nothing they haven't seen before, he told himself. And neither of them made remarks. They measured the bags, cut them off, pulled them over his shoes and up his bare legs. They wound the plastic tightly around him. They bound it in place with strips of tape. The back of Francine's hand brushed against his genitals once while she taped his thigh. She murmured, 'Sorry,' and didn't do it again.

When the plastic leggings were snug, he stood up and got into his jeans. He unclipped his holster, set it on the desk, and took off his belt.

Lisa cut head and arm holes in a bag. Trev took off his shirt, put the bag on. It hung down to his knees. Francine took the scissors from her daughter and slit the sides so the bag wouldn't inhibit his leg movements.

Then they fashioned coverings for his hands and arms, wrapped them snugly, and taped them tight around his wrists and upper arms.

Lisa chopped off the bottom of another bag. She slipped the bag over his head. While Francine held it in place, the girl carefully snipped out eyeholes and a breathing slot. Then they taped it in loosely around his neck.

'All set,' Francine said. 'No way you'll get wet.'

'Course, you look like something out of a horror movie.'

'Oughta do the job,' Trev said. 'Really appreciate it.' His voice sounded muffled and strange to him. Probably because his ears were covered.

The women helped him into his shirt and buttoned it for him.

'What about his eyes?' Lisa asked.

'The hat,' he said.

The bag over his head made crinkling sounds as Francine pushed the hat down firmly over it.

'That should do it,' he said. 'Thanks.' He took a step toward his desk, picked up his belt, and fastened it around his waist. With every movement, his ears were filled with quiet noises as if someone were wadding up plastic wrappers nearby. He clipped the holster to his side. He unsnapped its guard strap, drew his revolver, then explored the trigger with his covered index finger.

It was like wearing thin, rather slippery mittens.

He supposed he could fire the gun if he had to.

He holstered it.

'Go, and get your handbag,' he told Francine,

figuring she must've left it in the interrogation room.

While she went to get it, Trev stepped to the other side of the counter. He picked up Patterson's revolver, carried it into the public restroom at the far end of the reception area, and held it under the faucet. The hot water spilled over it, showing a shadow of gray as it ran into the sink. Then the water was clear against the white enamel.

Trev turned off the faucet, shook excess water from the gun, and dried it with paper towels.

Back in the main room, Francine and Lisa watched as he crouched over Lucy's body. He used her skirt to make sure that no trace of water remained on the weapon. Then he broke it open and cleared the shell casings from the cylinder. He wiped the cylinder.

'Do you know how to use a handgun?' he asked Francine.

She nodded. 'I used to go with a deputy.'

He stepped up to her and offered Patterson's .38.

She stared at it. 'I don't think . . .'

Lisa snatched it from Trev's hand.

'No!'

'It's all right. See?' She switched the gun to her left hand, and held her right hand open in front of her mother's eyes. 'See? Clean.'

'OK, give it to me.' Francine took the weapon.

'Go on and load it,' Trev told her, nodding toward the open box of cartridges on his desk. 'Then put the box in your purse. You'll have to do the reloading for both of us if things get bad.'

She started sliding rounds into the cylinder.

'I'll be back in a couple of minutes. I'm going out back. If I come in acting weird, don't be afraid to use that piece on me.'

Francine looked up at him, eyes narrow.

'Be careful, officer,' Lisa said.

'It's Trev,' he told her. Then he hurried to a cabinet behind the counter. It contained keys for three off-duty patrol cars. He gathered them, and ran for the rear exit of the station.

He thrust open the door. He stepped outside, hesitated for just a moment under the portico, then took a deep breath and held it and entered the downpour.

The rain pattered softly on the felt cowboy hat, the shoulders of his shirt. It tapped the plastic covering his hands and shoes. Though the lights of the parking lot were masked by rain, the area ahead wasn't totally dark. He could see that the rain was falling straight down, so at least he didn't need to worry about it blowing in beneath the wide brim of Patterson's hat, getting into his eyes or mouth.

He made out the faint shapes of the three patrol cars straight ahead. Over to the right were the personal cars of Lucy, Patterson, and the four cops who were out cruising (maybe wet and crazy by now and blowing away citizens).

Crouching at the rear of the nearest black and white, he tried keys until he found one that fit the trunk. The lid swung up. He felt around in the darkness of the trunk until he found the 12-gauge Ithaca riot gun. He took it out, slammed the trunk, and trotted to the next car. As he opened its trunk and lifted out the shotgun, he considered using one of these cars instead of his own.

And decided against it.

With all hell breaking loose, he sure didn't want to be driving around town in a cop car. Too damn conspicuous. The crazies might zero in on it.

Shotgun braced under each arm, Trev walked toward the station.

He resisted an urge to run.

Slip on the wet pavement, go down on your back, and in comes the rain through the face holes.

He wished he hadn't thought of that. It made him feel cold and shaky in the bowels.

But at least that cheerful scenario hadn't occurred to him until now, when he was on his way back.

I'll have to wash off these Ithacas before we go, he realized. Shit. Another delay. Might already have waited too long. *God, Maureen, hang in there.*

He switched one of the shotguns to his other arm, pulled open the station door, stepped into the light, flinched at the sight of Francine aiming a revolver at his face, slipped on the tile floor and fell on his butt.

7

'Let's clean her up,' Buddy said, nudging the body with his toe. 'See what our tarbaby looks like under that shit.'

'I still think we should call the cops,' Sheila said.

'Get real,' Buddy told her.

'I mean it. She tried to bash your brains out.'

'No cops.'

'Yeah,' Doug said. 'Let's keep her.' Grinning at Buddy, he said, 'We were one babe short. Now we got one for you.'

'Crazy bitch,' Buddy muttered.

Lou couldn't stop staring at the young woman. She gave him the creeps, black like that. Ever since he'd come into the foyer with the others and seen her, he'd felt cold and shaky. Last night, they'd done all that to Chidi. Now, a gal brings pizza to the house and *she* shows up covered with wet stuff that makes her as black as a nigger and she tries to whack Buddy. Like she was some kind of avenging phantom, or something.

Fucking weird.

They'd checked outside and the *rain* was black. If it *was* rain.

Lou had tried to tell himself that this was just an ordinary woman who came to bring the pizza and got caught in the storm. But that didn't ease his fears. Why in hell was *black* crap coming down out there? Why in hell did she try to brain Buddy?

He couldn't rid himself of the awful feeling that, somehow, Chidi was behind it.

Buddy and Doug were spooked, too. Even though they kept joking around and stuff, he could see it in their eyes.

'Yeah,' Buddy said after a few moments of silence. 'Let's lug her into the john.'

'I don't know if we should touch her,' Sheila said.

Doug, mocking her in a trembling voice said, 'Oh, my, it might be contagious.'

'It's nothing to kid about. I mean, we don't know what that stuff is. It's *black*.'

Buddy spread his arms and smiled at her. His shirt and pants looked smudged with soot from his struggle with the woman. His hands didn't appear stained, but they'd been black before he wiped them on the legs of his trousers. Some faint, gray blotches still showed on the inner sides of his wrists.

'If it's contagious, I've got it. And I'm gonna *get* you!' He lurched forward like a zombie, reaching for Sheila.

'Stop it!' she cried out, quick-stepping away from him. 'You're not amusing.'

Baring his teeth, Buddy pivoted toward Cyndi. She stood her ground. 'Just quit it.'

He dropped his act. 'Look, gang, I got that stuff on me and it didn't do anything.'

'How do you know there isn't an incubation period?' Sheila asked.

'What kinda period's that?' Doug asked, grinning.

'That's when gals bleed from their incubators,' Buddy explained.

'I mean it, guys.'

Deciding to take some of the heat off Sheila, Lou said, 'What she means is, maybe a space of time has to go by before you show any symptoms.'

'I know what she means, asswipe,' Buddy said. 'And it's stupid. The rain only started a minute or two before this babe went berserk with her rock. It's been – what? – five or ten minutes since I nailed her.'

'Good point,' Doug told him.

'So it doesn't do shit, touching her.'

Doug seemed convinced, 'I'll help you,' he said.

Buddy looked at Lou. 'OK,' Lou said.

'You guys take her feet. Whatever you do, don't drop her, she'll fuck up the carpet.'

Lou followed Doug around to the feet of the sprawled woman. She was wearing low heels. A little bit of green still showed where the shoes weren't stained with black. She didn't wear stockings. Her shins and ankles were streaky. The damp skirt of her dress reached down just past her knees, and looked glued to her legs. Here and there, its fabric was still green.

Lou realized that Doug had already lifted her left ankle off the floor.

He didn't want to touch her.

But he wrapped both hands around her right ankle. He'd expected her skin to feel cold. It was warm, though. It felt good. Some of his dread seemed to ease.

She's just a normal woman, he told himself, and lifted. Doug brought her other leg high. Buddy, squatting, grabbed her under the armpits. He straightened up. The sudden increase in weight nearly pulled her ankle from Lou's grip.

'Heavy mother, ain't she?' Doug said.

Sure heavier than she looks, Lou thought, taking careful steps as Buddy walked backward with her. The woman looked slim. Pretty tall, though.

'Is her skirt dragging?' Buddy asked.

'Just a little,' Cyndi said.

'Well, get it off the floor, damn it.'

Wrinkling her nose, Cyndi rushed in from the side. She reached under and pulled a handful of skirt toward her and folded it over the gal's thigh. Then she scowled at her hand.

'I told you, there's nothing to worry about.'

Buddy changed direction toward the foot of the stairs.

'We're going upstairs?' Doug asked.

'My room,' Buddy said.

Lou had figured they would carry her into the guest restroom on the ground floor. But he realized, now, that it only had a sink and toilet, no tub or shower. Buddy's bedroom, on the second floor, had its own john with a big bathtub.

And we're going to put her in it.

He wondered if they would take her clothes off. The girls won't stand for that, he thought. Maybe *they'll* strip her but make us leave.

Buddy started up the stairs. The top of the gal's head was pressed against his belly. Her shoulders were bare except for straps that looked like wide ribbons. The dress was low cut, but not *that* low. It didn't show any of her breasts or cleavage. Her breasts were there, though, making the fabric bulge. And they shook just a little as she was jostled.

Oh, man, Lou thought.

Sheila and Cyndi, behind him on the stairs, weren't saying anything.

They probably don't like this.

He suddenly wished the girls were gone. As much as he liked Sheila, she had a real prissy streak. She still wouldn't let him get into her pants, even though they'd been going together since summer. She *sure* wouldn't go along with it if they wanted to mess around with this gal.

Cyndi wasn't as big a prude as Sheila. But she was likely to throw a fit if they tried something. Especially Doug.

Shit.

This gal's our captive. She's at our *mercy*. We could do *anything* to her.

But not with Sheila and Cyndi here.

Lou was surprised when he found himself at the top of the stairway. The climb had been a cinch.

Cyndi sidestepped by, and led the way to Buddy's bedroom.

Maybe she'll be OK, Lou thought.

They followed her into the room. She hurried ahead of them and turned on the bathroom light.

Looking over his shoulder and changing course for the john, Buddy said, 'We'll put her right in the tub so this stuff doesn't get on anything.'

When they reached the tub, Buddy stepped over its side. He lowered her while Doug climbed in with her left leg. Lou leaned over the edge and put her right leg down.

'OK,' Buddy said. 'Everybody out.'

Doug's mouth fell open. 'Huh?'

'Go on downstairs, all of you. Look in the kitchen,

find something to eat, have some more drinks.'

'I thought we were gonna give this babe a bath.'

'Not we. Me. She's mine.'

'Hey, man, we helped you get her up here.'

Lou, feeling robbed, nodded but didn't speak.

'Yeah, thanks,' Buddy said. 'Now get out.'

'That's not fair.'

'Come on,' Sheila said, taking hold of Lou's wrist. 'We don't want any part of this.'

Speak for yourself, he thought. But he didn't argue. He let Sheila guide him toward the bathroom door.

'Shit,' Doug said. 'This really sucks.'

'Let's go,' Cyndi told him.

'Buddy.'

'Get off it,' Cyndi said, sounding a little miffed. 'What do you want with her, anyway? You got me. Besides, she's *old*.'

'She's not that old.'

Moments later, Doug followed Cyndi out of the bathroom. His face was red. He looked as if he might either start to cry or take a swing at somebody.

'One of you shut the door,' Buddy called.

Doug turned around. He slammed it.

'Don't be such a sourpuss,' Cyndi told him, and thrust her fingers under his belt buckle and pulled him up against her.

Lou wished Sheila would do something like that to him. But dragging him toward the door, she said, 'Let's go down and find some food.'

8

Denise unplugged the cord, put aside the lid, and dumped the popcorn into the plastic bowl. When she set the popper down, Kara tossed in a chunk of butter. It met the hot metal, sizzled and started to melt.

'I'll do the butter and salt,' Kara said. 'You can get the drinks. I think I'll have a New York Seltzer. Do you know what Tom likes?'

'He's big on Pepsi, if you've got some.'

'Oh, sure we do.'

Denise went to the refrigerator. It was loaded: cans of Bud, Diet Coke and Pepsi, bottles of New York Seltzer and Michelob, a jug of white wine. She took out two Pepsis and a bottle of cherry-flavored seltzer.

'I hope he gets here pretty soon,' Kara said. 'Popcorn's best when it's hot. It's OK after it's cooled off, but I think it loses something, don't you?'

'Definitely.'

'What'll we do when he gets here?' Kara asked, looking away from the melting butter and furrowing her brow with concern. 'I really don't think we should bore him with the birthday party, do you?'

'We can put on whatever you want.' Denise took three glasses down from a cupboard, then returned to the refrigerator for ice cubes.

'I have some movies Mom taped off cable for me.'

As Kara started to name them, Denise thought about the tapes she'd rented for tonight. She wished she hadn't left them at home. They might not be suitable for Kara, but . . .

Why don't I ask Tom over to my place? Lynn said they'd be back early. He can follow me home, and maybe we can watch one or two of them. And it'll give us a chance to be alone.

The idea made her nervous and excited. She really shouldn't have him in the house with her parents gone, but it'd sure be neat. As long as they didn't get *too* carried away. And as long as nobody ever found out.

'So what do you think?' Kara asked. 'Maybe one of those? Maybe not the Disney stuff, you guys are too old for that. But maybe *Goonies* or *The Stuff*. Have you ever seen *The Stuff*?'

'I don't think so.'

'Oh, it's great.' With a potholder, Kara lifted the popper and tilted it over the bowl, dribbling butter onto the popcorn. 'See, there's this white goop kind of like marshmallow topping? Only thing is, people can't stop eating it and it turns them into these *awful* yucky monsters. It's really gross, but it's funny, too, and it's not really a kid movie. You think Tom'll like it?'

'We can give it a try. But you must've already seen it.'

'Oh, I like to watch movies over and over again if they're good.' She shook the popcorn bowl and jiggled it up and down. 'I bet I've seen *Willy Wonka* a hundred times.'

'A hundred?'

'Well, maybe just seventy-eight or eighty. I never actually counted.' She set the bowl on the counter and started to sprinkle salt onto the popcorn.

And the doorbell rang.

'He's here!'

'Made good time, didn't he?' Denise picked up the Pepsis and seltzer. 'Do you want to bring the glasses in?' She watched while Kara gathered the glasses, pinning one between her wrist and chest, holding the others in her hands. 'Now, be careful.'

'I don't drop things. I'm not like Dad.'

The girl followed her into the living room. The doorbell rang again as Denise set down the cans and bottle on the table in front of the sofa. 'Coming!' she called.

She hurried for the door, leaving Kara behind to unload the glasses.

She slid the guard chain off its track. 'What's the password?' she asked.

'C'mon, open up.'

She did.

Tom, face shiny black, lunged across the threshold thrusting the steel tip of his umbrella at Denise's mid-section. She gasped and twisted away. The dull point plunged under the placket of her shirt and streaked across her skin. Half the closed umbrella rushed against her belly, slick and wet, before its tip poked a hole through the side of her shirt. As she fell, she grabbed it with both hands.

The floor pounded her shoulder and hip. Keeping her hold on the umbrella, she rolled over on it. The weapon was wrenched from Tom's grip and snapped against the tile.

He kicked the side of her thigh.

'STOP IT!' Kara shouted. 'YOU STOP THAT!'

He kicked her in the ribs.

Why's he doing this!

Clutching the shoulders of her shirt, he yanked Denise backward to her knees. Buttons flew off. She tried to squirm out of the shirt, but only managed to free one shoulder before Tom clamped an arm across her throat. He jerked her head against his belly, bending her spine back, choking her.

Denise felt her head starting to go warm and numb. Her ears rang. The lights, the furniture, Kara watching with her mouth wide – all were rimmed with flashing electric blue.

She reached behind her. Hooked the backs of Tom's knees. Jerked them forward and tried to throw her weight against him.

His knees folded.

He fell, keeping his chokehold and tumbling Denise onto him. She heard his wind blow out. With both hands, she forced his forearm away from her throat. He grabbed his wrist. She didn't have the strength to resist the power of his two arms. But she tucked her chin down to protect her throat. As his forearm shoved against it, she writhed and pushed and sank her teeth into the sleeve of his jacket and clamped down with all her might.

Crying out, Tom tore his arm from her mouth.

Denise flipped over, rolled off him.

He rolled, reaching out as she got to her hands and knees. He jerked her arm out from under her, tugged her toward him.

And Kara, standing behind him, swung a fireplace

poker like a golf club. Its brass handle struck him above the ear. The impact knocked his head sideways. His grip on Denise went loose. She fell against him as he flopped onto his back.

She pushed herself up.

Tom was sprawled out motionless, Kara raising the poker for another swing.

'No, don't!'

She lowered it.

On her knees, panting for air, Denise rubbed the front of her neck and stared down at Tom. His hair, normally the same light shade of blond as Denise's hair, was slicked down and black. Only the lids of his closed eyes and an area under his chin were unsoiled by the ebony liquid.

'Did I kill him?' Kara asked. Her voice sounded high and frightened.

The soaked front of Tom's jacket rose and fell, so he was breathing.

'No,' Denise gasped. 'You only knocked him out.' She looked up at Kara. 'Thanks.'

'Why'd he go and do that?'

'I don't know.'

'Gads.'

'I've never ever seen him fight with *any*one. I just can't . . . it's like he lost his mind. It's crazy.'

'What *is* that all over him?'

'I don't know.'

'Is the rain *dirty* tonight? It looks dirty. I thought rain was always supposed to be clean. Do you think he got mad at you because he came over and got all dirty like that?'

'I doubt it. Maybe the rain's toxic or something, I don't know.'

'You mean like poison?'

'Maybe. I don't know.'

Kara's red face contorted and her chin began to tremble. 'Well, Denise . . .' Tears came to her eyes. 'You've got it on *you*.'

Denise looked down. Below her white bra, her skin was smeared dark gray from the umbrella. She also noticed a red mark left by the steel tip. Though the dull point hadn't broken her skin, the mark felt hot. She rubbed it gently.

Raising her eyes, she saw Kara weeping silently, her face flushed and tears running down her cheeks.

'Don't worry, OK? I feel fine. Just a little beat up. But I don't feel weird or poisoned or anything.'

'Are you sure?'

'Yeah.' She straightened her shirt and pulled it shut. All the buttons were gone except for one just below her throat, which hadn't been fastened. With shaky hands, she pushed that one into its hole.

'Maybe you'd better wash,' Kara said. 'You know? Just in case . . .'

'Can you find something we can use to tie him up? Rope or something?'

Nodding, Kara wiped a sleeve across her wet face.

'Let me have the poker.'

Kara handed her weapon to Denise, then hurried away.

Hanging onto it, she walked on her knees to Tom's feet. She set the poker down. As she pulled his legs straight and pressed them together, she watched his face closely for signs that he might be regaining consciousness.

God, she thought, what if he *doesn't* come to? What if he's in a coma, or something, and never comes out of it? Or he wakes up, eventually, but his brains are scrambled and he's nothing but a vegetable for the rest of his life?

He'll be OK, she told herself. He'll be fine. People get knocked out all the time and come out of it OK.

She took off her belt, wrapped it twice around his ankles, pulled it tight, and fastened it. The buckle was on top, so she slid the straps until it disappeared behind his ankles.

He could still get to it, but not easily.

She picked up the brass poker and watched him.

As much as she wanted Tom to regain consciousness, she hoped he wouldn't do it too soon. Not before Kara got back and they had time to tie his hands.

Maybe when he comes to he won't be crazy anymore.

But if he is . . .

God, I don't want to hit him.

But I can't let him get loose and attack us.

Kara, where are you?

She heard quick footfalls behind her, looked back, and saw the girl rushing forward with a couple of jumpropes. 'Will these be OK?'

'Fine,' Denise said, though she wished the ropes

didn't have those wooden handles. She pulled Tom's arms down, crossed them over his belly, and started tying them together with one of the ropes.

'Do you think we'd better call the police?' Kara asked.

Denise shook her head. 'I don't know. I don't want to get him in trouble.'

'Yeah, but he tried to *kill* you, didn't he?'

'He can't do anything once he's all tied up.'

'He kind of scares me.'

'I know. He scares me, too. But maybe he'll be normal again when he comes to. Maybe whatever was wrong with him will go away. And even if he's still nuts, he won't be able to hurt us. We'll make sure he doesn't get loose.'

'How? You mean like bonk him on the head again?'

'If we have to.'

'Well, *you'll* have to do it, then. Not me. It's your turn.'

Nodding, Denise tugged the red wooden handles to tighten the bundle of knots. 'He won't get out of that,' she said.

She took the second rope from Kara. She made a slip knot near one of its handles, then lifted Tom's head off the tiles and put the loop around his neck. She slid the knot up against his skin. Holding the other handle, she scooted backward to take most of the slack out of the rope, sat down on the floor and crossed her legs.

'He causes any trouble,' she said, 'I'll give him a yank.'

'Sort of like a dog?'

'Exactly.'

A reluctant smile curled up a corner of Kara's mouth. 'Neat idea.'

'Why don't you go get the popcorn and our drinks? And maybe a couple of cushions to sit on.'

'Oh, this is really weird. You mean we're going to go ahead and have our party right here?'

'Might as well. We'll watch Tom instead of the television. We'll have a guardin' party.'

'A what?'

'Garden party, guarding party. Get it?'

Kara laughed softly and shook her head. 'I think you might be even weirder than my Dad.' Then she went to get the refreshments.

Captives

1

It was like driving blind. The eyeholes in the bag killed most of Trev's peripheral vision, dark rain spattered the windshield faster than the wipers could clear it, the parking lot lights were so dim that they might've been on rheostats turned way down, and his head-beams only seemed to penetrate fifteen or twenty feet into the heavy downpour before fading out completely.

Though he couldn't see worth a damn, he drove fast and hoped for the best.

Too much time had already gone by.

Crazies might've already overrun O'Casey's, might've already gotten to Maureen.

She'll be OK, he told himself.

His wheels bumped over the curb. He drove across grass, steering closer to the hedge by the station wall until bushes squeaked against the right side of his car. He spotted the portico's nearest support post. Slowing down, he passed between it and the station's front door. His tires rolled onto the walkway's smooth pavement. Rain stopped hitting the hood, the windshield. He eased forward until it went silent above his head, then set the emergency brake and looked over his shoulder.

His back door was out of the rain and lined up with the station's door. He reached over the back of the passenger seat to unlock it. Then he beeped the horn.

Light spilled out of the station as the front door swung open. Francine and Lisa came out, each carrying a shotgun. They had plastic bags draped over their heads and shoulders in case water should run off the car while they entered, and their arms were covered to the elbows.

Francine, in the lead, opened the back door of Trev's car. She climbed in. Lisa ducked in after her and shut the door. Trev watched them push the covers off their heads.

'Everybody OK?' he asked.

'It's insane, going out in this,' Francine said.

'Better than staying in there with a couple of stiffs,' Lisa told her.

'I'm not so sure anymore.'

Trev decided they were acting normal. Turning away from them, he shifted to reverse. He slowly backed his car out from under the shelter. When its front was clear, he started forward and headed for the parking lot.

'So where is it we're trying to go?' Francine asked.

'O'Casey's Pizza.'

'God, it's so dark out here,' Lisa said. 'Will you be able to find the place?'

'I'll find it.'

Somehow, he thought.

'It's just a straight shot up Guthrie and a left on Third,' he explained as his front tires bounced down from the curb onto the parking lot's pavement.

In normal weather, the drive shouldn't take more than five minutes. With this kind of visibility, he knew they would need some luck to make it at all.

We'll probably get creamed.

'This is really the pits,' Lisa muttered.

Trev drove straight forward until his headbeams met the bushes of the narrow strip that separated the station's parking lot from the sidewalk and Guthrie Avenue. He was tempted to plunge through the barrier. The possibility of tire damage stopped him. So he turned to the right. Stepping on the gas, he sped alongside the landscaped area to the entrance lane. There, he swung out onto Guthrie.

Nothing broadsided him.

Maybe we'll be lucky, he thought. Nobody but an idiot would be out driving in this crap.

An idiot, or somebody without any choice.

Or crazies, already wet and cruising for action.

He eased toward the middle of the road until he came to the broken yellow center line.

Keep watching the line, he thought. When you come to an intersection, there'll either be a left-hand turn pocket or the line will end.

He ran the names of the cross-streets through his mind. Should be seven before Third Street.

'Why don't you try turning on the radio?' Francine said.

The center line stopped. He looked both ways, saw

no hint of approaching headlights (you won't see them anyway until it's too late), and tromped on the gas pedal to get through the intersection as fast as possible. When the line reappeared, he slowed down. He turned on the radio.

Glen Campbell was singing 'Wichita Lineman.'

'Try to get some news,' Francine said.

'This is as close as we're gonna get to a local station,' Trev told her.

'What is it, Bakersfield?' Lisa asked.

'Yeah.'

'Do you think they'd be playing music if . . . ?'

'No, I doubt it. Bakersfield must be OK.'

'Maybe it's only happening . . .'

'That was good ol' Glen Campbell, and this is Bronco Bob for KLRZ, bringing you all the best in country music. We're coming up now on seven-forty in the P.M., and we've got a chilly fifty-nine degrees outside so snuggle up to your honey and stay tuned in. Waylon's coming up, along with Ronnie Milsap, The Judds, and Miss Robin Travis.'

'Nothing about any rain,' Lisa said.

'Well, we're some hundred miles from Bakersfield.'

'Maybe it's just happening here.'

Trev sped through another intersection. Two down, five to go. He eased off slightly on the gas.

'If it *is* just happening here,' Francine said, 'we ought to be grateful. I'd hate to think this was going on everywhere, wouldn't you?'

'I wonder if anyone out there even knows about it.'

Trev flinched as something pressed his shoulder. Then he realized it was Francine's hand.

'You know,' she said, 'maybe we can drive out of this if we just keep going. If it's the rain making people nuts and we get out from under the storm . . .'

He hit the brakes and jerked the wheel, shouting 'Hold on!' and they skidded and slammed the side of a station wagon blocking the lane. The force of the impact jerked him, tried to throw him over onto the passenger seat, but he kept his grip on the wheel.

Behind him, the women were gasping and moaning.

'Anyone hurt?' he asked, twisting around to look back.

Francine had been hurled against Lisa, and Lisa was hunched down against the right-hand door.

'I think I'm OK,' Lisa muttered.

'I can't believe this,' Francine said, pushing herself up. 'I just can't believe this.'

'At least we didn't break any windows,' Trev said.

'What're we *doing* out here?' Francine blurted.

Great, he thought. She's losing it.

'Just take it easy,' he said.

'Take it easy? You almost got us killed, you fucking maniac!'

'Mom, cut it out.'

'Well, he did!'

'I didn't expect there to be a goddamn car stopped *sideways* in the middle of the street.'

'If you hadn't been driving like a maniac . . . !'

'I'm sorry. I really am.'

'Lot of good sorry does.'

Trev turned his attention to the windows. His car appeared to be flush against the side of the station wagon. He couldn't see anyone inside.

But as he studied the car, he saw another in the glow of his headlights. A compact Dodge. Its rear against the front bumper of the wagon.

'Oh, man,' he muttered.

'What?'

'*Two* of them.'

'What?'

An intentional roadblock?

He stepped on the gas pedal. His car lurched forward with sounds of scraping, crunching metal. Then it parted with the side of the wagon and the noises stopped.

'What's going on?' Francine demanded.

Trev didn't answer. He backed up, watching the wagon. Parked at its rear was a pickup truck.

'Trev! Answer me!'

'It's a trap,' he said, trying to keep his voice calm.

'A what?'

'Make sure your doors are locked,' he said, and the car rocked on its shocks. He darted his eyes to the rearview mirror. Couldn't see anything but darkness. Couldn't see the man or woman scuttling over the trunk toward the back window. But the slight shaking of the car told him someone was there.

A hard thud against the rear window. He shot the car forward and heard a muffled outcry.

'What was *that*?'

'Lost a visitor,' Trev said, and wrenched the wheel,

turning away from the roadblock. The sweep of his headbeams lit four black shapes rushing in. Coming at them. A man with an axe. A woman with a tire iron. A woman who seemed to have no weapon and a kid maybe twelve or thirteen from the size of him with something bigger than a softball swinging at his side.

From behind Trev came a quick, high sucking sound.

'Oh my God!' That was Francine.

It isn't a softball, Trev realized as he rammed the pedal to the floor.

It was the head of a girl, and the kid was swinging it by its long hair.

He figured he could speed through the group. Not touch any of them.

But if he tried that, the bastard with the axe might bash the windshield, let the rain in. So he steered for the axeman.

The guy didn't try to dodge clear. He met the car face on, swinging the axe down from straight overhead with both hands as if he planned to split a log. It chopped into the hood. Then its handle caught him in the belly, hoisting him off his feet.

Something whacked the windshield in front of Trev's face.

The head. Face first. The blow mashed its nose flat. Teeth broke from its open mouth. Pale blurs of eyes glanced in at him. Then the head bounced away and through his side window Trev saw the kid stumbling backward, still hanging onto the thing's hair.

'*Jesus*!' he gasped.

He realized someone was shrieking in his ears.

And he realized he hadn't lost the axeman.

He sped away from the roadblock, away from all the attackers but one.

The head of the axe was still buried in the hood. And its handle seemed to be buried in the man who'd put it there.

The center line ended. An intersection. 'Detour!' Trev yelled.

He swung a hard right. But not hard enough to lose his guest. The guy stayed put, riding through the rain like a big, limp hood ornament.

2

Maureen thought, the pizzas are getting soaked. She knew she should stop this and get up and put her clothes back on and take the pizzas to the door, but it felt so good to be sprawled on the grass with the hot rain splashing down on her. She didn't want to get up ever.

When the rain filled her mouth, she choked. She raised her head and opened her eyes.

She was in a bathtub, not on the lawn. Not her bathtub. It wasn't rain coming down, but spray from a shower nozzle. There was a curtain rod, but no curtain enclosed the right side of the tub.

And she wasn't alone.

Someone was down low, peering in at her.

She sat up fast. Too fast. The sudden motion made her head spin, her vision cloud, her stomach churn. She grabbed the rim of the tub, hunched forward, threw her legs wide and vomited between them. The spasms wracked her. Pain throbbed through her head. Tears filled her eyes.

When she was done, she stayed bent over. She gasped to catch her breath. Water pounded against her head and shoulders and back. It ran down her face. She blinked the wetness of water and tears from her eyes. While she watched her mess spread out and slide toward the drain, the dizziness faded. It left confusion, shame and fear.

I'm naked in someone's bathtub. Who is that guy? What's happening?

He's the guy I tried to smash with a rock, she realized.

Why the hell did I want to do that?

What's he doing with me?

'Hope you didn't get any on you,' he said.

Maureen didn't look at him. She stopped holding onto the side of the tub, and wrapped both hands around her upthrust knees.

'What's your name?' he asked. He sounded friendly. The friendliness seemed mocking.

'Maureen.'

'Name's Buddy,' he said. 'I'm gonna be *your* buddy.'

He touched her back. His hand moved gently, making slow circles.

'You tried to knock my brains out,' he said.

'I know. I'm sorry.'

His hand moved higher and he began to massage the nape of her neck. 'Why did you do that?'

'I don't know.'

'You don't know?'

'Huh-uh.'

'Were you mad at me?'

'I don't know you.'

'Did somebody send you?'

'I just came with the pizzas.'

'And you just suddenly got an urge to brain me?'

'Yeah.'

'Don't like my face?'

'It wasn't you. I just wanted . . . to kill whoever came to the door.'

'Real nice.'

'I'm sorry.'

'What do you think we oughta do about it?'

He didn't call the police, Maureen realized. He brought me in here and stripped me, instead.

'Maybe you should call the police,' she murmured.

'Would you like to be arrested? Would you like to go to prison? You assaulted me with a deadly weapon. That'd be a prison term for sure, wouldn't it?'

'Maybe.'

I'd rather take my chances with the police, she thought.

Trevor. Oh God, Trevor. If Rory hadn't been sick . . .

One hand continued to rub her neck. The other, his

right, slipped beneath her armpit and closed gently around her right breast. Squirming, she dug her fingernails into her knees.

'No, don't,' she said. 'Please. Come on.'

'I think maybe you should be very nice to me, and maybe we won't have to bother the cops with this.'

His hand moved in a slow circle, palm stroking her nipple.

Maureen let out a shaky breath.

'You like that, don't you.'

'Come on, stop.'

'Bet it feels a lot better, now you're awake to enjoy it.' Laughing softly, he thumbed her nipple. 'Yeah, I already felt you up pretty good. This is better, though. This is a lot better.'

The hand slid down from her breast, down her chest and belly. And lower. When he fingered her pubic mound, she grabbed his wrist with her left hand and jerked it toward her hip. She rammed her right elbow back. It missed Buddy. Her upper arm collided with his face as he fell toward her, but she knew she hadn't done much damage.

And she knew she was in trouble.

The hand at the back of Maureen's neck shoved her away. She released his wrist. She flung her arm up. The far wall of the tub smacked her arm down against her side. A hand covered her face, pushed her down.

It went away. As she struggled to push herself up, Buddy rose from his crouch beside the tub. He wore nothing. He was grinning. He had a wide neck. His arms and chest were bunched with heavy muscles. His penis was erect. Big and thick and pointing high.

He climbed into the tub.

His broad body blocked the shower.

Maureen kicked at his shins until he squatted and grabbed her ankles. The water came again, splashing her face and torso. He spread her legs wide. He pulled her toward him. She twisted and bucked as her back slid over the slippery bottom of the tub.

Buddy sank to his knees. He tried to shove his hands under her rump, but she knocked them away.

'Naughty naughty,' he said, and punched her just below the navel. Right fist, then left, then right again. The blows bashed her breath out, made her guts feel hot and mushy, tore all her strength out.

She tried to struggle, but couldn't move.

Buddy stuck his hands under her rump. He clutched her buttocks and lifted.

Spine bent, arms hanging limp, the back of her shoulders and head sliding along the tub's bottom, she was dragged forward and impaled.

3

John, along with several other men, carried the bodies into the kitchen. It was Dr Goodman's suggestion.

Earlier, someone had called the police and Goodman had phoned for ambulances. While the doctor's call had at least been picked up, he'd been told that no units were available. So there would be no cops, no ambulances. Not for a while, anyway. Maybe not for a long while.

Dr Goodman thought it best, for everyone's sake, to remove the bodies from sight.

Among the dead were Andrew Dobbs, the reporter from *People Today*, and the female photographer who'd charged into the restaurant with him. She had no purse, no identification. The man she'd bludgeoned to death with her camera was Chester Benton, a local real estate agent. The man whose throat had been ripped open by Dobbs's keys was Ron Westgate, a high school teacher.

Four dead.

And John, himself, had killed the woman.

According to Goodman, she'd probably suffocated as a result of a collapsed trachea. John could've told him that, but he'd feigned ignorance. Why draw attention to himself?

Steve Winter, lugging her by the arms, knocked open the door to the kitchen. John followed him into the brightness with the woman's legs.

The savory aromas of the kitchen stirred his hunger.

After things had settled down a little, Cassy had ordered the cooks and dishwashers (who'd rushed out with knives and cleavers too late for the action) to return to their jobs. She planned to see that everyone ate.

Good for her, John thought as he followed Steve past a bank of ovens.

'I'm famished,' Steve said. Apparently, the wonderful odors were working on him, too.

'At least we don't have to worry about starving,' John told him. 'Good place to be in time of siege.'

'You going to stick around?'

'Aren't you?'

'Carol wants to go home.'

'I want to get home, too. Hell, my kid's with a sitter. I don't know about going out there, though.'

'What do you think's happening?'

'Shit if I know.'

'You think it's the rain?' Steve asked.

'I've never heard of rain making people homicidal.'

'I've never heard of rain being black.'

'Hold up,' John said.

They stopped and waited while two men came out of the freezer, looking pale and cold.

'OK. Go on ahead.'

John followed him into the walk-in freezer unit. The air felt like cold water seeping through his shirt. He wished he'd kept his blazer on. Until he remembered where it was and thought about Cassy's warm bare skin against its lining.

Looking over his shoulder, Steve stepped alongside the body of Andrew Dobbs.

They set the woman on the floor beside him.

Steve scowled down at her black face. Then he met John's eyes. 'Do you think this is it?'

'It? What do you mean?'

'You know.'

'The end of the world?'

'The Big One. World War Three. Only they didn't nuke us, they hit us with some kind of biological shit.'

That had already occurred to John. He supposed it must've occurred to everyone.

'Let's get out of here before we freeze up,' he said.

He waited for Steve. The two walked side by side toward the freezer door.

'So what do you think?' Steve asked as they stepped into the warmth of the kitchen.

'I don't know what's going on, but I don't think it's Doomsday. I sure hope not.'

Steve let out a nervous laugh. 'You and me both.'

'For godsake, don't bring up anything like that in front of the women. They're spooked enough as it is.'

They stepped aside as two men approached with the body of Chester Benton, and John wished he'd been quicker to take out the camera woman. Maybe it wouldn't have helped, anyway. For all he knew, the first blow might've been the fatal one that rammed a shard of skull into the poor guy's brain.

'If it's not the Big One,' Steve said, 'what do you think it might be?'

'Something of ours?'

'We're not supposed to be developing chemical weapons.'

'What we're supposed to be doing and what we *are* doing ain't necessarily the same thing. You know? Maybe the honchos decided to test out their new secret weapon on the citizens of Bixby.'

'No, that's . . .'

'Or maybe something just went wrong. Maybe that

135

boom wasn't thunder. Maybe it was some kind of military transport blowing up, and it had a nasty cargo.'

'You think so?'

'Hell, I don't know. I'm a *painter*, for godsake. You're the science teacher around here.'

'I'm no great research chemist. An MA in biology, that's it. And a secondary credential.'

'You must keep up on new developments.'

'Yeah, well *Scientific American* hasn't run any articles on black shit that gives people the hots for murder.'

'Maybe you missed that issue.'

Steve suddenly burst out with laughter. His face went red and he covered his mouth. 'John, you're weird.'

'That's what my kid tells me. Come on, let's get out of here and cheer up the ladies.'

They stepped around a couple of guys carrying the last body.

'I don't know about you,' Steve said, 'but I'm going to wash my hands.'

John glanced at his own hands. There was no black on them. He'd thought there wouldn't be. He'd checked the woman's ankles before picking her up, and they'd looked clean. Apparently, the legs of her slacks had protected them.

But he'd been touching a dead woman.

'I'll go with you,' he said, and followed Steve from the kitchen.

The dining room was dimly lighted. Most of the

people had returned to their tables. Lynn was now seated across from Carol at a booth near the front wall. She had a fresh margarita in front of her, and there was an additional Mai Tai on the table. Waitresses were scurrying around, most of them carrying trays of drinks.

He spotted Cassy sitting with an arm around a sobbing woman, Chester Benton's widow.

He turned away and walked with Steve to the entryway.

A couple of chairs had been brought over. Men sat in them, facing the doors and the prone body of Bill. A meat cleaver rested on the lap of one of the men. He had a croissant in one hand, a martini in the other. The second man held a carving knife and a glass of red wine. The young parking attendant was glaring at his guards, but lying still, making no attempt to free himself from the belts that bound his hands and feet.

'Behaving himself?' John asked as he stepped in front of the guards.

'I guess he knows what'll happen if he doesn't,' said the man with the martini.

'Well, keep up the good . . .'

Someone knocked on wood. John snapped his head sideways and stared at the doors. The knocking came again. Not a rough pounding, but a rather polite rap of knuckles.

The skin prickled on the back of his neck.

'Oh, shit,' Steve muttered.

John looked around at the two seated men. The one with the knife had slopped red wine onto the front of his camel jacket, but he didn't seem to be aware of that. He was gazing with wide eyes at the door. The martini man stuffed the remains of the croissant into his mouth and lifted the cleaver off his lap.

The knocking continued.

'If I were you guys,' John said, 'I wouldn't answer the door. Come on, Steve.'

Steve watched the door over his shoulder as he followed John into the cocktail lounge. Then he met John's eyes and said, 'This is really bad shit. I don't know. I don't know.'

'They seem like pretty sturdy doors. If you want to worry about something, worry about the windows.'

'Oh, thanks for mentioning it.'

'You're the guy who wants to go home.'

'I think I'll pass on that.'

John scanned the dimly lighted room. A few men and women were seated on bar stools. Small groups sat at some of the tables. 'Must be close to twenty people in here,' he said. 'Maybe about thirty others, including the help. That's a lot of manpower if the place gets stormed.'

'Stormed? Oh, Jesus. Great.'

'I'm not saying it'll happen.'

In the alcove at the far end of the room, people were lined up to use the two pay phones. John wished Lynn were among them instead of back in the dining area sopping up margaritas and chatting with Carol.

As he stepped through the group, he heard a woman at one of the phones say, 'In the nightstand drawer on your father's side of the bed. It's loaded, so be careful and don't let Terry get his hands on it. There's a box of bullets in the top dresser drawer, so make sure you get that, too.'

John groaned and kept moving.

God, he wished *he* had a gun in the house. He hated the things. He had vowed never to use one again. And he'd always felt secure in the knowledge that he rarely left Lynn and Kara by themselves. He worked at home. When he went out, they usually came with him. And he always figured he could defend them, if the need arose, without using a firearm.

Then this happens.

He rammed open the men's room door. It just missed crashing into someone about to come out.

'Sorry,' he muttered.

'Take it easy, partner,' the guy said.

Inside, a young man in a corduroy jacket was bent over, holding onto the sides of the sink and gazing at his face in the mirror. He didn't look away from his reflection when John and Steve entered.

John stepped up to the sink beside him. 'How you doing?' he asked, starting to wash his hands.

The kid kept staring into his own eyes.

He was about twenty. He sported a thin, blond mustache which was probably meant to make him look older.

'Everything'll be OK,' John said.

The kid looked at him. 'We're all gonna die.'

'It's not that bad. I know how you're feeling, but it's not that bad. What's your name?'

'Andy.'

'Andy, I'm John. This is Steve.'

Steve, at the sink to the left, leaned forward and raised a sudsy hand.

'I've been in a lot worse than this, Andy. And I'm here, all in one piece. You'll be fine. We'll all be fine. Are you here with somebody?'

'My . . . friend. Tina?' He said the name as if he expected John to know her.

'Where is she?'

'In the bar.'

'And probably scared half to death,' John said. 'Go out there and sit with her. Give her a hug. You'll both feel better.'

Andy just stared at him.

'Do it. Now.'

The kid hurried for the restroom door.

'Nice little pep-talk,' Steve said.

John rinsed the soap off his hands. 'I'm gonna get in the phone line. Would you mind telling Lynn? I'll be along as soon as I've gotten through to the house. You stay with the gals, OK?'

4

He shut off the water and climbed out of the tub. 'So,' he said, 'was it good for you?'

Maureen didn't answer.

She thought, I'm going to kill you, you rotten bastard.

'I usually don't go off so quick.' He sounded chipper. 'Guess you're just too hot for me.'

Maureen lay still, gasping and sobbing. Her knees were up. She felt Buddy's semen rolling slowly inside her. Some of it leaked out and flowed down. She clenched her buttocks together. The stuff felt like thick glue.

A big, white towel flopped onto her belly.

'Let's go,' he said. 'Dry off. I've got some friends I want you to meet.'

Holding the towel to her belly, she sat up. She wanted to stuff it down between her legs and swab away the sticky mess, but that would ruin the towel. So she shook it open and started with her hair. While she dried herself, she felt more and more of the stuff dribble out of her. It tickled a little bit. It made her anus itch.

Finally, after she'd dried her legs, she struggled up to a squatting position and tried to rub away every trace of the fluid.

'Squeaky clean?' Buddy asked.

She looked at him. He was smiling, doing a merry little dance as he rubbed an open towel across his back. His penis was red. It was sticking out straight, partly erect, bobbing and swinging as he moved.

'Want some more?' he asked.

She turned her face away, dropped the towel and stood up. She stepped over the side of the tub. Though dry, the skin between her buttocks still felt a little tacky.

Her dress was heaped on the floor, partly covered by

Buddy's discarded shirt and trousers. Crouching, she reached for it.

'No way, babe,' Buddy said.

Ignoring him, she clutched a corner of green fabric and pulled it toward her.

Buddy flicked his towel at her. There was a quiet *whap*, and the damp end of it stung Maureen's shoulder. Wincing, she grabbed her hurt.

'I'm the master,' he said. 'You're the slave. This is my whip.' He swung the towel beside his leg, the circular motion winding the towel around itself. 'Would you like another taste of the lash?'

Maureen shook her head. She stood up, leaving her dress on the floor.

'Excellent.' Turning sideways, he stretched the towel between his hands and twisted it. 'You're an excellent wench. I'm growing very fond of you.' And he snapped the towel at her again. It unfurled, striking toward her right breast. Lurching backward, Maureen jerked her arm up. The moist tip lashed her forearm.

She almost reached out to snatch the towel from his hand, but stopped herself.

He's the master, she thought. I'm the slave.

'You don't have to hit me with that,' she told him. 'Just tell me what you want. OK? I'll do whatever you want.'

His smile widened. 'Right now, I want to eat. Into the bedroom with you.'

Maureen turned to the door. She opened it. The towel smacked her rump. Her throat tightened.

Buddy followed her into the bedroom.

'Sit down.'

She sat on the side of the bed.

He went to a dresser, dropped his towel to the carpet, and opened a drawer. Looking over his shoulder, he said, 'My first command, don't try to get away. That would carry extremely severe penalties, including but not limited to torture, gang-bang and probable execution.'

He removed a white T-shirt and a pair of faded red gym shorts from the drawer.

He came toward the bed and tossed them to her.

'Get 'em on,' he said.

Maureen picked up the shorts, bent down, and slipped her feet into them.

'My second command is to do precisely what I ask of you. No questions, no delays. If you're a very good girl, you might just survive the night.'

You won't, she thought, nodding submissively as she drew the shorts up her legs.

5

Denise and Kara sat cross-legged on cushions, watching Tom. Denise kept her hold on the jumprope looped around his neck. But he hadn't moved since being struck.

'Aren't you going to eat some?' Kara asked, her voice muffled by a mouthful of popcorn.

Denise raised her right hand.

'You could always wash it.'

'I don't want to leave you alone with him.'

'I could always go with you.'

'We've got to watch him.'

'It's OK if you want to go and wash,' Kara said. 'Just don't take all night. I'll yell my head off if he moves a muscle.'

'Are you sure you don't mind?'

'I think I'd like it if you didn't have any of that stuff on you. It gives me the willies.'

'OK.' Denise slid the jumprope handle across the tiles toward the girl's knee. 'I'll be quick,' she said, stood up and rushed for the kitchen.

At the sink, she squirted liquid soap onto one hand and turned on the hot water. She worked up a lather. She rinsed. Before reaching for the roll of paper towels, she shut the water off. She listened for sounds from the front while she dried her hands.

So far, so good.

She checked her hands. Clean.

She unfastened the button at her neck and spread her shirt open. Then she wadded some fresh towels, dampened them, and rubbed the skin of her belly that had been soiled by Tom's umbrella. The stains came off as easily as if they were nothing more than muddy water. When she was done, the wet ball of paper towels was flat where it had pressed against her. It looked like a rag used to clean off a window sill that hadn't been dusted for a year.

Still, no yell of alarm from Kara.

She dropped the wad onto the counter. With a fresh handful of wet towels, she rubbed her face. The paper came away clean. But it was black when she looked at it after scrubbing her neck. She wondered if she'd gotten it all. She wished there was a mirror. The bathroom had a mirror, but that was too great a distance from Kara.

With some dry towels, she wiped her neck and belly. She fastened the button of her shirt. Then she tore off a yard of towels, moistened them, and left the kitchen.

Hurrying through the living room, she saw Tom still lying motionless near the door, Kara sitting on one of the cushions and reaching into the popcorn bowl beside her.

The girl looked over her shoulder as Denise approached. 'Did you get it all off?'

'Hope so.' On her knees beside Kara, she set down the damp towels and spread the collar of her shirt. 'Did I miss any?'

'I don't think so. There's none on your skin, anyway. Your shirt's dirty. Maybe you could borrow one of Mom's blouses or something. You want me to get one for you?'

'Not right now. I want to do this first.' Picking up the towels, she moved closer to Tom. 'Thought I might as well clean his face off.'

'Do you think that's a good idea? I mean, what if it wakes him up?'

'We've got him tied good.'

'Yeah, but still . . .'

'He won't look nearly as scary once he's cleaned up a little,' Denise said, and gently rubbed the wad of damp paper across his forehead. He didn't stir. In the wake of the towels, his skin looked clean and pale. She wiped his right cheek and jumped as the telephone rang.

'I'll get it,' Kara blurted.

'No, I will.' She lurched to her feet and dropped the towels.

'I bet it's Mom and Dad.'

'Probably. You watch him.' She ran for the kitchen. The phone rang three more times before she got to it. 'Hello?'

'Denise? It's John. Is everything all right there?'

'Yeah, fine.'

'You're both OK?'

'Sure.'

She heard him sigh into the phone. 'Well, look, I don't know what's going on but people are going nuts outside. It apparently has something to do with the rain. The rain's black out there. We just had three people go crazy and come into the restaurant and kill some people.'

'My god,' Denise muttered.

It isn't just Tom, she thought. She'd felt sure that he wasn't to blame, but knowing that other people had also gone crazy made her feel better about him.

'Are you and Lynn OK?' she asked.

'We're fine. But we're stuck in here. I don't know when we might get out. We'll get home as soon as we can, but it might not be for hours. I just don't know. We have to stay until the rain stops.'

'Well, I'll stay here till you show up.'

'You've got to. You can't go outside. Make sure Kara doesn't go out, either. And whatever you do, don't let anyone into the house.'

'No. I won't.'

'People might try to break in,' he said, and Denise felt a squirmy coldness in her bowels. 'I just don't know. I don't want to upset you. But it's possible. I want you to round up some weapons just in case. There's a hammer in the kitchen in one of the drawers. Kara knows where to find it. And there're plenty of knives. Grab a couple of big ones. The bathroom door has a lock. It isn't much, but it's better than nothing. You can lock yourselves in if there's trouble.'

'OK,' she said, and stiffened as Kara appeared beside her.

'Is it Mom?' the girl whispered.

Denise shook her head, and waved her away.

'One more thing,' John said.

'Dad?' Kara whispered.

Nodding, Denise frowned and jabbed her finger toward the front of the house.

'I know Kara won't be thrilled by this, but I want you to turn off all the lights in the house.'

'Can I talk to him?'

Denise shook her head sharply and kept pointing, but Kara stayed.

'If the house is dark, I think there's less chance of someone trying to break in. They're after people. At least that's what I'm guessing. So they might not waste time with a house they think is deserted.'

'OK. I'll do that as soon as I hang up.'

'Fine, fine. Is Kara there?'

'She sure is. Just a second.' Denise covered the mouthpiece. 'Don't mention Tom,' she warned, then passed the handset to the girl.

'Oh, hi, Dad.' She stared at Denise while she listened. She had a nervous look in her eyes.

Don't tell him!

'Yeah, everything fine. We're having a nice party. We made some popcorn, and . . .' She fell silent. Her lower lip strained down, baring her teeth. 'Oh, gosh.'

I'd better check on Tom, Denise thought.

But she wanted to hear Kara's end of the conversation.

'I will . . . OK . . . I love you, too . . . Bye.' She reached high and hung up the phone. When she turned to Denise, she wore her spooked-by-the-boogeyman look, but there was no hint of amusement. 'What're we going to do?'

'What did your father say?'

'He said I should do whatever you tell me and not give you any argument.'

Denise gently squeezed the girl's shoulder. 'Everything will be OK.'

Her face changed. She looked as if she might be considering something that was very personal and very embarrassing. 'I hate to say this, but I think maybe we oughta hide.'

'Probably a good idea. But your dad mentioned a hammer. Do you know where it is?'

'Oh, sure.'

'Why don't you get it and pick out a good sharp knife for me? I'll be right back.'

Denise strode quickly through the dining room, into the living room.

She halted when she saw the foyer.

Tom was gone.

'Oh my God,' she muttered.

He'd left his shoes behind. Along with Denise's belt, coiled and abandoned on the tile floor beyond the cushions and popcorn bowl and soda glasses. The two jumpropes were missing. So was the fireplace poker.

Breathless, she took a few steps backward, then whirled around and raced into the kitchen. 'He got loose.'

Kara's eyes spread wide and she sucked in a quick breath. In one of her hands was a claw hammer.

Denise rushed up to her and took it. She slipped a butcher knife from the wooden block on the counter.

'What'll we do?' the girl whispered.

'I don't know.'

'I don't think I want to go around hunting for him.'

'Me neither,' Denise said. She hurried to the kitchen entrance and looked out. 'Let's just stay right here. At least he won't be able to take us by surprise.'

6

'Mom! Mom!'

Francine kept wheezing.

Trev slowed the car and looked back. Lisa was shaking her mother by the shoulders so roughly that the woman's head was flopping.

'That isn't doing any good,' Trev said. He faced the front again. 'Just try holding her or something.'

'What's *wrong* with her?'

'Does she have asthma?'

'No.'

'It's probably a panic attack.'

'Mom!'

The woman went on sucking air with high, whiny gasps.

Should've left them in the station, Trev thought. If he'd known the gal was going to lose it . . .

Hell, she has every right.

Trev himself felt as if he were hanging over a cliff by his fingertips and the slightest push might send him plunging down into a chasm of panic.

He kept seeing the four black figures coming toward his car. He kept seeing the severed head slam against the windshield. And the body speared by the axe handle, still bouncing and swaying in front of the hood, kept it all from receding into the past.

He wanted to *lose* the damn thing.

But the guy was stuck fast.

He'd considered jumping out into the rain and just

yanking him off the axe. It would've been worth the risk of getting wet or being attacked by other crazies. But he'd decided it was not worth the loss of time.

The crash and detour had stolen four or five minutes from him. From Maureen.

Let the bastard have his ride.

Trev hadn't returned to Guthrie. He'd gone one block over, made another right, and now he was speeding up Flower Avenue, parallel to Guthrie. He'd lost count of the cross-streets. He'd quit slowing down for intersections. He suspected he must be getting close to Third.

We'll either crash and burn, or we'll be there pretty quick.

He wished Francine would stop making those awful gasping noises. He had half a mind to climb back there and shut her up.

The center line ended. He hit the brakes. His car fishtailed into the intersection. When it slid to a stop, he peered out the windows. His headbeams lit the side of a red Porsche. It seemed to be parked at a curb.

If his sense of direction wasn't screwed up, the skid had taken him across the northbound lane of the cross-street. This should be O'Casey's side of the street.

If this is Third.

The restaurant would be near the middle of the block.

He steered away from the Porsche, drove slowly alongside it, passed a Subaru, and came to an alley. He swung into the alley and stopped.

'Wait here.'

'You can't leave us!' Lisa blurted.

Francine kept wheezing.

'You can't get out,' Trev said. He shut off the wipers and headlights, and stuffed the keys into a front pocket of his jeans. 'I'll be back pretty soon. Just keep your eyes open. Give me one of those shotguns.'

Lisa passed an Ithaca over the seat back.

'Keep the other one handy. And your mom's got Patterson's revolver. Get it out of her purse and have it ready.'

'Please!' Lisa cried out.

'I'll hurry. Just take it easy.' He flung open the door. Clutching the forestock of the shotgun, he climbed out into the rain. He punched down the lock button and slammed the door.

He took a couple of steps toward the front of the car. Holding the shotgun by its barrel, he leaned over the hood and pressed butt plate against the dead man's shoulder. He shoved hard, thrusting the body away. The axe handle came out. The guy tumbled backward and dropped out of sight.

Trev saw no point in wasting precious time to wrench the axe out of the hood.

He walked quickly past the rear of the car, stepped out of the alley and headed up the sidewalk to his left. A nightlight illuminated the interior of the shop beside him. The place looked deserted. The sign near the top of its display window identified it as Ace Camera, and Trev's heart quickened.

This was Third, all right. Ace Camera was adjacent to O'Casey's.

Please, he thought. Please, let her be OK.

Just ahead, the overhang of O'Casey's awning blocked out the rain. Beyond the curtain of darkness, light spilled onto the sidewalk. Trev hurried toward it. He thought of Hemingway and the clean, well-lighted place. This was a dry, well-lighted place. A safe refuge from the storm.

Though he ached to get there, he also felt dread.

What if . . . ?

Don't think about it.

Then he was under the awning, out of the rain, standing in the light. He gazed through the open space where O'Casey's window used to be. He felt as if his brain were squeezing itself into a cold, dark ball.

Numb, he made his way to the open door.

He entered and scanned the restaurant. Nothing moved. He felt half blind, trying to see through the eyeholes. With one hand, he pulled off Patterson's hat and dragged the plastic hood over his head. He set them on the nearest table and breathed deeply and realized he was making wheezy noises just like Francine.

He wanted to call out for Maureen and Liam, but he knew he didn't have enough breath for that.

He moved carefully through the room. The hardwood floor was slick with patches of dark water, spilled beer and blood and slabs of pizza. It was littered with window glass, overturned benches and tables, broken steins, wine and soda glasses, pitchers and plates. There were knives and forks on the floor. Glass shakers of salt and pepper, parmesan cheese and red pepper flakes. And bodies. So many bodies.

He tried not to see the kids. He only glanced briefly at the male adults. None was stocky and red-haired. Two of the men, blood mixed with the black of their skin and clothes, must have been assailants from outside.

One of the dead women was also black.

Of the other females, one was obese. She lay on her back with a wedge of pizza still in her mouth and a wedge of glass in her throat. One, facedown, looked tall and slender like Maureen, but had blonde hair. One, curled on her side with her arms around a small boy, was pregnant.

Trev squeezed his eyes shut.

I've gotta get out of here.

But he couldn't leave, not without knowing.

One female, head out of sight under a table, wore a denim skirt that was rucked up around her waist. She had heavy legs. She wasn't Maureen.

That left a slim, long-legged female sprawled on her back across the top of the last table before the order counter. Trev knew that he'd found Maureen. He couldn't see her face or the color of her hair. The way her head hung over the far end of the table, only the underside of her chin was in sight. But he knew.

And he knew that they'd done more than murder her.

Why her?

It was obvious. Because she was so beautiful. Her

looks must've turned on one or more of the invaders.

She usually wore corduroy pants or jeans. They were gone. Both her shoes were missing. She wore white socks. A torn rag of red panties dangled from her left ankle. Her thighs were mottled with gray smudges. On the table between her legs was a pizza. Her blood covered it. And blood concealed the true color of her pubic hair. Where her torso wasn't sheathed with gleaming crimson, her skin bore dark streaks and stains. A mouth-sized chunk of flesh was missing from her right breast. Most of her throat had been chewed out.

Saliva kept flooding into Trev's mouth. He knew he was about to vomit. He swallowed quickly, but more saliva poured in.

He took a few more steps, staggering past the side of the table, and saw the woman's face.

She wore a mask of blood. Her wide mouth showed broken teeth. Raw pulp remained where her nose should've been. One eye was gone, and all that remained was a sloppy red pit.

Her hair hung toward the floor in thick, matted ropes of red.

But here and there, blood had missed it.

The hair was blonde.

Blonde, not the auburn of Maureen.

Thank God, Trev thought.

He threw up.

When he was done, he looked across the aisle. There were no bodies near the table there. Its surface was clear except for a glass of red wine and a stein of beer. He stepped over to it. The stein was half full. He picked it up and began to drink. The beer was cool, but not chilly.

Maybe Maureen and Liam escaped, he thought. He knew that the kitchen had a rear door. They could've fled out into the rain. Or maybe they hid.

He was certain he would find their bodies in the kitchen area.

Please, he thought. Don't let them be dead.

He set down the empty stein. He took a deep, trembling breath, then strode to the open side of the counter and entered the kitchen.

He saw no one.

Stepping past the ovens, he felt their heat. Probably pizzas in them right now, as black as the crazies who had committed the slaughter.

He found dials, and turned the ovens off.

He considered opening them and looking in. As he reached for a handle, however, he remembered a book he'd read a few years ago. *Phantoms*. The oven of an abandoned bakery had a severed head or two inside. So he stepped away from the ovens.

'Maureen?' he called. His voice sounded high and strange, and much too loud. But he forced himself to call out Liam's name.

No response.

He found Liam on the floor behind the food preparation island. The Irishman's body was sprawled on top of a woman. Her slim, bare legs were stretched out between Liam's. Her head was out of sight beneath him.

Trev felt his mind shrivel and darken just as it had done when he stood outside and first looked in at the massacre. A vague, shadowy image came to him of Liam throwing his body on Maureen to protect her.

But there was so much blood on the floor around them.

He tumbled Liam off the woman. The handle of a knife jutted from the middle of his chest.

The crescent blade of a two-handled pizza cutter was embedded deep in the woman's neck.

They'd killed each other.

Her black face was intact.

Not Maureen.

Her skin was stained ebony from head to toe. At first, Trev thought she was naked. Then he realized she wore a string bikini.

A bikini in November?

Changed into it, all the better to enjoy the sudden warm downpour?

Trev's dazed mind pictured a bikini-clad young woman prancing through puddles, dancing around a lamp post, singing in the rain.

Gene Killer.

He heard himself chuckle.

He thought, Fuck, don't lose it. Hang on.

And he hung on while he searched the rest of the kitchen.

7

'What's he doing?' Kara whispered.

'I don't know.'

'Maybe he left.'

Denise supposed that was possible. Since discovering that Tom had gotten loose, she and Kara hadn't seen or heard anything to suggest that he remained in the house. He *might've* gone straight out the front door.

Or he might be waiting for them just beyond the dining room entry.

'Your dad said we could lock ourselves in the bathroom,' Denise whispered.

'We can't get there.'

'We can if Tom left the house.'

'But what if he didn't?'

'I don't like waiting here,' Denise said, watching from the kitchen doorway. 'I know we'd be able to see him coming, but we've got no door at all. He can get right at us. If we could just make it into the bathroom . . .'

Kara shook her head. 'He'd get us.'

'Maybe not. Not if it's dark.'

A look of alarm filled the girl's eyes. 'Oh, I don't think I like that idea. Not even one little bit. He might just sneak right up on us.'

'I know it'd be scary, Kara. But it'd be just like we're invisible. If we don't make a sound, we might be able to creep right past him, and he'd never even know we were there. Do you know where the fuse box is?'

'Sure, but I don't think . . .' She shut her mouth, probably recalling her father's command to obey Denise. 'It's right over there,' she said. She turned from the doorway and nodded toward a closed door just beyond the stove.

'It's not outside, is it?'

'Huh-uh.'

'Where are those flashlights and candles you talked about right after we heard the thunder?'

Kara looked relieved. 'Everywhere. Well, not everywhere. I've got a couple of flashlights in my bedroom and Dad has a big red thing by his bed. It's *real* bright.'

'Is there one here in the kitchen?'

'Yeah, right where I got the hammer from.'

Why hadn't she mentioned that in the first place? Come on, Denise told herself. She's just a kid.

'OK, what about candles?'

'You mean just in the kitchen? Because we've got candles in a lot of . . .'

'Just here in the kitchen.'

'Yeah. Mom keeps some in her junk drawer.'

'Matches?'

Without saying a word, Kara turned around and reached high. She snagged a wicker basket off the top of the refrigerator and pulled it down. The basket was filled with matchbooks. 'Mom collects them. Wherever she goes, she gets matches. They're souvenirs. These are extras, though. She won't mind if we use them.'

Denise switched the butcher knife to her left hand.

She reached into the basket. She lifted out a handful of matchbooks and dumped them into the breast pocket of her shirt. She took out a second handful. The right front pocket of her corduroys held the hammer, stuffed in headfirst. With her knife hand, she swept the hanging front of her shirt out of the way. She thrust the second bunch of matchbooks into the pocket on her left.

'That should do it,' she said. Kara set the basket onto the refrigerator. 'OK. I'll keep watch here. You hurry and round up the flashlight and candles.'

While the girl was away, Denise stared through the dining room, into the living room beyond its entryway.

She felt tight and sick inside. Though she hoped Tom had left the house, she couldn't bring herself to believe it. By now, he'd had plenty of time to work his hands free of the rope. He would be waiting for them. Even in a house that was pitch black, their chances of sneaking past him to the bathroom were slim.

Tom, why are you doing this to us?

She was terrified of him. At the same time, she hated the idea of being forced to hurt him. If he attacked, she would have to defend herself and Kara.

What if I kill him?

But I can't let him kill us.

Just make it to the bathroom, she thought, and we'll be safe. He can't get us there, and we won't have to fight him off.

Kara returned with the flashlight and four long, pink candles.

Denise took two of the candles and slid them into a

seat pocket of her cords. 'You keep those,' she said.
'Take some matches, too, just in case we get separated.' She removed a couple of matchbooks from her
shirt, and gave them to the girl. 'Do you want to keep
the flashlight, too?'

Kara nodded.

'OK, turn it on and come with me.' Denise stepped
past the stove. She opened the door and entered a small
room. It contained a water heater, a mop, a couple of
brooms, a dust pan, a yard stick, a rag bag and a collection of neatly folded grocery sacks. On the far side was
a door. She pointed at it. 'What's through there?'

'The weather.'

'Not a porch or anything?' she asked.

'No. That stuff'd get us all wet if we went out.'

'Guess we don't want to do that, huh?'

'I don't think so.' Kara pointed the flashlight beam
at a gray metal panel on the wall. 'There's the fuse
box,' she whispered.

Denise stepped up to it. She clamped the knife
between her knees so she could use both hands, slipped her fingertips under the edge of the thin over-
lapping door, and tugged. The door popped open
with a squawk. She yanked the other open. Within the
panel were two main switches and rows of clear glass
circuit breakers. 'Ready?' she asked.

'I guess so.'

She flicked both switches down. The light from the
kitchen vanished. The refrigerator ceased its quiet
hum. 'Turn off the flashlight,' she whispered.

Kara shut off its beam.

Reaching down, Denise slipped the knife from between her knees. She pressed the flat of its blade against her belly. She decided to leave the hammer in her pocket so her right hand would remain free.

'OK,' she whispered. 'Now, stay behind me. Maybe hold onto my shirt tail.' She stepped past Kara and felt a small tug as the girl clutched her shirt.

They left the small room and slowly crossed the kitchen. Their sneakers made quiet squeaky sounds on the tile. Denise couldn't see a thing in front of her. She reached out, hand exploring the area ahead. After a few steps, her fingertips brushed the refrigerator. Keeping to its side, she moved straight forward.

The dining room carpet silenced their shoes. Denise heard nothing except rain pounding the roof, her own thudding heart and shaky breathing, and Kara's trembling breaths behind her.

She touched the back of a chair, pictured the layout of the dining room, and turned in the direction of the entryway. She half expected Tom to be waiting just inside the living room. Any second, he would jump them.

He can't see us, she told herself.

But he might be able to hear us.

She had a sudden, strong urge to whirl around and race for the kitchen.

She kept moving forward, sweeping the area ahead with her open hand.

We must be in the living room by now, she thought. So far, so good. Maybe we've already snuck past him. Hell, he might be anywhere. He might be right in

---

front of me. One more step, and I'll touch him.

Denise took that one more step. Felt nothing. Took another. And another.

And gasped as her fingertips prodded something that felt like fabric. She lurched backward, jerking her arm away from it, and Kara bumped against her. A second later came a quiet crashing noise. A pop of glass.

The sounds of a lamp striking the carpeted floor, its bulb bursting.

You hit its shade, she thought. You knocked it over. And Tom knows right where we are.

No more point in sneaking.

She shoved the knife handle between her teeth. She fumbled a matchbook out of her shirt pocket. She flipped it open, tore out a match and struck it. A blinding bright flare, then the fire settled to an orange bloom. In its glow, she saw the lamp on the floor at her feet. She saw the sofa and much of the room beyond it. No Tom.

Thank God.

She spun around. He wasn't rushing at them from the rear.

'Turn on your flashlight,' she whispered. 'We'll make a run for it.'

The flashlight shot its beam against Denise's belly, then swung away. She shook out her match. She pulled off her shirt. Matchbooks spilled from the pocket as she wadded it. She wrapped the sleeves around the clump of fabric to hold the bundle together, knotted the sleeves once, and clamped shirt between her knees. Then she struck another match.

She lit her shirt on fire.

'You're gonna *burn* yourself.'

'Probably,' she muttered.

As flames climbed around the fabric, she grabbed the knot, pulled the shirt from between her knees, and turned away from Kara. She took the knife from her teeth. 'Go first,' she said. 'Run for the john. Don't stop for anything.'

The girl rushed past her.

Knife in her left hand, the blazing wad of shirt in her right, Denise dashed through the living room. She kept her arm high, carrying the fireball overhead like a torch.

Kara, a few strides in front of her, cut to the right at the foyer and dashed for the hallway.

No Tom. So far.

Where is he?

Denise's shoes slapped the tiles. She turned. Raced after Kara. The pale beam of the girl's flashlight skittered over the hallway carpet, the walls and dark doorways. Then the carpet was under Denise. Her torch cast orange light into the gloom ahead, fluttered against the walls and carpet. She felt heat surrounding her hand. So far, she didn't think she was being burnt.

So your hand gets burnt, she thought. You can live with it.

Just get to the john.

And a dark shape lunged out through a doorway and blocked the hall and whipped the fireplace poker at Kara's face. The girl ducked under it. Her head

rammed Tom in the belly. Instead of knocking him
down, the blow sent Kara stumbling backward. She
landed on her rump. Denise leaped over the girl.
Tom swung the poker. Its brass bar whapped against
her side. She shoved the blazing shirt at his
face.

Dropping the poker, he lurched to the side and
slammed a wall as he flung up both arms to shield his
face. Denise thrust the torch against his arms. She
knew his midsection was unprotected, knew she could
drive the knife straight into him with her left hand.
But she refused.

'KARA!' she shouted. 'GO! GO!'

The flames flapped against her face, curled hot
around her fist and forearm. But she didn't stab Tom.
She just kept jamming the fireball against his crossed
arms.

Kara rushed by.

Made it into the bathroom.

Denise pumped her knee into Tom's groin. His
breath exploded out. He spasmed against the wall.
Denise lurched away from him, dashed to the bathroom, hurled the flaming remains of her shirt into the
sink, swung around and drove her shoulder against
the door, slamming it shut. Her thumb jabbed the
lock button down.

She slumped back against the door. As she gasped,
coughing on the smoky air, Kara turned on a faucet.
Water splashed down. The burning shirt hissed. Its
glow faded. In seconds, the bathroom was dark
except for the beam of the flashlight.

Denise's right hand and forearm felt as if they were still burning. She stepped to the sink, and set down her knife, and splashed cool water against her skin.

'Are you hurt bad?' Kara whispered.

'I don't think so. How about you?'

'I'm OK. Did you stab him?'

'No.'

'How'd you get away?'

'Kneed him in the nuts.'

'Huh?'

'Never mind. Why don't you light a couple of the . . .' Denise jumped as something crashed against the door. From the sound, she guessed Tom must've struck it with the poker. She pulled her arm out from under the water, hurried to the door, and pressed her back against it.

The next blow jolted her.

That was a kick, she thought.

While she braced the door, Kara lit a candle, dripped some paraffin onto the side of the sink, then stood the candle upright in the small puddle.

Tom struck the door again.

Kara said, 'Somebody better keep that gizmo in.' She stepped up close to Denise and clutched the doorknob. Her small thumb pushed against the lock button. 'It can get popped out real easy,' she whispered. 'It doesn't even take a key.'

She held the button in.

Denise curled a hand around the back of the girl's head. As she caressed the soft hair, Kara leaned forward, slumped a little against her, and rested a cheek against her chest.

8

'What are they *doing* up there?' Cyndi said. She studied the kitchen ceiling as if it might give her a clue.

'I don't want to know,' Sheila said.

'Maybe I oughta go up and check on 'em,' Doug offered.

Cyndi glowered at him. 'Oh, you'd like that.'

Lou sipped his vodka and tonic, then squatted down and peered through the glass of the oven's door. The frozen, fried chicken pieces spread out on the cookie sheet looked as if they might be done pretty soon. The crust, getting darker, was shiny with juice or oil that bubbled. He could hear faint sounds of sizzling and crackling.

The sounds reminded him of last night. Chidi tied to the goalpost, wrapped in flame. That kid's skin had sizzled and crackled.

The memory gave Lou a heavy, sick feeling.

I didn't do it, he told himself. I didn't do any of it.

He knew that wasn't quite true. He hadn't done the *bad* stuff, though. He hadn't cut on the kid or burnt him. He hadn't killed him.

All I did, he told himself, was help snatch the bastard and strip him and tie him up. I trashed him just a little, maybe, but nothing serious. Nothing that even would've put him in the hospital for godsake.

Buddy never should've done that stuff.

Now I'm in just as much trouble as him, and I

didn't do a damn thing. Lisa's gonna spill the beans on us. We'll be fucked.

We oughta be shutting up Lisa, not having a goddamn party.

And Buddy's upstairs with the pizza gal as if he doesn't have a worry in the world.

The whole thing's crazy.

And it's storming black shit outside and the crazy bitch tried to *kill* Buddy, and we're all acting like nothing's wrong. The whole damn world's gone nuts.

'How's the chicken doing?' Sheila asked. She crouched beside Lou and looked into the oven. 'A while longer, huh? I like it good and crispy.'

You should've seen Chidi. He was good and crispy.

Sheila leaned against him. She caressed his back. He felt her breast pressing his upper arm. Breath tickling his ear, she whispered, 'Do you think we can get out of here?'

'Not while it's raining,' Lou whispered. 'Or whatever it's doing out there.'

She kissed his ear. Lou knew she was doing this so Doug and Cyndi would think they were making out, whispering endearments or something. 'I don't like this. We oughta get away. I just know Buddy's raping that woman.'

'Probably.' The feel of Sheila and images of Buddy putting it to the pizza gal started to make Lou horny. He slipped a hand under the back of Sheila's sweatshirt. Normally, she wouldn't have allowed that with people around. But she didn't protest. Her skin was warm and smooth. 'It's not like we're accomplices or anything,' he whispered. 'We're down here, you know? He's up there. They might just be talking.'

'Oh, sure.'

'Besides, she tried to knock his head off.'

'That's no excuse to . . . violate her.'

'I know,' Lou whispered. He moved his hand over the cross-strap of Sheila's bra. He knew she would go ape if he tried to unhook it.

The lucky son-of-a-bitch, Buddy. Up there with the pizza gal. Bet he got the bra off *her*. Everything else, too. The bitch was in no position to argue.

Bet he violated her but good.

'Maybe Buddy's got some raincoats and umbrellas around,' Sheila whispered. 'If we covered up really good . . .'

'It's too risky.' Then Lou came up with an idea that he knew should please her. 'Besides, there's no telling what Buddy might do to the gal.'

'That's what scares me. I don't want to be around . . .'

'If we stay, we might be able to keep him in line, you know? Stop him from . . .'

'Nobody stopped him upstairs.'

You didn't, either, Lou thought. But he didn't want to say anything that might turn Sheila against him. He rubbed her shoulder, sliding the bra strap out of his way.

'I won't let Buddy do anything *really* bad,' he said.

'Oh, raping someone isn't *really* bad? What do you call *really* bad?'

'I don't know. Like if he wants to get rid of her or something.'

'That's what I thought you meant. 'Cause I'm thinking the same thing. How's he planning to keep her from going to the cops about this if he doesn't . . . like waste her?'

'Well, she *is* the one who started it.'

'I'm not gonna be here for something like that.'

'We won't let it happen.'

'Yeah, sure.'

'I mean it. I'll stop him.'

'Will you?'

'Damn right.' Just like I stopped him last night, Lou thought. 'I'm not gonna let him kill someone in front of us.'

'How's the chick-chick coming?' Doug asked, stepping up behind them.

'A few more minutes,' Sheila said. She patted Lou's back, then stood up. Lou stood up, too, keeping his hand on her shoulder.

'I wish Buddy'd get down here,' Cyndi said.

'He's probably already eaten, anyway.'

'Very funny. Maybe one of us *should* go up and . . .'

'Help him,' Doug said.

'You're really asking for it.'

'Think I'll get it?'

'Not . . .'

'Hi ho, everyone,' Buddy said, stepping into the kitchen with the pizza gal beside him. 'What's cooking?'

'We found some chicken in the freezer,' Cyndi told him. 'It's about ready.'

'Well, we're just in time.' He smiled at the pizza gal and patted her rump. 'Friends, this is Maureen.'

Lou's hand dropped out from under Sheila's sweat-shirt.

Incredible, he thought.

'Turned out to be a white girl,' Buddy said.

'Holy shit,' Doug muttered.

Holy shit is right, Lou thought. She's a fucking knockout.

She was taller than Buddy, but slender. Even from across the kitchen, Lou could see the brilliant emerald of her eyes. Her hair must've been blow-dried. It seemed to float around her face, a rich curtain of brown and rust and gold. Lou couldn't recall ever seeing such a beautiful face. Not in the flesh, at least. Maybe on movie screens, in magazines, never in the same room with him.

She wore a white T-shirt. One of Buddy's under-shirts? It was much too large for her. It hung down so low that it covered all but the bottom inch of her red gym shorts. It seemed to drape from her shoulders, hardly touching her body anywhere except her breasts. There, the shirt was pushed outward, smooth over the soft mounds, peaked at the very front by the thrust of her nipples. Her skin showed through the thin fabric. Pink except for the darker disks at the tips of her breasts.

Like the T-shirt, the shorts were far too big. They looked as if they might fall down. Their legs gaped around her slim thighs, so loose and baggy Lou figured there was probably room to stick your head inside either one of them.

He thought about doing just that.

Buddy, you lucky bastard.

Buddy rubbed her rump. She stood rigid, letting him. Her lips were pressed tightly together, her fabulous green eyes fixed on the floor. 'Maureen has agreed to be our servant for this evening. I'm her master, of course, but you're the guests and she will be acting accordingly.'

'What a load,' Cyndi said.

Doug stepped toward Maureen and offered his hand. 'I'm Doug. Pleased to make your acquaintance.'

She smiled at him, the corners of her mouth trembling slightly, and held out her hand. Doug gripped it. With a silly grin, he hopped up and down, pumping her arm.

'Grow up,' Cyndi muttered.

'My friend, Cyndi, doesn't find me amusing.'

'Oh, that's right. Just great. Tell her all our names, why don't you.'

'It doesn't matter if I know your names,' Maureen said, meeting Cyndi's eyes. 'I'm not about to tell on anyone. I assaulted Buddy. Now, I'm paying for it. He's my master and I'm his slave. It's fair. Besides, the way I see it, Buddy may have saved my life.'

Buddy looked surprised and pleased. 'Really?' he asked. 'How's that?'

'This oughta be a good one,' Cyndi said.

'It's simple,' Maureen said, facing Buddy. 'You cleaned me. You made me all right again.'

'I bet he made you, all right,' Doug said.

'Shut up,' Buddy told him.

'Could I have a drink?' Maureen asked.

'Sure,' Buddy said. 'Why not.'

'I'll get you one,' Lou told her, and caught Sheila giving him a sour look. 'What would you like? How about a vodka and tonic?'

'That would be nice. Thank you.'

While Lou hurried to prepare the drink for Maureen, Cyndi complained, 'I thought she was supposed to be *our* servant.'

'Dry up,' Doug said.

'Oh, real nice. Looks to me like *she's* all of a sudden ruling the fucking roost around here.'

'I only asked for a drink,' Maureen said, her voice soft and apologetic.

'Yeah, well, screw you.'

'That's already been done,' Doug said.

Lou, at the counter, looked over his shoulder and saw a blush spread over the young woman's face. 'That wasn't necessary, Doug,' she said. 'I'd like to be your friend. I know that I sort of crashed the party, and I'm sorry about that. I really had no choice in the matter. But since I'm here, I'd like to be friends with all of you.'

'You can be my friend any old time,' Doug told her.

'She's pulling your chain, you dork.'

'No, I'm not,' Maureen said.

'Fuck you.'

'I love this.' Doug grinned at Buddy. 'They're fighting over me.'

'Wouldn't be any match,' Buddy said. 'Maureen would clean her clock.'

'Up yours,' Cyndi blurted.

Buddy's face lost its smile. 'Why don't we find out?'

'Why don't we eat?' Sheila suggested. Turning around quickly, she pulled open the oven door.

9

Denise's thigh muscles shuddered from the effort of bracing the door with her back. She had taken over the job of holding the lock button down, though Tom hadn't attempted, so far, to pop it open from the other side. He seemed content with crashing against the door.

Each time he struck it, the door jolted Denise.

She knew that only her body prevented it from ripping out the latch and flying open.

Sweat streamed down her face, stinging her eyes, dripping off her nose and chin. It rolled down her chest and sides, tickling her, making her itch. It made the wood slick against her back. The knife was so slippery in her right hand that she feared she might drop it. The sweat seemed even more irritating than the soreness of her back or the tight hot throb of her spasming leg muscles.

'Get a towel and wipe me,' she gasped.

Kara whipped a towel down from a bar near the tub, hurried over to her, and started to mop her face. 'What're we going to do?' the girl whispered.

'I don't know.' She winced into the soft towel as the door hit her back. 'I can't do this much longer.'

'What about the window?' Kara asked.

'Even if we get out in time, we'd be in the rain. It'd make us like him.'

Kara was silent for a moment as she rubbed the towel over Denise's shoulders and chest. 'What if we *pretend* to go out?'

'I don't . . .' Another blow. 'TOM! QUIT IT! THIS IS DENISE. YOU DON'T WANT TO HURT ME!'

Even as she yelled, the hammer was tugged from her front pocket and Kara hurried past the bathtub toward the louvered window. She boosted herself onto the counter. With quick blows of the hammer, she smashed the slats. Glass exploded outward, bounced off the screen and clattered down on the counter at her knees.

Hissing, spattering sounds of the rain came in.

Tom hit the door again. Denise gritted her teeth.

Kara struck the frame of the screen with her hammer. Again and again until the screen dropped into the night.

She jumped down from the counter. At the sink, she grabbed the flashlight. She raced with it to the

175

window, turned it on, and rested it on the sill so its beam was aimed at the door. Back at the sink, she pointed toward the bathtub. Then she puffed out her candle.

Tom hit the door again, pounding agony through Denise.

Kara climbed into the tub. It had sliding shower doors of clear glass. In the dim glow from the flashlight, Denise saw her crouch down at the back of the tub and beckon to her with the hammer.

It'll never work, Denise thought.

Neat idea, but it'll never work.

She let the door ram her one more time, then thrust herself away from it and raced for the tub. She stepped over the side. She brought her other leg in. She eased the shower door shut, stepped backward, and raised the knife from her side. She pressed its pommel hard against her belly, blade straight out.

Fall for it, Tom. Please. I don't want to stab you.

She flinched when the bathroom door burst open.

Tom lurched into view, stumbling. He almost fell, but got his balance and hurried alongside the tub. He still had the fireplace poker. He went straight for the window, leaned over the counter, reached to the sill and picked up the flashlight.

Then he turned away from the window.

He played the beam across the shower doors.

Denise squinted when its glare jabbed her eyes.

'I *seeeee* youuuu,' he said in a mad, cheery voice.

He strode toward the tub. Toward Kara's end of the tub. He shined his light down at the crouched girl.

'Leave us alone!' Kara blurted.

'Oh, I don't think so.' The light went out.

'OVER HERE!' Denise shouted. She threw the shower door wide, putting a double thickness between Tom and the girl, and braced it there with her knife hand.

She heard a quick *whiss*. A clink. The knife jerked and dropped from her hand. A blind, lucky swing of the poker must've struck its blade. Denise's fingers tingled, but the poker had missed her hand.

Gazing into the blackness straight ahead, she stepped backward. Some kind of hose brushed against her left arm. As her back met the cool tile wall behind the tub, she reached up.

A clank, and the shower doors shook. He must've whipped his poker across the opening and hit the metal frames.

Denise found the shower nozzle. One of those removeable things with a handle. She tugged it from its mount, pulled it in close to her face.

She heard Tom's harsh breathing.

It came from straight ahead.

She didn't hear the poker swing, but felt a quick fiery streak across her belly.

Suddenly, a harsh rolling rumble. The shower doors. Someone thrusting them shut in front of her? For an instant, Denise thought that Tom must've gone back to the other end of the tub to get Kara. Then he grunted. The rushing doors must've caught him.

Kara, back in action.

Denise dropped to a squat, fumbled in the dark as

the doors clamored. She pictured Kara at the other end, trying to keep them shut, Tom in front of her, shoving at them.

She found a faucet. She turned it on all the way. Water rushed from the faucet, pounded the bottom of the tub, splashed her. Cool, but getting warmer.

She hoped the Foxworth's kept their water heater turned up high – hot enough to scald.

Fingering the top of the spout, she found the shower knob and lifted it.

Water stopped thudding into the tub. The nozzle throbbed in her hand. She aimed it upward where Tom's face should be. Heard a few sputters, a *shhhhhhh* as the hot water shot out. Then hard drumming. The spray was hitting the shower door, not Tom. Hitting it and flying back at her and it was hot. Not scalding, maybe. But damn hot.

Whimpering with pain, she squeezed her eyes shut and turned her face away and shoved herself up to get her bare skin away from the spray.

The shower doors skidded. Kara yelped. Tom squealed. Something clattered against the floor of the tub, slid against Denise's shoes. The poker?

'You bitch!' Tom cried out.

She aimed at the sound of his voice.

Heard him splash into the tub. Heard breathless, whiny noises from him. Her hand was knocked aside. A fist struck her just below the left breast. Hooking an arm around Tom, she squeezed him hard against her. With her other hand, she clubbed his head with the plastic nozzle.

As he clutched her neck, she tried to knee him in the groin. Hit something that made him grunt – probably just his thigh – and he threw her sideways by the neck. Her feet slipped out from under her. She fell, keeping hold of the nozzle, felt a rough tug when it reached the end of its hose, heard a crack of breaking plastic.

Her back slammed against the tub but something cushioned her head as it snapped down. Kara?

Tom came down on top of her, mashing out her breath, squeezing her throat. She pounded the nozzle against the side of his head. Water no longer sprayed from it. But water was spouting down, anyway, probably from the shower arm. Not hitting Denise. Shooting against Tom. And starting to fill the tub, burning against her buttocks and back.

Dropping the nozzle, she cupped water in both hands and flung it at his face. He cried out. His stranglehold loosened. She grabbed his thumbs and tore them away from her throat. His hands plunged into the water, splashing it up against her face and shoulders, and she yelped as the droplets stung her.

'Denny?'

Tom's voice. Alarmed.

'Oh my God, Denny, what am I *doing* to you?'

'Tom?'

'God, I'm sorry. I'm so sorry.' His cheek pressed the side of her face.

10

The car's dome light came on when Trev opened the door. Francine and Lisa were still in the backseat. Francine looked as if she'd recovered from her panic. But her eyes were wide and frightened. So were Lisa's.

Lisa had Patterson's revolver pointing at his face.

'Everything OK?' he asked.

Neither of his passengers answered. Lisa said, 'Are *you* OK?'

'I didn't get wet,' he muttered, then slid his shotgun across the seat, climbed in and shut the door.

'Did you find your friend?' Lisa asked.

'No. Thank God,' he muttered. 'It was a massacre in there. Her father's dead.'

'What'll we do now?'

Trev shook his head. He wanted to sit here and do nothing at all. What *is* there to do?

Maureen had been staying at Liam's house. He'd called there from O'Casey's, and the phone had gone unanswered. She was either out somewhere, or home but unable to pick up the phone. He'd pictured her dead, sprawled out, stripped and bloody, savaged like the woman he'd found on the table top.

'I'll tell you what we'll do,' Francine said. 'We'll drive the fuck out of here. That's what we should've done in the first place, drive till we get out of this fucking rain and madness.'

'I can't leave without Maureen.'

'The hell you can't.'

The plastic crinkled and pressed against the nape of his neck. Through the thin layer of garbage bag, he felt a ring the size of a quarter.

The muzzle of a shotgun.

'Mom, for godsake!'

The muzzle jabbed him. 'Let's get moving.'

Trev didn't move a muscle.

'Now!'

'Maybe you should,' Lisa said, a pleading sound in her voice.

'I'll *shoot* you! Nobody'll even blame me. They'll think the wet people did it.'

'Lisa will know who did it,' Trev said. Though he realized that the woman was desperate enough to pull the trigger, he felt no fear. He just felt weary, a little numb. 'Besides, if you fire that thing, you'll probably blow out the windshield. How do you feel about letting the rain come in?'

'How do you feel about being dead?'

'Mom!'

'I'm doing this for you, honey. We've gotta get out of this town.'

'You can't kill Trev. That'd be murder. You'd be just as bad as the wet people. Worse, even. You know? I don't think they have any choice. I think the rain *makes* them do it. But you'd be doing it because you want to. That's a lot worse.'

'I don't want to. Shit!'

'Well, put it down.'

'No.'

Trev heard the *snick-clack* of a cocking revolver.

'If you shoot him, I'll shoot you.'

'Lisa!'

'I mean it! They murdered Maxwell last night, and it was all my fault. I'm not gonna sit here and let you murder a man right in front of me. I don't care if you *are* my mother. You just can't do it. Put the gun down!'

Trev felt the muzzle ease away from his neck.

'OK? *OK?* Are you happy now?'

Lisa didn't say anything.

After a while, Francine said, 'Are we just going to sit here?'

'How about if I take you home?' Trev suggested.

'Fine. Just fine.'

'Is there a way in that's sheltered?'

'The carport's covered,' Lisa said. 'The kitchen door's right there.'

'OK. Let's do it.'

He started the car, put on its wipers and headlights, and backed slowly out of the alley. He glimpsed the black heap of the axeman before turning his eyes to the rearview mirror.

'Will you stay with us?' Lisa asked.

'We'll see,' he said. He had no intention of staying with them.

'That means no,' Francine said.

'It means we'll see. Where do you live?'

'4823 Maple.'

'OK.' He swung out onto Third Street, started forward. Easing down on the gas, he suddenly realized that the visibility had improved. Though the rain still came down, it no longer splashed a black sheet against the windshield, no longer deadened his headlights so much or blanketed the street lights. Trev could actually see cars parked along both sides of the road, and the glow of shop windows. He felt a swelling of hope. But it dwindled when he noticed the dim shapes of people in the rain.

The dead and the living.

'Oh, my God,' Lisa muttered.

Francine sucked in a quick breath.

It was better when we couldn't see, Trev thought. He wished the rain would come down in a heavy shower like before and hide all this.

He glimpsed several bodies. Some were sprawled in the street, others on the sidewalk. He saw a man draped out the window of a pickup truck, torso split open and ropes of entrails hanging to the pavement. He saw a German Shepherd tugging at the leg of a child, trying to drag the small body over a curb. He swerved to miss the carcass of a woman in the middle of the road – a twisted jumble of broken limbs, head mashed flat. She looked as if she'd been run over many times.

The sights of the dead sickened Trev. The sights of the living terrified him.

Alone or in small groups, some skulked through the darkness like phantoms searching for prey. Others pranced around like revelers. Others raced in mad pursuit of fleeing victims. Many had discarded their clothing.

He saw a naked woman sprawled on the pavement,

squirming and rubbing herself as if the rain had triggered a fit of erotic ecstasy. He saw a couple rutting on the hood of a car. The man was on top, and Trev couldn't be sure whether the woman jerking beneath him was alive or dead. At the corner, he spotted two women and a man hunched over a corpse, tearing at its clothes and flesh.

Those people, distracted from their chore, turned their heads and peered toward Trev's car. A chill prickled the back of his neck. He shoved down hard on the gas pedal.

In the back seat, Francine was wheezing again.

No sounds at all came from Lisa.

'At least we can see where we're going,' Trev muttered.

He wondered if Maureen was among those he'd seen, demented or dead.

Maybe she's safe, he told himself.

I'll drop these two off and drive to her house. Maybe she's there, safe and sound, and I can stay with her and protect her.

'What could do this to people?' Lisa asked, her voice high and shaking.

'I wish I knew. Poison in the rain? Chemicals? Germs? I've got no idea. Hell, maybe God's finally decided he's had enough crap from humanity . . .'

'God wouldn't do this,' Lisa said.

'No, you're probably right. Maybe it's the Devil.'

A teenaged kid darted into view from behind a parked van. He sped toward Trev's car on a skateboard, waving a machete overhead. He wore nothing but undershorts and a ballcap.

Trev swerved.

Not to avoid this one, to hit him.

The kid flipped high as the bumper knocked out his legs. He lost his machete. His ballcap spun away. He missed the axe handle. He bounced on the hood and tumbled. His knee thumped the windshield. Then he flew upward out of sight. Trev heard some rough bumps on the roof before the kid toppled off.

'*I can't stand it!*' Francine blurted.

And Lisa said, 'Maybe it's Maxwell's grandpa.'

'What?' Trev gasped.

'He's some kind of a witch doctor. Maybe this is his revenge, or something.'

Ridiculous, Trev thought.

But what mad, poetic justice if it were true. White boys murder a black kid. Next thing you know, down comes the rain making *everyone* black and kill-crazy. Revenge in spades.

But black magic? Come on, Trev.

'What do you know about him?'

'Just that Maxwell . . . he wouldn't ever let me meet his family. He said they wouldn't like him going out with someone like me . . . you know, someone white. But especially his grandfather. He said the old man might do something weird if he ever found out. Like put a hex on me. I told Max I wasn't afraid of any hexes, but he said I *oughta* be. He said his grandpa was really into that stuff, and it worked. He even told me some stories about how his grandpa got back at enemies, and stuff. How he'd cripple them up, or make them go crazy, or even die. Like there was a doctor back on the island they came from, and he gave Max's grandmother some drug she was allergic to and she died. So Max's grandpa put a spell on him, and the doctor went crazy and carved up his whole family, his wife and kids and everything, and when they found him he was still alive but he'd cut off both his own feet and his left hand, and even his you-know-what . . . his dick. And he'd poked out both his eyes.'

'Oh, wonderful,' Francine said, her voice high and shaky.

'I mean, Max really *believed* his grandpa made the doctor do all that. And he was afraid the guy might hurt me if he found out we were going together. It kind of scared me, you know?'

'So you never met the grandfather?' Trev asked.

'I never met anyone in his family. Except his sister. She's in the tenth grade. She promised not to tell on us.'

'Did Max ever mention black rain?'

'No. Huh-uh. I would've caught on right away, if he ever had. It was just, you know, when you said that about the Devil. I never even thought about Max's grandpa till you said that. It just sort of clicked, you know? That maybe this is all some kind of a curse and maybe the old guy's *making* it happen.'

'That's insane,' Francine said.

'What isn't?' Trev muttered.

'You don't honestly think . . .'

'It makes as much sense as anything else,' he said. 'It makes a hell of a *lot* of sense. The motive, anyway.

I'm not saying a guy could actually *do* this. But if he could, it'd be a damn nifty way to get back at the town he blames for murdering his grandson.'

'Oh, for godsake.'

'I know it sounds weird, Mom. But what if he *is* doing it? You know? And what if there's a way to make him stop? Maybe the rain'll end.'

'Did the grandfather live with the family?' Trev asked.

'Yeah. He had his own room in their house.'

Trev knew that he'd seen the address on reports. Fairmont Avenue, but he couldn't recall the house number.

Near the north end of town, and he was heading south.

'Do you know the address?' he asked.

'Huh-uh.'

Trev made a U-turn.

'Our house is *that* way,' Francine protested.

'First things first,' Trev said. His headbeams swept past the tattered body of a man bound to a lamp post. Like Chidi tied to the goalpost standard. This guy was black, but hadn't been born that way. And hadn't been burnt. He had a gaping pit below his ribcage.

'You can't do this!'

'Mom!'

'Damn it! It's a waste of time, and you'll get us all killed.'

'Maybe I can end the whole mess.'

It might be too late for Maureen, he thought.

But if Chidi's grandfather was responsible, and if

Trev could get to the house, there was a chance he could put a stop to the downpour and save lives.

'You can't seriously believe some damn *witch doctor's* behind all this.'

'Of course I don't,' Trev said. 'But I'm going to proceed as if I do. Lisa, do you know if they're listed in the phone directory?'

'Yeah, they are.'

'I'll have to make one more stop, then we'll head straight out to Chidi's place and see what the bastard's up to.'

11

Soon after John joined the others in the booth, Peggy brought plates of top sirloin, baked potato and green beans. She explained that the menu had been dispensed with, and the meal was complementary.

Lynn and Carol asked for fresh margaritas.

John and Steve exchanged glances. 'I'm fine,' John told the waitress. He was halfway through his second Mai Tai. A third would be nice, but it would also be enough to impair his faculties.

'I'll pass on another one, too,' Steve said. After Peggy left, he added, 'Hate to get busted for DWI on the way home.'

Lynn laughed. 'I'd say that's the least of your worries.'

'What *about* going home?' Carol asked.

'Too dangerous,' Steve said, and started cutting into his meat.

'If I could think of any way to get home,' John said, 'we wouldn't be here. I'd give anything to be with Kara right now. But I just don't see how it can be done. Maybe I'd be able to handle whoever's outside, I don't know. I don't know how many there are, or how they might be armed. But the problem's the rain. If I get wet, it's all over. I'd be just like them. Hell, I might just turn around and come in to nail *you* people.'

'We just have to wait for the rain to stop,' Steve said.

'Eat, drink and be merry,' Carol muttered. She tongued some salt off the rim of her glass. 'I hope Peggy hurries with those drinks. If I'm gonna die, I want to be good and sloshed.'

'Nobody's going to die,' Lynn told her.

'Tell that to those poor slobs in the freezer. I'm sure the news would cheer them up considerably.'

'We're all going to be fine,' Lynn persisted. John reached around her back and caressed her shoulder.

You tell them, honey.

'Before we know it,' she said, 'the rain'll let up and we'll all go on home and this'll be just like a bad dream. Isn't that right, honey?'

'Yep.'

'Bullshit,' Carol said.

'Eat your food,' Steve told her.

'We're perfectly safe in here,' Lynn said. 'Look how

many of us there are. And we've got plenty of sharp cutlery if push comes to shove.' She twirled her serrated knife in front of her eyes.

'A lot of good steak knives'll be against a horde of raving lunatics.'

'What horde?' Lynn said. 'There's no point in blowing things out of proportion. One person's knocking on the door. For all we know, nobody else is out there.'

'Maybe half the town's out there,' Carol said.

'We could open the door and see,' Steve suggested.

'Oh, great. Why don't you just go and do that.'

'As long as they're making no serious effort to break in,' John said, 'it really doesn't matter a whole lot. We're safe right now. I think we should go ahead and eat, and try not to worry about it.'

'Yeah, sure.' She gave him a sullen look, then lowered her head and began to cut her meat.

Peggy showed up with the drinks.

'All quiet on the western front?' John asked her.

'Some nut's still pounding on the front door. Other than that, not much is going on. A lot of folks are getting pretty polluted. And there's a bunch in the bar I think are getting ready to abandon ship.'

'Don't they know what'll happen to them?' Steve asked.

'They just want to go home.' Peggy shrugged, then carried her tray to the next booth and set a martini in front of Chester Benton's widow. Cassy, still sitting with her, met John's gaze and smiled slightly.

He returned the smile, then looked down at his

plate. Don't think about her, he told himself, and pictured her sprawled on the floor, the doctor cutting her laces, spreading her bodice.

Knock it off!

'What about those people in the bar?' Steve asked.

John took a bite of beef. 'What about them?'

'Maybe we ought to see what they're up to.'

'That's not a bad idea,' Carol said. 'What if they've figured out how to get out of here?'

'It's worth a check,' Steve said.

'Should probably try to talk them out of it,' John muttered. He didn't want to get involved. Let them do what they want, he thought. If they're fools enough to go outside . . . It's not my job to save people from their own stupidity. But they get wet, and they might be *our* problem.

He remembered the guy in the men's room. Andy. After calling home, he'd noticed Andy and the girl, Tina, holding hands across their small table in the cocktail lounge. They'd looked like a couple of kids, helpless and terrified.

What are their chances if they go outside?

He took one more bite, then looked up at Steve. 'I think I'd better go on over there and . . .'

The window beside the next table exploded. Cassy twisted away from the flying glass, squeezing her eyes shut and hurling up an arm to shield her face. The Benton woman, closer to the window, squealed and lurched sideways against her. John realized she must've looked toward the source of the sudden noise. Her face was a mask of raw rips, studded with shards. A triangle of glass jutted from her left eye.

Lynn grabbed John's sleeve and yelled 'Don't!' as he lunged from the booth and a fat bald man, shiny black, leaned through the broken window and caved in the woman's forehead with a tire iron. John pulled free. He didn't bother to dodge Steve, who was leaning out and starting to rise. He shouldered him out of the way, rushed past the empty bench and table, clutched Cassy's arm and tugged her from the booth. She came up brushing against him, gasping warm breath against his face.

The man in the window grabbed a handful of Mrs Benton's hair and dragged her limp body toward him.

At least he's not coming in, John thought.

Taking her. Taking her out with him.

John swung Cassy away. He sprang onto the cushioned bench. It was soft and springy under his shoes. He took only one step before the man hurled the tire iron at him, sidearm. He shot up a hand to block it. The bar struck his wrist. Instead of bouncing away, it took a quick flip around his wrist and smashed him across the brow.

A strobe flashed behind his eyes.

He fought to stay on his feet.

Gotta stop him!

It didn't matter that the woman was probably dead. Didn't matter much, anyway. Dead or not, John didn't want the bastard to take her.

He brought up his knife hand. The knife seemed to be missing. He stared at his empty hand. He was sure he'd had the knife a second ago.

He looked up.

He couldn't see much. The lights were just too faint. But he could see enough to realize the guy was using both hands, now. The woman's head was clamped between them, and he was pulling her toward the window.

John knew he was about to go down.

He teetered backward.

NO!

He waved his arm, struggling against gravity and unconsciousness, and managed to correct the direction of his fall.

He tumbled forward.

Onto the moving body. It dropped, trapped against the seat and wall. Some glass in the woman's face cut John's cheek.

He wrapped his arms around her.

You won't get her now!

He was vaguely aware of commotion around him. There were shouts. The edge of the table shook against his side. More sounds of breaking glass. Then people were pulling at his legs. He held onto the woman. Together, they slid over the cushion. Her legs went out from under him. His knees followed, jabbing into them, and he murmured 'Sorry' and tried to get off her.

He released her. Then he was carried backward and lowered to the floor.

Someone bending over him. Lynn.

'Oh, you idiot. You fool.'

'I didn't . . . let 'im get her.'

'No, you didn't. God, John.'

He tried to sit up, but she pushed him down, pinned his shoulders to the floor. 'Just stay put, honey.'

Then Cassy was on her knees beside him, patting his face with a cloth napkin.

'Are you OK?'

'He took an awful knock on the head,' Lynn said.

Lynn stopped holding him down. She stroked his hair while Cassy dabbed at the cuts.

'I keep some bandages in my purse,' Lynn said. 'Stay with him?'

'Sure.'

When she was gone, Cassy said, 'You keep coming to my rescue.'

'Glad to help,' he said. He noticed the way the blazer drooped, closed only by its two low buttons. He glimpsed her shadowy right breast, then forced his eyes away from it and watched the way her short, glossy bangs swayed above his face.

'Come away from there!' Carol snapped.

'*Jesus!*'

'Steve!'

'Where'd they all *come* from?'

'How many?' asked a voice John didn't recognize.

'I don't know. A bunch.'

'Let's block up that window.'

12

Trev parked in the alley near O'Casey's. His head-beams lit the black heap of the axeman. He shut them off, killed the engine and stuffed the keys into his jeans.

'Hurry, OK?' Lisa said.

'I'll be as fast as I can.' He grabbed the shotgun and climbed out. The rain came down on him. More of a soft shower than a downpour.

Making his way toward the street, he avoided puddles. Though he hadn't checked the bottoms of his feet, he was sure that his earlier walking must've worn holes in the plastic under his shoes. The thick rubber soles of his sneakers should keep his feet dry so long as he didn't step in anything much deeper than half an inch.

I keep wandering around in this stuff, he thought, and I'm bound to get wet.

At the front of the alley, he checked both ways. A body on the sidewalk to the right, several yards away. At the corner, someone darted by and vanished behind a parked car. But that was a good distance away. Trev didn't think he'd been seen.

He turned to the left. The sidewalk ahead looked clear. He walked quickly toward O'Casey's.

He knew what he would find in there. He didn't want to see those bodies again. Probably every shop on Third Street had a telephone directory. He could've gone into any one of them to look up Chidi's address. But he *didn't* know what he would find in other places. He didn't want surprises.

Also, the alley seemed like a good place to leave the car. The women had been safe there, last time.

He stepped under O'Casey's awning and paused, glad to be out of the rain. He took deep breaths. Though he hadn't exerted himself, he felt winded.

Something trickled down the back of his neck.

A chill crawled up his spine.

Oh, my God!

Another droplet ran down his neck.

And he realized it was only sweat. He let out a quiet, shaky laugh, and hurried into the restaurant.

He scanned the bodies. They looked the same. He headed for the kitchen, stepping around the bodies and broken glass, being careful not to slip on the wet floor. As he walked, more sweat trickled down his neck and face.

He'd probably been sweating like a hog, all along, and simply hadn't paid attention to it. The hair at the back of his head was dripping. The garbage bags felt slick and greasy against his skin. Only his socks and underwear kept him from being completely encased by the slimy, clinging plastic. And they were sodden.

He had a sudden urge to strip free of the damned wrappings. Feel the cool air on his body. Strip down to his briefs and *stay* here. Have some beer. Throw together a pizza. Forget about going back out in the rain.

The body of the woman sprawled across the rear table put a quick end to that.

She looked *so much* like Maureen.

He stopped beside her drooping head, blinked sweat out of his eyes, and studied her hair until he spotted some blonde.

What if Maureen had bleached her hair?

Trev considered getting a wet rag and cleaning the gore from her pubic hair, just to make sure *it* wasn't auburn.

Don't get crazy. That isn't her.

Stop wasting time.

He stepped into the kitchen, removed Patterson's hat and slipped the hood off his head. The fresh air felt wonderful. He set them and the shotgun on the counter.

He glanced at Liam. His friend. Maureen's father.

The poor girl. Both her parents gone.

She might be dead, herself, by now.

Trev turned away quickly and hurried to the telephone. He threw open the directory. His plastic mitten dripped dark liquid onto the pages as he flipped to the Cs.

Chidi, Clarence was at 4538 Fairmont. He memorized the address, then searched through the Os until he found Liam's number again. He snatched up the handset, picked up the same pen he'd used before to punch in the number, and jabbed the keys.

He heard the quiet ringing.

Answer it, answer it, answer it! Come on, Maureen!

Maybe she'd been in the shower, last time.

It rang eleven times. Then it was picked up.

Oh, thank God. 'Maureen?'

No answer.

'Maureen? It's Trevor Hudson.'

'Hi, Trevor.' A woman's voice, low and husky, and not Maureen.

'Who is this?'

'Maureen.'

The skin on the back of his neck prickled.

'Come on over, honey. It's lonesome here. We'll have us a party.'

He closed his eyes. He felt as if his breath were being squeezed out. 'You're all alone there?'

'Sure am, sweetheart.'

'Have you got any bodies?'

'Mine. And it wants you, Trevor. Real bad.'

'I want dead people,' he said.

'Maybe we can go out and find some.'

'None in your house, though?'

'I wish there was. But you come on over, now. OK? We'll have us a real good time.'

'Fine,' he said. 'See you.' He set the phone down on its cradle and struggled to fill his lungs.

13

Tom held the flashlight on the fusebox, and Denise flicked the switches. They stepped out of the small room. Denise squinted when she met the brightness of the kitchen. Kara, waiting there, let out a sigh as if her world had just undergone a tremendous improvement.

Denise smiled. 'Better, huh?'

The girl bobbed her head. 'Darkness is not one of my favorite things.'

'This is better, all right,' Tom said.

His eyes shifted upward quickly to Denise's face, and she felt herself blush. In spite of the towel draped over her shoulders to cover her bra, she suddenly felt almost naked. It hadn't bothered her earlier, while they dried themselves in the bathroom and made their way through the house by flashlight. Nobody could see much, and she'd been too relieved by the change in Tom to care much about modesty.

'Maybe we should get into some dry clothes,' she said. She turned to Kara. 'You don't think your folks would mind us borrowing . . .'

'Oh, no. Let's go and change. This feels yucky.'

'Could I use the phone first?' Tom asked her. 'I want to call home and make sure my parents are OK.'

'OK, sure.'

He thanked her, then picked up the kitchen extension. He tapped in the number. He smiled nervously at Denise. His gaze dropped for a moment. He looked away fast. 'Hi, Mom, it's me . . . No, nothing's wrong. Can I talk to Dad, though?' Covering the mouthpiece, he said, 'Sounds like everything's fine over there.' He took his hand away.

'Yeah, hi Dad. Nothing weird's going on over there, is it? . . . Well, some guy tried to break in over here. The rain's black, Dad . . . No, I mean it. And it's really dangerous. It's making people into killers. I heard they broke into the Edgewood, too, and killed some people there . . . No, I'm not *on* anything. It's really true. I don't know what's going on, but I wanted to make sure you're all right and warn you and Mom. You oughta get out one of your guns and keep it around. Don't let anybody into the house . . . I don't know why there haven't been any reports on the TV. Maybe nobody knows about it . . . Look, if you don't believe me, take a look at the rain. But be careful, OK? Don't get any on you, or it'll make you want to kill people . . . You can't talk to them, they're not here . . . They're at the Edgewood. They called from there . . . Yes, I knew. I'm sorry. But jeez, it's no big deal . . . If I try to come home, *I'll* get wet. Besides, I have to stay here and take care of Denny. She's all alone, and there's no telling what might happen . . . OK, then ground me. For godsake, Dad, this is a real emergency. I'm not kidding. Something really terrible's going on, and I don't understand it, but it's sure happening . . . Just get a gun and watch out, OK? I've gotta go.' He hung up. His cheeks puffed out, and he blew air through his pursed lips.

'Guess you're in hot water,' Denise said.

He laughed. 'Well, at least they're safe. Dad might want to kill me, but they're safe.'

'Do you want to call your parents?' Kara asked Denise.

She shook her head. 'They're out of town.'

'I hope it isn't raining where they are.'

'Me, too. But it's a long way from here.'

'Can we change, now?'

'Yeah, let's.'

Kara led the way. Denise turned off the kitchen lights and followed, Tom walking close behind her. It felt good to know he was there.

So weird, she thought. A while ago, he was a raving lunatic and you were scared to death of him. Now, it's like he's your protector. All it took was enough hot water.

'Maybe we can find me some aspirin,' he said.

She looked around at him. 'Are you all right?'

'Just a headache, mostly.' In a louder voice, he said, 'You've got a mean swing, Kara.'

She looked back, contorting her face. 'I'm awful sorry.'

'Hey, I'm glad you did it. God. I just can't believe I was actually . . .'

'Don't worry about it,' Denisé said. She paused in the living room to pick up the lamp she'd knocked over.

'I hate it that I hurt you.'

'I know. But you couldn't help it. And I got you pretty good, too.' At the other end of the sofa, she turned off the next lamp. 'I'm just glad you're back to normal.'

'Thank God we ended up in the bathtub.'

201

Denise crossed the foyer. As she reached for the switch panel, Kara frowned. 'You're not going to make it dark again, are you?'

'You can turn on the hallway light. But your dad thought we'd be safer if the house looks deserted.'

'Most people leave lights on when they're gone,' Tom pointed out.

'Yeah, you're right. OK.' She dropped her hand away from the switches.

Kara started up the hallway, then halted. 'Maybe it'd be better if somebody else goes first.'

Denise stepped forward. 'Let's go together.' She took the girl's hand.

'Can I change first?'

'Sure.' The hallway smelled smoky. Though there didn't seem to be any ashes on the beige carpeting, Denise's burning shirt had left a grimy trail along the ceiling. She wondered if soap and water might take care of it.

When they came to Kara's bedroom, Denise reached around the doorframe and turned on the light. They entered. Tom stopped in the doorway. 'Are there fresh towels somewhere?' he asked.

'Oh, that's a good idea. They're in the closet by the bathroom.'

He went to get some.

'Do you think he's OK?' Kara whispered.

'I think so.'

'Me, too. He seems really nice. Though he does tell a lot of fibs.' She sat on the edge of her bed and started to undress. 'I try never to tell a lie, especialiy to

---

my Mom and Dad. I'm sure that I would never get away with it, anyway.'

'Doesn't look as if Tom's getting away with it.'

She laughed. 'He's in trouble, all right. But I'm sure glad he isn't weird anymore. Do you think it was just washing off the black water? That cured him?'

'It sure looks that way.'

'Yeah. I guess that's a good thing to know.' Leaving her underpants on, she stepped to her dresser. The panties looked damp and clinging. The backs of her legs had blotches of a faint reddish hue from the bath water.

'Do the burns hurt?' Denise asked.

'Oh, not very much.'

'Kind of like a little sunburn?'

'Yeah.'

'Me, too.'

'You got a lot more on you than I did,' the girl said. 'Should I put on my nightie, or what?'

'Might as well. I don't think we'll be going out.'

She pulled open the top drawer, took out a pink night-gown and fresh panties, and looked past Denise as Tom came into the room. Her eyes went wide. Denise whirled around. Some neatly folded towels were pressed to Tom's side. His other hand was full with the fireplace poker, hammer and knife. 'Don't worry,' he said. 'I just thought we'd better keep this stuff with us.' He stepped toward Kara. 'Do your parents have any guns?'

'No. Dad doesn't like them.' She put on her night-gown.

'Here.'

Kara pulled a towel out from under his arm. Tom

turned away as she reached under her nightgown. She took off her panties, spent a few moments drying herself from the waist down, then stepped into the dry underwear. She went to her closet. She put on a pair of Alf slippers.

Then she led them down the hall to her parents' room. 'What do you suppose you want to wear?'

'It's up to you,' Denise said.

'How about warmups? They'd be good and cozy.'

'Fine.'

Kara searched some drawers. She took out a royal blue warmup suit for Denise. The jacket had a hood, a zipper front, and white piping up the sleeves. The pants matched, with piping up the sides of the legs. 'Snazzy,' Denise said.

Kara gave her the suit, and a pair of white socks.

'Dad hasn't got anything as neat,' she told Tom.

'Whatever,' he said.

She found a gray sweatsuit and white socks for him. He dropped the weapons onto the bed, and she handed the garments to him.

'I'll change in the john,' he said.

'We ought to stay together,' Denise said. 'Why don't you just go in the closet?'

He left a towel behind for her, stepped into the roomy closet, turned on its light, and pulled the door shut.

'Don't come out till I say so,' she warned him.

'Aw.'

She laughed. She undressed in front of the closet door. It had a full-length mirror.

'You *really* got wrecked,' Kara said.

Denise nodded while she dried her hair. She looked as if she'd sunbathed in the nude and stayed out too long. And maybe as if there'd been a tree above her, a few leaves blocking out the sun so she ended up with pale blotches here and there. The red was very faint, though. She suspected it would go away entirely in an hour or so.

The discoloring across her throat was a deeper red than the burns. Where Tom had choked her. That would probably turn into a bruise. The same with the patch under her left breast. Where he'd punched her. She had two crimson streaks across her belly. One from the tip of the umbrella, a longer one from the point of the fireplace poker he'd whipped at her while she stood in the tub. The umbrella hadn't broken her skin at all, but the poker had scraped off a layer. The skin was ruffled up around the edges of the wound, leaving a strip that looked raw and juicy.

She pointed to it for Kara's benefit. 'I'll have a nice scab there.'

'I had a really bad one on my knee. I had it forever.'

'Did you pick it off and eat it?'

'Oh, gross!'

'Hey,' Tom said. 'I'm missing all the fun.'

'Just admiring the wounds you gave me.'

'You should see what you did to my arm.'

'Sorrrry.'

Kara laughed.

'Can I come out, now?'

'No way. Stay put.' Though Denise's skin wasn't

very wet anymore, it seemed moist and clammy. The towel felt good. Her burns were a little tender, but didn't hurt much. She gently patted the streaks on her belly.

When she was done, she stepped into the warm-up pants and pulled them up. They were soft and clingy. They seemed to trap in the heat of her skin, making the burns feel slightly worse. Otherwise, they felt wonderful. She put on the jacket. She raised its zipper to her throat, then lowered it a few inches to let some air in.

She rapped on the mirror.

'Yo.'

'I'm dressed. Are you?'

'Yep.' He opened the door and came out. The sweatsuit came with him. Drooping and baggy. He looked like a kid lost in the clothes of a giant.

Denise laughed. Kara, grinning, shook her head.

'Your dad must be a pretty big guy,' Tom said.

'Oh, he is.'

'You aren't gonna lose your pants, are you?' Denise asked.

'If I do, you'll be the first to know.'

'I'm not sure *anyone* will know,' she said.

'Look at this,' he said, and pushed his right sleeve up to the elbow. His forearm showed a red crescent of teeth marks. But the skin wasn't broken.

Denise pursed her lips. 'I did that, huh?'

'You should see what you did to her,' Kara said.

Denise lifted the bottom of her jacket.

'Yeah, I know. You weren't wearing that before, remember?'

She blushed. That seemed to make her burns feel even hotter. She pulled the jacket down again.

She went to the bed, sat down, and put on the socks.

'What'll we do now?' Kara asked.

Tom picked up the fireplace poker. He frowned at it, and turned it slowly in his hands. 'Well, I came over here for some popcorn.'

'Yeah. Why don't we make a new batch and have a nice party and watch some TV.'

'Might as well,' Denise said. 'It might be a long night.'

Warriors

1

'Messy, messy stuff,' Buddy said. He dropped the last of his chicken bones onto the paper plate on his lap, then leaned forward and set the plate on the coffee table. He settled back against the sofa. Smiling, he raised his hands to show the others.

Lou, from his seat across the room, could see the shiny grease and flecks of chicken fat on Buddy's fingers.

'What're you trying to do,' Sheila said, 'make us sick?'

'It's just so messy. Sticky. Ick.' With that, he turned sideways and held his dripping hands in front of Maureen's face. 'Be a good girl and lick them clean for me.'

'For godsake,' Sheila muttered.

Cyndi grinned. Doug tore a chunk off his drumstick and turned his head to watch.

Maureen swallowed her mouthful. She stared at Buddy, her eyes narrow.

'Do you have a problem with that?' he asked.

She shook her head. With the back of her hand, she wiped the grease from around her lips. Buddy took the plate off her lap. She sat up straight. Then she opened up, and he slid his right thumb into her mouth.

'Suck it, honey, suck it.'

Lou's heart started thumping. Maureen shut her eyes. She was breathing hard through her nose, her breasts rising and falling under the thin shirt. Buddy plucked the thumb from her mouth. It came out with a wet slurpy sound. He stuck in his index finger.

'This is disgusting,' Sheila said.

Buddy grinned at her, then pushed against Maureen, his hand pressing her down until she was slumped against the sofa back. The breath hissed through her nostrils. She writhed a little. He took out the finger and slid his middle finger into her mouth.

'Yeah, suck it hard, baby.'

'Oh lordy,' Doug murmured.

Her legs swung apart and she pushed at the floor and one side of her shorts gaped. Lou could see up the leg hole. He gazed at the shadowy smoothness of her inner thigh. He almost had a view of her groin, but not quite. If he got down and sat on the floor . . . But Sheila would catch on.

He squirmed. It's a good thing I can't see any higher, he thought.

'When you're done with him,' Doug said, 'I could use some of that. Don't know how I got chicken grease all over my dick, but . . .'

Cyndi jabbed his arm.

'Just kidding, just kidding.'

'Shithead.'

Buddy popped his middle finger out of Maureen's mouth, and poked in his ring and pinky fingers together. 'Ooooh,' he said. 'So tight and wet. Love it. Suck, honey, suck.'

Sheila, sitting on the floor near Lou's chair, twisted her head around and scowled up at him. He knew his face was red. He knew he was panting some. He hoped Sheila didn't know the reason why, and just thought he was upset. At least his legs were crossed so she couldn't see the bulge. He shook his head to show her just how disgusting he considered Buddy's behavior.

'Thank you so much,' Buddy said. He took the fingers from her mouth, clutched her breast and squeezed it through the shirt. She gasped and her lips peeled away from her teeth. 'Just drying off,' he said. He turned his hand over and wiped its back against her shirt. Lou watched how it pushed her breast in, and how the breast came springing back when it went away.

'I don't believe you,' Sheila said.

Buddy grinned at her. 'If you don't like it, go home.'

'I don't think we should all just sit here and let him *do* stuff like this.'

'Buzz off,' Cyndi told her. 'She deserves anything she gets.'

Buddy jammed his left hand into Maureen's mouth. All four fingers at once. She choked, grabbed his wrist and shoved his hand out. As the fingertips cleared her lips, he drove his right fist into her belly.

Her breath gusted out. She lurched forward, hunching over her thighs, and wheezed for air.

'You're such a bastard,' Sheila said. 'It's no wonder Lisa dumped you.'

The mention of Lisa made Lou go tight and cold inside. For a while there, he'd been able to forget about her, forget what they'd done to Chidi.

Buddy grinned at Sheila. 'She didn't dump me. She just got a hankering for some dark meat. That's all over now.'

'Done,' Doug said. '*Well* done.'

Buddy chuckled.

'That's sick,' Sheila muttered.

Lou reached to the lamp table for his drink. He picked it up. The cold, wet glass was slick in his sticky fingers. He thought about Maureen sucking his fingers clean, but the idea of it didn't turn him on. This damn talk about Lisa and Chidi.

Maureen was still bent over, huffing for breath.

'I sure hope Lisa's all right,' Buddy said. He looked at Cyndi. 'You said she's babysitting tonight?'

'Yeah.'

'You wouldn't know where, would you?'

'Oh, sure. They live just down the block from me. The Foxworths. That's where she is.'

'I think I'll give her a call and check up on her.'

'She isn't interested in you,' Sheila said.

'Oh, don't be too sure about that.' He grabbed the back of Maureen's neck and pushed, using it like a handle to help himself off the sofa, shoving her down hard against her thighs. 'Keep a sharp eye on my honey, folks. But no feelies. That means you, too, Sheila.' He winked at her.

She gave him the finger.

That's twice in one night, Lou thought. She's sure getting brave with Buddy. Any braver, and she would probably get herself stomped.

Buddy laughed and strode out of the room.

Lou finished his vodka.

'Don't you gals need to use the powder room?' Doug asked.

'Take a leap,' Cyndi told him.

'I think we've all got to stand up to Buddy,' Sheila said. 'We shouldn't just sit here and let him *do* things to this woman. It's horrible.'

Maureen raised her face. She looked at Sheila. 'Thanks,' she murmured.

'You shut up,' Cyndi said.

'Lou!' Buddy called. The faint voice came from far away. 'Get in here, would you? Lisa wants to talk to you.'

Lou's heart thumped. He felt as if he were falling. But he got up from the chair. On wobbly legs, he stepped past Sheila and headed for the kitchen.

What does she want to talk to me for? It doesn't make sense.

Thanks a lot for murdering Maxwell, you fucking bastard.

I didn't kill him. It was Buddy.

What's going on?

He entered the kitchen. Buddy was standing by the wall extension. But he didn't hold the phone. It was hanging where it belonged. Buddy had the directory open in his hands.

'Did she hang up?' Lou asked.

'I didn't call her, numbnuts. Are you kidding?'

Thank God.

'What's going on?'

'Checking out the address. We're gonna pay the cunt a visit.'

'What?'

'Are you deaf or just stupid?'

'What do you mean, pay her a visit?'

'I been thinking about her all day, man. Sooner or later, she's gonna lose it and squeal on us.'

'Yeah. I think she might.'

'You, me and Doug are gonna go over and take care of her. It's perfect, man. We tell the gals we're all done messing with Maureen and want to take her back to her place. They'll be glad to get rid of her, you know? They're both so fucking jealous you can taste it. We leave them here. They'll be our alibi, you know?'

'I'm not so sure Sheila'll lie for us.'

'Don't worry about that, man. She'll do whatever we say.'

'So we leave them here and take Maureen with us?'

'That's the idea.'

'What'll we do with Maureen?'

'Anything we want. You're both aching for her.'

Lou moaned. 'You'll let us . . . ?'

'Damn right. Then we'll dump her and drop in on Lisa. Take care of her.'

'Kill her?'

'Don't worry, man. I'll do it.'

Lou leaned back against the doorframe and stared at Buddy.

He's gonna let me at Maureen.

'Then we'll all be in the clear. Neat, huh?'

'Wait. Wait. What about the rain?'

'What about it?'

'If we get wet . . .'

'So, we don't get wet. No big deal. I've got umbrellas, raincoats. Go on back and tell Doug to come here. Then keep an eye on our babe. Those gals might let her get away if they get the chance.'

'This is wild,' he muttered. His mind felt numb.

Buddy slapped him on the shoulder, and he headed for the living room.

We can't do this, he thought.

But, oh, we sure will.

2

Trev, shaken by his talk with the stranger at Maureen's house, pulled the plastic hood down over his head and put on Patterson's hat.

The way she'd talked, it was obvious that she'd been out in the rain. A crazy. A killer hoping for some action. Hoping I'll come by so she can nail me.

She might just get the chance, Trev thought. He picked up the shotgun and made his way toward the door.

She'd claimed there were no bodies in the house. She could've been lying. But he wanted to believe her. If Maureen wasn't dead in the house, then she might still be alive. Either in the house, hiding, or away somewhere.

So how do you play it? he wondered.

Maureen didn't seem like the kind of woman to run and hide if she realized someone was breaking into her house. Hell, no. She'd attack.

But who's to say the intruder went in alone? She could've been with a whole gang. Just because she'd claimed to be there by herself, lonesome . . .

They jumped him as he stepped out onto the sidewalk. One leaped onto his back and hooked an arm around his throat. Another, a skinny naked man, came in from the front driving a knife toward his chest. He rammed the muzzle of his shotgun into the knifeman's belly and pulled the trigger. As the blast slammed the guy away, he pumped a fresh shell into the chamber.

He pivoted, planning to ram backward against the doorframe, and saw a third assailant, out of sight until now because the damn hood killed his peripheral vision. This one swung a baseball bat at his face. He had no time to aim. He tugged the trigger. The shotgun bucked. Its load ripped through the man's upper arm, tore it away in a mess of flying tissue and bone, and spun him.

Staggering beneath the weight on his back, Trev turned in a full circle to make sure there were no others.

None.

Then he went blind as the arm across his throat jerked sideways, shifting the plastic bag and sliding the eyeholes away from his eyes.

He stumbled backward. Struck something that made the person on his back grunt. Sounded like a woman. Probably is a woman, he thought. Not much force in the choke hold. More like she was just trying to hold on and ride him.

He took a step forward, then threw himself back hard, pounding her against the obstruction. This time, the impact brought more than a grunt. She cried out in pain. The pressure on Trev's throat eased. Reaching up with his left hand, he yanked the arm away. She slid down his back. He pulled her sideways just enough to give himself a target, then shot his elbow into her body. A good solid blow that pounded the air out of her. He felt her start to slump, trapped between his back and the wall or whatever it was that he'd battered her against.

Lurching away from her, Trev adjusted his mask until he found the eyeholes. He was standing over the man who'd come at him with the knife. The guy wore sneakers. He had a cave just above his groin.

Trev pumped the shotgun. As he started to swing around, he saw a man standing by the curb, trying to fit his severed arm onto the gushing stump below his shoulder. Trev blasted him in the chest. The guy flopped backward and slammed against the side of a parked car.

He whirled toward the woman.

She was on her rump, legs stretched out, back against the doorframe of O'Casey's. Her arms were folded across her belly and she was gasping for air. She gleamed black in the light from the restaurant. Her eyes were squeezed shut. Her pained grimace showed the white of her teeth.

Trev pumped the shotgun and aimed at her face.

A kid. She looked no older than fifteen or sixteen.

Her bangs were pasted to her forehead. She wore a jumper over a blouse with a frilly collar. Her sodden, pleated skirt clung to her thighs. She wore knee socks and loafers.

Kid or not, Trev thought, she's a killer now. If I don't shoot her, she'll go on her merry way and maybe nail someone.

Tie her up, leave her in O'Casey's?

He didn't want to waste the time. Besides, she might get loose and end up hunting for victims again. Or other crazies might find her and kill her.

Do they kill their own?

They'd either kill her or set her free.

'Come on,' he said. Crouching, he grabbed the girl's wrist and dragged her to her feet. She tried to pull away. He tugged and she stumbled forward. With a growl, she drove her head into his stomach. Trev brought his knee up. She folded and dropped. 'Now *stop it*! I want to help you.'

He reached down. He clutched the black rope of

her pony tail and pulled, trying not to hurt her but applying enough force to give her the message. She stood up. Left hand gripping the pony tail, right hand pressing the shotgun to her spine, he guided her toward the alley.

'Just stay cool,' he said. 'You'll be all right. Just keep walking. You'll be fine.'

He hoped nobody was coming up behind him.

Only once did the girl try to struggle free. Trev yanked her hair back and jabbed the muzzle into her back, and she yelped and settled down.

'It's OK,' he told her. 'It's OK. We're almost there.'

He swung her into the alley. The car was there, and he heard the rain drumming on it as he pushed the girl closer to its rear. 'Get down,' he said.

She tried to turn around, so he tugged her pony tail. She went to her knees. He nudged her with his knee until she turned sideways. Then he forced her down onto the pavement. He stepped over her. With a foot on her rump to keep her from getting up, he propped his shotgun against the bumper. He dug out his keys and unlocked the trunk.

He straddled her, jammed his hands under her armpits, and picked her up. The girl squirmed. She kicked backward, the heel of her shoe striking his shin. 'Damn it!' he gasped, and shoved her headfirst into the trunk. Then he slipped a hand under her skirt, clutched the side of her right thigh, and swung her legs up and over the side. She tumbled into the dark trunk. He slammed the lid.

Picking up his shotgun, he hurried to the driver's door. Francine unlocked it for him. He climbed in, jerked the door shut, and locked it. 'Everything OK?' he asked.

'What happened?' Francine asked. 'What did you put in the trunk?'

'A girl.'

'One of *them*?'

'Yeah. Just a kid.'

'You're taking her *with* us?'

'It was either that or kill her.'

'You should've killed her.'

'I told you, she's just a kid. She didn't ask for any of this. She's a victim, same as everyone else.'

'She's one of *them*!'

'She's one of us, now.'

'Great. Just great.'

'We heard some shots,' Lisa said.

Trev poked his key into the ignition and started the car. He turned on the headlights. 'That was me. Three of them tried to nail me when I came out of O'Casey's.'

'Are you all right?' Lisa asked him.

'I had to drop a couple.'

'And bring one along,' Francine muttered.

'They didn't hurt you?'

'I'm fine.' He started backing the car out of the alley.

'Did you find the address?' Lisa asked.

'Yeah, I got it.' Eyes on the rearview mirror, he swung the car onto Third Street. He started forward.

Heading north. Toward Chidi's house. But also toward the home of Liam O'Casey, where a strange woman had answered the phone.

Both on the north side of town. Chidi's house a couple of miles closer.

Trev knew what he ought to do – hit Chidi's first. See if the grandfather's playing with magic. More important to stop the rain than to bust into Liam's on the chance Maureen might be there.

But if he could save Maureen . . .

You've got a few miles to go before you have to make up your mind, he told himself.

He told himself that. He already knew his first stop would be Liam's house.

3

Following John's instructions, Steve brought the people from the cocktail lounge into the entryway, where they joined the restaurant staff gathered by Cassy, and John's group from the dining room. John stood with his back to the double doors. For the moment, nobody was pounding on them. The only pounding was inside his head. He rubbed the lump on his brow. He hoped the aspirin would kick in soon.

'I think everyone's here,' Cassy told him.

'OK,' he muttered. Then he raised his voice. 'Could I have your attention, please?'

The murmuring faded.

'We need to get organized, here. You're probably all aware that a guy broke through a window a few minutes ago and killed Mrs Benton. Well, apparently there's quite a crowd outside.'

'Just how many are we talking about?' asked a stocky, florid man near the front of the group.

'Steve?'

'I just took a quick look out the window,' Steve said. 'I didn't have time to make an accurate head count, but I'd guess anywhere from twenty to thirty.'

'Oh, dear God,' a woman muttered.

Other people moaned, shook their heads, moved closer to their spouses or friends, whispered.

'They were scattered along the sidewalk in front,' Steve went on. 'There was a pretty good bunch right outside the doors.'

'Why are they *doing* this?' asked Tina. Her boyfriend Andy squeezed her shoulder.

'They're after the fine cuisine,' said a small guy in a plaid jacket.

'This is no time for levity,' Dr Goodman pointed out.

'Levity in the face of disaster is a hallmark of the American character.'

'Oh, shut up,' said a woman John figured must be the guy's wife.

'They're outside,' Cassy said, 'because they want to come in and kill us. That's pretty obvious, isn't it?'

'But *why*?' From Tina.

'It doesn't matter why,' John said. 'I'm sure it has something to do with the black rain. But that's not our concern, right now. What we need to do is get organized so we can protect ourselves.'

'Hey,' said a big guy with a beer mug in his hand. 'Who died and made you king shit?'

'It's all yours,' John told him. 'You can be king shit.'

The guy sneered. 'You trying to be a wiseguy?'

'I'm totally serious. You take over. I don't want this, anyway.'

Cassy frowned at him. 'Hey, John, come on.'

'I don't even want to be here, much less be the guy giving orders. Let macho man . . .'

'Look, buddy . . .'

'Hey, shove it,' Lynn told him. 'If we waste time arguing, those jerks are going to break in and God only knows what'll happen to us. So just shut up and listen to John. We've got to have a leader and I don't know most of you people, but I know my John and he's the man for it.'

John looked at her. He felt a swell of pride at the way she was taking on the bastard, but he wished she would shut up. He didn't *want* to be the leader. The only reason he'd gotten involved was because someone had to take control fast and nobody else was doing it.

'Gimme a break, lady,' the guy said. 'I know who he is. He's the fuckin' *painter*.'

I'm not so anonymous after all, he thought.

'Yes, he's a painter,' Lynn said. 'He's an *artist*.'

'We want a pansy artist running the show?'

'He also served two tours in Vietnam,' Lynn said. 'And he holds a third degree black belt in Karate.'

Thanks a lot, John thought.

But the guy who'd called him a pansy grew a sickly smile and took a step backward.

Everyone stared at John.

Now they think I'm a miracle worker. Really appreciate it, Lynn.

'OK,' he said. 'I see that quite a few of us already have weapons. After we break up here, I want everyone to get a knife.'

'Some of you got them with your dinner,' Cassy added. 'We'll bring more out from the kitchen in just a minute.'

'We should also make ourselves some clubs,' John said. 'Legs from tables and chairs, maybe. A good blow to the head'll put a man out in record time.'

'How about putting knives on the ends of the clubs?' Andy suggested.

'Whatever you can think of. Use your imaginations. Just put together the meanest weapons possible.'

'What've *they* got?' asked the red-faced man who'd asked about their numbers.

'Some of them must've gotten into a hardware store,' Steve said.

'Handyman's down at the end of the block,' Dr Goodman said.

'Figures. I only took a glimpse, but I saw knives, tire irons, hammers, hatchets and axes.'

A woman let out a quiet whimper. There were moans from several others, including men.

'I want us to split up into groups,' John said. 'Cassy's told me that the rear door opens out into the alley. It has no handle on the alley side, it's a solid door and it's locked. Our main areas of vulnerability are the windows and the front doors here.

'I want a group of men at the doors with me. Steve. You,' he said, nodding at the man who'd called him a pansy. 'You.' He indicated an oriental wearing a chef's floppy cap and holding a meat cleaver. 'And you two,' he said, giving the nod to a pair of husky men from the cocktail lounge.

'OK. The rest of you, form into two groups. One group will be stationed in the bar area, one in the dining room. Your job is to watch the windows. Anyone tries to break in, deal with him. Or her. Don't let it stop you if the invader's a female. Remember, it was a woman who killed Chester Benton.'

'Equal opportunity maniacs,' said the guy who believed in levity.

'If there's any kind of concerted assault, just call out and the rest of us'll come over to reinforce you. Any questions?'

'What about getting out of here?'

'Yeah. Some of us have kids at home.'

'So do I,' John said. 'But we won't do our kids any good if we get killed.'

'Won't do 'em any good staying here, either.'

'If you want to leave,' John said, 'be my guest. But you've got a street full of bloodthirsty nuts outside,

227

and the rain. From all appearances, the rain'll turn you into one of them. But if you want to risk it, go on ahead. It's pretty clear to me that we stand the best chance by sticking together in here and holding down the fort.'

'They come in here with axes and shit, we're dead meat.'

'Yeah, what if they overrun us?'

Overrun.

The word sent a shock of cold through John.

'We're not going to let that happen,' he said, trying to keep his voice steady.

'Yeah, and how do we stop it? All they gotta do is bash in the doors, thirty of 'em coming pouring in with their damn hardware. We won't stand a chance in hell.'

'What'll we do then?' a woman blurted.

'We're all gonna die,' Tina muttered.

John saw panic spreading through the group like a brush fire on a windy day. Eyes widened. Faces blanched. Tina and another woman began to sob. A small, long-haired man near the back whirled around and ran off into the cocktail lounge. Men and women hugged each other and spoke in low, urgent tones.

As if sharing a silent cue, Lynn and Cassy both raised their arms at once.

'Please,' Cassy called out.

'Everyone just calm down,' Lynn snapped. 'We'll be all right.' As the group quieted down, she looked at John. 'Tell them, honey.'

Fighting his own fear, he lifted his voice. 'The guy's

right. If we're overrun, we're in deep trouble.'

'John!' Lynn gasped.

'So we have to make sure that doesn't happen.'

'Good plan,' said the humorist.

'I do have a plan,' John said. 'First we arm ourselves and take our positions. Like I told you, my group mans the doors. Then we let 'em in.'

'*What?*'

'He's flipped.'

'That's the craziest damn thing I ever heard.'

'We let 'em in *one at a time*.'

'Oh, right. Sure.'

'One at a time, two if we can't help it. Yank 'em in, slam the door on the rest, take care of the ones we've got. Put 'em out of commission one at a time, thin out their force.'

Lynn squeezed his arm. Cassy frowned at him, nodding, her lips a tight line. Steve shook his head. 'That *is* crazy,' he said. 'Let's do it.'

4

'What's the deal with Lisa?' Cyndi asked when Buddy and Doug came back into the room.

'She's just fine,' Buddy said. 'Wants me to take her out tomorrow night. That's if things are back to normal with the rain.'

'Has she had any trouble?' Sheila asked.

'Nope.'

'Maybe everyone else is OK,' Lou said. 'Maybe it wasn't the rain that made Maureen do that.'

'It was the rain,' Maureen said.

'Why don't we turn on the TV and see if there're any reports about it?' Lou said.

'Feel free.'

He got up from his chair, went to the television and turned it on.

Buddy sat down beside Maureen. She stiffened as he reached toward her. But he frowned and drew back his hand. Looking from Cyndi to Sheila, he shook his head. 'I guess I didn't realize how much I still . . . care for Lisa.'

'Yeah,' Sheila said. 'You've really been *acting* like you care for her.'

'I know,' he muttered. 'I know. I feel like a . . . a pig.' He met Maureen's eyes. 'Look, I'm sorry. I'm sorry about all this, about everything. I just don't know what got into me.' He contorted his face to show his misery.

This is all a damned act, she thought.

'At least you had an excuse for your behavior,' he said. 'The rain got you. You couldn't help what you did. I just . . . I feel awful. Can you forgive me?'

Maureen said, 'I forgive you.'

What's going on? she wondered.

Lou, squatting in front of the television, flicked from channel to channel with the volume low.

Buddy turned and looked at the others. 'I'm going to take her home.'

'You're kidding, right?' Cyndi asked.

'No, I'm totally serious.'

'You idiot, you raped her. You can't just let her go.'

'I won't tell,' Maureen said.

'I believe her,' Buddy said. 'She tried to kill me.' To Maureen, he said, 'We're even, right?'

'Yeah.'

'You're out of your gourd,' Cyndi told him.

'I'm all for it,' Sheila said. 'I think he *should* take her home.'

'It'll be risky,' Buddy said. 'But it's the right thing to do.'

'Since when have you cared?' Sheila said.

'I never should've . . . messed with her. Talking to Lisa just now . . . God, I've never felt so rotten.' He glanced from Doug to Lou. 'You guys'll come with me, won't you?'

Maureen's stomach went cold.

'Now hold on,' Sheila said.

Lou turned off the television. 'Nothing,' he said. 'Just the regular shows.'

'So, you in with me?' Buddy asked him.

'You mean, taking Maureen home?'

'Yeah.'

'Sure.'

'I don't know,' Doug said. 'We shouldn't leave the gals here alone.'

'They'll be a lot safer here,' Buddy pointed out. 'We don't know what's going on in the streets. That's why I want you two along with me – in case we run into trouble between here and Maureen's place.'

'Just put her out the door,' Cyndi said.

'Good idea,' Sheila said.

'I can't do that.' He gave Maureen a miserable, guilty look. 'I owe her. After all this, the least I can do is make sure she gets safely home.'

'What're you trying to pull?' Cyndi asked.

'I'm not an animal, for godsake. I feel bad, OK?'

'Yeah, sure.'

'I think it's the right thing to do,' Lou said. He turned his eyes to Sheila. 'Don't you think so?'

'I guess. But what about me and Cyn?'

'You'll be fine here,' Buddy said. 'We'll be back before you know it.'

'This really sucks,' Cyndi muttered.

'What kind of car do you have?' Buddy asked Maureen.

'A Jeep. A Cherokee.'

'We'll have to take that. My folks went off in the BMW, and we can't all fit in the Austin. Where's the Jeep, out front?'

She nodded.

'Do you have the keys?'

'No.' She rubbed her face, and tried to remember what she'd done with them.

In my coat pocket.

She'd taken off the coat, thrown it down on the front lawn just after the rain got her.

'You can't even get to her Jeep,' Sheila said. 'You'll get wet.'

'I'll cover up and go after it,' Buddy told her. 'I'll

pull it into the garage. That way, they won't have to worry about the rain.'

'You have it all figured out, huh?' Cyndi said. She gave Maureen a sweet smile. 'And guess what happens to you, cutie, when the three of them get you alone.'

Maureen didn't need the hint. She'd already figured it out. 'I trust them,' she said.

'We're not going to lay a finger on her,' Buddy protested.

'Who's talking about fingers?'

'*I'm* not gonna touch her,' Lou said, giving Sheila a solemn look.

'Me neither,' Doug said.

'If you do,' Cyndi told him, 'I'll know it. I'm gonna check you out when you get back.'

He laughed. 'Is that a promise?'

'Damn right. And if you think I won't know the difference, man, you've got another think coming.'

'Jeez, can't wait.'

'If they try anything,' Buddy said, 'I'll bust their heads.'

'Yeah, sure.'

'I left the car keys in the ignition,' Maureen said.

'Thanks.' He slapped her thigh, but not very hard. Then he got up and hurried from the room. Maureen saw Doug and Lou exchange glances. She heard quick thuds as Buddy raced upstairs.

Doug slipped an arm around Cyndi's back. 'How's about a little something for the road?' he asked, and pulled her closer.

'Get real. I'm sure I'm gonna get you all turned on and then you go off with *her*.'

'Oh, come on. Be nice.'

'We'll see about being nice. When you get back.'

'Please?' He put a hand on her breast. She shoved it away. 'Come on. There's no telling what might happen to me out there.'

'I know what better not happen.'

'We could all get killed.'

'Wouldn't *that* be too bad.'

'If it's that dangerous,' Sheila said, 'you shouldn't go.' She faced Lou. 'I don't think I want you going out there.'

'We'll be careful.'

'He doesn't want to miss his chance at Miss Pizza Pussy,' Cyndi said.

'That's not true,' he snapped.

Sheila stared at him. 'If you do fool around with her, you can just forget about me. I mean it. I won't have anything to do with you. Ever.'

'I promise. We're just going to drive her home. Honest. I don't even *want* to go. But I have to. They'll need me if there's trouble.'

Maureen heard Buddy rushing down the stairs. Her heartbeat quickened. It pounded so hard that she felt sick. Her lungs seemed tight, constricted. She couldn't bring in enough air to fill them. Her hands, pressed tight against her thighs, were wet and cold.

Take it easy, she told herself. Don't let them suspect anything.

Buddy came into the living room. He wore a black

raincoat, heavy gloves of red leather that looked as if they were designed for snow skiing, and rubber boots that reached nearly to his knees. In one hand was an umbrella. He was grinning. 'This oughta do the trick, huh?'

'Haven't you got anything for us?' Doug asked.

'What for? No need for anyone to leave the car except Maureen.' He looked at her. 'You can use this stuff when you go to your house.'

She nodded. She knew it was a lie, like everything else he'd been saying. When they finished with her, they would just throw her out.

They won't get me *in*, she told herself.

'OK,' Buddy said. 'You folks can take her out to the garage and open the door for me. I'll be with you in a minute.'

That's about how long I've got, Maureen thought. About a minute before he gets to the Jeep, sees that the keys aren't there, and comes running back.

She got up from the sofa, 'Be careful,' she said, and squeezed Buddy's arm through the slicker. 'Don't get wet.'

He looked a little surprised. He smiled. Maureen held onto his arm, and they walked together, the others close behind. When they reached the foyer, she released his arm and stepped away. He opened the umbrella. He raised it overhead, pulled the door wide, and said, 'Here goes nothing.'

'Don't get any on you,' Doug warned.

Buddy's smile looked a little nervous. 'No way,' he said. Then he stepped out.

Maureen swung the door shut and locked it. She snatched up the dangling guard chain and fitted it into the slot before a hand yanked her arm away and spun her around.

'What the hell are you . . .' Cyndi blurted.

Maureen's fist crushed her nose. Cyndi stumbled backward, crying out, clutching her face. She bumped into Sheila. They both staggered away, Sheila grabbing the girl to keep her from falling. 'Guys!' Sheila cried out.

Lou stood there with his eyes wide, his mouth hanging open. Doug hurled himself forward, slamming Maureen's back against the door. As her breath blasted out, she wrapped her arms around him. She squeezed him tight against her body. He squirmed, trying to get loose. Until her mouth found his lips. She kissed him hard. His mouth opened. She thrust her tongue in. Then he was moaning.

'Doug!' Lou shouted.

'Look what she's *doing*!' Sheila cried out.

Maureen let go of Doug and pulled her shirt up. His hands went to her breasts.

'Make her stop!'

As Doug's greasy hands groped her breasts, Maureen tugged open his belt.

'Oh, my God,' Lou muttered.

'Lou!'

She unfastened the button at Doug's waist, pulled his zipper down.

'Stop her, damn it!'

She slipped her hand down the front of his underwear, curled her fingers around him. Gently stroking, she eased her mouth away. Doug, writhing, sucked the side of her neck. 'Lou,' she gasped. 'I want you, too. Now. Quick.'

'Don't you . . . !' Sheila let go of Cyndi and grabbed Lou's arm. While Cyndi sank to her knees, Lou shoved Sheila hard. 'You bastard!' she shrieked.

Lou came forward. He was gasping, his face scarlet.

Maureen held Doug's penis with one hand. With the other, she pushed his pants down around his thighs. 'On your knees, honey,' she gasped. 'On your knees.'

'Buddy'll kill you!' Sheila blurted.

Cyndi looked up, but didn't move. She just knelt there, bloody hands cupped to her nose, eyes blinking.

Lou came in from the side as Doug, on his knees, pulled Maureen's shorts down. She took Lou's hands and pressed them to her breasts. They stayed there, fondling her. She felt Doug's mouth between her legs. With a hand behind Lou's head, she drew his face to hers. She kissed him.

Sheila, letting out a wild squeal, launched herself at Lou. She yanked his hair, pulling him away. Lou whirled around, swinging at her.

Maureen shot her knee up.

It caught Doug under the chin, hurling him backward.

Lou's fist missed Sheila's chin. She plowed into him, driving him back, snatching his hair again with one hand. As Sheila's other hand raked his cheek, Maureen yanked her shorts up and leaped over Doug's sprawled body. He grabbed her foot, but she jerked it free.

She ran.

Ran from the foyer, through the dining room, into the kitchen.

Heard nobody in pursuit.

Snagged the door latch down.

Tugged open the sliding glass door and rushed outside into the rain.

5

'You bastard! You bastard!' Sheila cried, driving Lou back to the wall as she punched him and clawed him and tore at his hair.

'Stop it!' He caught one of her hands. The other punched his cheek. 'She's getting away!'

'You bastard!'

Then Doug was behind Sheila, throwing his arms around her, hurling her aside. She tripped over her feet and hit the floor hard.

'Buddy's gonna kill us!' Doug yelled as they raced for the kitchen.

'We'll get her,' Lou gasped.

'We'd better!'

We're screwed, Lou thought. The bitch! Made me do that right in front of Sheila.

He knew Sheila was done with him. All Maureen's fault. And Buddy would go ape when he found out they'd let her get away.

She hasn't gotten away yet!

In the kitchen, Lou saw the open door just as Doug lurched to a stop.

She went out?

Maybe a trick.

Lou halted beside Doug. They both scanned the kitchen. No Maureen. No spaces where she might be crouched, hiding. No cupboard or pantry doors that looked large enough to conceal a person.

Their eyes met.

'We've gotta get her,' Lou gasped.

'Here goes nothing.' Doug rushed outside, Lou at his back.

The warm rain splashed Lou's face, tingled against his scalp, soaked his clothes. And he realized he'd been foolish to fear it. There was nothing bad about this rain. It felt great. He spread out his arms and tilted back his head, moaning as a strange excitement pulsed through his body.

He ached with desire.

For a moment, he didn't know what he desired. Then it came to him.

His head snapped down and he grinned at Doug.

Doug, already turning, rushed him. Grinning, too. Teeth white in his black face. Doug dropped low. He drove his head into Lou's stomach. As Lou's breath exploded out, he glimpsed Maureen.

Someone, anyway.

The black smudge of a head that seemed to be floating on the surface of Buddy's swimming pool several yards away.

But he didn't care. He cared only about the pain in his belly, the hot desire pounding through his blood. His chin hit Doug's back, crashing his teeth together. He was carried backward and down. As his rump struck the patio's concrete, he grabbed Doug's sides. The momentum slammed him down, but he kept his grip on Doug and the boy tumbled over him, landing on him, mashing his face. His teeth clamped down on the seat of Doug's jeans. Felt flesh under the heavy fabric. He bit hard and Doug yelped and flinched.

He tried to catch Doug's head between his thighs. Got it for an instant. But the head twisted free. He spread his legs, hoping to scissor it again, but the head dropped and struck his groin.

Pain blasted his body.

Through the daze of agony, he realized that Doug had scurried off him. He rolled onto his side, clutching his genitals and curling up.

6

Maureen, watching from the middle of the pool, wanted to join in.

Rip them up. Tear their flesh. Lap up their blood. Yes!

She slipped beneath the surface and swam for the side and thought, *Am I nuts?* They're at each other. This is my chance to get away.

Her urge to savage the two boys was gone, leaving her with a heavy feeling of repugnance.

How could I even *consider* . . . ?

The rain.

Oh, Jesus.

The black, warm rain. It had soaked her when she dashed from the house, and she remembered how she'd suddenly wanted to turn around and rush back inside and kill them all. But she'd been moving too fast to halt herself before plunging into the backyard pool. The water had engulfed her, and the urge had passed. It had returned when she stood up and watched the boys come out.

The same vicious impulses would take hold again if she came up for air.

Some rain on my head, I'll be just like them.

Staying underwater, Maureen turned herself around. She breast-stroked for the middle of the pool, angling downward, fighting her buoyancy that was like a balloon in her chest trying to lift her to the surface.

Gotta stay down!

Her lungs burned. They seemed to be squeezing themselves tight, wanting to force her breath out to get ready for fresh air.

Maureen let the breath slip from her mouth. As she felt herself begin to sink, she tugged the baggy gym shorts down her legs and off.

She draped them over her head.

She guided herself slowly upward and broke the surface, the shorts hanging like a big, floppy hat. She sucked air into her lungs.

She was facing the deep end of the pool.

And the diving board.

She slipped beneath the water, caught the sodden rag as it started to drift away, and swam for the board. She needed to get under it. There, she might be able to breathe without the rain touching her, making her crazy.

Her left hand touched the slick tile wall at the end of the pool. Staying below the surface, she peered up. But she saw only dark water. She pressed the shorts to the top of her head and surfaced.

A yard to the left of the board.

She plunged under, kicked and came up again directly beneath the board. She turned sideways, reached out and clutched the pool gutter. With her other hand, she plucked the shorts off her head.

She felt the cold water encasing her body. No warm rain striking her head or shoulders or outstretched arm. No urges to rend flesh or taste blood.

Satisfied that she was all right, she turned her gaze toward the patio.

Doug was standing, pulling Lou's arm. Helping him up?

A chill gripped Maureen's bowels.

Lou got to his feet. He was hunched over slightly as if hurting, but he nodded eagerly.

She knew what would happen next. They would come for her.

She heard a sharp laugh.

Then the two guys, side by side, turned away.

And Maureen saw Sheila dash through the lighted kitchen, arms stretched out, face twisted with terror. Cyndi ran into view, and for a moment Maureen thought Cyndi was chasing the girl. Then she understood.

They were racing for the door.

Doug, apparently realizing what they intended, suddenly bolted for it.

Sheila reached the door first and hurled it sideways. Over the sound of the splashing rain, Maureen heard the door rumble across its rails and thud shut.

Doug slid to a halt. He yanked the outside handle. The door didn't budge.

The girls on the other side of the glass gazed out. Sheila started backing away. Cyndi wiped blood off her lips and chin. They both jumped when Doug hammered his fists against the pane. Sheila, shaking her head, shouted at him. Cyndi darted behind her and vanished. Doug pounded the door again, then slammed his forehead against it. Maureen heard the thump. The glass held.

At the sound of a clank, Maureen looked away from the brightly lighted scene. She saw Lou over to the side, a black shape against the darkness of the wall, lifting the iron lid off a barbecue kettle. He snatched something off a nearby tray. Carrying the lid in front of him like an odd, dome-shaped battle shield, he ran toward the door.

In the kitchen, Cyndi rushed up beside Sheila. She passed a butcher knife to Sheila and kept one for herself.

Doug dodged out of the way. Lou punched the iron lid against the door. The glass shattered, blasting inward, throwing shards at the girls as they staggered backward.

Lou leaped through the opening, shield first, right hand waving a yard-long barbecue fork overhead.

7

He went for Sheila, but Cyndi lunged in from the side, shrieking like a madwoman. As she stabbed downward, he whipped her across the face with the rod of his fork. The blow turned her head. Her body followed, and the blade cut only air. Doug, diving, took her down.

Lou flung the barbecue lid to the floor. It struck with an awful, ringing clamor that made him cringe and grin. Sheila glanced around at him, then hurled herself through the doorway and into the dining room. Lou raced after her.

Great fun, he thought. Great fun!

Sheila slapped a chair, tumbling it away from the table to block his path. Lou, laughing, leaped over it.

He chased her into the living room. Gaining on her. But not too quickly. He was enjoying himself so much that he didn't want to end this. Not right away, anyhow. He watched the way her glossy hair bounced and swayed, the way her sweatshirt shook, and how her pumping legs pulled the jeans tight against the flexing mounds of her rump.

In the foyer, she turned toward the front door. She glanced back at Lou. Then she struck the door with her shoulder and reached up for the guard chain.

The door shot open. The chain snapped taut, trapping Sheila's fingers as it bumped her away. She shrieked and yanked her hand free, flesh ripping from her fingers. As she dashed for the stairs, Lou glimpsed Buddy's black face grinning at him through the gap.

'Hey, pal, let me in.'

'Busy!' Lou cried out.

'Hey!'

He took off, chasing Sheila up the stairs, closing in on her as fast as he could. No more time to waste. Buddy was back, and changed, and would try to steal the kill once he got through the door. The guard chain might keep him out for a while, but not for long.

Sheila was almost to the top when Lou thrust the barbecue fork upward. Its tines popped through the seat of her jeans. They sank into her right buttock and she squealed. He shoved. The fork slipped in deeper. Instead of stopping her, it seemed to speed her up. He felt the wooden handle twitching with the flex of her muscles. A patch of blood began to spread over the denim surrounding the twin holes.

He rammed again. She reached back and grabbed the fork as she bounded up the final stairs, but she couldn't dislodge it. Lou leaped to the top, driving her ahead of him. He steered her across the corridor. He slammed her against the wall and pulled out the fork.

Sheila whirled around, slashing at him with the knife. He lurched backward. The blade flashed across his chest, missed, but sliced through his right sleeve and nipped his upper arm. She swept it at him again. Lou took another quick step back and swung the fork at her arm and his foot came down on air.

Yelping, he flung the fork from his hand. He reached out for the banister. His fingers hooked over the rail, but the weight of his tumbling body tore his hold away. His back struck the stairs. He saw his wet, black legs fly up. His neck twisted. He felt his legs kicking high, flipping him over, coming down. His knees thumped the carpeted stairs and he slid down, treads rubbing their way up his body like the rungs of a ladder. They bumped his face. One edge caught his genitals and mashed them up against his crotch. Then another did the same, and another.

At last, he came to a stop. He lay sprawled on the stairs, pain roaring through his body.

He heard quick footfalls.

Sheila hurrying down to finish him off?

'Asshole.' Buddy's voice. 'Should've let me in when I asked you.'

The stairs on which he was lying shook a little as Buddy climbed past him.

He *is* going to steal my kill, Lou thought.

'No!' he gasped.

He tried to push himself up, whimpered as the strain sent spears of pain radiating out from his testicles, and sank back against the stairs.

8

Denise lifted the popcorn bowl off her lap, leaned forward and set it on the table beside her glass. She picked up the glass. As she drank the last of the Pepsi, Tom's hand went to her back. It moved in an easy circle, sliding the warmup jacket against her skin.

She finished drinking. She set the glass down. Instead of settling back against the sofa cushion, she rested her knees on her elbows.

Tom's hand was warm through the jacket. The fabric was very soft. Her mind seemed a little foggy from all that had happened. She felt peaceful and lazy. The good feel of his hand made her eyelids heavy.

'There you are again,' he said.

Lifting her gaze to the television screen, Denise saw herself in a sunny backyard, laughing hard and trying to dodge a water balloon hurled by Kara. As she twisted away, the balloon caught her in the hip. It burst to shreds. Clear, gleaming water exploded out, darkening her red shorts, gluing her T-shirt to her side, splashing down her leg.

Tom laughed.

Kara didn't. Not even when two of her friends charged into view and nailed Denise with more balloons, drenching her, and she cried out and snatched up the garden hose and went after them.

Denise looked over her shoulder. Kara, with her Alf slippers resting on the edge of the table, was slumped back against the sofa asleep.

'Our little friend's zonked,' she whispered.

'I know,' Tom said.

She looked at him. From his smile, she realized that Kara's dropping off had been his cue to reach for her. 'We might as well turn this off,' she said, and picked up the remote.

'Hey, I'm enjoying it.'

'Kara wouldn't like us watching it without her. She's the star.' Denise pushed the 'off' button. The birthday party vanished, replaced by a Jeep commercial.

'Aw. It was just starting to get good.'

'We can turn it back on if she wakes up.'

'Can't we at least rewind and watch you get wiped out again?'

Smiling, she shook her head and settled back against the sofa. Tom's arm was trapped for a moment. Then it worked its way up. As he curled his hand over her shoulder, she swung her legs onto the cushion and leaned against his side. She patted his thigh. 'Why do you want to watch me on the tube when the real McCoy's right here?'

'That way, I get you in stereo.'

The commercial ended, and a Clint Eastwood movie came on. One of those old spaghetti westerns. Clint looked gritty and cool, squinting as he lit the stub of a thin cigar.

'*Fistful of Dollars*,' Tom said. 'It's a great one.'

'How many times have you seen it?'

'Who knows? I never counted.'

'Kara does,' Denise said. 'She counts. She's seen *Willy Wonka* eighty-nine times, or something.'

'My kind of kid.'

'Mine, too.' Face relaxed in sleep, Kara looked so peaceful. Like an infant. As if the world's troubles had never touched her. 'God, she's so cute.'

'She's really neat. I usually can't stand the little ankle-biters, but she's something else.'

'I hope I have a kid just like her someday.'

'That wouldn't be so bad, huh?'

'It's a spooky world, though.'

'Yeah,' Tom said. 'I've noticed. Sometimes, I think I shouldn't ever have any kids. Because of that, you know? What with nuclear bombs, and all the crime, and the environment getting shot to hell. Like it wouldn't be right, bringing kids into such a mess.'

'I think there's plenty around to make it worth the risk,' Denise said. 'I'm glad *I'm* alive, even if it does get creepy.'

'Yeah. Me, too. I guess.'

'Glad to hear it.'

'But jeez, there's so much that can go wrong.'

'But we're in here, safe and sound. It's nice. It's almost as if there *isn't* the black rain out there.'

'Thanks for reminding me,' Tom said, and she felt his hand tighten on her shoulder.

'It'll end sooner or later. Everything will be fine again.'

'I sure hope so.' When he said that, Denise felt his breath stirring her hair, warm or her scalp, tickling a little. 'At least . . . I'm glad we're together.'

'Me, too.'

He gently kissed the side of her head. Then his lips went away. Denise snuggled against him and yawned. 'I'm so wiped out,' she muttered.

'Do you feel like sleeping? I can move over to a chair so you can stretch out.'

'Don't do that. I like you just fine here.' She snuggled against him and sighed with contentment.

Tom's hand moved gently from her shoulder to her elbow, then up again. 'This is pretty nice.'

'Maybe I will take a little nap,' Denise said. 'Would you mind?'

'Heck, no.'

She scooted away and lay down, resting her head on his thigh, bringing up her knees so her feet wouldn't interfere with Kara. The movements rucked up her jacket so it bulged out from her chest. The opening at the top of the zipper was like a pyramid-shaped window. It gave her a clear view of the shadowy sides of her breasts.

She murmured, 'Woops,' and wondered if she'd said that to draw Tom's attention to the gap. His head was higher, though. He wouldn't be able to see in. Not quite so far, anyway. And she could feel that the jacket had come up enough to reveal a band of bare skin at her waist. Maybe he was looking there. Or maybe his eyes were on the Eastwood movie.

She imagined his hand slipping inside the gap, drifting over her skin, cupping one of her breasts.

He wouldn't do that in a million years, she thought.

And if he did, I probably shouldn't let him.

She gripped the elastic around the bottom of the jacket and tugged. The bulge came down. The fabric pressed snug against her. She folded her hands on her belly.

The opening was gone. But her thoughts about Tom's caresses had excited her. The mounds where her breasts pushed the jacket up were tipped with blunt peaks.

Oh, Lord, she thought.

She felt a blush spread over her skin, heating up the mild burns.

She willed her nipples to soften, to melt down flat. But they didn't obey.

Sighing, she closed her eyes.

This is just so embarrassing, she thought.

Maybe Tom hasn't noticed.

Of course he has.

He squirmed a little, shifting his position beneath Denise's head, and she wondered if he had an erection.

Maybe I should sit up and watch the movie.

But she didn't move. With each breath, she felt the soft rub of the fabric. She waited for the feel of Tom's hand.

Then it came.

But not to either breast. His warm fingertips caressed her forehead, brushing some hair aside. She felt him trace the curve of one eyebrow, then the other. His gentle touch was soothing. Heat seemed to pass from him, seep into her skin and go inside her skull and fill her head with a heavy, dark calm.

9

Lou, sitting at the bottom of the stairs, wrapped a handkerchief around his cut arm. As he pulled the knot tight with his teeth and left hand, Buddy came down.

His face was more red than black. He had Sheila's knife. Its blade was slick with blood.

'She was mine,' Lou complained.

'Guess not. She was too much for you, man.' Buddy stopped in front of him. He shifted the knife to his left hand. Lou noticed that he no longer wore the ski gloves. His right hand was crimson. It was slick and sticky when Lou grabbed it and Buddy pulled him up. The weight on his legs made him wince.

'You OK?'

'I'll live,' Lou muttered.

'Sorry you missed the fun.'

'You owe me.'

'I don't owe you shit.'

'Yes, you do.' Lou hobbled alongside the staircase. He crouched, groaning with the effort, and picked up his barbecue fork. As he straightened up, he frowned at Buddy. 'You've gotta let me have Maureen.'

'I don't gotta anything, dickhead.'

Lou waited while Buddy shut the front door. The guard chain, ripped out of its mount on the door-frame, dangled from its track.

Some lock, he thought. If it had held, Sheila would've been mine.

'So where is she?' Buddy asked, and started through the living room.

'Maureen?'

'Who do you think?'

'She's in the pool.'

'The pool? How the hell did she get away from you bozos?'

Buddy wouldn't like the truth. 'Sheila and Cyndi helped her,' Lou said.

'Figures. The bitches.'

'That's how we got wet. We went after her. Me and Doug.'

'But you didn't get her, did you.'

'Doug tried to kill me. Then we figured it'd be a good idea to come back inside and nail the gals.'

'Great. She's probably long gone by now.'

'We'll get her.'

'She lied about the fucking keys,' Buddy muttered.

'We still gonna go after Lisa?'

'You bet. We'll take the bikes. But we gotta take care of Maureen first.'

'Let me, OK? It's only fair. You got Sheila.'

Then they entered the kitchen. Lou's heart pounded, his mouth went dry and heat surged through him when he saw Doug with Cyndi. Breathless, he limped toward them. But Buddy grabbed his arm.

'Stay put,' Buddy said. 'Doug, cut it out. Come on, we got business.'

Doug paid no attention, kept wallowing.

Buddy stepped closer, slipped on the bloody floor and almost went down. But he caught his balance in time. He kicked Doug in the hip.

'Hey!' Doug looked back over his shoulder, scowling.

'Let's go!' Buddy snapped.

'Shit.'

'You dorks let Maureen get away. Now, *come on*!'

Shaking his head, Doug pushed himself up. His hands flew out from under him. He splashed down on Cyndi and laughed until Buddy grabbed the back of his collar and dragged him off. 'OK OK,' he said. 'Let me go.'

Buddy released him. On hands and knees, Doug searched through clumps of fleshy debris beside the body. He found Cyndi's knife. Then he stood up. He stared down at her. 'She sure made a mess of your kitchen.'

Buddy punched his shoulder. 'Let's move.'

Their shoes crunched on broken glass as they walked toward the door. Lou was first to step outside. It felt good to be under the rain again. Striding toward the pool, he rolled the makeshift bandage down his arm. He peeled his sodden shirt off, and sighed with pleasure as the rain found his skin.

'OK,' Buddy said. 'So where is she?'

Lou scanned the dark surface from end to end as he pushed the knotted handkerchief back up his arm to cover the gash. No sign of Maureen.

'She supposed to be in the pool?' Doug asked.

'That's what Louie says.'

'I saw her. She was right there watching us.' He pointed toward the middle.

'Well, she ain't there now.'

'Maybe she ducked under.'

'I'll check,' Doug said, and rushed for the edge.

'Damn it, don't . . .'

Even as the words left Buddy's mouth, Doug leaped.

'Bastard! I'm gonna make *you* clean it!'

Doug, standing in shoulder-deep water, turned around and grinned. 'What, you don't want any Cyndi in the pool?'

Lou started to laugh, but suddenly realized that Doug might beat him to Maureen. 'I'll help,' he said. Before Buddy could protest, he dived in.

The water shocked him. He'd supposed it would be like the rain, but it wasn't. It was frigid. It felt like icy arms squeezing his breath out. As he kicked for the surface, he pictured Cyndi's mutilated carcass on the kitchen floor. He imagined Buddy upstairs, ripping Sheila. And horror gripped him. Freezing, suffocating horror. *What have we done!*

He burst to the surface screaming.

The warm fingers of the rain tapped his face, entered his mouth, and his scream twisted into laughter.

'What's so funny?' Doug wanted to know.

'Everything's beautiful.'

'It'll be beautiful if we find her.'

'I call first tibbies.'

'Bullshit.'

'Hey, you got Cyndi and Bud got Sheila. It's my turn.'

'Whoever finds her first,' Doug said. Turning away, he called in a sing-song, 'You-whoooo, Maureeeeen. Where *arrrre* youuuuuu?'

Lou scanned the dark surface.

No Maureen. Could she hold her breath this long? he wondered. What if she'd drowned? Better for her to drown than get away. But the idea pulled at him with disappointment. He wanted her alive. He wanted to make her blood burst out. He wanted to bury himself in her hot gore.

Lights suddenly pushed away the darkness around the pool. Peering through the black shower, Lou saw Buddy by the switch panel at the rear of the house. Then the pool lights came on. Instead of the brilliant shimmering blue that Lou remembered from summer night parties, the water looked murky. Like used dishwater. Its surface, calm except for ruffles set in motion by Doug swimming toward the deep end, was spickled with tiny geysers spashed up by the raindrops.

Lou turned in a slow circle, scanning the depths. Though the water was cloudy with gray, he could see the bottom. At least at the shallow end. When he studied the other end, he realized he couldn't make out the drain at the deepest point. So the gloom obscured the very bottom.

Maureen couldn't be that far down, he thought. Not if she's alive.

And dead, wouldn't she float to the surface?

Doug stopped beneath the diving board, reached up and grabbed its edge. 'I don't think she's in here,' he called to Lou.

'Me neither.'

Buddy walked out to the end of the board and gazed down.

'You see her?' Doug asked.

Buddy shook his head. 'Dive on down and check the bottom.'

'Thanks, but no thanks.'

'Do it.'

'You and the horse you rode in on. I went under a minute ago and it scared the shit out of me.'

'Scared of the dark?'

'You wanta check the bottom, help yourself. Have fun.'

'Fuckin' woos.'

'I don't think she's in here, anyway,' Lou called. 'She must've climbed out and run for it.'

Shivering, he waded to the side of the pool. He tossed his barbecue fork onto the concrete, then boosted himself up. At once, the rain began to soothe his chill. Twisting around, he sat on the edge and scooted backward. He stretched out. The rain poured down on him, caressing away the cold from the pool, melting his goosebumps, covering him like a warm blanket. He shut his eyes and opened his mouth.

It felt so good.

He didn't want to move.

His drifting mind imagined that the rain was blood. Maureen's blood. She was suspended above him, maybe in some kind of a harness that held her horizontal over the ground. She was naked and sobbing. Blood poured from wounds all over her body. Blood from her face spilled onto Lou's face. Blood from the severed stub of her tongue dripped into Lou's mouth. Blood from her breasts splashed against his chest. From her vagina came the blood that pattered the front of his pants and soaked through, hot against his groin. He imagined the harness lowering her slowly. Closer and closer. Soon, she would be on him.

'Get off your ass!' Buddy shouted. 'Doug, get

out of there. We gotta find that bitch and put her down.'

Yanked from his fantasy, Lou groaned. But then he realized it had only been make-believe. When we find her, he thought, it can get real.

10

Trev steered up the driveway and stopped under the carport.

'Do you want me to come with you?' Lisa asked. 'I know Maxwell's sister.'

He shut off the lights and engine. 'This isn't Chidi's house.'

'What?'

'It belongs to the man who ran the pizza parlor. I've got to see if his daughter's here.'

'Oh, for godsake,' Francine muttered.

'I won't be long. Sit tight.' He opened the car door, then hesitated, wondering whether he should leave the key in the ignition. A crazy woman had answered the phone. She might still be inside. She might not be alone. If something should happen to him . . .

But if he left the key, Francine might just drive away.

'What is it?' Lisa asked.

'Nothing. You two keep your eyes open. Don't be

afraid to use those guns if there's trouble.' He pulled out the ignition key. Then he dragged the shotgun across his lap. He climbed out, locked the door, and shut it.

As he stepped past the rear of his car, he heard thumping from the trunk. His prisoner. He wondered if she had enough air.

Don't want her to suffocate, he thought.

So he propped the shotgun against the bumper and unlocked the trunk. The lid sprang up, shoved by the girl. 'Hey!' he yelled as she scurried to her knees. 'Get down!'

She snarled. Before she could leap, his fist caught the point of her chin. Her arms flew out. Her head snapped back and rang against the underside of the trunk lid. As she started to slump away from him, he reached in. With both hands, he grabbed the shoulder straps of her jumper. He tugged her forward and down so the lid wouldn't hit her, then slammed it shut.

'Damn!' he gasped. He struggled for air.

Just trying to be a nice guy, and she goes for me!

He felt angry and betrayed, but mostly he felt scared.

As if he'd offered a nice chunk of meat to a stray dog, and the damn thing had turned into Cujo.

Should've expected it, he told himself. He picked up the shotgun. Consider it a lesson. Don't trust anyone, and watch your ass or they'll take it apart for you.

Still shaken by the encounter, Trev stepped around

to the passenger side of his car. He climbed two stairs, tried the knob of the house door, then peered through the glass.

Liam's kitchen. Its lights were on. He saw no one, alive or dead.

On the table were Liam's salt and pepper shakers. China Leprechauns. Trev's throat went tight. He'd spent a lot of time at that table, drinking Guinness and laughing with Liam and Mary. They'd seemed a bit like leprechauns, themselves. Full of blarney and mischief. They never tired of joking about themselves, a couple of folks from County Kerry coming to the States and opening a pizzaria. *Sure, 'n there's no accounting for the whims of a Kerryman.*

Trev's vision went blurry. He blinked his eyes clear, then stepped down to the driveway.

If the woman who'd answered the phone claiming to be Maureen wasn't a guest, she'd broken into the house. Better to find where she entered, and go in that way, than to smash through a door or window.

Keeping his shotgun ready, Trev passed the bushes at the corner of the house. He looked over the low stucco wall of the porch. The front door – what remained of it – was shut. Light spilled out through a ragged gap above the handle.

Someone had bashed through the door.

Trev pictured a wild, axe-wielding woman bursting into the house, going after Maureen.

She would've had some warning, though. All that noise. Maybe she got out in time. If she was inside, at all. And if she didn't try to defend the place.

At the door, Trev crouched and peered through the gap. The living room lights were on. He didn't see anyone. On the carpet just inside were dark water drops and footprints, but they faded away after the intruder had gone a short distance.

Only one set of footprints. Made by sneakers. Large for the shoes of a woman, but it had been a woman who answered the phone.

A big gal. But apparently alone.

He tried the knob. It turned, and he eased the door open until it met the wall. He stepped into the house.

He closed the door. He pulled off his hat and plastic hood, and dropped them to the floor. That was a lot better. Now, his vision wasn't limited to the eyeholes. The cool air felt good on his face.

A few strides took him to the center of the living room. The sofa, easy chairs, lamp tables and television stand were flush against the walls. Nobody could be hiding behind them. Nobody seemed to be lurking in the corners. He saw no bulges in the window curtains.

Trev moved slowly toward the dining room. The chandelier above the table was dark. The only light was that which spilled in from the living room. Stopping in the archway, he sank to a crouch. He peered through the bars of chair and table legs. Staying low, he scanned the rest of the room. Nobody.

Over to his left, the kitchen door was shut. A strip of light showed at the bottom. He had checked the kitchen from the door beside the carport, but someone might've entered after he'd headed for the front.

Leave it for last, he decided.

Beyond the kitchen door was the opening of the short hallway that led to the two guest bedrooms and the bathroom. The master bedroom was on the far side of the table, just to the right. Its door stood open. It was dark inside.

Trev rose from his crouch. He sidestepped silently to the right. As he rounded the end of the table, he could see down the hallway.

Dark. Except for a strip of light beneath the bathroom door.

His breath hitched. His heart kicked.

Easy, he told himself. The light doesn't mean she's in there. Go charging, she might just pop out of a room and plant an axe in your head.

He crept to the doorway of the master bedroom. He scanned the darkness. Nothing moved. All he heard was his thudding heartbeat. Bracing the shotgun with his left hand, he eased into the room and elbowed the light switch. Lamps came on at both sides of the bed. He studied the beige carpet and found no water stains. To the right of where he stood, the closet door was shut.

She might be in there. Or hiding at the far side of the dresser or bed.

Probably in the bathroom, he thought. But this was no time to take anything for granted.

Trev strode quickly forward, stepped up onto the bed, and walked across it. The mattress was springy under his feet. The bed creaked a little, but he doubted that the noise would carry beyond the room. Nobody beside the dresser. Nobody hiding alongside the bed. Turning around, he made sure the closet door was still shut. Then he stepped down, knelt, lifted the hanging coverlet, and checked the space beneath the boxsprings. Suitcases. He let out a trembling breath, then got to his feet.

Only the closet remained. He dreaded opening its door. But he had no choice.

He stared at it as he made his way around the end of the bed.

If the woman was in there, she'd probably heard him walking on the bed. She might even be able to hear his approach. Though his shoes were silent on the carpet, the plastic bags encasing him in their slick heat made crinkling sounds that might be picked up by keen ears behind the door.

He imagined her waiting in the darkness, the axe raised overhead.

He took a deep breath and held it. Reaching out, he closed his hand around the knob. He clamped the shotgun's stock tight against his side, hooked his mittened fingertip over the trigger, jerked the door open wide and leaped back.

Nobody lurched out at him.

He saw only rows of clothing on hangers. Liam's shirts and pants along the right side, Mary's blouses, slacks and dresses to the left.

Liam hadn't gotten rid of her things yet. Now, he wouldn't have to.

Shoes on the closet floor. Trev crouched to make sure nobody was hiding among the hanging garments.

And saw a pair of feet, legs bare to the knees where they vanished behind curtains of clothes. His breath shot out and he lurched backward. His calves struck the bed. He dropped onto the mattress.

'You in there.' His voice was high and shaking. 'Come out. Right now.'

Silence from the closet.

What if it's Maureen?

Maureen would've answered.

'Maureen?' he asked.

No answer.

'OK, lady. Come out or I'll shoot.'

'Trevor?'

A chill squirmed up his spine.

'Are you Trevor, the guy that called?' Whoever she was, she sounded scared.

'I'm Trevor.'

'You . . . you're one of *them*.'

'I pretended to be one of them when we talked. I'm a police officer. Come out of there. Now.'

'Did you get the stuff on you?'

'No. But you did.'

'Yeah, but . . . I don't wantcha killing me.'

'Just come out.'

Deep in the shadows of the closet, Mary's clothes slid toward the front. Trev heard hangers skidding on the rail. A woman squeezed her way clear, stood up straight and faced him.

'Don't you shoot me, now.'

Trev got to his feet. He kept the shotgun trained on her chest.

She stepped forward.

Trev let her stride through the doorway, then said, 'Hold it right there.'

'Yes sir.' She halted and stared at him. She looked terrified.

She was a big woman, just as her footprints had indicated. Probably over six feet tall, with broad shoulders. Her brown hair was matted down. She looked to be in her mid-thirties. A pretty face, with hints of creases where they'd be if she grinned and laughed a lot.

She wore a faded green bathrobe. Probably Liam's. It was tight across her shoulders. The sleeves ended well above her wrists. Her chest wouldn't let the front close completely, but the edges of the robe met at her waist where the cloth belt was tied. The robe reached almost to her knees.

Trev saw no black on her skin.

'You came in from the rain,' he said.

'Yeah, I did. And I know what you're thinking. But I ain't one of them. Not any more.'

She didn't *seem* like one of them. But Trev kept his guard up and kept the muzzle pointed at her chest. Her skin looked pale and sleek between the lapels of the robe.

'I'm OK,' she said. 'Honest.'

'You didn't sound OK when we talked on the phone.'

'Well, I *weren't* OK then. I still had the black on

me. But then I took me a bath and now I'm OK.'

He stared at her, confused. 'What do you mean?'

'Well, it passed. You know? I just went real wild when the rain got me. I was out for a walk and the rain got me and I just run around wild for a spell. I just didn't know what to do with myself. Then I got my hands on a hatchet out in a tool shed and I busted in here. I gotta tell you, I was all hot to bust some heads. I ain't in here but a few minutes, and you called up. You said you'd come on over, so I figured I'd knock *your* brains out.' She frowned at Trev. She nibbled her lower lip. 'I'm right sorry about that. But it was like I had a hoodoo on me? I wanted to bust your head something fierce.'

'But not now?' Trev asked.

'Not after I got clean. I stripped down and took me a hot shower. You know? The rain out there, it felt so darn good. But I didn't want to go outside, what with you coming over. So I figured the next best thing'd be a hot shower. But it didn't feel the same, at all. And before I know it, I don't feel like bashing heads no more.'

'The shower *cured* you?'

'Well, it's like I said. All that wild feeling just leaked right out of me. All I felt then was scared. So I come in here and hid.'

'There's nobody else in the house?'

'I sure don't think so. I ain't seen anybody but you.'

'Let's have a look. You go first.'

He followed her out of the room.

'What's your name?' he asked.

'Sandy Hodges.'

'In there,' he said. Sandy stepped into the first guest room and turned on the light. 'Stand over there and don't move.' She stepped to the far wall. She watched while Trev searched. He found no blood, no body. A woman's clothes were hanging in the closet, and he supposed they must belong to Maureen.

Where *are* you?

At least she wasn't in this room.

Nor was she in the next. The second guest room had a convertible sofa that was still pulled out. Green pajamas were wadded on top of the sheets. For a moment, Trev wondered who'd been sleeping here. Then he remembered that Liam had mentioned using one of his spare rooms. The poor man hadn't been able to sleep in his own bed since Mary's death.

'Are you OK?' Sandy asked.

He shook his head. 'I knew the people who lived here.'

'Well, I hope they're OK.'

'Let's check the bathroom.'

She led the way, opening the door and stepping over the damp, black clothes heaped on the floor: socks draped over sneakers, corduroy pants, a flannel shirt with panties and a bra on top.

A moist white towel hung from the shower curtain rod. The tub was empty, its enamel still beaded here and there with clear drops of water.

Trev leaned against a wall. He felt weak with relief.

She's not in the house. Sandy didn't bash her head in. God knows, Maureen might be dead or in bad trouble, but at least she isn't here. She could be all right.

'Where's your hatchet?' he asked.

'Under my duds,' Sandy said.

Stepping away from the wall, he nudged the pile with his shoe until he spotted the wooden handle.

'You'd better get dressed,' he said.

Sandy raised her upper lip. 'I can't put them things on. They'll get me all dirty and I might go wild again.'

He supposed that was true. 'You don't want to go out in that,' he said.

'Well, I don't much wanta go out at all.'

'I can't leave you here.'

'I don't see why . . .'

'Maureen might come home.' There was a roughness in his voice that made Sandy draw her head back.

'Well, I wouldn't hurt her or nothing.'

Softening his tone, he said, 'I'm not going to leave a stranger in her house. Besides, she might come home wet. If that happens, she'll attack you. I don't want either one of you getting hurt.'

'Well, I don't wanta get wet again.'

'I've got a car just outside the kitchen. It's not in the rain.'

'Where do you aim to take me?'

'Just away from here. You won't have to leave the car. Come on.' He backed his way out of the bathroom, watching her. She stepped over the pile of clothes, taking a long stride to avoid them, the robe slipping away from her thigh. She made no attempt to snatch up the hatchet.

She's either all right, Trev thought, or she's putting on a good act.

But he didn't think he was ready to turn his back on her.

He waved her into Maureen's room, and followed her in. 'Find something to wear,' he said.

She pulled open a dresser drawer and lifted out a pair of black panties. She frowned at him. 'You don't gotta watch me, do you?'

'Put them on.'

'Well, shoot.' She turned away from him, bent over and stepped into the panties. She drew them up beneath her robe, groaned and pulled them down again. 'These little things'll cut off my dang circulation.'

'We're wasting time. Try the closet. Maybe she's got a coat or something.'

Sandy entered the closet. She pulled a string to turn on the light bulb, then searched among the hanging clothes. 'Reckon this is a pretty big gal,' she said. 'Not as big as me, but she's tall, ain't she?'

'Yeah.' The talk of Maureen made him feel empty.

'Now, here.' She pulled a tan trench coat off a hanger. 'This oughta do just fine.' Still in the closet, she faced Trev. 'You just *gotta* watch me?'

Shaking his head, he turned around.

'That's a sight better,' she said.

'Don't try anything.'

'You sure don't trust me very much.'

'I'm just trying to keep alive.'

'Well, same here.' A few moments later, she said, 'OK, I'm decent now.'

Trev turned. She came out of the closet with the robe in one hand. Maureen's coat was tight across her shoulders and chest, but the sleeves reached to her wrists and the bottom of the coat covered her to the knees. Though she hadn't been able to button it, the belt cinched it shut.

'You'll need shoes,' Trev said. 'You'll have to wear your own, I suppose.'

Nodding, she stepped to the dresser. She took out a pair of white socks. 'These'll probably fit OK. Maybe you can wash off my shoes for me. You got them bags on.'

'Let's go.' He waved her ahead, and followed her toward the bathroom.

'Maybe we can dig up some trash bags for me,' she said.

'We've already wasted too much time. We'll just get your shoes ready, and take off.'

'You're sure in a mighty rush to get out in that rain. You sure we shouldn't just oughta stay right here and be safe?'

'I've got to make one more stop. Then we'll see about finding a place.'

11

So far, the trick was working fine.

They'd taken care of three outsiders, one each time, keeping the right hand door of the restaurant latched with the steel pegs at its top and bottom, shoving open the door on the left, grabbing the first crazy to squeeze in, and taking him down while Terry and Rafe jerked the door shut again by tugging on the table cloth they'd passed through its handle.

They'd killed one intruder. He was a skinny, giggling man who came in swinging a crowbar. As John chopped his arm, Gus jammed a steak knife into the side of the guy's neck and severed the carotid artery.

'Let's not kill them if we don't have to,' John had said while they dragged the body out of the way.

'We don't kill 'em, what'll we *do* with 'em?' Gus wanted to know. He was the one who'd called John a pansy.

'Let's try to disable them, then maybe tie them up.'

'Great. That how you handled the VC? No wonder we lost the fuckin' war.'

'This isn't a war. These people are just like us except they happened to get caught in the rain.'

'Like a mutt happens to get rabies.'

'John's right,' Steve said. 'We should try to take them alive if we can.'

'More risky that way,' said Roscoe the chef.

'Fuckin' right, more risky.'

'I'll handle the next one,' John told them.

The next one had charged into the restaurant with a knife in each hand. John broke both his arms, then his nose. The screaming man was dragged into the cocktail lounge where people huddled over him and bound his feet.

The third outsider was a teenage boy with a Mohawk haircut and a monkey wrench. John took the wrench away. Gus clobbered him with an upper-cut that lifted him off his feet. The first part of the kid to hit the floor was the back of his head. From the noise it made, the stiff brush of hair hadn't been much of a cushion. He was taken into the cocktail lounge to be trussed.

'We do much more of this,' Gus said, 'folks are gonna start running low on belts.'

'Let's worry about one thing at a time,' John told him.

'This is working pretty good so far,' Steve said.

John stationed himself at the door. He glanced at Terry and Rafe, off to the side with the table cloth. Steve stood next to him. He checked the rear. Gus and Roscoe, waiting, nodded.

'Let's do it,' he said.

Terry and Rafe let the cloth droop. John shoved the door open. This time, those outside were ready. Two of them hit the door, forcing it wide. The crowd surged forward.

'Oh shit!' Steve cried out.

The first to rush in was a woman in a nightgown. She drove a screwdriver down at John's face. He blocked it, slammed a fist into her belly, and hurled her sideways for Steve. An elderly man tried to bring down a golf club, but it was too long. Its head knocked against the top of the doorframe. John chopped both sides of his neck, grabbed the front of the man's jacket, kneed him in the groin, then swung him aside for Roscoe. A kid rammed his head against John's hip. John's elbow punched into the back of his neck. The kid flopped and two men blocked the doorway, elbowing each other as they tried to squeeze through at the same time.

John yanked the knife from his belt. He shoved it up under the ribs of the man on the right. John recognized him. Henry, the night man from the Shell station.

Damn!

He pulled the knife out and kicked high, the blow shoving Henry into the crowd. Gus crashed a chair leg down on the head of the man on the left. As that guy started to slump, John slashed his throat and shoved him. That one knocked against the pair bracing the door open. John ducked, snatched up the hanging table cloth and threw himself backward.

A woman with a clawed gardening tool leaped over Henry's body. She managed to get her arm inside. The door slammed on it. She shrieked and dropped the weapon. John gave the cloth some slack. The woman's arm jerked out of the gap. With a quick tug, he jerked the door shut. Steve rushed in from the side and locked it.

John stepped over to the wall. He leaned back against it, gasping, and let his legs fold. He slid down the wall until his rump met the floor.

It seemed as if everyone from the restaurant had poured into the entryway. Some just stood around looking shocked. Others were gathered in small groups, probably surrounding the crazies he'd brought in. He heard quiet murmurs, weeping, voices high-pitched with alarm, the thumps of blows landing on the kid, the golfer and the woman. He thought he should get up and tell them to stop, but he just sat there.

Too close. It had been too damn close. His trick had backfired, could've gotten everyone killed.

He saw Cassy push her way into one of the groups, heard her snap, 'Quit it! That's enough.'

Then Lynn came through the crowd and sat down beside him. She slipped an arm across his shoulders. 'Pretty rough?' she asked.

'God,' he muttered.

'You're not hurt, are you?'

He shook his head. 'So much for brilliant plans.'

'You did fabulous, though. Really. The plan really *did* work. You got . . . how many of them? Six?'

'Plus two outside.'

'So eight. That's fabulous. That's really whittling them down, honey. We got eight of them and they didn't get any of us.'

He faced Lynn. She had a forced smile and a sad, rather frantic look in her eyes.

She'd led a peaceful, sheltered life and there was no reason in the world for her to understand. But she did. John could tell. She knew this wasn't pretend, knew that lives had been lost, that he had killed people whose only crime was getting caught in the black rain, and that he hated all this.

'I'm so sorry I made you come here tonight,' she said.

'We didn't know what would happen.'

'If Kara gets . . .'

'She'll be fine.' He wished he could believe that.

Lynn was silent for a while. Then she said, 'I used to have these horrible daydreams. About earthquakes and nuclear war. I always thought, what if something like that happened and we weren't all together? I'd see myself out grocery shopping or something, and I knew I couldn't get home. And that was the worst part, not being with you and Kara . . . at the end.' Sobbing quietly, Lynn lowered her head.

'This isn't the end,' John said. He put his hand on her thigh, and realized he was touching skin. He looked down. Her leg had come out of the slit side of her gown. He'd given her a rough time about wearing the outfit. Hurt her feelings. Over something as minor as a dress. They might not survive the night. Kara might . . .

Kara will be all right, he told himself.

He moved his hand up the smooth warmth of Lynn's thigh. 'It *is* a nice dress,' he said.

She sniffed. 'Oh, sure.'

'Really.'

'I wore it for you, you know.'

'I know.'

He eased his hand under the slick fabric, and felt a quick surge of desire when he realized she wore no panties. She caressed his shoulder. More of her leg came out of the slit. He touched her soft curls, slipped his hand lower and spread his fingers, opening her. She squeezed his shoulder. Breath hitching, she squirmed a little, rubbing herself against his hand. He curled a finger into her. She moaned.

With her free hand, she wiped tears from her face. She looked as if she didn't know whether to keep on crying, or laugh, or beg him to stop, or reach for his zipper. She said, 'Jeez, John.'

'Jeez yourself, lady. You got nothing on under there.'

'All these people . . .'

'I'm sorry I gave you a bad time about it. About coming here. About everything. I love you.'

'I love you, too.' She gave a loud, wet sniffle. She moved his hand away, but didn't let go of his wrist as she got to her feet. 'Come with me,' she said.

John stood up. As she led him through the foyer, he saw that people were busy with belts, binding the three he'd let in. Nobody paid attention to him or Lynn.

She hurried ahead, pulling him through the cocktail lounge. One woman was hunched over the bar, nursing a drink. Otherwise, the room was empty.

'Where are we going?' he asked.

'Not far.' Lynn glanced over her shoulder at him. Her smile was crooked and strange.

'You're kidding,' he said.

'Oh, yeah?'

'They might need me out front.'

'They can do without you for a while. Can't they?'

'They'll have to, I guess.'

Lynn pushed open the door marked Damsels and pulled John in. The restroom appeared deserted. As the door swung shut, she leaned back against it. She pulled at her single, glossy sleeve, baring her shoulder. As the sleeve descended her arm, the top of her dress peeled down from her breasts. She shook her hand free. With a funny half-smile, she used both hands to twist the dress at her hips. Its slit came to the front. She slipped the dress higher until golden hair filled the peak of the opening.

'Holy smoke,' John whispered.

Lynn said nothing. Gazing into his eyes, she pulled at the knot of his necktie. The movement made her breasts sway a little. He held them, caressing the stiff nipples with his thumbs while she opened the buttons of his shirt.

Cassy came into his mind. The way she'd looked when she stretched back to put his blazer on.

Even before he could feel any guilt for thinking of Cassy, he forgot about her as Lynn guided one of his hands down between her legs. He stroked her there. She was wet and slippery. Moaning, squirming, she unfastened his pants. They dropped around his ankles, and she pulled at his shorts, dragging them down, freeing him.

She curled her fingers around his straining penis. They glided down it, and up, and down again.

'I'm not quite sure how to go about this,' he said.

Lynn chuckled. 'You'll think of something.'

'Hope nobody comes in.'

'Then we'd better get on with it.'

'What about the floor?'

'Yuck.'

'And hard on my knees.'

She swallowed. She shook her head. She looked as if she were in pain. Her tongue darted out and licked her lips. 'Just fuck me right here against the door,' she said.

Fuck me? John had never heard her say that before. Somehow, the words didn't sound foul. Just blunt and urgent.

'Fuck me,' she said again.

And he no longer cared how, as long as he did it.

He moved forward and Lynn spread her knees wide and he went up against her feeling the firm soft push of her breasts, her arms going around him. When he tried to crouch, the door at Lynn's back stopped his knees. He pulled her away from it, clutching her buttocks through the slick dress, urging her closer.

And he slid up into her as she sank down, wet and tight and hugging.

Her legs came up around his hips. They seemed to be climbing him. The higher they climbed, the deeper he plunged.

Then he had her pinned to the door. He kissed her mouth. It got away, and his lips met her chin. Her mouth was a moving target, and he stopped trying to kiss it. He watched her eyes, and she watched his as the hard thrusts jammed her upward and she slid down against the door only to be pounded up again. She grunted and bit her lips and whimpered. She whipped her head from side to side. She let go of him with her arms. Slumped back against the door and jerking up and down against it, she rubbed and squeezed her breasts.

John had never seen her like this before.

12

'Denny?'

She awoke with a start and found herself lying crooked on the sofa, her legs hanging to the floor and her head resting on Tom's lap. Kara still slept at the other end.

'News bulletin,' he said. His hand, just above Denise's face, pointed at the television. 'They broke into the show.'

She turned her eyes to the TV and recognized Chris Donner, the Eyewitness News anchorwoman.

'. . . been receiving sketchy reports that a crisis has developed in the nearby town of Bixby. Our news staff received its initial telephone call from a citizen of Bixby shortly after seven-thirty this evening, in which we were informed that a storm was dropping rain onto the town which appeared to be black. We were further told that the caller's spouse, caught in the mysterious storm, quote "went out of her senses and attacked me for no good reason" unquote.

'In our attempts to verify the story, we tried to make contact with various Bixby officials. Our calls to the mayor, fire department and police department have gone unanswered.

'Since that time, we have received numerous calls from people in that area. We have determined that an emergency situation exists in Bixby, and we have notified officials in surrounding areas.

'It appears that the storm began shortly after seven

o'clock this evening, that it is generally confined to the city limits of Bixby, and that the black rain-like substance falling from the sky may be causing those who come into contact with it to commit acts of violence. We understand that affected citizens are roaming the streets, and breaking into business establishments and homes in search of victims. Though the reports we've received have been sketchy, we understand that an undetermined number of people have been killed by these roaming marauders.

'Let me repeat that, at this time, the crisis is occurring only in Bixby and in the areas immediately surrounding its city limits. The situation is not taking place in any of the neighboring towns. If you are not a resident of Bixby, there is no cause for alarm.

'We ask that our viewers who *are* in Bixby remain indoors. Under no circumstances should you venture outside. Also, it is imperative that you avoid contact with anyone who has been exposed to the rain. Many of those people have armed themselves, and they should all be considered extremely dangerous.

'We take you now to Stan Fisher, live at the scene. Stan?'

'Thank you, Chris.' The screen showed a tidy, middle-aged man wearing a bow tie and an open sweater. He was standing in lights beside a van marked 'Eyewitness News.' Staring grimly into the camera, he said, 'I'm here at a roadblock set up by the CHP on Route 12 two miles south of the town of Bixby. County and local law enforcement agencies are cooperating with the Highway Patrol in an effort to seal off all roads leading into the stricken community. Nobody is being allowed to enter the area.'

The TV showed Chris at her news desk, the picture of Stan Fisher on a screen behind her as she spoke into a telephone. 'Stan,' she said, 'is anyone coming out?'

'As a matter of fact, Chris, three cars have come out just since we arrived. Unfortunately, we haven't been able to interview any of the survivors. They were immediately taken into custody. I presume that authorities are questioning them even as I speak to you.'

'In effect, they're being quarantined?'

'That seems to be the case, Chris.'

'Do you know whether they had come into contact with the rain?'

'It appears that they hadn't.' Stan again filled the TV screen and the camera pulled back, showing a man in uniform beside him. 'Chris, this is Commander Brad Corkern of the Highway Patrol. Sir, what can you tell us about the situation in Bixby?' He held his microphone toward the man.

'Well, Stan, I'm afraid we don't know a whole lot at the present time. As you've mentioned, we're doing what we can to prevent people from going into the rain area. We've had a total of eleven people come out since the time we established the roadblock here.'

'How were they?'

'Rattled. Plenty rattled. But they don't appear to be infected.'

'Infected. Is it a disease of some kind?'

'We don't know what it is. We've talked to these

people, and they indicate that anyone who gets wet from the rain – or whatever it might be – takes on violent behavior. Many of them reported witnessing assaults, and they saw quite a few dead bodies before they got out of the area.'

'Do you have any idea what might be causing such violence?'

'The dope,' Tom said. 'The guy already told him . . .'

'It's like I said, Stan, we can't explain it.'

The TV showed Chris in the studio as she said, 'Ask him if it's something like acid rain.'

The camera stayed with her, showing Stan in the background as he touched a button in his ear, nodded and said to the commander, 'Could this have anything to do with acid rain?'

'This is *black* rain, Stan. I don't know from acid rain. Isn't that something to do with Canada?'

From Chris again, 'Are there chemical plants in the area?'

'Could this be caused by a problem at a local chemical plant?'

'We're looking into that, Stan. We're also looking into the possibility that some kind of biological agent has infiltrated the area.'

'By "biological agent," you're referring to a bacteria or virus that may have gotten into the rain?'

'Something like that, yes.'

'Is there a possibility that Bixby has been subjected to any kind of biological or chemical warfare weapon?'

'I'd say that's highly unlikely. I don't think it's in anyone's best interest to speculate about such things. We've got enough on our hands without folks jumping to conclusions and panicking about some kind of war breaking out. This is purely an isolated situation. Nobody who isn't in Bixby has anything to worry about.'

Chris said, 'Stan, ask if the storm is moving, and in which direction?'

'Does the storm appear to be moving toward any other populated area?'

'From all we can tell, it's stationary over Bixby. Like I said before, there's no call to alarm anyone. If it does begin moving, we'll let folks know in plenty of time to evacuate or take protective measures.'

'Stan, ask if any rescue efforts are under way.'

Stan nodded. 'Is any effort being made to send authorities into the area to restore order?'

'We're looking into the possibility. Until we've been able to determine the cause of the contamination, however, we're extremely reluctant to take that measure. If we send in armed men, not knowing what they might be up against in terms of the conditions at the root of this thing, we'd be risking the possibility that they'll become infected and turn their weapons on innocent civilians. Right now, I'm afraid, our wisest course of action lies in adopting a wait-and-see posture, preventing people from entering the town, and making sure that nobody who's been infected is allowed to get by us and possibly carry the problem to other areas.'

The camera pulled in close on Stan. 'That's the latest from Commander Brad Corkern of the Highway Patrol, here at the scene on the outskirts of Bixby. This is Stan Fisher reporting for Eyewitness News. Back to you, Chris.'

'Thank you, Stan.' She hung up the phone. The screen at her back went blank for a moment, then showed a map of central California with a black circle ringing Bixby. 'Our mobile news unit will remain at the scene, and we'll bring you further reports as the situation develops in Bixby, where a black rain of mysterious origins appears to be contaminating the residents, breeding violence and death. This is Chris Donner for Eyewitness News, returning you now to our regularly scheduled program.'

A commercial for Excedrin came on.

'Cute,' Denise muttered. 'What's this, Excedrin headache number three?'

Tom looked at her, narrowing his eyes. 'People are driving right out of this mess.'

'Some are.'

'Maybe we should give it a try.'

Her stomach went tight and cold. 'Are you kidding?'

'If we can make it to one of those roadblocks . . .'

'Tom, too much could go wrong. We're safe here.'

'Right now, we are. But God, who knows? This could go on for a long time. Sooner or later, some of those lunatics might break in. What'll we do then?'

'I'd rather take my chances here. Really.'

'I think we should get while the gettin's good.'

13

Lou, searching the alley behind Buddy's house, caught a glimpse of someone ducking behind a garbage can.

All *right*! he thought.

When Buddy had ordered them to split up and search for Maureen, picking Lou to hop the high redwood fence and check the alley, he had nearly given up hope of being the one to get her. He was sure she'd gone a different way, probably fleeing along either side of the house and escaping through a gate rather than trying to climb the fence at the rear. Buddy and Doug had taken those routes. One or the other of them would end up with Maureen, and Lou would be out of luck.

Now, he realized how wrong he'd been.

She *had* gone over the fence.

She's mine, all mine.

Lou's heart thudded wildly as he strode toward the garbage can. The rain felt great splashing against his bare skin, running down his body in hot rivulets. He thought about stopping long enough to take off his pants so he could feel the rain all over him. And feel Maureen's body and blood all over him when he took her. Too tricky, though. He knew he couldn't get his pants off without removing his shoes. Then he would have to put the shoes on again because what if she made a run for it and he had to chase her? He sure didn't want to go racing down the dark alley barefoot.

Nail her first, he decided. Get her down so she can't run. Then you can take your time stripping and doing her.

His breath came in rough gasps as he halted in front of the garbage can. The can was just off the alley blacktop, set in a strip of weeds alongside someone's fence.

She might think she was hidden just fine, but Lou could see the faint dark curve of the top of her head.

'Come on out, honey,' he said.

She didn't move. She didn't make a sound. Lou heard only his own heartbeat and ragged breathing, the rain pattering against his skin, hissing on the alley pavement, thumping the hard rubber lid of the garbage container.

He kicked the barrel aside. It skidded, tumbled over.

Maureen, beautiful Maureen in her clinging wet T-shirt and baggy shorts wasn't cowering in front of him.

Lou muttered, 'Fuck.'

Squatting in the strip of weeds was a bony, naked man who leered up at him, said, 'Hi-ya, honey,' and sprang. Lou leaped backward as the man lunged at him, driving the jagged end of a broken bottle at his stomach.

'NO!' Lou yelled.

He lashed out with his barbecue fork and sucked in his belly, expecting the glass fangs to bite deep. The man jerked his head back. The tines missed him, but the bottle jabbed short. Lou grabbed his wrist. He shoved it sideways an instant before the man smacked against him. They both went down. The bottle shattered, off to Lou's left, and then his back hit the alley and the man pounded down on top of him and pinned both his hands to the wet asphalt.

'Get *off* me!' Lou squealed. 'Get *off* me!'

'You're mine,' the man piped.

Lou twisted and bucked. The man's skin was slippery and hot against his chest and belly. Something was pushing against his groin. He realized what it was, and he whimpered.

'Get *off* me, you bastard!'

A crazy thought came to Lou's mind: he ought to be just as turned on as the filthy madman writhing on top of him. It had been that way when he fought Doug by the pool and when he'd gone for Sheila. This shouldn't be any different.

But it sure was.

He felt no lust, just terror and revulsion.

Lou opened his mouth to scream, and the man's mouth came down, slimy against his lips.

He's kissing me! Oh my God no!

Before Lou could twist his face away, the teeth chomped in on his lower lip and yanked, and he shrieked as his lip was ripped off. The man spat it out. It stuck to Lou's cheek and the head darted down again and he felt the man suck on the raw wound.

Lou jerked his head aside. Growling, the man clutched both sides of his face and wrenched it upward and clamped his mouth to the wound again.

He sucked furiously, his growls softening to moans of pleasure. His fingernails dug into Lou's cheeks. He licked and sucked and gnawed on the open flesh. He writhed, rubbing himself against Lou's body.

And Lou, through the pain and horror, realized that the man's hands were holding onto his face. They weren't pinning his own hands to the alley. Not now. They couldn't be.

Stretching his right arm out sideways, he lifted the barbecue fork. He swung its long rod up, and eased it down until the tines were an inch from the side of his assailant's neck.

He rammed them in.

A harsh gasp blew spittle and blood into Lou's mouth. The man twitched and shuddered. Lou rolled, throwing him off and tugging the fork from his neck. The guy was on his back, mouth and eyes wide, one hand clutching his throat as if he were trying to strangle himself. His heels were shoving at the alley, thrusting his rump off the asphalt, scooting him along on the backs of his shoulders and head.

Lou crawled toward him. Past the man's head. The guy scooted closer. Lou caught the head between his knees. Holding it there, he raised the long fork overhead with both hands and drove it down. He missed his target and the tines ripped furrows in the guy's left cheek. He tried again. This time, he hit where he wanted. The bridge of the nose. One of the twin tines on each side. They punched into the corners of the eyes and went deep.

The orbs burst. The man's shriek only lasted an

instant. While he flapped and bounced, Lou pressed down hard on the fork handle and shook it.

Stir him up a little.

He grinned, but winced as the pulling sensation burnt the raw tattered flesh where his lower lip should've been.

He got me. He sure got me. But not as good as I got him, the dirty old shit.

After the man stopped moving, Lou waved the fork back and forth a few more times. Then he pulled it out. As he licked the tines clean, he remembered Maureen.

Buddy and Doug had probably gotten her by now.

They probably sent me on this wild-goose chase just so they could have her without me.

Lou got to his feet. Staring down at the dead man, he cautiously tongued his wound. Some of his lip was still there. He'd thought the whole *thing* had been ripped off, but only a thin strip, right in the middle, actually seemed to be missing. He touched his cheek where the piece had landed. It wasn't there now.

He stomped on the man's face.

Then he rushed back to Buddy's section of fence. He tossed his fork over the top, grabbed the edge, boosted himself up and dropped to the other side.

Nobody in sight. The patio and pool lights were still on. Lou picked up his fork. He studied the murky depths of the pool as he hurried around it, wishing Maureen would come to the surface and he could jump in and have her all to himself. But the pool looked empty.

'Lou!'

He spotted Doug by the corner of the house.

'Any luck?' Doug called.

He shook his head, afraid of how it might feel if he tried to speak. But he smiled and the pain came, anyway.

If Doug was asking about *his* luck, it meant they hadn't found Maureen.

He ran to meet his friend.

'Shit, man. What happened to you?'

'I ran into a guy,' he said, and realized that those particular words hadn't required him to move his jaw or mouth. No extra pain.

'You kill him?'

'Yeah.'

'Hot damn.' Doug slapped his shoulder. 'We haven't turned up Maureen or anyone else. Buddy's kicking up a shit fit. Come on.'

Lou followed him alongside the house and through the gate.

In the driveway, Buddy was sitting on his Harley. 'Did you find her?' he asked.

Lou shook his head.

'What the fuck happened to your mouth?'

'A guy got . . .' He closed his lips to form the m of 'me' and felt as if burning oil had been dumped on his wound.

'Lou murderated him.'

'Big deal. You dickbrains let Maureen get away.'

'She's gotta be somewhere,' Doug said.

'Yeah, well we can't waste the whole night looking for the bitch. Saddle up. We're gonna pay Lisa a visit.'

Lisa? Lou wanted Maureen, not Lisa. Then he remembered. Last night. That Chidi bastard. Lisa might tell on them. They really ought to kill her.

But she wasn't like Maureen. She wasn't tall and slim and beautiful. She was short and her tits were too big.

'I want N'reen,' he said.

'Tough shit. You should've thought of that before you let her get away. Now let's move it!' He kick-started his Harley. Its engine thundered.

Doug clamped his butcher knife between his teeth as if he were a pirate. Then he mounted up.

Lou stepped to his bike. He swung a leg over it, and lowered his rump against the warm puddle gathered on its seat.

He wished he could stay behind. Maybe he could find Maureen.

But he didn't want to be left alone.

There might be others around like that horrible man in the alley.

Besides, Maureen might be far away by now. Better Lisa than nobody, even if she was kind of a pig.

She's babysitting, Lou reminded himself. Won't be alone. There'll be a kid, maybe a couple of them. Maybe girls.

Yeah!

He pushed the fork under his belt so it pressed against his side like a saber, then fished out his keys.

Collision Course

1

Maureen, flat on her belly under her Jeep, head just below the front bumper, squirmed backward as the three boys swung their motorcycles around and roared down the driveway. They turned away, however, so she needn't have worried about headlamps finding her.

As the bikes sped off, she scooted herself farther back until she was clear of the tire. Then she scurried out from under the Jeep, dragging her coat beside her. Still sprawled on the road, she waited until the bikes disappeared around a corner.

Seconds later, she was sitting behind the steering wheel. She dug into a pocket of her coat, found the keys, and slid the Jeep key into the ignition.

'Now I've got you,' she muttered.

Grinning, she started the engine. She pulled away from the curb. As she picked up speed, she put on the windshield wipers. But she left the headlights off.

By the time they know I'm coming, she thought, it'll be too late.

This was working out even better than Maureen had hoped. Earlier, when she'd climbed out of the pool, she'd ached to rush straight into the house and find whatever weapons might be handy and tear the boys apart. The boys *and* their damn girlfriends. But she'd known she wouldn't stand much chance against the four of them . . . five, if Buddy should come back in after discovering she'd lied about the keys.

As much as she'd wanted their blood, caution had won out. So instead of blundering into the house, she'd raced to the front. She'd rounded the corner just in time to see Buddy burst in through the door and slam it shut. Then she'd snatched up her coat and taken shelter under her Jeep.

To wait for them, to watch for her chance.

Waiting, she'd heard distant screams, some far-off bangs that sounded like gunshots. Somewhere, people were getting creamed. She imagined bodies being ripped by knives, blown open by bullets. She saw guts spilling from a slashed torso. She saw herself kneeling over a stranger, sucking blood and clots of flesh from a bullet wound. Thinking about such things took her breath away and made her moan and squirm against the pavement.

A couple of cars had gone by, their tires swishing over the wet road.

Then she'd heard a strange, quiet rumbling sound accompanied by clicks and clatters. Roller skates? Sure enough, when she raised her head and peered back she saw a guy on skates dancing and whirling his way up the middle of the street. He must've been well over six feet tall. He appeared to be entirely hairless. He was shiny black under the streetlights. All he wore

was a long scarf wrapped around his neck. Its tails
should've been flying behind him as he sped along,
but when he twirled Maureen saw that they were plas-
tered to his bare back.

He carried an assault rifle with a banana clip.

Watching his approach, Maureen had wondered
about her chances of jumping him and taking the gun.

If she got her hands on that sucker, she could blast
Buddy and Doug and Lou and Sheila and Cyndi. She
could blow their heads off.

He'd blow off mine if I tried, she thought.

Then, fearing that he might spot her, she'd scurried
deeper into the dark beneath the Jeep.

He'd pranced and twirled past her hiding place, and
the sound of his roller skates had faded to silence.

Some time later came the quick smack of footfalls
on the sidewalk. Maureen had pushed herself sideways, savoring the rough rub of the street against her
breasts and belly and groin, and peered over the curb.
Two women – fat things in hair curlers and clinging
housecoats, were chasing a kid. One of the women
brandished a cordless electric carving knife. The other
didn't seem to be armed. Those were probably her
scissors sticking out of the kid's shoulder. The kid
wore pajamas. He looked no older than seven. He
seemed to be outrunning the gals.

Maureen wanted the electric knife.

It was no assault rifle, but a lot better than nothing.

She started to squeeze up between the curb and the
undercarriage.

But the squawk of gate hinges warned her in time,

and she slid back under the Jeep moments before Buddy appeared beside the house. She watched his feet as he rushed around. Then someone joined him. Either Lou or Doug, she supposed. She heard voices, but the pounding rain and the distance prevented her from making out what was being said.

When one of the boys approached the Jeep, Maureen knew she was about to be found. More excited than frightened, she'd wondered whether to stay in the tight space, or scurry out and attack. But the kid never looked under the vehicle. Apparently, he just peered in through the windows. Then, he'd gone away and there was more talk.

Working her way toward the front, she'd seen Buddy and Doug standing by their motorcycles near the top of the driveway. After a brief conversation, Doug went through the gate. Buddy waited by his bike.

Alone.

Now, driving her Jeep in pursuit of the boys, Maureen was glad she'd resisted her urge to go for Buddy while he was waiting by his bike. She'd been very tempted. She'd wanted to crawl out from under the Jeep and let him see her, pull off her T-shirt and shorts as he approached. The rain would feel wonderful on her bare skin. She would caress herself, tell Buddy how much she wanted him. And he would put his knife away to free his hands for touching her.

It had worked with Doug and Lou in the house. It would work with Buddy.

And just when he was so overcome with lust that he

didn't care about anything else, she would strike. Crush his balls. Grab his knife. Rip him open.

It would've worked. It would've been great.

But she'd stayed under the Jeep thinking about it and was still there, savoring the fantasy, when Doug showed up with Lou.

It's probably a good thing I didn't try, she told herself. Something might've gone wrong. And this way I can get all three of them. Without any risk.

They were a block ahead of her, riding abreast up the middle of the street.

The noise of their engines should keep them from hearing her approach.

She pressed down harder on the gas pedal and felt the surge of speed press her back into the seat. The three boys on their choppers grew. Lou, on the right, didn't have a shirt on. Maureen grinned as she imagined how the pavement would shred his skin. But she steered for Buddy. The Jeep wasn't wide enough to take down all three at once, and she wanted to nail Buddy on the first pass. He rode between the other two. Smash him down. Maybe get Doug at the same time, then swerve to the right and try for Lou.

The distance closed.

Four car lengths separated Maureen from her quarry. Then three, then two.

Buddy glanced back over his shoulder.

'*Adios, bastard!*' Maureen yelled, and floored the accelerator.

As she roared down on him, lights pushed in from

the left. A car. Just ahead. Speeding toward the inter-section.

Oh, my God!

Maureen shoved at the steering wheel and braced herself for the impact.

2

Moments before spotting the headlights and motor-cycles speeding in from a cross-street, Trev figured he was about a mile from the Chidi house. A few more minutes, and he would be there. With his carload of women.

Sandy had seemed relieved when she stepped out the kitchen door and found two other females in the backseat of his car. 'You got yourself quite a collection here,' she'd said.

'There's another in the trunk.'

'You ain't gonna put me back there, are you?'

'She's one of *them*,' Trev said, and opened the passenger door.

Sandy said, 'Howdy, ladies,' as she climbed in.

Trev hurried around to the driver's side and slid in behind the wheel. As he backed his car out of the driveway, Sandy turned around in her seat. Her knee pushed against the side of Trev's thigh.

'I'm Sandy Hodges,' she said.

'I'm Lisa Walters. This is my mom, Francine.'

Trev swung onto the street. He started forward. The knee nudged him. He looked down. Through the eyeholes in his mask, he saw that Sandy's leg was out of the trench coat, bare all the way up her thigh.

He felt a strange mixture of desire and sadness. That was Maureen's coat, but not Maureen's leg, not Maureen's groin just out of sight under the draping fabric.

He wondered if he would ever see her again.

Damn it, he shouldn't have been so timid about getting to know her. If only he'd realized that time was so short.

It's too late for regrets, he told himself. You can't go back in time and change anything. Just gotta live with your mistakes. And your losses.

'I sure am glad to meet you two,' Sandy said. 'It was getting to where I was starting to feel like there wasn't anybody else sane but me in the whole darn world.'

'I'm not sure how sane we are,' Francine said, and let out a peculiar laugh as if to prove her point.

'Well, you're sure a sight for sore eyes, I tell you that.'

'I bet you were awfully glad Trevor showed up,' Lisa said.

'Thought he aimed to kill me, is what.'

'We bundled him up real good so the rain wouldn't get to him.'

'Wish I had me an outfit like that.'

'They're garbage bags,' Lisa explained.

'And they feel horrible,' Trev said. 'Be glad you're not wearing these things.'

'Well, I feel right naked.'

'Are you and Trev . . . do you go together?' Lisa asked.

'Never seen him before tonight.'

'I thought you were his girlfriend, or something.'

'Me? Nope.' To Trev she said, 'Is Maureen your gal?'

'Not exactly. She's the daughter of a friend.'

Sounding annoyed, Francine said, 'So she wasn't even home? You took us all the way over there for nothing?'

'Mom.'

'Shit. He's been dragging us around all night on this wild-goose chase of his, looking for this woman. He's damn near gotten us killed. And he *still* hasn't found her. We could've been out of here by now.'

'You been searching around like she says, Trevor?'

'Tried a couple of places.'

'We could get out of this rain and be safe if he'd just quit this damn nonsense.'

'Mom,' Lisa said again.

'I think that's mighty noble,' Sandy said. 'Your Maureen's a lucky gal, having a fella like you searching high and low for her.'

'Noble, my ass,' Francine said. 'You'll think he's noble when he stops again to go looking and we get jumped by crazies and they kill us all.'

'You got quite a burr up your hindquarters, lady.'

Lisa laughed.

'What sort of a hick are you?' Francine snapped. 'You fall off a haywagon on your way to the rodeo?'

'Gosh, Trevor, how long you been putting up with this gal?'

'Seems like ages,' he said, smiling.

'I reckon as how I'd of given her the boot if I was you.'

'It's crossed my mind. But she's Lisa's mother. Lisa's a good companion.'

'Lisa's what got us into this mess,' Francine said. 'But you wouldn't know that, would you, Daisy May? My wonderful daughter here took up with a jungle bunny and . . .'

'I don't like your mouth one whit, lady.'

'Thank you,' Lisa murmured.

'*You* tell her,' Francine said. 'I'll bet she'd be very interested in knowing all about it, so she'll know just who to blame when one of these maniacs murders her.'

'I started going out with this guy,' Lisa said. 'And some kids killed him last night. Because I was going with him. And because he was black.'

'I'm mighty sorry,' Sandy said.

'Oh, you haven't even heard the best part yet. Tell her the best part, honey.'

'We don't even know it for sure.'

'The coon's grandpa is some kind of a witch doctor,' Francine explained. 'He's put a hex on the whole town. That's what's happening here. That's why we've got the black rain. It's grandpa's idea of payback.'

'Well, that's a load if I ever heard one.'

'It might be true,' Trev said. 'We're going over to his place right now to check on it.'

'You're telling me this *is* a hoodoo?'

'I plan to find out.'

'Well, don't that just beat all? What're you aiming to do about it?'

'Make him stop.'

'Aren't you scared he'll hex *you*?'

'I guess he might try.' Trev realized he hadn't given any thought to that possibility. But the idea of it didn't frighten him, and he wondered why.

Maybe because you don't really believe the old guy has any special powers.

If he doesn't, why are you bothering to check him out?

Just on the off-chance he *does*?

I'll find out soon enough, he thought. Can't be more than a mile from the Chidi house.

A few more minutes, and he would be there. With his carload of women.

Beyond the yard of the corner house, the headlights of three motorcycles pushed pale beams through the night. Trev flinched and Sandy yelled, 'Look out!'

The riders were black. Crazies. For an instant, Trev considered taking them down. But he thought better of it. Those were big bikes. A collision might put Sandy through the windshield. He swerved to the right, hoping to cut behind them.

He shouted, 'Hang on!' His front tire bounced over the curb. Then the rear tire hit and the car tilted and he heard Francine squealing behind him but it was OK, he'd missed the bikes, the nearest speeding by just ahead of his bumper as he came off the corner and he waited for the jolt of his tires coming down and something hit them.

It felt like the sledgehammer of a giant bashing the rear side of the car. He heard screams, a roar of sundered metal and bursting glass.

The blow slammed his teeth together and threw him against the door, knocking Patterson's hat off his head, then hurled him back against his seat. The world outside the windshield twisted and tipped sideways. Something clipped his cheek. The shotgun? Sandy dropped onto him. Sparks flew at the windshield, tossed up by the side of the car skidding over the pavement.

He glimpsed the red brake lights of whatever had hit them. Then the spin of his car wrenched the lights out of view.

3

Maureen's quick swing to the left had almost taken her past the rear of the car that came racing in over the corner of the block, tipped up and riding on its outside wheels. Almost. Her bumper caught it just behind its back wheel.

The jolt thrust her forward, stiff arms folding at the elbows. But she was well braced. The impact wasn't as severe as she'd expected. She didn't even hit the steering wheel.

She plowed right through, bashing the car out of her way, then saw that she was speeding toward the far corner. A mail box there. A tree beyond it. She wrestled the steering wheel to the right.

And spun out.

She gasped. Her Jeep twirled. She saw the car she'd hit skidding along on its driver's side. Then it was whipped out of sight like something glimpsed from a carousel.

When she came to a stop, she couldn't believe her luck. Her Jeep was upright near the middle of the intersection, facing in the very same direction she'd been driving before the accident.

The lights of the motorcycles were specks in the distance.

Maureen stepped on the gas. Nothing happened.

She twisted the ignition key. The engine roared to life.

Far away, the bikes turned to the right and disappeared.

She jammed the gas pedal down. The tires grabbed, and she sped after her prey.

4

Trev, pinned on his side between the door and Sandy, suddenly realized he could only see with one eye. He started to panic, then remembered the bag on his head. He pulled an arm out from under Sandy and tugged the bag off. He could see again.

Sandy's head. Hanging hair hid her face as she shoved at the window of his door in an effort to push herself up.

'You OK?' he asked.

'I been better,' she gasped.

From behind Trev came moaning sounds. 'Lisa? Francine?'

'I think Mom's knocked out,' Lisa said in a squeezed, breathless voice.

'You OK?' Trev asked.

'Kind of.'

'How are the windows back there?'

Silence for a moment. Then he heard a quick, high suck of breath. 'Oh my God, Trev! The whole rear window's busted!'

The rear window, he told himself. Not the back passenger window. Otherwise, rain would be pouring down on Lisa and her mother.

'Is rain getting in?' he asked.

'I can't . . . Just some trickles.'

'For godsake, don't let any of that water touch you.'

'It's OK so far. But it's kind of starting to run.'

'Don't let it touch you!'

'I'll try.'

'Gotta do better than try.'

'This is some fix,' Sandy said. She sounded fairly calm about it.

'We'll be all right,' Trev said.

'How do you figure that?'

'Cause we're the good guys.'

'Reckon that's what they said at the Alamo?'

'If you can get off me, I'll try to get out the back window.'

'That'll do us a heap of good.'

'You'd better do something quick!' Lisa blurted.

'Try to cover up the window with those bags you've got back there.'

He heard the rustle of plastic.

'It's just kind of running in along the . . . MOM! Oh God, Trev, Mom's face is in it! I didn't see . . . There's a *puddle*!'

'Don't touch it!' he snapped. Twisting so his back was against the door, he shoved at Sandy's shoulder and chest. She got a knee onto his hip. Then she put her other foot against the door. 'Try to stand up,' he told her. Then, to Lisa, he said, 'Your mom's still out cold, isn't she?'

'Yeah. I think so. She's moving a little, though.'

'Oh shit.'

Hanging onto the steering wheel, Sandy pulled herself up. Her weight lifted off Trev's hip. As she rose, her head bumped the passenger window. She hunched down some.

'I think Mom's starting to wake up,' Lisa said.

'The guns! You've got the revolver and shotgun back there! Get rid of them! Throw them out the window!'

'If I can find 'em.'

'Don't let your Mom get them!'

Trev struggled to sit up. He reached under the hanging tail of Sandy's coat, clutched her leg, and pulled at it. She wobbled a little, but held steady. Then she bent down. She grabbed the front of his shirt and tugged. He squirmed and kicked, and came to rest with his rump on the window. The car wobbled slightly as he slumped backward against its ceiling.

He turned his head toward the rear and found Francine close enough to touch. She was slumped against the side of the car, face against the window. She was moaning softly. The darkness hid her eyes. He couldn't tell whether they were shut or open.

Lisa was half standing, her back to Trev, right foot on the window sill below her mother's chin, left knee propped on the woman's hip. As he watched, she tossed the shotgun underhand through the high, narrow gap of the rear window. Its barrel clamored against the open lid of the trunk, bounced back toward the window and dropped out of sight.

The trunk!

Trev remembered the girl he'd left there.

He suddenly felt sick.

The right rear of the car must've taken a terrible impact to pop open the trunk that way.

She can't be alive, he thought.

A kid. Just a kid. A girl in a jumper and knee socks.
I killed her.

The revolver, tossed by Lisa, clunked against the
trunk and fell.

If she's not dead, we've just given her two guns.

Francine raised her head. Trev leaned toward her
and pounded it down. It struck the window with a
thud, and the woman went limp.

'What'd you do?' Lisa blurted, looking around at
him.

'Hit your mom. We can't have her waking up and
going crazy on us.'

'Jeez.'

'I'm sorry,' he muttered.

Fingers suddenly clenched Trev's hair. 'Hey,'
Sandy said. 'I got me an idea. Why don't we see we
can't knock the car back down on its wheels? Get on
up here.' She pulled his hair.

Trev stood up, his back rubbing along the ceiling.

Sandy maneuvered until she was standing in front
of him. She pressed her body against his. 'Give me a
hug,' she said.

He wrapped his arms around her.

'Lisa,' she said, 'you stand there on the back door.
On the count of three, we'll hit the seats. Trevor, you
just throw me backward hard as you can. Lisa, tackle
your seat.' She pushed her cheek against the side of
Trev's face.

'I guess I'm ready,' Lisa said.

'Here we go. One, two, *three*!'

Trev rammed Sandy backward, smashing her

against the seat. Her breath gushed hot against his ear. The car rocked away beneath the impact, teetered, and started to fall.

My God, it's working!

The car seemed to drop for a long time. Then Sandy was smashed up against him, grunting. He felt the tires bounce. And heard a rip and clank and knew at once that the front axel had given out.

'We did it!' Lisa sounded as if she might cheer.

Trev grabbed the seatback and pulled himself up. Kneeling between Sandy's legs, he looked out the windshield. The wipers swept back and forth, clearing off the black raindrops.

The car had a tilt, thanks to the axel, but Trev was glad to see the world right-side up again. He smiled at Sandy. Her face was a pale oval that showed white teeth.

'I guess we're still in a fix,' he said. 'But at least we're down.'

The engine had quit. The headlights were still on, driving pale tunnels into the darkness ahead. The car had come to rest near the right corner of the intersection. He peered through the windshield, then through the windows on each side. He saw nobody.

Lisa leaned forward and crossed her arms on the back of the seat above Sandy. 'What are we going to do now?' she asked.

'We won't be driving anywhere,' he said. He crawled backward until the door stopped his shoes. Sandy raised her knees. The trench coat spread open to its belt. Trev looked away while she scooted backward and sat up. She tugged at the coat to cover herself, then leaned back against the passenger door. Smiling at Lisa, she reached up and stroked the nape of the girl's neck.

'Seems to me,' she said, 'we either stay right here or we don't. We stay put, we got water coming in the rear and we got Francine already wet. She's bound to go for us when she comes to her senses.'

'We could tie her up,' Lisa suggested.

Trev said, 'There's no telling who might come at us from the outside.'

'We *can't* leave the car,' Lisa said.

'Well now,' Sandy said, 'we can if we want to. We'd get wet and wild, but that ain't necessarily the worst thing in the world. I been there, you know. And your mom, she's already that way. Trevor, you'd have to get yourself wet along with us.'

Trev's heart suddenly felt like a fist trying to punch its way out of his chest. 'We'd turn into killers,' he said, his voice shaky.

'That don't mean we'd have to kill each other. Back when I was wet, I ran into some others in the rain. I had kind of a hankering to go for 'em, but I was plenty more interested in getting after folks that was still dry. If we was all to step out and get ourselves soaked . . .'

'Were you still able to think straight?' Trev asked.

'Pretty much. Just that I had these nasty desires, is all. Except for that, I was pretty much like normal.'

'So do you think the four of us . . .' Trev had to

pause and catch his breath. 'Could we walk on over . . . to the Chidi house? And take care of business?'

'Don't see why we couldn't. After we get there and finish up whatever we've gotta do, we can shower off and be OK again.'

'Would we kill everybody there?' Lisa asked.

'I reckon we'd sure want to.'

'But if it's only the grandfather causing the trouble . . .'

'Lisa's right,' Trev said. 'Maybe the whole family's in on it with the old man. But maybe not. We might end up killing some innocent people. And not just at the Chidis. Maybe we won't be able to control ourselves and we'll stop along the way. Once we're changed, we might not even *care* about getting there. What if we just go on a rampage?'

Sandy shook her head. 'Well, we might.'

'I don't want to go around killing anyone,' Lisa said.

'OK,' Trev said. 'Look. I can go out on my own and not get wet. With any luck, I should be able to make it to the Chidi place on foot in six or seven minutes. We're only about a mile away. If it is the grandfather . . .'

The door behind Sandy flew open. The overhead light came on. Sandy gasped with surprise and flung her arms wide as she flopped backward. Her right arm swung out into the rain. Her left hand clawed at the door frame. Lisa's hand darted down and grabbed a lapel of her coat, but the coat merely pulled open and didn't stop her fall. Trev gripped her ankles.

And cried out 'NO!' as the girl from the trunk hooked an arm under Sandy's chin and tried to drag her from the car.

Not dead. The crash had freed the teenager, not killed her.

At least she hasn't got the guns, Trev thought.

He heard himself groan as he watched the raindrops splatter black against Sandy's face and coat and chest. She was stretched out straight, only her rump and legs still on the car seat, the girl tugging at her head. She writhed and kicked against Trev's restraining hands.

He let go of one ankle and reached for his revolver. Her other ankle jerked free. Her legs slid away from him. He snatched the weapon from its holster. He brought it up, hating what he had to do, feeling betrayed by the girl he'd tried to save, thinking *It's her or Sandy* but knowing it was already too late for Sandy as he pointed his .38 at the girl's chest just above the bib of her jumper and tried to find the trigger through his slippery plastic mitten and Lisa threw open her door.

'Don't!' he yelled.

Ignoring him, she leaped out into the rain at the same moment Sandy's thrashing legs dropped toward the pavement. The girl from the trunk couldn't handle a woman of Sandy's size. She fell backward, pulling Sandy down on top of her. Lisa rushed at them. Her pale sweater looked as if it were being eaten by the darkness. She dropped to her knees beside the two, and tried to tug the girl's arm away from Sandy's throat.

Trev, holstering his weapon, crawled across the seat.

Don't do it, he told himself. Get your hood on first.

But he knew he had to get wet. He had to be like them.

No!

If the rain got him, he might lose control. He might never make it to the Chidi house.

He twisted away from the open door, spotted his plastic hood crumpled on the far edge of the seat, reached back and grabbed it, then snatched Patterson's cowboy hat up off the floor. His shotgun was there. He made a quick decision to leave it. The 12-gauge would require both hands. Besides, a blast from that would almost certainly be fatal, and he didn't want to kill any of the girls.

He pulled the bag over his head, blind for a moment until he found the eyeholes, then jammed the Stetson down to hold it in place.

He crawled across the seat and climbed out.

Sandy was sprawled on top of the girl from the trunk. Lisa had one of the girl's arms pinned to the street. Sandy was trying to sit up.

Her trench coat was wide open, still on her shoulders but leaving the rest of her body naked except for her socks and sneakers as she pushed backward at the pavement. Her skin gleamed black under the streetlight. Trev stared at her, feeling an unexpected rush of heat. Then he hurried forward, careful not to step on any legs. He ducked down, grabbed Sandy's coat by the shoulders, and pulled her up.

She threw herself against him. As he staggered backward a step and braced himself, Sandy ripped open his shirt. He felt her fingernails through the thin plastic. Before they could tear it, he caught her wrists. He shoved her arms down against her sides, then forced them up behind her back. She came tight against him.

'Sandy!' he yelled in her face. 'Stop it!'

She shook her head and squirmed. Through the plastic glued to his chest, he could feel the heat of her skin, the rub of her breasts, the stiffness of her nipples.

Her head darted toward his face.

He rammed her arms up higher. She squealed and tossed back her head, rising as if going up on tiptoes, arching her spine. He felt a soft, curved ridge pressing his groin and realized he had an erection.

'Damn it!' he snapped. 'Settle down or I'll break your arms off!' He gave them an upward yank. She shrieked and tried to climb his body.

Letting go, he shoved her away. She stumbled backward and fell to her rump beside the struggling girls.

Trev pulled his revolver. He aimed it at her chest.

'Come at me again, I'll shoot you! You're gonna do what I tell you!'

She sat there, glaring up at him.

Trev kept the gun on her, and turned his eyes to the girls. They were a rolling, snarling tangle as they punched and bit and scratched one another. Trev rushed forward and kicked. His shoe caught Lisa just under the armpit and sent her tumbling off the other girl.

Standing above her, he aimed at her face. 'Get up slow or I'll kill you.'

Lisa bared her teeth.

Glancing from her to Sandy, he stepped over to the girl from the trunk. She'd obviously been no match for Lisa. She was sprawled on her back, whimpering as she gasped for breath. The bib of her jumper had been torn down. Her blouse was ripped open and pulled off one shoulder. The skin of that shoulder looked mangled. In the glow from the street light, Trev saw blood there, mixed with the running black rain water. Her pleated skirt was rucked up around her waist. A knee sock had come down and was bunched above her ankle. Trev nudged that ankle with his shoe.

'Get up,' he said.

He stepped backward, sweeping his weapon from side to side.

'I'm in command,' he told the women as they slowly rose to their feet. 'You'll do whatever I say. Anybody causes trouble, I'll shoot. If you behave yourselves, we might all get through this mess alive. Is that . . . ?'

From behind him came the metalic snick-snack of someone working a pump action.

He whirled around.

Francine. She stood by the car's open door, grinning, a shotgun at her hip.

The one he'd left in the car.

Jesus!

He jerked his trigger. In the instant before the hammer dropped, he heard a clack from the shotgun and realized it was empty. He had no time to turn his muzzle away. The revolver bucked. Its blast crashed in his ears. Francine flinched. Her mouth fell open. She lowered her head and turned it as if trying to find the stain of something carelessly spilled. Dropping the shotgun, she lifted a hand and touched her sweater midway between her left shoulder and the top of her breast. She took the hand away, turned sideways and looked at her fingers in the light from the car. Then she looked at Trev. 'You shot me, you bastard,' she said. 'You . . .' She pitched forward and fell flat. Trev cringed at the sound her face made hitting the pavement.

Lisa rushed in, and he realized he'd forgotten about the women at his back.

He swung around. Sandy and the girl from the trunk, both hurrying forward, abruptly stopped.

Standing sideways, he was able to keep them covered and still watch Lisa.

He felt sick. He'd shot her mother.

The girl, on her knees, pulled Francine onto her back. She tore the sweater off the woman's shoulder, jerked the bra strap out of her way, sank down and pressed her mouth to the wound.

'Lisa!'

She ignored him. He heard sucking sounds. He rushed forward, kicked her sprawling, then crouched beside Francine. He pressed an open hand against the woman's chest, felt her rib cage rise and fall.

She was breathing.

Keeping his eyes on the other three, he holstered his revolver. He grabbed Francine under the armpits and pulled her up. Careful not to knock the Stetson off his head, he hoisted her onto his shoulder. He clamped his left arm across the backs of her legs, and stood. He drew his gun. 'OK ladies,' he said. 'Let's go.'

5

John was waiting by a sink when the door opened and Tina, Andy's girlfriend, entered the restroom.

'Oh!' she gasped.

A blush warmed John's face. He smiled. 'Just waiting for my wife,' he said, and nodded toward a toilet stall.

'Is she all right?' Tina asked.

'Yeah, she's just fine. Thanks. Anything happening out there?'

'It's all just so awful.'

'What?'

'Well, you know.' She sighed and shook her head. Her eyes were still red from crying, her face smudged and streaked with makeup that had dried after running. 'Just everything.'

'They haven't opened the doors again, have they?'

'Oh, no. They sure haven't. Not since you did it and everybody tried to get in.' She drew her arms in close to her sides and shuddered. 'Everyone's just so scared and crazy. And they're wondering where you went off to.'

'Thought I'd better stay with Lynn,' he said. Then he called out, 'Honey, I'll wait for you right outside the door.'

'OK. I won't be much longer.'

To Tina, he said, 'Sorry if I startled you.'

'No, that's all right.'

He went out the door, noticed that no one was using the pay telephones, and stepped over to one. He dug into his pocket for change. He lifted the receiver off its hook. Its black plastic was slippery with his sweat. He realized he was suddenly trembling.

Reaching toward the coin slot, he hesitated.

What if nobody answers?

But he knew that he had to make the call. Denise would probably pick it up. He could talk to her, to Kara. If everything was all right, it would lift a terrible weight off his mind.

He took a deep, shaky breath, then dropped a quarter into the slot. He punched in his home number.

Some hissy sounds.

A ringing.

Answer it! Come on!

It rang four times. Five.

Sweat trickled down John's sides.

Six. Seven. Eight.

Damn it! Please!

A soft click and clatter. 'Hello?'

'Denise!'

'Mr Foxworth?'

'Thank God.'

'We're OK.'

'Thank God,' he said again.

'Are you and Mrs Foxworth all right?'

'Fine. We're fine. It's insane around here, but . . . we're holding on. Nothing's happened at the house?'

Silence.

'Denise?'

'Yeah?'

'Is something wrong?'

'No. But look, I have to tell you something. My boyfriend's here. Tom? I didn't mention it before, but . . . anyway, Lynn said it'd be OK if he came over.'

'Your boyfriend?'

'Yeah. Tom Carney.'

'When did he show up?'

'It was after the rain started, but . . .'

'Oh, my God. He didn't get *wet*?'

'Well, yeah. But he's OK now. Nobody got hurt. He got . . . washed off, and he was fine.'

'What?'

'Yeah. You know the rain? At least with Tom, he stopped being crazy once it was cleaned off. He was just the same as usual.'

John gazed at the phone. His mind seemed to be reeling.

They had a guy with them. He must've come in crazy, maybe even attacked them. But they were OK. They hadn't been hurt. And somehow, the black stuff had been washed off and he'd returned to normal.

It doesn't make them permanently nuts.

The implications of that . . .

'Mr Foxworth?'

'I'm here. Are you sure Tom was all right again after he got clean?'

'I'm positive.'

'Jesus,' he muttered.

'Kara's right here. Do you want to talk to her?'

'Sure.'

'But don't hang up,' Denise said. 'I want to talk to you about something.'

'Fine. OK.'

A moment later, Kara said, 'Oh, hi, Daddy.'

Oh, hi. As if it came as big news that he was on the line. Those were always her first words into a telephone, even when she was the one instigating the call.

Tears filled John's eyes. 'Honey.'

'How are you?' she asked.

'Mommy and I are just fine,' he said through the tightness in his throat. 'We're still at the restaurant. How's everything there?'

'Pretty neat. We had popcorn and I had a New York seltzer and we watched my birthday on the VCR but I fell asleep.'

'Sounds like you're having a great time.' John used his sleeve to wipe his eyes, but more tears came. 'Wish I was there,' he said.

'Me, too. When're you and Mommy coming home?'

'I don't know, honey. I think we'll have to wait till the rain stops.'

'Can I stay up till you get home?'

'Well, stay with Denise and Tom. You don't have to go to your bedroom. Sleep on the sofa if you get tired.'

'I'm not tired now.'

'How's Tom?'

'Oh, he's real nice. I guess Denny told you what happened, didn't she?'

'A little.'

'Well, we beat up Tom real bad and knocked him out. I bonked him right on the head. But he's fine now.'

'You're a tough little monkey, huh?'

'I am not a monkey, Daddy.'

'No, you're not. I love you, honey.'

'I love you, too. Can I talk to Mommy?'

'Not right now. She's in the bathroom.'

'Oh. OK.'

'You be good, honey. Now, let me talk to Denise again.'

'OK, bye.'

A moment later, Denise said, 'Me again. What I wanted to tell you, there's been some news on the TV. They said this is only happening here in Bixby.'

'Well, that's good to know.'

'Yeah. But the thing is, Tom has this idea about the three of us trying to drive out. You know, go where it isn't raining? He's got an umbrella, and he's already found your raincoat and some galoshes. I don't know. I think we ought to stay here. What about you?'

'*Yes*. For godsake, don't leave the house. There's no telling what you might run into.'

'Yeah, that's the way I see it, too.'

'Let me talk to him.'

'Sure. Just a second.'

John heard a quiet whoosh behind him, realized it must be the restroom door opening, and turned to see if Lynn was there. She met his gaze. And suddenly went rigid. Her face lost its color. A frantic, stricken look came to her eyes.

I've been crying, he thought. Shit!

He said fast, 'Everything's fine.'

Lynn shut her eyes. She let out a breath, went a little limp, and leaned her side against the door frame.

'Mr Foxworth?' A stranger's voice.

'Hello. Tom?'

Lynn opened her eyes. She looked confused.

'Yes. Denny said you wanted to speak with me.'

Nodding, he forced himself to smile for Lynn. 'I want you to stay in the house, Tom. Forget about trying to get out of town, OK?'

'Well, you know, if we can get to one of the CHP roadblocks, we'll be safe.'

'Don't try it. Not with my daughter. And not with Denise. If you want to go by yourself, that's up to you. But what I'd really like you to do is stay in the house and take care of the girls.'

'Well . . . I wouldn't go off and leave them, sir.'

'Then you'll stay put?'

John heard nothing for a few moments. Then came a quiet sigh. Tom said, 'Yes, sir. I'll stay. I'll protect them as best I can if anything happens.'

'Good man.' Lynn pushed away from the wall and stood up straight again, frowning as she stared at John. 'Is it true what Denise said about you getting wet?' he asked.

'Yes, sir. The stuff got on me when I came to your house from my car. But I didn't hurt anyone. Denise, a little. But she's OK. I never touched Kara.'

'I'm glad to hear it. But you're all right, now?'

'Yes, sir.'

'You got clean, and then you were all right?'

'Uh-uh.'

'That's great news, Tom. It's been nice talking with you.'

'You, too, sir. And you can count on me. I'll stay right here and take care of everything.'

'I really appreciate it.' He smiled again at Lynn. 'Is Kara still there?'

'Sure,' Tom said. 'You want to talk to her?'

'Her mother does.'

'Here she is.'

John stepped aside and held the handset out for Lynn. Her eyes filled and her chin started to tremble. She rushed forward and took the phone. 'Kara?' A moment later, in a choked voice, she said, 'Oh, hi to you, too.'

While she talked, John stood next to her. He caressed her back. It shook against his hand each time she sobbed.

She's really been through it tonight, he thought. We all have.

Now she's weeping, overcome with love for Kara and relief that the girl is OK and probably despair that she might never see her again. A few minutes ago, she'd been mad with lust.

It's having death right outside the door, John thought. Death trying to get at you. Makes life so urgent and sweet.

His hand drifted down to her rump. He squeezed it gently through the slick fabric and she smiled at him and sniffed and told Kara, 'We'll be home pretty soon, honey.'

After she hung up the phone, she turned to John and held him tight. 'I want us to be home with her,' she said.

'I know. So do I.'

'What'll we do?'

'We'd better get back to the others.'

'Can't we leave?'

'You know we can't. Not yet.'

He took Lynn's hand and led her through the cocktail lounge to the foyer. Everyone seemed to be gathered near the closed doors. 'Can I have your attention?' John called out.

People turned to him. The talking faded.

'Where the hell've you been?' Gus snapped.

'I was on the phone.'

'For ten fucking minutes?'

'Shut up,' Lynn told him.

'I found out a couple of things,' John said. 'I talked with someone who saw a newscast, and Bixby's the only place where this is happening. Every place else is fine.'

Some of the people appeared relieved. He heard

murmurs of 'Thank God,' and 'Well, that's something, anyway,' and 'At least we're the only ones.'

Gus muttered, 'Lot of good that does us.'

Dr Goodman said, 'Do they know what's causing the situation?'

'I don't know,' John said. 'But I think it's reassuring that it's confined to this area. Authorities are aware of it. Apparently, the Highway Patrol has set up some roadblocks nearby.'

'Will they be coming in to rescue us?' Carol Winter asked.

'I don't know.'

'We can't depend on that,' Cassy said, stepping toward the front of the group. She smiled at John, then turned to scan the others. 'We've got to take care of ourselves.'

'They haven't tried anything for a while,' said an elderly woman.

'Probably waiting for us to open the doors again,' Peggy said.

John raised a hand to regain their attention. 'I found out something else. The madness isn't permanent. Once the rain has been washed off, the people apparently become normal again. Now, we've got several of them tied up in here. Those who haven't been disabled can help us defend this place if we clean them up. So let's form a group and take them into the kitchen.'

'Throw 'em in the dishwasher,' suggested the little man who believed in levity.

'There are a couple of wash tubs,' John said. 'Let's get started.'

6

Maureen slowed her Jeep as she drove through an intersection. She glanced both ways. Cars were parked in driveways and along the curbs, but the street looked deserted.

'Where *are* they?' she muttered.

The last she'd seen of the three motorcycles was just after the collision when they'd been turning right onto a sidestreet. By the time she'd reached the corner, however, they'd been gone.

She'd headed down that road, looking for them. Maybe the bastards had reached their destination, and she would spot their bikes in front of a house.

She'd scanned the curbs, the driveways, the front lawns of the houses along the street. She'd checked both ways at the corners, peering down the cross-streets in search of their lights.

But this was the fifth or sixth intersection she'd passed without finding any sign of them.

They'd had a big headstart. Still, if they'd gone this far, she should've seen them when she first turned onto the road. So they must've taken one of the earlier sidestreets.

Maureen swung across the road, pulled into a driveway, reversed her way out, and started back in the direction from which she'd come.

I'll find them if I have to drive down every street in the whole damn town, she thought. Find them and waste their sorry asses.

If that car hadn't cut in front of her . . .

Snarling, she pounded the steering wheel.

For a few moments, she considered driving back to the scene of the accident and killing the ones in that car. She'd caught a glimpse of those inside. There'd been three or four in there. She could have a field day. If they were still hanging around. They're probably long gone, she thought. Unless they were hurt.

And they might be armed.

Also, they were strangers. Killing them wouldn't be half as good as killing Buddy and Doug and Lou. Those guys had messed with her. Buddy, for godsake, had raped her. She remembered how she'd wanted to kill him for it even before she escaped from the house and got herself wet again.

Her mind went back to the rape. She could feel herself sprawled on the slick bottom of the tub, the hot shower pouring down, Buddy pulling at her buttocks and thrusting into her. The memories took her breath away. She felt heat spreading outward from her center. Her nipples tingled as they pushed against the damp fabric of her T-shirt. She imagined herself reaching up for Buddy, pulling him down against her, sinking her teeth into his throat. Blood spurting down her throat while his cock twitched deep inside her, pumping her full of semen.

Trembling, she let out a sigh.

That would've been just incredible.

She remembered how she'd felt only pain and outrage and shame when Buddy had actually taken her.

No thrill at all. Even the desire to kill him hadn't brought any feelings of lust.

I was sure different then.

'Weird,' she muttered.

She suddenly had an urge to feel the rain, so she cranked down her window and put her arm out. The warm drops splashed against it. How nice it would be to have a convertible, to feel the rain pouring down on her. She cupped some in her hand. As she rubbed it over her face, she glimpsed a stop sign.

I could stop and get out, she thought. Just for a minute.

No, I've got to find them.

The rain would feel good on her. But their blood would feel better.

Then she realized she had just gone through the intersection without even looking for the guys.

She stepped on the brake. The Jeep came to a stop, and she shifted to reverse. She started to back up, but changed her mind.

They'd probably gone up one of the streets closer to where they'd turned onto this road. One of the first few.

She continued driving forward while she thought about the matter.

They'd probably made a left. A right would've taken them parallel to Buddy's street, and back in the direction they'd started from. If they'd wanted to do that, they would've headed the other way when they came out of Buddy's driveway.

Maureen grinned.

It was so obvious. They'd gone left.

That means I make a right, she told herself, since I'm coming from this direction.

I'll start at the first street they could've turned onto, check it out for a while, then work my way back on the next one.

She sped up.

She'd gone two blocks when a man dashed out of a driveway. She pressed down harder on the gas pedal, hoping to hit him. But he was running too fast. He would get by her in time, and she was reluctant to make a swerve for him, fearing she might spin out and crash. He suddenly flung his arms wide and seemed to dive at the pavement. He skidded to a halt right in front of her. Maureen saw the feathered shaft of an arrow upright in the middle of his back. She looked to the side and glimpsed the man with the bow. Standing on a front lawn. Wearing a breechclout, a feathered band around his head. Drawing another arrow from his quiver. Then she bumped over the body in the street.

Moments later, something thunked her Jeep.

An arrow? The bastard shot at *me*!

She had a sudden urge to back up and go after the guy, run him down.

Hell no, she thought. Keep wasting time, and I'll never find Buddy and his pals.

7

'Does anybody want to see more of my birthday party?' Kara asked as *Fistful of Dollars* came to an end.

'I think we should keep this channel on,' Denise told her. 'They might have another news report.'

'Oh. OK.'

Denise, smiling, patted the girl's knee. And gripped it when she heard a growling rumble of engine noise. She glanced at Tom, then stared at the front door. The roar seemed to be coming from beyond it. As if a motorcycle or a souped-up car was thundering by on the street outside. She waited for the sound to fade away. But it grew louder and louder and ended abruptly.

A chill squirmed up her back.

'Uh-oh,' Tom said.

She turned to him. He was gazing at the door. He looked as if someone had just invited him to eat a worm.

'Is something the matter?' Kara asked.

Denise ducked forward, snatched the remote control off the table, and shut off the television. 'Somebody stopped in front of the house,' she whispered.

Kara's lips formed an O, then stretched away, baring her teeth as her eyebrows climbed her forehead.

'Sounded like motorcycles,' Tom whispered.

'More than one?' Denise asked.

He shook his head. 'Three or four, maybe.'

'Does that mean somebody's coming *here*?' Kara asked.

'We don't know,' Denise said. 'Let's be real quiet. If they think no one's home . . .' Her voice trailed off.

Kara snuggled up against her. Tom put a hand on her back. The three sat motionless on the sofa, gazing at the door.

They all flinched when the bell rang.

Denise glanced at the table beyond her knees. The fireplace poker was there, along with the hammer and butcher knife.

The doorbell rang again.

'Should we see who it is?' Kara whispered.

'Shhhh.'

Someone pounded on the door. Each blow shook it. Each blow felt to Denise like a punch in the stomach. She struggled to breathe. Her cheeks tickled. She rubbed them with one hand, and found the skin pebbled with goosebumps.

'Lisa!' a voice called through the door.

'Lisa?' Kara whispered, frowning up at Denise. 'She was supposed to be sitting for me tonight.'

'Yeah. I know.'

'It's Buddy,' the voice called. 'Come on, open up.'

'Buddy Gilbert,' Denise muttered.

'Oh, great,' Tom said. 'And he thinks Lisa's here.'

'They go together,' Denise said.

'They did till she started running around with Max.'

333

He pounded the door again. 'Open up, Lisa! Come on, I know you're in there.'

'He's probably got Doug and Lou with him,' Tom said.

'Lisa!' Buddy shouted. 'Let me in! Right now! Or I'll bust the fucking door down!'

'The F word,' Kara whispered.

Tom leaned forward. He snatched the poker off the table and got to his feet.

'What're you doing?'

'I'd better tell him Lisa isn't here. Maybe they'll go away.'

'Fat chance.'

A hard blow rattled the door in its frame.

As Tom hurried toward the foyer, Denise picked up the hammer. She went after him, glanced back and saw Kara following, the knife in her hand.

Tom pressed his shoulder to the door. 'Buddy?'

'Who the hell are you?'

'Tom Carney.'

'What the fuck are you doing there, Carney?'

'Lisa isn't here.'

'Bullshit. Let me in.'

'It's the truth,' Denise said. 'Lisa was supposed to be here, but she canceled out.'

'Who're you?'

'Denise Gunderson.'

'Denise, huh?'

The way he said her name, she thought of how he leered at her in school. The look had always made her feel crawly.

She heard some quiet voices through the door. Then Buddy said, 'You're bluffing. I know damn well Lisa's there. She got you two for body guards, or what?'

'She's not here!' Tom shouted.

'Bullshit.' He crashed against the door.

'We've got guns!' Tom yelled. 'Now knock it off! Get out of here or I'll start shooting! I swear to God, you hit the door one more time and I'll put some bullets through it!'

Denise heard more faint conversation from outside. Then silence.

She stared at Tom. Grimacing, he shook his head as if he thought the warning about guns was a pretty lame idea, but the best he could do.

He looked surprised when the motorcycles grumbled to life. A grin spread across his face. He whispered, 'I'll be damned.'

'Get away from the door,' Denise said, suddenly fearing that Buddy might try to ram it down with his bike.

'You don't think . . . ?'

'I don't know.' She rushed over to the picture window and swept the drapery out of her way. Clamping the hammer between her knees, she cupped her hands against the glass and peered out.

Far to the right, she saw the three boys mounted on their motorcycles. The bikes turned in tight circles near the end of the driveway, their headlights sweeping across the window. Then the bikes roared down to the street, swung right and sped out of sight.

Denise stepped away from the window. Tom and Kara gazed at her, their eyes wide. 'I don't believe it,' she said. 'They really left.'

Kara beamed. 'They just didn't want to get shot to smithereens.'

Tom, with a weary smile, sagged against the door. 'God,' he muttered. 'That was a close one.'

'I wonder if they'll be back,' Denise said.

'Yeah. I wouldn't put it past those creeps. Did you see who was with Buddy?'

'Two other guys. I didn't get a very good look, but I think they were probably Doug and Lou like you thought.'

'Probably. Those three are always together.'

'I wonder what sort of plans they had for Lisa.'

Tom shook his head. 'Did you hear what happened at the dance last night?'

Denise had agreed to miss the football game and the dance that followed so her parents, being away for the weekend, wouldn't have to worry about her.

'It was on the news about Max,' she said.

'Well, that was afterward. But I saw Jim Horner today, and he said Buddy and Doug and Lou showed up drunk and really gave Lisa and Max a bad time. They got themselves booted out.'

Denise felt herself sinking inside. 'You don't think . . . you don't suppose they're the ones who *did* that to Max?'

She saw Tom's face go red. His lip curled up.

'What happened to Max?' Kara asked.

'Somebody murdered him last night,' Denise explained.

'Oooo, yuck.'

She frowned at Tom. 'Kara's mom . . . she told me on the phone that Lisa couldn't come here because her mother was taking her to the police station. It sounded like Lisa wanted to tell the cops something about the murder.'

'Oh, my God,' Tom muttered. 'I guess it'd crossed my mind that those guys might've . . . But . . . I can't believe they'd actually do that to someone. They're real jerks but . . . I mean, to actually . . .'

'Can we change the subject?' Kara asked.

Denise glanced at her, then met Tom's eyes. 'I bet they came here to kill Lisa.'

'They're wet,' he said. 'They'll kill anyone they can.'

'But if they think she's here . . .'

'Maybe they're heading for her house.'

'Or maybe they just rode away to trick us,' Denise said, 'and they'll come back on foot.'

8

Lou hadn't wanted to leave. Not with Denise there.

But he followed Buddy and Doug away down the street, hurting with disappointment.

They swung into the driveway of a house at the end of the block, only four homes away from the Foxworth place. Lou shut off his engine, kicked down the stand and climbed off.

'Why'd we stah here?' he asked, being careful not to move his lower lip, forming the words deeper inside his mouth than usual. He knew they sounded garbled, but he didn't care. 'I thought we were going to Lisa's.'

'We *are* going to Lisa's dickhead.'

Lou's heart quickened. 'Huh?'

Doug shook his head, smirking at him. 'You didn't believe that shit they handed us back there, did you?'

He hesitated. 'I guess not.'

They strode down to the sidewalk and started back.

'Those asswipes were probably lying about the guns, too,' Buddy said. 'But just in case, we're gonna go in careful. Find ourselves some windows.'

Lou nodded. He wasn't sure how going in carefully would solve the problem of being met by firearms. It wasn't likely, after all, that windows had been left unlocked. Glass would have to be broken. The noise would ruin any chance of taking them by surprise.

Lou didn't want to get shot.

But Lisa had to be killed, that was for sure.

And Denise was in the house. Denise Gunderson.

We're going back. Oh yeah, we're going back!

He'd missed his chance for Maureen, but Denise . . . whenever he saw her in school, he ached with strange feelings of desire and sadness. She was more than just beautiful. There was something fresh and innocent about her that made him hollow inside.

Lou remembered the empty feelings of loss that she always stirred in him. But they weren't here, now.

'Cause I'm going to get her, after all. Tonight.

He pictured her tied spread-eagle to a bed. He saw himself ripping her clothes off. Pushing the tines of his barbecue fork against one of her breasts. Watching the skin dent as she writhed and screamed. Seeing the points break through her skin and slide in. And that would just be the start.

Lou's heart pounded like a hammer. His breath came in shaky gasps. His penis strained against the front of his pants and he wanted to let it out but the guys would laugh at him.

Buddy halted in front of the house next door to the one where Denise waited. 'Let's go around the back,' he said. 'Find us some windows.'

'All *right*!' Doug said.

Lou grinned, and winced with pain from his torn lip. Then he slid the barbecue fork out of his belt. 'I want Denise,' he said.

'You get who you get,' Buddy told him.

9

Trev knew they weren't making good time. It slowed him down, lugging Francine around on his shoulder. And it slowed him down, keeping the others covered in front of him.

Without the women, he would've been at the Chidi house by now. But he couldn't leave Francine to die from her wound or be killed by any of the crazies he sometimes glimpsed in the distance. Nor could he allow the other three to run wild and maybe kill innocent people.

For one reason or another, all four women were here because of him. They were in his care. They were his responsibility. He planned to make sure they lived through the night.

No matter how much they slowed him down.

Only a couple more blocks to go, he told himself.

Lisa was the worst. She kept walking backward, staring at him and Francine. Trev was sure that his gun was the only thing that kept her from attacking.

The girl from the trunk behaved herself. She walked beside Sandy, her head low. Trev supposed that her injuries must've taken her spunk out.

Sandy hadn't caused much trouble, so far. She'd thrown Maureen's trench coat to the pavement soon after they began their journey, and Trev had told her to put it back on. She'd drawled, 'You aim to plug me if I don't?' and kept on walking. He had decided it wasn't worth fighting about. And he found that he didn't mind watching her stride along, naked except for her socks and sneakers. Sometimes, she turned around, grinning and rubbing herself. Trev wasn't sure whether she was trying to be seductive in hopes of getting close so she could put her teeth into him, or whether she was simply aroused by the feel of the rain.

'Why don't you turn around before you trip?' he told Lisa.

Instead of obeying, she halted, crouched, spread her arms and growled.

Trev aimed his gun at her face. 'Keep moving.'

The girl from the trunk continued walking forward, but Sandy pranced up behind Lisa and slapped the side of her head. 'Do like he tells you,' she said.

Lisa whirled around. 'You bitch!' she snapped. 'We can take him!'

'You're dumber than a dead dog's butt, girl. He'd put holes in us sure.'

'He won't shoot us.' Lisa bared her teeth at him. 'You like us, don't you.' It wasn't a question. 'You want to *save* us, don't you.'

'My own skin comes first, Lisa,' he told her.

She lurched toward Sandy and grabbed the woman's arm. 'Come on. Help me.'

'Not on your life, gal.' Sandy tugged her arm from Lisa's grip and the blast of a gunshot crashed in Trev's ears and Lisa's head jerked sideways as if it had been kicked. A mess flew out from her left temple.

'Down!' Trev shouted.

He dropped to a crouch as Lisa toppled to the pavement. Sandy threw herself flat by the curb. The girl from the trunk turned around slowly as if confused.

'Get down!' Trev yelled at her.

Another shot. A bullet kicked sparks off the hood of a parked car. The way the girl leaped backward, it must've just missed her. She squatted quickly beside the car.

Trev dumped Francine off his shoulder. He spread himself out flat on the street.

A slug whined off the pavement near his face.

He twisted his head to the left. Lost his eyeholes. With one hand, he turned the bag until he could see again.

A man in plain sight. An old, bald guy in a plaid shirt, standing some fifty feet away under the shelter of his porch roof. The porch was lighted. Even as Trev spotted him, the geezer levered his rifle and put another shot through the screen. The bullet chopped the curb near Sandy.

He's not wet!

He killed Lisa and he's not even fucking wet!

'Hold your fire, damn it!' Trev yelled. 'I'm a police officer!'

'Whoop-de-doo, fella!' He swung the barrel in Trev's direction and fired again. The bullet struck the street somewhere behind Trev's head.

'Stop it! Just let us pass. We've got no business with you.' *Except you killed Lisa*, Trev thought.

'I got business with you!' the man called. He levered another round into the chamber as Trev shoved himself up to his knees and the bag blinded him and he threw it off along with Patterson's hat and he could see again and the rain felt good on his head and he braced his aiming hand and the man sighted in on him and fired. Something stung Trev's thigh. Something else slopped against it, and Trev snapped off four shots as fast as he could pull the trigger. The old man jerked, staggered backward and fell out of sight.

Trev looked down. A mess clung to the leg of his jeans. A chunk of skull, hair still clinging to its patch of scalp, slid down the denim. It had come from Francine's head. There was a cavity above her right ear.

He set his revolver on the pavement and tugged the plastic bags off his hands.

There was a slash at the side of his jeans just above the knee.

Like one of the cuts in Lisa's jeans.

I'm a fashion plate, he thought, and chuckled softly.

His skin under the slash felt burnt. The bullet must've nicked him.

I'll live, he thought.

He touched the glop that had splashed the leg of his jeans. It felt spongy and warm. He scooped some off and stuffed it into his mouth. Moaning at the good taste of it, he shoved his fingers into Francine's head and started to dig out more.

'Trevor!'

Sandy stood in front of him. He took his fingers out of Francine's head and reached for her. He wrapped his slippery hands around her buttocks and drew her closer. When he pressed his mouth between her legs, she grabbed his hair. She yanked his head backward. He gazed up between her breasts at her frowning black face.

'Grandpa Chidi,' she said. 'Remember him?'

Trev nodded. He remembered. But he didn't care. He strained against Sandy's grip, trying to get his mouth on her again, but she jerked his hair so hard that tears filled his eyes. He cried out.

'I reckon we gotta finish what we started,' she said.

'OK, OK.'

She released his hair and stepped back.

Trev reached down for his gun.

She stepped on his hand. Her knee crashed against his forehead. The blow knocked him backward. His hand pulled out from under her shoe. But without the gun.

He pushed himself up.

Sandy had the gun. It was aimed at his face. 'Get up off the street,' she said. 'We got us a job to do.'

10

Of those from outside the restaurant who'd been taken– alive, the kid with the Mohawk haircut remained unconscious and one man had broken arms. There was no point in washing either of them.

Four others were in good enough shape to help defend the place: Bill the parking attendant; a kid of about sixteen wearing only a T-shirt; a young woman dressed in a nightgown; and the old fellow who'd tried to strike John with his golf club.

Bound and struggling, they were carried into the kitchen and placed on the floor near the wash tubs.

The tubs were about two feet deep. Each looked large enough to permit someone to sit down or kneel. John stoppered the drain of one, and turned on the water.

'Let's do Bill first,' Cassy suggested.

Roscoe the chef dragged the young man to his feet. John held a knife on him while Roscoe removed the belts lashed around his arms and legs. Lynn and Cassy held onto his arms. He struggled against them until John pressed the blade to his throat. 'Calm down, pal.' Bill glared, but stopped resisting.

Steve and Carol kept watch on the other three as Roscoe, Lynn and Cassy stripped Bill down to his underwear. He was mostly black to his neck. From his shoulders to his feet, he looked clean except for his hands. Apparently, he hadn't been under the rain long enough for it to penetrate his clothes to the skin.

'I don't think we'll have to put him in,' Cassy said.

'Yeah,' John agreed. 'Just dunk his head and hands.'

Roscoe shoved Bill against the sink and pushed his head down into the water. Lynn and Cassy plunged his hands in. The three of them held him under, Roscoe rubbing his hair. The water turned murky gray. Then they let him up. He lurched out of the water, gasping. His hair was blond, his face red. He looked around, blinking.

Cassy gave him a dish towel. He frowned at her.

'How are you?' she asked.

He shrugged. 'OK. I guess it worked, huh?'

'Did it?' Cassy asked him.

'I guess I hurt you, huh? When I came in?'

'Yeah.'

His face flushed to a deeper shade of red. 'Jeez, I'm really sorry.'

Cassy met John's eyes. She smiled. 'It really did work,' she said. 'This is great.'

'Let's do the rest,' John said. 'Bill, you can get your clothes back on and go out to help the others.'

He scowled down at his wet, stained clothes.

'It's all right,' John told him. 'Secondary contact doesn't seem to bother anyone.'

'What do you mean by that?'

'It means the rain actually has to get you,' Cassy explained. 'You can touch someone who's black, or you can touch their clothes, and it doesn't make you weird.'

'That doesn't make any sense,' Bill said.

'Maybe not,' Cassy told him. 'But it's true.'

Bill wrinkled his nose, then crouched and picked up his clothes and moved out of the way.

'OK,' Lynn said. 'Who's next?'

'Her,' Roscoe said. He pulled the woman up by her arms, stepped behind her and began to remove the belts while Lynn and Cassy held her.

Unlike Bill, she looked as if she'd been out in the rain for a long time. Her hair was black, matted down and stringy. Her nightgown was a sodden, clinging rag. The women peeled it up and dropped it to the floor. John saw that the rain had seeped right through it. She was black from head to toe.

Steve gave the chef a hand and they lifted her into

the sink. She sat down in the water, knees up.

John stepped aside to make room for the women. They went to work with dish rags, starting at her head. In seconds, her hair was blonde again. Water streamed down, sluicing through the black, leaving strips of pale skin. They scrubbed her face, her neck, her shoulders. John watched rivulets run down her breasts, drops fall from her nipples. Then Lynn blocked his view and he looked away.

Do the kid next, he thought. Probably a better fighter than the old man.

'That should just about do it,' Lynn said.

'Missed some on her shin,' Roscoe told her.

The woman in the tub began to weep.

The boom of a gunshot made John jump. Lynn's head snapped around. Her eyes were suddenly frantic.

Faint shouts of alarm came from somewhere beyond the kitchen. Screams. Another explosion.

John raced for the kitchen doors.

'No!' Lynn yelled.

'Stay here!' He slammed through a door and burst into the dining room. Men and women rushed by, some hunched low, others glancing back in panic. A few ducked under tables. Dr Goodman hurled a chair through a window. As the glass shattered, he dived out into the rain.

'My God!' It was Steve. Behind him.

'What's happening?' Carol's voice. She must've come out with Steve.

Another blast.

John ran toward the foyer, but stopped abruptly when he saw that the doors stood wide open. Crazies were already in, throwing themselves onto those who'd stayed to fight. In their midst stood a man with a short-barreled shotgun. A gunbelt laden with equipment hung around his waist. On the chest of his drenched shirt, a shield gleamed. A police badge.

As John watched, the cop shoved the muzzle of his shotgun into the belly of a waitress – Peggy – and pulled the trigger. The blast folded her in half and lifted her feet off the floor.

She was still in the air when John whirled around. He glimpsed Steve and Carol dashing for the broken window.

Planning to take their chances with the rain.

Better that, maybe, than staying to be slaughtered in the restaurant.

John rammed through the door into the kitchen. He saw Roscoe running for the alley exit, pulling the naked woman from the tub along behind him.

Lynn and Cassy were still by the tub. They both held knives. They both stared at John with terrified eyes.

'This is it,' he gasped. 'We're being overrun.'

Overrun. Like his firebase.

He'd survived that. He would survive this. The same way. But with Lynn and Cassy. This time, he wouldn't be the only one to make it.

'What'll we do?' Lynn asked.

'Get invisible,' he said.

They looked at him as if he'd lost his mind.

'Strip,' he said. He snatched the clump of black nightgown off the floor and tossed it to Lynn. 'Put it on.'

As she caught the gown, John saw the look in Cassy's eyes. She seemed to understand what he had in mind. And to understand that there was only one black nightgown, and he'd given it to his wife. She looked like a kid who hadn't been picked for a game, and was trying not to show her letdown.

She flinched at the sound of a gunshot. This blast had a hard, flat sound. Not the shotgun. A revolver.

'Get your clothes off,' John told her.

Two more shots.

In the wake of the blasts, John heard screams and shouts and wailing and giggles. Sounds of a madhouse where slaughter was in full swing.

Dropping to his knees, he cut through the belt that bound the teenaged boy's hands together. The kid started to fight him. John slashed his throat. Clamping the knife between his teeth, he tugged off the boy's wet T-shirt. It had been all black a moment ago. Now the black was mixed with red. He threw the shirt to Cassy.

She looked stunned by what he'd done. But she pulled the shirt over her head. It came down halfway to her knees.

Lynn already wore the nightgown.

Both women looked sickly pale where they weren't covered by the garments.

'Come here,' he snapped. 'Quick.'

They rushed up close to him.

John flung blood at their bare legs from the pumping throat of the boy.

'Get plenty on you. Quick!'

Crouching, they cupped blood and spread it over their hair and faces. Lynn washed her shoulders with it. John painted their legs.

Then he got up. 'The freezer!'

'Where?' Lynn asked.

He pointed at the freezer door. 'Hurry,' he gasped. 'Get in there and play dead.'

'What about you?' Lynn blurted.

'I'll be all right. Go!'

The women ran for the freezer, Lynn glancing back, her face dripping crimson, a look in her eyes as if she thought she might never see him again.

John crouched beside the body of the boy he'd killed. When he heard the heavy thud of the shutting door, he clamped the knife between his teeth and lifted the body.

11

They sat on the sofa, Kara watching while Denise and Tom fashioned their weapons.

Tom had broken off the ends of a broom and a mop they'd found by the water heater, leaving each shaft with a jagged point. Kara had fetched a ball of twine from a kitchen drawer. They'd gathered more knives and returned to the living room.

The living room, Denise thought. The heart of the house. Its center.

She supposed this wasn't precisely the center, but it was close enough. From here, they should be able to hear anyone attempting to break in, and get to the trouble spot fast.

She worked quickly, lashing the handle of a long, serrated carving knife to the blunt end of her broom handle.

Tom finished making his spear and offered it to Kara.

'Can't I just use my poker?' she asked. 'I'm pretty good at bonking people.'

Grinning, Tom rubbed the lump on his head. 'Yeah, I noticed.'

'Keep your poker,' Denise told her. 'But I want you to have a knife, too.'

'OK.'

'We'll wipe 'em out with these things,' Tom said.

'Maybe they won't show up,' Denise said. She gripped the bound handle of the knife and put some pressure on it. The twine made quiet creaky sounds. The knife didn't wobble at all. 'Decent,' she muttered.

'Sheena.'

'That's me. God, I hope we don't have to use these things.'

'I wonder if we should split up, kind of stand guard at different parts of the house.'

'We do not want to split up,' Kara said. 'They do

that in all the movies, and it's absolutely silly.'

Denise smiled. 'She's right.'

'I don't know if we should just sit here. We could patrol the house.'

'Together?' Kara asked.

'I think we're better off . . .' A noise of crashing glass stopped Denise's voice. Her heart kicked.

Tom leaped up, staring toward the opening of the hallway. 'A bedroom?'

'Sounded like it.'

'Oh, gosh,' Kara muttered.

'Let's get 'em!' A knife in one hand, his makeshift spear in the other, Tom ran for the hall.

Denise leaned forward with her spear and snatched another knife off the table. She got to her feet and waited for a moment while Kara gathered up her poker and knife. Then she went after Tom. The girl was quick. Denise didn't need to hold back. Kara stayed close behind her as she ran to the foyer, cut to the right and raced up the hall.

She caught up with Tom when he stopped in the doorway of the master bedroom. He elbowed a switch. Light filled the room. Peering past him, Denise saw no broken window. She stepped aside. Tom rushed past her, and she followed him to Kara's bedroom.

Again, he flicked on a light. This time, he didn't stop in the doorway. He dashed across the room. Running in after him, Denise checked the windows but her view of the one on the left was blocked by Tom's body.

'Careful,' she gasped. Lurching sideways, she caught sight of the window. A hole near the bottom. As big as a head. Splintered edges.

Nobody was reaching in.

She saw only darkness through the break.

Tom stopped a yard from the window to avoid stepping on glass with his stocking feet. He crouched toward it and gazed out.

'See anything?'

'Huh-uh.'

Denise scanned the pale blue carpet. It was littered with shards and bits of glass. She saw nothing that might've been hurled through the window.

'The screen's still on,' Tom said.

'Maybe it was a trick,' Kara said.

'What do you mean?' Denise asked.

The girl frowned. 'You know. A division?'

Tom whirled around. 'A di*ver*sion!'

Denise felt her stomach drop. 'Oh my God,' she muttered.

12

John dropped the dead boy to the floor beside the freezer door. Lying down, he pulled the body on top of him. He grimaced as its cheek pressed the side of his face.

It was worse last time, he told himself. Last time, he'd buried himself under three bodies. One was Lieutenant Becker, and Becker's belly had been split open and his guts were all over John. He'd been underneath the corpses so long that, by the time he finally struggled free, Becker's intestines had dried against his fatigues. They'd come with him when he got up. He'd had to peel them off.

Hours under those corpses.

This won't be as bad, he told himself.

He wondered how long Lynn and Cassy could last inside the freezer.

They shouldn't have shut themselves in, he realized. With the door shut, the cold would build up too fast. And he wasn't sure whether the door could be opened from the inside. If something happened to him, they might be trapped.

He listened. Screams and laughter and shouts still came from the other areas of the restaurant. But he didn't think anyone had entered the kitchen. Not yet.

He shoved the body off, got to his feet, took a quick look around, then tugged open the freezer door.

Among the bodies of the journalists and two men who'd been killed by them, Lynn and Cassy lay sprawled on their backs. They should pass for crazies, all right, in their soiled wet nightgown and T-shirt. But one glance convinced him that they wouldn't pass for dead. The blood in their hair, on their faces and arms and legs made them look damn gory, but hardly concealed that they lay there stiff and shivering.

He whirled around to make sure once again that no one had entered the kitchen.

'Come out of there,' he said. 'It won't work. Hurry.'

Lynn pushed herself up on her elbows. 'What's the matter?'

'Don't ask questions,' Cassy said, saving John the trouble.

Both women got to their feet. Hunched over, they rushed to the front. Lynn's teeth were gritted and she was rubbing her arms. Cassy hugged her chest for warmth. Then they were out and John threw the door shut.

'What'll we do now?' Lynn gasped.

'Stick with me.'

They followed John as he hurried to the old man who'd tried to bash him with a golf club. The guy was still bound with belts and sitting near the tub with his back against a counter. He wore a sport jacket over his knit shirt. Some of the jacket's plaid still showed, but it was mostly stained black by the rain.

John kicked him in the head. The man fell onto his side, dazed but conscious. John slashed the belt that bound his arms behind him. He tore off the jacket and struggled into it.

'Get your knives,' he said.

Lynn and Cassy searched around and found the knives where they'd dropped them before getting into the wet garments.

'Now what?' Lynn asked.

'We go out there. We act like the crazies.'

'You're kidding,' Lynn said.

'Let's go.'

As he rushed for the kitchen doors, he heard Cassy behind him say, 'Here goes nothing.'

13

Denise let Tom take the lead. She ran close behind him, Kara at her side.

They'll be in by the time we get there, she thought.

Probably smashed the window and headed for the other side of the house while we were on our way to check it out. We got into Kara's room and couldn't even hear them breaking in for real.

She raced out of the hallway. Had enough time for one quick look at the living room – long enough to see that nobody was there – and then the house went dark.

'Uh-oh,' Kara murmured.

'Hold up,' Denise gasped at Tom. She skidded to a halt near the front door. Kara brushed against her arm.

The thud of Tom's footfalls stopped. Denise saw his faint shape moving toward her. She heard him panting for breath.

'They're at the fuse box,' she whispered.

'Someone is. Or was.'

'Maybe the juice went off,' Kara suggested.

'Hang on.' Denise stepped in the direction of the door. Holding her spear upright, she reached out until she touched the wood. Then she moved sideways, running her hand over the door, its frame, the wall. Draperies brushed her knuckles. She clamped the shaft between her legs, fingered the draperies, found their drawcord and pulled.

The drapes slid open. A hazy, gray glow came in from the window. She glanced out. Through the falling rain, she saw a streetlight casting dim silver onto the top of Tom's car. Across the street, a porch light burned.

'It's not the power,' she whispered. 'They're in the house.'

'Get away from the window,' Tom said.

She wrapped her hand around the shaft of her spear and stepped backward. Turning to face the living room, she gazed into the shadows. The light from the window helped. She could make out the dim shapes of the sofa, the lamps, the television.

The entrance from the dining room was as black as the mouth of a cave.

'We oughta be able to see them coming,' Tom whispered.

His face was a faint oval blur. His gray sweatsuit was slightly less visible than his face. Though Denise couldn't see him clearly, he didn't blend in with the darkness around him. Neither did Kara in her pink nightgown. She looked down at herself. Her warmup suit was royal blue, but it appeared to be black. Her hands were dusky gray. Her white socks almost seemed to glow.

'They'll see us, too,' she said.

Tom squatted down. Denise and Kara did the same.

'Where the hell are they?' he muttered.

'They're being sneaky. They think we've got guns, remember?'

'I sure wish we did,' Kara whispered. 'Wouldn't it be neat if you could wish for something and make it come . . . ?'

'Shhhhh,' Denise warned her.

From off in the distance beyond the living room came the sound of a thud. Someone muttered, 'Shit!'

'Stay with Kara,' Denise muttered.

'What're you . . . ?'

'Shhhh.' She lowered her spear to the floor, shifted the knife to her right hand, and crawled toward the living room.

I'm out of my gourd, she thought. She struggled to stop breathing so loudly. Her heart wanted to pound the air from her lungs. She felt as if she might wet her pants. But she kept moving.

Away from the front door. Away from Tom and Kara. Closer to the three unseen intruders who'd come here to kill them all.

She sank to her belly and squirmed forward. She passed an end table. Made her way into the narrow gap between the coffee table and the front of the sofa. Through it and past the other end table. Across an area of open floor to the front of an easy chair close to the wall. The wall that stood between her and the dining room.

She got to her hands and knees. The chair blocked her view of the dining room entrance, but she could see the area through which the boys would have to pass when they went for Tom and Kara.

She waited. She held her breath until her lungs burned and she feared her head might explode. Then she let her air out slowly and inhaled. Sweat stung her eyes. The handle of her knife felt oily.

Come on, she thought. Let's get it over with.

She wondered if this was the dumbest thing she'd ever done. Probably was.

Putting herself out here alone.

Seemed like a good idea at the time.

It *is* a good idea. I can't let those bastards get Kara. Or Tom, for that matter.

Off beyond the chair, something moved. A low, bulky shape that was darker than the darkness. Like a black animal creeping forward.

One of the guys. Crawling.

Denise stared at his head. She couldn't make out who he was. Probably Buddy. He was the worst of the three (if it's them at all), and he would be in the lead.

She suddenly feared that he might sense he was being stared at. She tried to force herself to look away, but her eyes refused to leave him. So far, he seemed to be watching the area in front.

At last, his head disappeared behind the sofa.

Denise saw another crawling shape behind him. This one had a faint sheen on its back. Whatever light there was seemed to be gleaming off its wet, black skin.

This is them, all right, she thought. One of the three had been shirtless when she'd watched through the window and seen them ride away.

Keep moving, she willed him. Don't look over this way. Just keep your eyes on Buddy.

The third crawled into view.

Denise held her breath. She waited. The feet of the second intruder vanished behind the sofa. Number three was out in the open. Then the sofa blocked her view of his head.

Do it!

She leaped up, took four quick strides across the carpet, saw the kid look back over his shoulder. 'Shit!' he cried out. She rammed the knife down. It sank into his back. 'No!' he squealed. 'Guys!'

She jerked out the knife and stabbed him again. This time, it struck something hard. The kid, shrieking, flopped flat. Denise tugged at the knife. It didn't come out. Her hand slipped off it. The blade must've gone into bone.

The other two guys were scurrying up, coming for her.

'Tom!' she yelled.

'Gotcha gotcha gotcha,' gasped the kid duck-walking toward her.

She leaped sideways, twisting in the air as she dived over the back of the sofa. Something stabbed her hip, tore skin and ripped the side of her pants. She landed on the cushions, face up.

Her knees caught the kid dropping onto her. His breath gusted out. She shoved at his bare chest, felt his weight shift, and saw him tumble away. He crashed against the edge of the coffee table and fell to the floor.

Denise flipped herself over. On hands and knees, she scuttled along the sofa. From the other side came thuds and grunts. Tom must've come to help her. Reaching out, she grabbed the table lamp. She hooked her other hand over the sofa back and pulled herself up.

Tom was there about to drive the knife end of his spear into the chest of the kid at his feet. But Kara, a running blur in her pale nightgown, came up behind him swinging her poker.

'No!' Denise blurted.

The brass handle crashed against the side of Tom's head. He dropped his spear and stumbled away, reeling.

'Kara!'

The girl chased after him and hit him again. He went down on one knee, covering his head.

'*What're you doing!*'

The sofa shook with a sudden jolt. A hand grabbed Denise's ankle.

'Gotcha!'

She swung the lamp off the table and twisted around. A dark arm darted up. She glimpsed a rod of some kind in the hand. Yelped as spikes jabbed deep into her right buttock. Then the base of the lamp clubbed the guy's face. His head was knocked back.

He released her ankle. The spikes were yanked from her rump.

She climbed onto the sofa's back. Straddling it, she saw Buddy down on the floor. Tom, over by the wall, was on his knees, both arms over his head to protect it as Kara struck downward again with her poker. It whapped his arms and he cried out.

'Kara! Stop it!'

Buddy sat up. Denise threw herself off the sofa. She dropped both knees onto him, smashing him flat. His arm hooked around her back. He rolled, hurling her to the floor beside him. 'What're ya . . . tryin' to do to me?' he gasped.

Not Buddy's voice.

'Tom?' She ran her hands over his chest. Felt a sweat-shirt. A dry sweatshirt. 'Oh God.'

That was Buddy who'd had the spear? And Tom on the floor about to be stabbed when Kara came along? Didn't seem right. But this was Tom on the floor beside her.

Denise rolled away from him as Kara yelped. Looked up. Saw Kara spin away. Her hands looked empty. Buddy – the real Buddy – had the poker. He swung it at her. Denise heard the rod hiss through the air. It missed the girl. Buddy staggered, fell to his knees.

Then hands dug into Denise's armpits and pulled her up.

'Your room, Kara!' Tom shouted. 'Run to your room.'

The girl glanced back, then ran for the front of the house.

Denise got her feet under her, stumbled as Tom thrust her forward. 'Go!' he snapped.

'We can finish 'em!'

'Go!'

She raced after Kara and heard Tom close behind her. Her buttock felt as if it were burning inside. Her pants were wet and clinging around the wound. Warm blood spilled down the back of her leg. Each time her right foot hit the floor, pain bolted through her body.

Shouldn't be running away, she thought. We almost had them.

With what?

Did we *all* lose our weapons?

Like some kind of a damn nasty joke. We go in armed to the teeth and now we've got nothing.

I got one of the bastards, she reminded herself. That's something, anyway.

Ahead of her, Kara lunged to the left and vanished into the doorway of her bedroom. Denise rushed in. She felt a shove. As she staggered forward, the door slammed.

'Gotta block it shut,' Tom gasped. 'I'll hold it. You two, get something over here. A dresser or something.'

14

Maureen was beginning to give up hope of ever finding them. Maybe the guys hadn't stopped, at all. Maybe they'd just kept on riding and were miles away by now.

I'll get them, she told herself. I'll get them if it takes forever.

But maybe this searching was pointless. She wondered if she should return to Buddy's house. Wait for them there. Sooner or later, they would probably show up.

She saw the motorcycles.

Three Harleys standing in the driveway of a corner house. But no Buddy. No Doug or Lou.

She knew they'd gone into the house.

Grinning, she swung her Jeep onto the driveway and stepped on the gas.

This'll bring 'em running!

Three hogs, all in a row. She hit the first bike, smashing it into the second before her front tires bumped over it and she rammed the second bike into the third. The third stayed up somehow – maybe locked to the front of her Jeep – and it skidded along sideways with shrieking rubber until she crashed it through the garage door.

It came loose when she backed up. She bounced her way over the other bikes, metal groaning and crunching, glass bursting. Then she was on smooth pavement again.

Maureen grinned at the debris.

She couldn't even see the third bike. It was somewhere in the darkness under the remains of the garage door.

She beeped her horn.

'Come on out, guys. See what happened to your hogs.'

She scanned the front of the one-story house. The porch light was off, but the draperies behind the picture window glowed. The draperies didn't stir. The front door didn't open.

Maureen honked again. This time, she kept the horn blaring for a long time.

Nobody came from the house.

'They deaf or something?' she muttered.

She shut off the engine, took the key from the ignition, and climbed out. The rain poured down on her. It felt even better, more exciting, than she remembered. She stopped at the rear of the Jeep, threw back her head and arched her spine, savoring the touch of the water as it splashed her face and soaked through the front of her T-shirt. One hand held the keys, but the other was free to peel the shirt up above her breasts. The raindrops made her bare skin tingle. They tapped against her breasts, teased her nipples, slid down her body like the tips of tongues. Trembling, she pulled the elastic band of the shorts away from her waist and let the hot little streams run down to her groin and thighs.

Take off your clothes and lie down on the grass, she thought. Forget about Buddy and his friends. Let the rain . . .

Buddy and his friends.

Maureen let the elastic snap back against her belly. She bent over the tailgate, very aware of how the rain now fingered her back, soaked through the seat of her shorts and streamed down her legs, but struggling not to let the exciting feel of it overwhelm her.

I'm gonna get those suckers, she told herself. I'm gonna roll in their blood and that'll be even better than the rain.

She held her right hand to steady it, and pushed the key into the lock. She twisted the key. She opened the tailgate. She leaned into the darkness, savoring the way her sodden shorts pulled taut against her buttocks but regretting the loss of the rain on her head and back. Soon, she found the jack. She dropped the keys, wrapped her hand around the steel bar of the tire tool, and pulled it out.

Turning away, she swung the bar through the air.

'Break their heads apart,' she muttered.

She rushed toward the house. The grass was thick and slippery. She wanted to dive onto it and roll over. But she kept running.

She pressed her way through shrubbery at the front of the big window. Leaves rubbed against her. Limbs poked and scraped her.

Then she was at the window.

She drew the tire iron back and hammered it through the glass.

15

'I think this is it,' Trev said.

'Well, is it or isn't it?' Sandy asked.

He'd checked the street sign at the corner. This was Fairmont, all right. Crouching, he looked more closely at the house number painted on the curb. 4538. Back at O'Casey's, he had memorized Chidi's address. He was pretty sure it was 4538 Fairmont.

But was that right?

He'd had to struggle so hard to remember the address. As if the rain had submerged it, hidden it at the bottom of a deep and murky pool, forcing him to go down through the dark heat and search.

'I'm pretty sure,' he said.

'Well,' Sandy said, 'I reckon we'll know soon enough.' She waved his revolver, gesturing him toward the house. 'Come on along, Rhonda,' she said to the girl from the trunk.

Trev stepped over the curb, crossed the strip of grass and then the sidewalk. Looking back, he saw Sandy and Rhonda a few strides behind him. Sandy had her left hand on the girl's good shoulder. As if Rhonda were her kid sister, or something.

Weird how she'd started acting.

She'd been like an animal in heat before the shoot-out. Then, all at once, she was different. She got serious. Trev didn't understand. Mostly, it pissed him off. But part of him, far down under the churning new desires, was glad she'd taken command. Down there was the memory of a mission – to stop the rain and somehow save Maureen. He knew the mission was important. He knew that he cared about it. But he also knew that too much was in the way. Hungers to rip flesh, taste blood, tear into throats and breasts and guts.

Sandy's and Rhonda's, for starters. Then, anyone else he could find.

But Sandy, gun in hand, kept all that from happening. And got him here to the Chidi house.

Under his dark heat and anger stirred a lost man who was grateful.

Walking backward over the lawn, he watched how Sandy's skin gleamed black in the light from the porch. He was pretty sure he'd fired four rounds at the man with the rifle. Before that, one into Francine. Which left only one in the revolver. Maybe Sandy would use it on the Chidis. Then he could get her.

He tripped and dropped down hard on the concrete stoop.

Sandy came closer, one hand still on Rhonda's shoulder. 'Get up,' she said.

Trev stood, climbed the two steps, and moved to the front door. There was no screen door, just a panel of dark wood with a handle and peephole.

'Want me to ring the bell?' he asked.

'Don't be a jerk, Trevor. See if it's locked.'

He tried the handle, then shook his head.

'Didn't reckon they'd make it easy for us,' Sandy said. 'OK, go on and kick it in.'

'They might be waiting and kill us,' Rhonda said.

Trev was surprised to hear her speak, though he knew she'd been talking with Sandy along the way.

'I'll go in first, honey. Trevor, get on with it.'

'You'd better hang onto me,' he said. 'The stoop's slippery. I'll end up on my ass.'

Sandy studied his eyes for a moment, then nodded. She pressed herself against his back and wrapped her left arm across his chest. Her right hand shoved the gun muzzle against his ribs.

Do it so we both fall, he thought.

Hell, it would probably happen anyway. Kicking open doors wasn't as easy as it looked on TV. His foot was likely to bounce right back at him and knock them both flat.

Of course, Sandy might pull the trigger.

But maybe she wouldn't. With a little luck, he could get the gun away from her once they hit the concrete.

'What're you waiting for?'

'Be careful with that gun,' he said. Then he raised his right leg, drew his knee in toward his chest, and drove his foot at the door. The heel of his shoe struck beside the handle.

Pain didn't streak up his leg. The door didn't throw his foot back at him.

Instead, he felt an instant of hard resistance and the door burst open and slammed the wall behind it.

He was still off balance when Sandy hurled him forward. He tripped on the threshold, staggered across some carpet, and fell to his hands and knees. Sandy rushed past him. She was crouched low, head turned away, sweeping the revolver from side to side.

Trev crawled toward her. She swung around and jabbed the muzzle against his forehead. 'Mind your manners, pal,' she said. Taking a step backward, she straightened up and looked toward the doorway. 'Come on in, Rhonda. Nothing in here's gonna hurt you.'

The girl stepped inside and shut the door. She gazed into the living room. 'Are they dead?' she asked.

Perplexed, Trev got to his feet. He looked past Sandy. A teenaged girl lay sprawled on the sofa. One arm hung toward the floor. Trev saw no blood on her tan corduroys or white blouse. She looked as if she might be asleep. But if she'd been sleeping, the clamor of their break-in should've shocked her wide awake.

An adult male was slumped in a reclining chair in a corner of the room. He wore gold-rimmed glasses, a pale blue sport shirt, dark slacks and black socks. A book lay open on his chest as if he'd dropped asleep while reading.

Nobody else was in the room.

'I reckon we got the right house,' Sandy said, her voice low.

'Yeah,' Trev said.

He'd never seen any of the Chidi family except Maxwell, the boy dead and charred, bound to the goalpost. But these two were probably his sister and father. It wasn't likely that Trev had gotten the address wrong. And there were only a few black families in town.

Not really black, he thought as he stared at the girl. *We're* black.

Her hair was black, all right, but her skin was a deep, rich brown.

Sandy went to the sofa and bent over the girl. In the bright lamplight, she didn't look nearly as good as before. Her wet skin gleamed, but it was streaky and Trev liked the soft brown of the girl's skin better than the dirty black of Sandy's.

'This gal's breathing,' Sandy said.

Trev moved closer. Sandy, keeping an eye on him, stepped over to the man.

He watched the girl's chest rise slowly and sink. He could see her white bra through the blouse, pale against her dark skin. He glanced over at Sandy. She was bending over the man.

'They musta been drugged or something,' she said.

He ripped the girl's blouse open and heard the sudden click-clack of a cocking gun.

'Just leave her be.' Sandy had the revolver pointed at his face.

'Hey, come on,' he said. 'Let me have her. You take him.'

'That's just the rain talking.'

'So what? You're wet, too. What's the matter with you?'

'I got it reined in, buster.' A half smile tipped a corner of her mouth. 'You'd best rein it in, same as me. We gotta find gramps and put a stop to all this. Now I can do it by myself, or you can help me.' She straightened her arm, closed her left eye, and seemed to be sighting in on him down the entire length of her arm.

'I'm on your side,' Trev said.

With her thumb, she eased the hammer down. She lowered her arm. 'Let's have a look around,' she said, and nodded toward the dining room.

Trev went first. He glanced back at the girl on the sofa.

Get back to you, he thought.

Just need to wait for Sandy to use that last bullet.

Nobody in the dining room.

He headed for the kitchen, and suddenly grinned. There was *no need* to wait for Sandy to use the last bullet. The fool had cocked the revolver and let the hammer down on its only live round. She'd have to go through five spent shells before the cylinder would bring the good cartridge back into firing position.

I've got her!

I've got them all!

Should be a knife in the kitchen, he thought. A good sharp knife would come in handy.

He entered the kitchen. The faucet was running. On the floor in front of the sink was a shattered plate. A woman sat at the table, arms folded beneath her face.

The mother, Trev thought.

She wore white jeans and a green blouse. The hair draping her face was glossy brown with red highlights. The look of it stirred something deep inside Trev.

Can't be her natural color, he thought.

Might be.

He frowned at the thick auburn tresses.

Hair just like Maureen's, he realized.

'I spect gramps must've doped their food,' Sandy said.

Hair just like Maureen's.

Maureen.

Trev tried to focus his mind on her. He remembered her smile and the soft, amused challenge in her eyes.

Hold onto it.

He stepped to the counter and drew a long knife from its wooden holder.

'Drop it, Trev.'

He turned to Sandy. She aimed the useless revolver at his chest. 'Pull back the hammer and let it go five times,' he said. 'That'll put a live round into position.'

One of her eyes narrowed, its lid twitching slightly.

'Try to save it for grandpa,' he said.

16

With Lynn and Cassy close beside him, John ran into the midst of the carnage. It was worse than he'd imagined. The air was dense with screams and shouts and growls, rippling with horrible giggles. It stank of excrement and urine. Everywhere he looked, people were being slashed and hacked and bludgeoned. The dead were being killed again. Clothes had been torn from bloody victims. He saw people being eaten, raped, sodomized. One man had his head completely buried inside the split torso of another like a dog searching for a hidden treat: even as he delved, a drenched woman chopped an axe into his spine and let out a wild laugh.

Shouldn't have come out here, John thought.

No, this is best. This is how we blend in.

He nudged Lynn toward a waitress scurrying nearby. The woman still wore the bodice of her costume, but her skirt was gone. The handle of a knife protruded from her shoulder blade. 'Get her,' John yelled. Lynn caught on and hurled herself onto the woman's back. Cassy, with a quick nod to John, leaped onto the two.

None of the real crazies joined in.

They were all too busy.

John scanned the crowd quickly, seeking a restaurant patron to attack.

He saw the cop.

Reloading.

The man was several strides away, standing motionless in the swamp of gore and thrashing bodies, his head down as he stuffed cartridges into the cylinder of his revolver.

John didn't want to go for him. He wanted to *blend in*, damn it, join in the fighting and be *invisible*.

I'm not a damn hero, he thought.

He just wanted to survive and make sure Lynn survived so they could get home to Kara.

He didn't want to go for the cop even as he leaped over someone squirming atop a body, elbowed a man aside, and saw the cop snap the loaded cylinder into place. He knocked the gun aside with one hand and smashed the heel of his other hand up against the underside of the cop's nose. The nose crunched, went soft and flat as John's blow drove its ridge bone up into the brain. The head flew back. The cop staggered away, stiff and twitching, and dropped to the floor.

Took him out of the picture, John thought.

That was all he'd intended – to stop the man from running amok with a loaded gun.

He suddenly felt like an idiot.

He could use the gun.

He saw a hand reaching for it. The bloody hand of a man on his knees, whose sweater was wet and black. John stomped down, popping the man's elbow. He ducked and snatched up the revolver, shot the man in the head, then looked at the cop.

He glimpsed a plastic name plate on the chest of the uniform. HANSON.

Hanson hadn't snapped his cartridge case after reloading. A dozen rounds had fallen out when he hit the floor. John dropped to his knees, scooped up a handful, and dropped the ammunition into his shirt pocket as he got to his feet.

He spotted Lynn and Cassy, still on top of the waitress. Cassy had tugged the knife out of the woman's shoulder. She held it in her teeth while she pinned the waitress down and Lynn pretended to chew on the nape of the gal's neck.

It's working, John thought.

They looked like the real article, and nobody was bothering them. Not yet.

John made his way toward them. Just get to them, he thought. Stay there, shoot anyone who tries to take them. But even with the extra bullets in his pocket, he knew he didn't have enough ammo to kill *all* the crazies.

He glimpsed someone rushing at him from the side. He whirled. A man with a steak knife. Black face grinning.

He swung the revolver up.

Steve Winter?

'No!' he yelled.

As the knife flashed down at his chest, John side-stepped and chopped Steve's wrist. The knife flipped away. He slammed the gun barrel against Steve's head. The man started to drop. John grabbed the front of his shirt and hurled him sideways, watched as he toppled over the back of a woman hunched over bloody remains, watched him roll and come to a stop near Lynn's feet.

Where's Carol?

John spotted Steve's wife near the open doors. She was on her knees, biting the face of a screaming man while a guy with a pocket knife split open the man's leg from hip to knee.

John rushed to get her. Somebody grabbed his ankle. He pulled free, leaped over a couple of struggling women, and saw the gal with the axe prance in from the right. She had the axe overhead. Maybe she wasn't going for Carol. John decided he didn't care who she was going for.

He aimed and fired.

She wore a sleeveless gown. The slug punched through her skin just under the armpit. Its impact nudged her sideways. She jogged along, knees pumping up the front of her dress, axe still raised. She angled toward the doors like a sleepwalker in a big hurry. The doorjamb at the far side stopped her. She struck it with her face, bounced off and fell back.

Rushing forward, John grabbed Carol's wet hair. He yanked, jerking her head up.

The man with the pocket knife glared up at him.

Dr Goodman.

'She's with me,' Goodman said, as if this was some kind of a damn prom and John was trying to put moves on his date.

The same knife he'd used to cut the laces of Cassy's bodice was now deep in the thigh of the man who was gasping and writhing on the floor.

Goodman tore the knife out and waved it at John. 'She stays with me!'

'No she doesn't,' John said, and shot him in the forehead.

He looked around quickly. Nobody rushing them. He jammed the revolver into a rear pocket of his slacks, chopped the edge of his hand against Carol's neck hard enough to black her out but not kill her, then hoisted her onto his shoulder and carried her toward the corner of the foyer – toward Lynn and Cassy and the waitress and Steve – where he would make his stand.

17

After searching the rambling house, Maureen returned to the living room. She saw bright red footprints on the gray carpet.

Someone had followed her into the house!

A chill spread goosebumps over her skin. She turned, watching the bloody tracks wind their way through the room toward the kitchen.

One set of tracks. One intruder.

She clamped the tire iron between her knees, rubbed her sweaty right hand on the side of her sodden shorts, then gripped the bar again.

She gazed at the tracks.

Whoever made them had been damn sneaky. She hadn't heard a sound while searching the house. She hadn't *felt* the presence of anyone.

From the feel of the house when she first came in through the window, she'd been sure it was deserted. Somehow, she'd known that nobody was here. But the Harleys had been left out front, so she'd gone ahead and searched and found nobody.

But damn it, *someone* had come in after her.

Someone awfully stealthy.

Stalking her.

That can work both ways, Maureen thought. She started to follow the bloody footprints. Her heart raced. Her stomach felt fluttery. Her skin crawled as if a basketful of spiders had been dumped on her head. With her left hand, she reached up to where her

T-shirt was still bunched above her breasts. She tugged it down.

What if he's creeping up behind me!

She whirled around.

Saw *two* sets of red footprints coming toward her across the carpet.

The second set ended at her own bare feet.

She stared at them.

She sighed.

'A Woozle,' she muttered.

Winnie and Piglet go hunting and almost catch a Woozle.

She remembered that long ago she'd been a writer of children's books. Long ago, this morning.

'And now I'm reduced to Woozle hunting,' she said.

She laughed softly. Then she sat down on the carpet and crossed her legs and gazed at her lacerated feet and wept.

18

The dresser rammed Denise's back.

It's like being in the bathroom again, she thought. Trying to keep Tom out.

But now Tom was beside her, helping to hold the door shut.

The dresser wasn't much of a barricade. Too light-weight. The first smash of the door would've toppled it over if they hadn't been bracing it up. Had it been any heavier, though, she and Kara might not have been able to push it to the door in time.

She was glad they'd done it. At least the dresser put a little distance between her back and the door – and the two crazy bastards on the other side.

They hit it again. Hard. The dresser's top edge jammed against Denise's back, shoving her forward, bending her knees. A drawer slid out. It pounded her rump, hitting her wound and sending a throb of pain down her right leg. She thrust her heels into the carpet. Wincing, she drove the dresser backward.

The door slammed.

Her right leg started to jiggle. She grabbed her thigh and tried to hold it still.

'We can't keep this up,' she whispered.

'We have to,' Tom said.

'Look what I found,' Kara said. A tube of frosty light suddenly appeared in front of the girl. She waved it. The tube carved a twirl of brightness through the air. 'My *Star Wars* light sword,' she explained.

Some weapon, Denise thought. It looked like a cylinder of translucent plastic attached to a flashlight. But she was glad Kara had found it. Better than being in the dark.

'I wish it was a real laser sword like Luke Sky-walker . . .'

'See what else you can find,' Tom gasped.

As Kara vanished into the closet with her light, the

door bashed the dresser forward. Denise winced and shoved herself back. Her right leg gave out. The door banged shut, and she dropped. The open drawer caught her rump. Wood splintered. The drawer broke away and she found herself sitting on a soft cushion of clothes. She flipped over, got to her knees, scurried forward and pushed her shoulder against the dresser just as the boys hit the door again.

The blow shook Denise, but she stayed on her knees. The dresser tipped for a moment before she and Tom could force it back.

'Buddy!' Tom suddenly called.

'Yeah?'

'Let's talk.'

'Nothing to talk about, dickhead.'

'Who do you really want?'

'Huh?'

'Can we make a deal?'

'Like what?'

'I can make it easy for you. I'll let you have the girls, but you've gotta promise to leave me alone.'

He's conning them, Denise told herself. Stalling for time.

Isn't he?

God, what if he means it?

'Yeah, sure, okay,' Buddy said.

'How do I know you won't try to nail me if I let you in?'

'You got my word, man.'

'Cross your heart and hope to die?'

'Yeah, fuck. Cross my heart.'

'And hope to die?'

'Yeah yeah yeah. Cut the stupid games and open up.'

'OK. Just a second.' He put a hand on Denise's head. She winced. He gently stroked her hair and whispered, 'Get ready for another hit.'

Denise turned her head as Kara came up behind her. In the glow of the sword, she saw that the girl held a small leather bag and a thick, foot-long pink pencil in her left hand. Clamped against her side was a metal baton.

'Your second's up, asshole,' Buddy said.

'Just hang on.'

Kara handed the pencil to Tom. She gave the baton to Denise. It had rubber bulbs at each end.

'He's just shitting us.' Someone else's voice. Lou?

They hit the door. The dresser rocked. Denise shoved her shoulder against it. Kara threw herself at it. Tom grunted as he pushed. The dresser dropped back and the door crashed shut.

Denise twisted the rubber bulb off one end of the baton. It popped off with a hollow, ringing sound.

'Let 'em in and try to take 'em?' she whispered.

'Jesus, I don't know.'

'I think the smart thing to do,' Kara said, 'is to go out the window.'

'We'd get wet,' Tom muttered.

'Better wet than dead,' Denise muttered.

'Maybe.'

Kara helped at the dresser as the boys struck the door again. Then she ran to her bed. She tore the top cover off, rushed past the end of the bed and threw the blanket on the floor beneath the window.

So our feet won't get cut, Denise realized.

Kara dropped her light saber onto the blanket. She stepped to the broken window, unlocked it, and shoved up the lower sash. Some glass fell off, clattering when it hit the sill.

Denise got to her feet. She dropped back against the dresser. Her right leg felt rubbery, its muscles still trembling but no longer twitching out of control.

She hoped the leg would carry her to the window.

The door jumped, slamming the dresser against her back. She dug her heels into the carpet. This time, the door didn't rebound and crash shut. Buddy and Lou were giving it all they had. She heard them grunting with effort. She felt the dresser start to scoot on the carpet.

Twisting her head around, she saw the dim shapes of fingers clenching the edge of the door. She shoved herself upward, the dresser's rim digging into her back. Then she was high enough to get her right elbow over the top. With a flick of her wrist, she whacked her baton against the fingers.

Somebody yelped. The hand jerked out of sight and the door slammed shut.

'Go!' Tom whispered.

Denise raced across the room. Ahead of her, Kara was shoving at the window screen.

19

Trev led the way through the Chidi house, Sandy and Rhonda close behind him. In the hallway, he glanced into the dark rooms until he came to a closed door.

He pressed his ear against it and heard soft mumbling sounds.

He looked over his shoulder. He nodded.

'Let's take him,' Sandy whispered.

With his left hand, Trev turned the knob and gently swung the door inward. Smoke, fanned by the opening door, rolled and swayed away in front of him. He smelled a terrible stench. He held his breath and tried not to gag.

He'd encountered the same odor last night. At the stadium. It had come from Maxwell Chidi. The reek of burnt hair and flesh. But Maxwell's stink had been mild compared to this.

What's the old bastard doing in here?

Trev could still hear the low, incoherent mumbling. It came from somewhere ahead and to his right. Through the swirling smoke, he saw the tongues of candle flames. Dozens of them. All around the room. In the direction of the voice, he saw a blur of slow movement. And a blaze too large for a candle.

He stepped silently toward it. He jerked to a halt as something brushed his arm. Turning his head, he saw Sandy beside him. She was squinting in the direction of the voice. Her eyes were red from the smoke, tears cutting pale streaks down her black face. Her left hand was clasped against her mouth, pinching her nostrils shut.

Trev blinked tears from his own stinging eyes. He looked again toward the side of the room. Though he tried to hold his breath, what he saw made him gasp.

Much of the smoke had cleared away. Probably poured out through the doorway. A murky, orange haze remained. Thin enough to let him see too much.

He gagged once, but the white-haired man didn't seem to notice. Maybe in a trance, Trev thought as he willed his throat to relax. Sandy suddenly hunched over and vomited. Still, the man paid no attention.

Trev wondered where Rhonda was. Maybe she'd stayed in the hall. Lucky her.

Grandpa was crouched, facing the wall. He was naked. His brown skin gleamed like polished wood. As he chanted softly, he ripped pages from a book that lay open on the floor. He rolled the pages into a tube, held them over a candle until they ignited, then raised his blazing torch to the charred and runny flesh of the corpse on the wall.

A female. Rather small, but not a child. Old enough to have breasts. She was nailed upside-down to the wall, her arms and legs stretched out wide. Trev could see no skin on her that hadn't been burnt. Her hair was gone.

On the floor beneath her head and shoulders was a plastic tub brimming with black fluid. Bits of gray ash floated on its surface. So did small, white globs of congealed grease.

As Trev watched, disgusted and amazed, the old

man filled his mouth with something from a golden urn in his left hand. He raised the blazing roll of pages to his lips, then spewed a fine spray through the fire. A gust of burning fluid swept across the girl's crusty black midsection, spread out and streamed down. Flaming rivulets slid over her breasts and between them, down her neck and face. Trev heard sizzling, crackling sounds, saw streamers of smoke rise from the fiery streams. When they ran off her shoulders and head, their fires died. Black drops fell like rain and splashed into the tub.

Grandpa, still mumbling, crumpled the remnants of the burning pages and snuffed them in his hand. He let the ashes drift to the floor, then reached down to the book. He flipped through several pages. Trev glimpsed a color plate of Jesus surrounded by lambs.

A *Bible*.

The old man ripped the pages from their binding. He started twisting them to form another torch.

Trev turned to Sandy. She was still doubled over. Her hands were on her knees. Trev dropped his knife, reached through strings of hanging mucus and took the revolver from her right hand. She made no effort to keep it.

He walked slowly toward the squatting man, who had already lit the *Bible* pages and filled his mouth from the urn. As fire sprayed at the girl, Trev pressed the muzzle against the base of the old man's skull and pulled the trigger.

For just an instant, he wondered if Sandy had turned the cylinder to the correct position.

She had.

The blast jerked the gun in his hand. The old man's head lurched as if it had been clubbed. Still squatting, he pitched forward. The top of his head smashed against the upside-down face of the girl. His knees hit the floor. He slid down, the wound above his neck pumping blood, his head rubbing the girl's face. The charred mess came apart like a shattered jigsaw puzzle, sliding down over bloody bone, bits of it clinging to his white hair.

His head splashed into the tub.

It went under.

The girl had lost her lips. She seemed to be grinning at the old man's fate.

20

Lou rubbed his shoulder.

'Come on, man,' Buddy muttered.

'It hurts.'

'Now!'

Together, they rammed against the door. This time, it wasn't shoved back at them. Something on the other side scooted away, then crashed to the floor. Buddy squeezed between the edge of the door and the jamb. Lou followed.

Saw Buddy hurl his spear. Its dim, fleeing target

dived through the window, and the spear stuck in the wall just beneath the sill.

Lou scanned the dark room. Nothing moved. Had they all managed to get out?

He caught up with Buddy. Side by side, they raced for the window. He whipped the barbecue fork from side to side, relishing his memory of stabbing its tines into Denise's firm rump, aching to sink it into her breasts.

Outside the window, a girl sprang up. Her arm shot over the sill. She flung something from a small bag, then dropped out of sight.

Buddy gasped, 'Fuck!' One of his legs flew sideways. He tumbled, crossing in front of Lou, tripping him. Lou fell over Buddy's back. His forehead bumped the shaft of the spear. The long fork in his right hand whapped the blanket spread under the window. His other hand pounded down, something like a small rock jamming its heel.

He picked the object up.

A marble!

Is that what the bitch had tossed into the room? A bunch of marbles?

Lou scurried off Buddy. He crawled onto the blanket. Beneath it, glass crunched. A tiny, hard ball dug into his knee. Another marble.

He got to the sill and pulled himself up. Poking his head out the window, he caught a glimpse of Denise, the girl and Tom dashing alongside the house.

He crawled through the window and jumped. Standing on the fallen screen, he saw the three disappear around the house's corner.

And realized that the night air was clear.

The rain had stopped.

He tipped back his head, scowling, wanting to feel the hot rain on his face, wondering where it had gone. Above him, the clouds parted. The glare of the full moon hurt his eyes and made him squint.

Buddy, spear in hand, leaped from the window. 'Let's nail 'em, man! Which way'd they go?'

Lou nodded toward the front of the house.

They ran over the slippery grass, Lou longing for the rain to come back but knowing he would soon have Denise – and that would be great.

21

John knew he'd blown it. He shouldn't have taken the cop's revolver. He shouldn't have gone on the quick rescue mission to save Carol. He'd made the crazies too damn aware of him. In spite of his bloody face and the wet, black jacket he'd taken from the old man in the kitchen, they seemed to realize he wasn't one of them.

Twelve, fifteen – maybe more – were converging on the corner of the foyer where he knelt with Lynn and Cassy.

Should've just played along. Might've made it.

Lynn and Cassy had given up their act. They were

crouched on either side of him. They held their knives ready. The waitress cowered behind Lynn, hanging onto her shoulders and gazing with terror at the approaching mob.

At least the crazies were holding back.

None eager to get shot.

But John knew he only had three rounds left in the gun. He could feel the weight of the extra cartridges in his shirt pocket.

A lot of good they'd do.

He wouldn't have time to reload.

Three bullets left.

Take out the ones with the best weapons: the bearded guy with the axe; the woman in panty-hose who had the hatchet; the fat naked guy with the meat cleaver.

That would still leave people with knives, hammers, screwdrivers, crowbars and one crazy bastard with pruning shears.

They'd all be on him the instant they realized his gun was empty.

John knew he was good. In hand-to-hand combat, he could take any of them.

But not all of them.

He glanced at Lynn. 'When I start shooting, run for it.'

She shook her head. 'I'm not leaving without you.'

'You've got to. You've gotta get out of this.'

'John.'

'Just do it. Get home to Kara.' He elbowed Cassy. 'Run for it when I open fire. You and Lynn.'

'Right,' Cassy said.

John aimed at the axeman, two yards away, and fired. The bullet knocked a hole through his chest. He staggered backward a few steps, bumping into those behind him. 'GO!' John yelled.

He got to his feet, sweeping his gun from side to side. The crazies, muttering and snarling, glared at him but stayed away. A few of them flung up arms to shield their faces.

He glanced to his right. Lynn was beside him, standing there, scowling at the black faces.

'GO!' he shouted.

She shook her head.

'Damn it!'

On his left, Cassy stood hunched over, jostling the knife in her hand like some kind of fifties delinquent eager to join in a rumble.

This is mad, he thought. We'll all be killed.

Three of us against the mob. Cornered.

They're still not attacking.

Let's at least get out of the foyer. Maybe make it to a window.

He sidestepped, nudging Cassy, taking quick aim at the nearest crazy, who gasped and ducked. Lynn stayed with him. They made their way to the entryway between the foyer and the main dining room. Cassy checked the rear.

Then they backed out of the foyer. The crazies came toward them, but none was foolish enough to charge.

'We'll try for a window,' John muttered.

It felt better, being in the big, open room. A little better, anyway.

They stepped past overturned chairs and abandoned tables. Some of the tables had been swept clear in the melee. Others were still cluttered with the remains of interrupted dinners: plates, glasses, silverware and wine bottles shimmering in the soft glow of the centerpiece candles; some plates loaded with food, others nearly empty.

As John and his women (he realized the waitress was still with them) backed their way through the room, the crazies fanned out.

Can't let them circle us.

Cassy tripped over a body. Her back pounded the floor. The fat man with the cleaver, maybe pushed beyond caution by what he saw as Cassy swung her legs up to roll clear of the body, rushed at her. Bellowing. Waving his cleaver overhead.

John fired. The bullet struck him under the left eye. The eye popped from its socket. The man veered away from Cassy, his piles of flesh flopping like a bloated bag of pudding. He crashed down on a table top.

Cassy scrambled to her feet as the table overturned.

One shot left, John thought.

'Go for the window!' he yelled.

A woman with a steak knife rushed in from the right. John swept his revolver past the others and put a bullet into her chest.

That's it.

But the others held back, not realizing his gun was empty.

Lynn was still beside him. John glanced toward Cassy. Saw her squat by the fat man and snatch up his cleaver. The guy was half buried under the linen tablecloth. A pile of linguini in red sauce was sliding slowly down his back.

Flame licked up from a corner of the tablecloth that had fallen into the shattered chimney of the table's candle.

Cassy, cleaver in hand, rushed over to John's side.

He ached to reload. The weight of the cartridges in his shirt pocket pressed against him like a cruel joke. The instant he broke open the cylinder . . .

He looked past Cassy at the fire. Half the tablecloth was blazing. The dead man's hair steamed. Flames leaped around his massive torso. His skin crackled and bubbled.

John stuffed his left hand into his pocket, clutched as many cartridges as he could, and threw them at the fire. They spread apart in the air. Some dropped into the flames, while others bounced off the body and rolled away on the hardwood floor.

A crazy yelled, 'Hey!'

'Dumb fuck!' shouted another.

Others looked surprised, others scared, some angry. A few whirled away and fled.

Cassy suddenly hurled her cleaver. It tumbled end over end, sliced off a man's ear and chopped into the chin of a woman behind him.

'Let's get 'em!' a man yelled.

Now she's done it, John thought.

Nobody charged, but the remaining ten or so crazies started moving in.

'Stop or I'll shoot!' John snapped.

Cassy threw her knife at the nearest man. He twisted away and ducked. The handle of the knife struck his side. The knife fell to the floor. He grinned.

Now Cassy had no weapon.

Had she lost her mind?

John was sure of it when she peeled the big, loose T-shirt over her head. The males among the crazies gaped at her.

'Cassy!' he shouted.

She rushed to the fire and threw her shirt into the flames. Then Lynn was beside her. Lynn yanked the nightgown up her body, and off, and flung it onto the fire.

As the flames surged high, devouring the clothes, the crazies attacked. Ignoring John's gun. Ignoring John. Apparently no longer caring about the bullets as they charged toward Lynn and Cassy.

'Run!' John yelled.

He lunged sideways. The nearest man dived for Cassy. John's kick caught him in the hip, turning him in midair. The guy dropped back-first onto the pyre and screamed. John drove his elbow into the face of a giggling lunatic. He pivoted and crashed his revolver against the forehead of an old woman.

He was hit hard in the back. Lynn shrieked and hurled herself onto someone behind him. He spun around in time to see her throw a skinny little guy to the floor. She landed on top. She pounded her knife into the guy's chest. A woman rushed in from the side, hatchet raised. She started to swing it down at Lynn's head. John's kick flung her backward.

Off to the side, two men had Cassy down. One pinned her arms to the floor. The other was sitting on her legs. She squirmed and writhed, twisted and bucked. But they had her. John saw the guy on her legs pull a screwdriver from between his teeth.

Gotta help her!

A woman dropped to her knees beside Lynn and bit the back of her thigh.

'No!' John yelled.

Before he could move to help either woman, arms grabbed him around the legs. Someone jumped on his back. He staggered, trying to stay up. An arm came down from the front, driving a knife toward his chest. He caught the wrist of the knife-hand. As he fought to hold the knife back, a blast crashed in his ears.

Blood flew from the head of the man sitting on Cassy's legs. His screwdriver was already speeding down. Its blade dented the skin below her left breast. Then the handle popped up from the man's fist. The screwdriver tilted and started to fall. He flopped down on top of her.

Another round of ammunition exploded in the fire. Then another. Something zipped past John's face.

He twisted the wrist. The knife fell from his assailant's hand. He shot his elbow backward, connected and heard a grunt through the ringing in his ears.

Then the rain came down.

Cold rain, pouring onto his head.

A woman with a hammer sprang at him from the front. His knuckles caved in her throat. Her weight struck him. He stumbled back, falling onto the one holding his legs and the one clinging to his back.

He blinked water from his eyes.

Above him, a ceiling sprinkler cast down its cold spray.

The fire, he thought. *Jesus, the fire did it.*

Cassy hadn't lost her mind, after all.

22

Denise and Tom raced over the wet grass, side by side, cutting diagonally across the front lawn, heading for the sidewalk at the end of the hedge.

And Denise suddenly wondered where Kara was. The girl had been right behind them when they'd come around the corner of the house. She heard no one back there, now. She looked over her shoulder.

Kara was gone.

She slid to a stop and whirled around.

At first, she didn't see Kara. Her stomach sank. Then she spotted the girl among the bushes near the front stoop.

'Kara!' she shouted.

Buddy and Lou came around the corner of the house, running slowly, heads turning.

They're gonna get her!

'Guys!' she yelled.

They sprinted toward Denise and Tom.

And didn't notice Kara there in the shrubbery. They ran right past her. Buddy had a spear in one hand. Lou waved some kind of long fork overhead and let out a whoop.

'Denny!' Tom gasped.

She couldn't move. She couldn't run off and leave Kara.

The boys dashed closer and closer.

Water suddenly shot up from the ground. Geysers of it, sprouting everywhere. Denise flinched as cold spray from a nearby nozzle seeped through her warmup suit.

Kara had turned on the lawn sprinklers?

Lou cried out as if he were being scalded. Buddy, laughing, leaped one of the showers. He stopped laughing when he slipped. He landed flat on his back.

Tom took hold of Denise's arm. He looked at her. In the moonlight, she saw him smile and shake his head.

'It'll be all right,' she said.

'That kid's amazing.'

'Yeah, isn't she?'

But Lou didn't stop and throw away his fork. He kept running toward them through the fountains of cold, clear water. And Buddy was already scurrying to his feet, lifting his spear.

Why aren't they quitting?

Maybe they haven't been washed clean enough yet.

Lou, bare to the waist, looked pale under the moonlight. Buddy's hair was blond again, his face white.

But the two guys acted the same as when they'd been black.

Buddy, still running, threw his spear. Tom shoved Denise aside. She stumbled, trying to stay up. Her foot struck a sprinkler head. Crying out, she fell sprawling. As she slid to a halt, she rolled onto her side and saw Tom running from Buddy. He only took a few strides before Buddy leaped and tackled him.

Then Lou walked out of the spray beyond Denise's feet. He had the fork in his right hand. His left hand was tugging at the belt of his pants.

'Leave me alone!' she gasped. 'It's over! Lou, it's over!'

'Huh-uh.'

She squirmed away from him, shoving herself over the grass with her heels and elbows. Lou unfastened the button at his waist. He started to pull his zipper down and Kara jumped onto his back. Denise jerked the baton up from her side. She rammed it upward with both hands. Lou fell, his belly striking the end of the metal tube, driving the baton down. She yelled as the weight of Lou and Kara pounded the baton's rubber knob against her ribs.

Lou shrieked as the pipe punched into him.

Denise bucked and squirmed. The weight shifted. Lou and Kara tumbled to the left. They hit the grass. Denise saw the baton jutting out of Lou. He had dropped his fork. He grabbed the baton with both hands and pulled. Inches of it slid out of him. The end made a hollow sucking pop when it came free. Blood poured from a hole the size of a nickel.

Kara, behind his back, got to her knees. 'Are you OK?'

'Yeah.' Denise sat up. 'Thanks. You . . .' She saw the spear come flying out of the spray too late to warn Kara.

The girl yelped with surprise when it hit her.

The knife ripped through the nightgown glued to her body, ripped through her skin, glanced off, and struck Lou's back with a heavy thunk. Kara grabbed her slashed thigh. She turned to look over her shoulder.

Buddy rushed in through the moonlit, silvery shower.

'No!' Denise cried out. She jerked the baton from Lou's limp hands. As Buddy grabbed Kara from behind and hoisted her overhead, Denise scurried over Lou.

He clutched the front of her jacket. 'Gotcha.'

Her knee rammed the bleeding hole in his belly.

Someone said, 'Put the girl down easy, you bastard.'

23

Buddy turned around, holding the little girl high over his head as if she were a barbell.

'Put her down,' Maureen said.

'Where the fuck did you come from?'

Maureen stood shivering in the cold spray. The lust

for killing was gone. But not the need. 'You raped me, mister.'

'Guess what? I'm about to do it again.'

Behind him and just off to the side, a girl crawled over Lou's twitching body, scampered to her feet and rushed forward. She tossed away a shiny weapon of some kind.

'All you're gonna do is die,' Maureen said.

The girl leaped, reaching up, grabbing the kid and pulling.

Buddy yelled, 'Hey!' He tried to hold onto her, and stumbled backward a step as the kid was yanked from his hands and fell into the arms of the girl. He looked over his shoulder to see what had happened.

Maureen thrust the tire tool into his belly. His breath huffed out. He doubled over. Maureen swung with all her strength. The steel bar crashed through his cheekbone, snapped his head sideway. He hit the grass and rolled, his back cutting off the spray of a sprinkler.

Maureen straddled his chest. She raised the bar over her head and swung it down with both hands, caving in the top of his skull.

Aftermath

1

Tom was sitting up when Denise and Kara got to him. 'Are you OK?' Denise asked.

He nodded and winced. His face looked battered and puffy. Blood no sooner spilled from the split skin above his eye than it was washed away by the spray.

'Buddy sort of punched my lights out,' he said.

Denise gripped one of Tom's arms. Kara took the other. They helped him up. The three of them walked over to the woman. She was sprawled on the grass beside Buddy, knees up, arms spread out, a tire iron resting across her belly. The bar went up and down, wobbling as she gasped for air. She squinted up at them through the rain of a nearby sprinkler.

'Hi,' Kara said. 'Thanks for helping us.'

'Glad to.'

'Would you like to come into the house?'

'I think so. Yeah.' She pushed herself up. The tire tool rolled down to her lap. She grabbed it, and got slowly to her feet.

Tom crouched down over Buddy. 'Jeez. What happened to him?'

'Me,' the woman said.

'Good going,' Tom told her.

'Where'd you come from?' Kara asked.

She pointed down the block. 'I'd just come out of the house over there. I saw what was happening.'

'Thank God,' Denise muttered. She stepped over to Lou and pulled the spear from his back. Looking around at the others, she said, 'We'd better keep some stuff, just in case.'

'And let's leave the sprinklers on,' Kara said. 'If anybody comes on the lawn, it'll make them good again.'

'It didn't make Buddy and Lou good,' Denise told her.

The woman made a funny sound. It was sort of a laugh, almost a sob. 'With them,' she said, 'I don't think it was just the rain. Where's the other one?'

'In the house,' Denise said. 'I stabbed him.'

'So that's it, then,' the woman said.

'Unless someone else shows up. Come on, let's get inside.'

2

With a towel wrapped around his waist, Trev stepped through the steamy bathroom. He stopped at the door. His hand hesitated on its knob.

They're still black, he thought. What if they try to nail me?

They won't.

Sandy has it 'reined in.' I hope.

He opened the door. Sandy stood in the corridor, leaning back against the wall, holding Rhonda by the shoulders. The girl was slumped against her, head resting between her breasts.

'You save some water for us, pal?'

'It's all yours.'

He stepped past them, and watched as Sandy pushed away from the wall and guided the girl into the bathroom. The door swung shut.

Trev hurried down the hallway. He averted his eyes from the closed door of the room where grandpa Chidi had worked his terrible magic.

In the master bedroom, he rid himself of the towel. He stepped into a pair of soft, dry corduroy pants belonging to the father. He put on socks and a pair of Reebok shoes that were slightly too large, then slipped into a flannel shirt.

He remembered that the woman in the kitchen was about Maureen's size. Maureen's clothes had been too small for Sandy. But the father's things should be about the right size. He gathered another pair of corduroy pants, a sweatshirt and socks. The man had a set of snake-skin cowboy boots in his closet. A smile worked its way across Trev's face as he picked them up.

They ought to suit Sandy just fine.

He carried his load through the hallway, and put it down by the bathroom door.

In another room, he found clothes for Rhonda: a

pleated skirt, a white sweater, socks and white tennis shoes. He put them beside the garments he'd picked for Sandy.

He went to the living room. The father and the teenaged girl still slept.

Whatever grandpa had used to drug them, Trev hoped it kept on working. He didn't want to be here when they woke up.

He entered the kitchen. In a cupboard near the sink, he found the family's liquor supply. He took out a bottle of Irish whiskey, carried it to the table, and sat down across from the woman.

Auburn hair. Just like Maureen's.

He twisted the cap off the bottle. 'I'm sorry for your troubles, lady,' he said. And then he drank.

3

'Uh-oh,' Tom said. He turned away from the picture window. 'A car's stopping out front.'

A sick feeling made Denise's stomach sink. She went ahead and pressed the bandage across the twin punctures on her right buttock, then pulled up her soggy pants. She winced as the elastic waistband was dragged over the torn skin of her hip.

Kara rushed toward the window. She had the fireplace poker in one hand while her other hand pressed a washcloth to her lacerated thigh.

Denise picked up the spear she'd taken from Lou's back.

Maureen, with her tire iron, hobbled toward the window on her bandaged feet.

Kara got to it first. She pressed her face against the glass. 'I think it's Mom and Dad!' She dropped her poker and rushed to the front door.

'Wait!' Denise snapped.

'Someone's getting out,' Tom said.

The girl unlocked the door, threw it open and left the house.

Denise ran after her. She found Kara standing just outside the door, eyes on the big, dark shape of a man dashing through the sprinklers with a knife.

She raised her spear.

'Dad!' Kara cried out.

'Honey!' He ran closer.

Denise recognized him. John Foxworth, all right. And he didn't look black.

'I think it's OK,' she said as Tom and Maureen came out.

John threw away his knife. He opened his arms. Kara leaped from the top of the stoop. Somehow, he managed to stay on his feet when he caught her. She wrapped her arms and legs around him.

While they embraced, Denise saw a woman hurrying across the lawn. She recognized the dress first. It was the slinky, one-armed gown with the slit up its side. The dress that Lynn had felt so uncertain about wearing.

The woman rushed closer, and Denise recognized her face.

Lynn went to her husband and daughter. She wrapped her arms around both of them.

Tom put a hand on Denise's back. She leaned against him and sighed.

Then another woman came striding through the sprinklers. She wore a skirt and a dark blazer. The blazer was buttoned at her waist. She didn't seem to be wearing a thing underneath it. She suddenly smiled. 'Maureen? Is that you?'

'Cassy?'

Maureen trotted down the stairs. Moments later, those two were embracing.

'I guess they know each other,' Tom said.

'Guess so.'

'Everybody's hugging but us.'

'Looks that way.' Denise dropped her spear. She turned to Tom, slipped her arms around him, and squeezed him hard.

4

In spite of the sun's warmth, Maureen felt a chill spread over her skin when she saw a splintery gap in the front door of her house.

'I'll go in first,' said the CHP officer. One of a

virtual army that poured through the streets of Bixby soon after the rain had stopped. He'd come to the Foxworth house a few hours after dawn.

His name was Jack Conroy. He'd already taken Cassy back to her apartment, and gone inside to make sure there were no lurking crazies. Then he'd driven Tom and Denise to Tom's home. He'd stayed with them, but hadn't needed to go inside because they were met on the porch by Tom's family.

Now, he drew his revolver. With his left hand, he threw the door open. He rushed into the house, crouching. 'Freeze!' he shouted.

Maureen went in behind him.

On the living room sofa, hands in the air, sat Trevor Hudson. When he saw Maureen, he clamped his lower lip between his teeth and looked as if he might be about to cry.

'It's all right, Jack,' she said.

'I guess he looks clean.'

'I'm clean,' Trevor said, his voice trembling.

'Do you know this man?' Jack asked.

'Yeah. He's a friend. An old friend of the family.'

'So, it's OK to leave?'

Maureen nodded. 'Thanks for the ride.'

'Glad to help. Take care.'

He left.

Trevor got to his feet. 'I hope you don't mind me coming in like this.'

'It's nice to see you.'

'It's nice to see you, too. God. It was a bad night.'

'No kidding.'

'But you made it. I'm so damn glad you made it.'

'Is Dad around?'

From the look on Trevor's face, she knew. 'Oh, my God.'

'Rory's fine. I talked to him. He's worried about you.'

'But Dad . . . ?'

'He didn't make it. I'm sorry.'

Maureen dropped onto the sofa. She didn't cry. She felt only stunned and weary. Trevor sat down next to her. She slumped against his side, and felt his fingers gently stroke her hair.